THE MAGNETIC NORTH

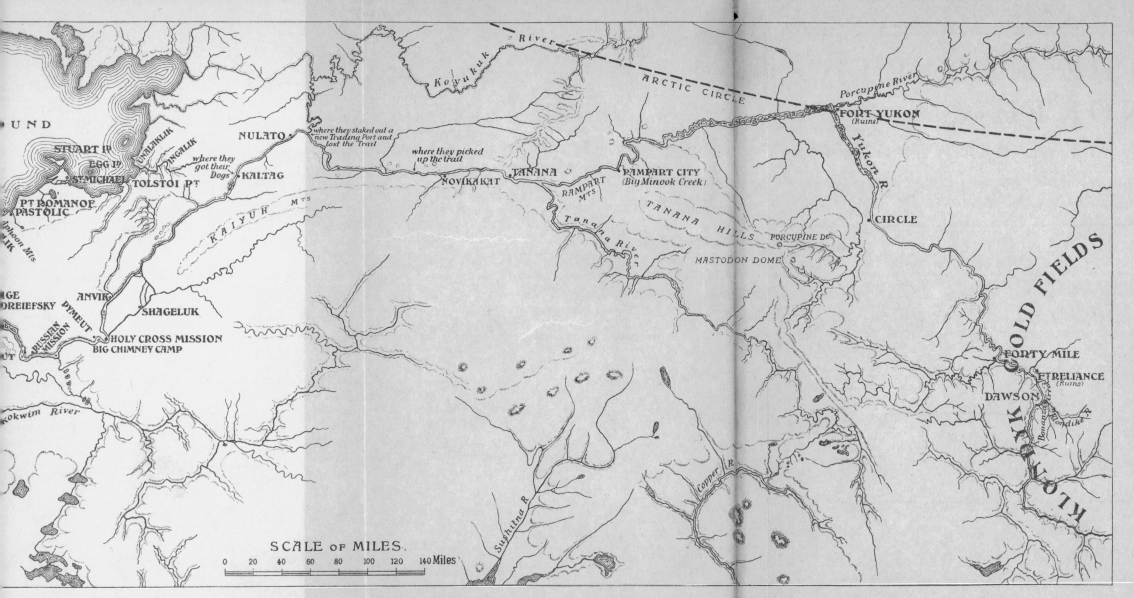

MAP OF THE KLONDYKE DISTRICT SHOWING THE VARIOUS POINTS MENTIONED IN THE NARRATIVE

THE MAGNETIC NORTH

By ELIZABETH ROBINS

(C. E. Raimond) Author of "The Open Question," "Below the Salt," etc. *With a Map*

New York · FREDERICK A. STOKES COMPANY · Publishers

CONTENTS

CHAPTER		PAGE
I.	WINTER CAMP IN THE YUKON	I
II.	HOUSE-WARMING	22
III.	TWO NEW SPISSIMENS	46
IV.	THE BLOW-OUT	62
V.	THE SHAMÁN	86
VI.	A PENITENTIAL JOURNEY	102
VII.	KAVIAK'S CRIME	125
VIII.	CHRISTMAS	149
IX.	A CHRISTIAN AGNOSTIC	173
X.	PRINCESS MUCKLUCK	190
XI.	HOLY CROSS	211
XII.	THE GREAT WHITE SILENCE	240
XIII.	THE PIT	250
XIV.	KURILLA	269
XV.	THE ESQUIMAUX HORSE	283
XVI.	MINÓOK	296
XVII.	THE GREAT STAMPEDE	320
XVIII.	A MINERS' MEETING	330
XIX.	THE ICE GOES OUT	346
XX.	THE KLONDYKE	371
XXI.	PARDNERS	388
XXII.	THE GOING HOME	403

THE MAGNETIC NORTH

CHAPTER I

"To labour and to be content with that a man hath is a sweet life; but he that findeth a treasure is above them both."—Ecclesiasticus.

OF course they were bound for the Klondyke. Every creature in the North-west was bound for the Klondyke. Men from the South too, and men from the East, had left their ploughs and their pens, their factories, pulpits, and easy-chairs, each man like a magnetic needle suddenly set free and turning sharply to the North; all set pointing the self-same way since that July day in '97, when the *Excelsior* sailed into San Francisco harbour, bringing from the uttermost regions at the top of the map close upon a million dollars in nuggets and in gold-dust.

Some distance this side of the Arctic Circle, on the right bank of the Yukon, a little detachment of that great army pressing northward, had been wrecked early in the month of September.

They had realised, on leaving the ocean-going ship that landed them at St. Michael's Island (near the mouth of the great river), that they could not hope to reach Dawson that year. But instead of "getting cold feet," as the phrase for discouragement ran, and turning back as thousands did, or putting in the winter on the coast, they determined, with an eye to the spring rush, to cover as many as possible of the seventeen hundred miles of waterway before navigation closed.

They knew, in a vague way, that winter would come early, but they had not counted on the big September storm that dashed their heavy-laden boats against the floe-ice, ultimately drove them ashore, and nearly cost the little party their lives. On that last day of the long struggle up the stream, a stiff north-easter was cutting the middle reach of the mighty river, two miles wide here, into a choppy and dangerous sea.

Day by day, five men in the two little boats, had kept serious eyes on the shore. Then came the morning when, out of the monotonous cold and snow-flurries, something new appeared, a narrow white rim forming on the river margin—the first ice!

"Winter beginning to show his teeth," said one man, with an effort at jocosity.

Day by day, nearer came the menace; narrower and swifter still ran the deep black water strip between the encroaching ice-lines. But the thought that each day's sailing or rowing meant many days nearer the Klondyke, seemed to inspire a superhuman energy. Day by day each man had felt, and no man yet had said, "We must camp to-night for eight months." They had looked landward, shivered, and held on their way.

But on this particular morning, when they took in sail, they realised it was to be that abomination of desolation on the shore or death. And one or other speedily.

Nearer the white teeth gleamed, fiercer the gale, swifter the current, sweeping back the boats. The *Mary C.* was left behind, fighting for life, while it seemed as if no human power could keep the *Tulare* from being hurled against the western shore. Twice, in spite of all they could do, she was driven within a few feet of what looked like certain death. With a huge effort, that last time, her little crew had just got her well in mid-stream, when a heavy roller breaking on the starboard side drenched the men and half filled the cockpit. Each rower, still pulling for dear life with one hand, bailed the boat with the other; but for all their promptness a certain amount of the water froze solid before they could get it out.

"Great luck, if we're going to take in water like this," said the cheerful Kentuckian, shipping his oar and knocking off the ice—"great luck that all the stores are so well protected."

"Protected!" snapped out an anxious, cast-iron-looking man at the rudder.

"Yes, protected. How's water to get through the ice-coat that's over everything?"

The cast-iron steersman set his jaw grimly. They seemed to be comparatively safe now, with half a mile of open water between them and the western shore.

But they sat as before, stiff, alert, each man in his ice jacket that cracked and crunched as he bent to his oar. Now right, now left, again they eyed the shore.

Would it be—could it be there they would have to land? And if they did . . . ?

2

Lord, how it blew!

"Hard a-port!" called out the steersman. There, just ahead, was a great white-capped "roller" coming—coming, the biggest wave they had encountered since leaving open sea.

But MacCann, the steersman, swung the boat straight into the crested roller, and the *Tulare* took it gamely, "bow on." All was going well when, just in the boiling middle of what they had thought was foaming "white-cap," the boat struck something solid, shivered, and went shooting down, half under water; recovered, up again, and seemed to pause in a second's doubt on the very top of the great wave. In that second that seemed an eternity one man's courage snapped.

Potts threw down his oar and swore by —— and by —— he wouldn't pull another —— stroke on the —— Yukon.

While he was pouring out the words, the steersman sprang from the tiller, and seized Potts' oar just in time to save the boat from capsizing. Then he and the big Kentuckian both turned on the distracted Potts.

"You infernal quitter!" shouted the steersman, and choked with fury. But even under the insult of that "meanest word in the language," Potts sat glaring defiantly, with his half-frozen hands in his pockets.

"It ain't a river, anyhow, this ain't," he said. "It's plain, simple Hell and water."

The others had no time to realise that Potts was clean out of his senses for the moment, and the Kentuckian, still pulling like mad, faced the "quitter" with a determination born of terror.

"If you can't row, take the rudder! Damnation! Take that rudder! Quick, *or we'll kill you!*" And he half rose up, never dropping his oar.

Blindly, Potts obeyed.

The *Tulare* was free now from the clinging mass at the bow, but they knew they had struck their first floe.

Farther on they could see other white-caps bringing other ice masses down. But there was no time for terrors ahead. The gale was steadily driving them in shore again. Boat and oars alike were growing unwieldy with their coating of ever-increasing ice, and human strength was no match for the storm that was sweeping down from the Pole.

Lord, how it blew!

"There's a cove!" called out the Kentuckian. "Throw her in!" he shouted to Potts. Sullenly the new steersman obeyed.

Rolling in on a great surge, the boat suddenly turned in a boiling eddy, and the first thing anybody knew was that the *Tulare* was on her side and her crew in the water. Potts was hanging on to the gunwale and damning the others for not helping him to save the boat.

She wasn't much of a boat when finally they got her into quiet water; but the main thing was they had escaped with their lives and rescued a good proportion of their winter provisions. All the while they were doing this last, the Kentuckian kept turning to look anxiously for any sign of the others, in his heart bitterly blaming himself for having agreed to Potts' coming into the *Tulare* that day in place of the Kentuckian's own "pardner."

When they had piled the rescued provisions up on the bank, and just as they were covering the heap of bacon, flour, and bean-bags, boxes, tools, and utensils with a tarpaulin, up went a shout, and the two missing men appeared tramping along the ice-encrusted shore.

Where was the *Mary C.?* Well, she was at the bottom of the Yukon, and her crew would like some supper.

They set up a tent, and went to bed that first night extremely well pleased at being alive on any terms.

But people get over being glad about almost anything, unless misfortune again puts an edge on the circumstance. The next day, not being in any immediate danger, the boon of mere life seemed less satisfying.

In detachments they went up the river several miles, and down about as far. They looked in vain for any sign of the *Mary C.* They prospected the hills. From the heights behind the camp they got a pretty fair idea of the surrounding country. It was not reassuring.

"As to products, there seems to be plenty of undersized timber, plenty of snow and plenty of river, and, as far as I can see, just nothing else."

"Well, there's oodles o' blueberries," said the Boy, his inky-looking mouth bearing witness to veracity; "and there are black and red currants in the snow, and rose-apples——"

"Oh, yes," returned the other, "it's a sort of garden of Eden!"

A little below here it was four miles from bank to bank of the main channel, but at this point the river was only about two miles wide, and white already with floating masses of floe-ice going on a swift current down towards the sea, four hundred miles away.

The right bank presented to the mighty river a low chain of hills, fringed at the base with a scattered growth of scrubby spruce, birch, willow, and cotton-wood. Timber line was only two hundred feet above the river brink; beyond that height, rocks and moss covered with new-fallen snow.

But if their side seemed cheerless, what of the land on the left bank? A swamp stretching endlessly on either hand, and back from the icy flood as far as eye could see, broken only by sloughs and an occasional ice-rimmed tarn.

"We've been travelling just eight weeks to arrive at this," said the Kentuckian, looking at the desolate scene with a homesick eye.

"We're not only pretty far from home," grumbled another, "we're still thirteen hundred miles away from the Klondyke."

These unenlivening calculations were catching.

"We're just about twenty-five hundred miles from the nearest railroad or telegraph, and, now that winter's down on us, exactly eight months from anywhere in the civilised world."

They had seen no sign of even savage life, no white trader, nothing to show that any human foot had ever passed that way before.

In that stillness that was like the stillness of death, they went up the hillside, with footsteps muffled in the clinging snow; and sixty feet above the great river, in a part of the wood where the timber was least unpromising, they marked out a site for their winter quarters.

Then this queer little company—a Denver bank-clerk, an ex-schoolmaster from Nova Scotia, an Irish-American lawyer from San Francisco, a Kentucky "Colonel" who had never smelt powder, and "the Boy" (who was no boy at all, but a man of twenty-two)—these five set to work felling trees, clearing away the snow, and digging foundations for a couple of log-cabins—one for the Trio, as they called themselves, the other for the Colonel and the Boy.

These two had chummed from the hour they met on the steamer that carried them through the Golden Gate of the Pacific till—well, till the end of my story.

The Colonel was a big tanned fellow, nearly forty—eldest of the party—whom the others used to guy discreetly, because you couldn't mention a place anywhere on the known globe, except the far north, which he had not personally inspected. But for this foible, as the untravelled considered it, he was well liked and a little feared—except by the Boy, who liked him "first-rate," and feared him not at all. They had promptly adopted each other before they discovered that it was necessary to have one or more "pardners." It seemed, from all accounts, to be true, that up there at the top of the world a man alone is a man lost, and ultimately the party was added to as aforesaid.

Only two of them knew anything about roughing it. Jimmie O'Flynn of 'Frisco, the Irish-American lawyer, had seen something of frontier life, and fled it, and MacCann, the Nova Scotian schoolmaster, had spent a month in one of the Caribou camps, and on the strength of that, proudly accepted the nickname of "the Miner."

Colonel George Warren and Morris Burnet, the Boy, had the best outfits; but this fact was held to be more than counterbalanced by the value of the schoolmaster's experience at Caribou, and by the extraordinary handiness of Potts, the Denver clerk, who had helped to build the shelter on deck for the disabled sick on the voyage up. This young man with the big mouth and lazy air had been in the office of a bank ever since he left school, and yet, under pressure, he discovered a natural neathandedness and a manual dexterity justly envied by some of his fellow-pioneers. His outfit was not more conspicuously meagre than O'Flynn's, yet the Irishman was held to be the moneyed man of his party. Just why was never fully developed, but it was always said, "O'Flynn represents capital"; and O'Flynn, whether on that account, or for a subtler and more efficient reason, always got the best of everything that was going without money and without price.

On board ship O'Flynn, with his ready tongue and his golden background—"representing capital"—was a leading spirit. Potts the handy-man was a talker, too, and a good second. But, once in camp, Mac the Miner was cock of the walk, in those first days, quoted "Caribou," and ordered everybody about to everybody's satisfaction.

In a situation like this, the strongest lean on the man who has ever seen "anything like it" before. It was a comfort that anybody even *thought* he knew what to do under such new conditions. So the others looked on with admiration and a pleasant confidence, while Mac boldly cut a hole in the brand-new tent, and instructed Potts how to make a flange out of a tin plate, with which to protect the canvas from the heat of the stove-pipe.

6

No more cooking now in the bitter open. Everyone admired Mac's foresight when he said:

"We must build rock fireplaces in our cabins, or we'll find our one little Yukon stove burnt out before the winter is over—before we have a chance to use it out prospecting." And when Mac said they must pool their stores, the Colonel and the Boy agreed as readily as O'Flynn, whose stores consisted of a little bacon, some navy beans, and a demijohn of whisky. O'Flynn, however, urged that probably every man had a little "mite o' somethin'" that he had brought specially for himself—somethin' his friends had given him, for instance. There was Potts, now. They all knew how the future Mrs. Potts had brought a plum-cake down to the steamer, when she came to say good-bye, and made Potts promise he wouldn't unseal the packet till Christmas. It wouldn't do to pool Potts' cake—never! There was the Colonel, the only man that had a sack of coffee. He wouldn't listen when they had told him tea was the stuff up here, and—well, perhaps other fellows didn't miss coffee as much as a Kentuckian, though he *had* heard—— Never mind; they wouldn't pool the coffee. The Boy had some preserved fruit that he seemed inclined to be a hog about——

"Oh, look here. I haven't touched it!"

"Just what I'm sayin'. You're hoardin' that fruit."

It was known that Mac had a very dacint little medicine-chest. Of course, if any fellow was ill, Mac wasn't the man to refuse him a little cold pizen; but he must be allowed to keep his own medicine chest—and that little pot o' Dundee marmalade. As for O'Flynn, he would look after the "dimmi-john."

But Mac was dead against the whisky clause. Alcohol had been the curse of Caribou, and in *this* camp spirits were to be for medicinal purposes only. Whereon a cloud descended on Mr. O'Flynn, and his health began to suffer; but the precious demijohn was put away "in stock" along with the single bottles belonging to the others. Mac had taken an inventory, and no one in those early days dared touch anything without his permission.

They had cut into the mountain-side for a level foundation, and were hard at it now hauling logs.

"I wonder," said the Boy, stopping a moment in his work, and looking at the bleak prospect round him—"I wonder if we're going to see anybody all winter."

"Oh, sure to," Mac thought; "Indians, anyhow."

"Well, I begin to wish they'd mosy along," said Potts; and the sociable O'Flynn backed him up.

It was towards noon on the sixth day after landing (they had come to speak of this now as a voluntary affair), when they were electrified by hearing strange voices; looked up from their work, and saw two white men seated on a big cake of ice going down the river with the current. When they recovered sufficiently from their astonishment at the spectacle, they ran down the hillside, and proposed to help the "castaways" to land. Not a bit of it.

"*Land* in that place! What you take us for? Not much! We're going to St. Michael's."

They had a small boat drawn up by them on the ice, and one man was dressed in magnificent furs, a long sable overcoat and cap, and wearing quite the air of a North Pole Nabob.

"Got any grub?" Mac called out. •

"Yes; want some?"

"Oh no; I thought you——"

"You're not going to try to live through the winter *there?*"

"Yes."

"Lord! you *are* in a fix!"

"That's we thought about you."

But the travellers on the ice-raft went by laughing and joking at the men safe on shore with their tents and provisions. It made some of them visibly uneasy. *Would* they win through? Were they crazy to try it? They had looked forward eagerly to the first encounter with their kind, but this vision floating by on the treacherous ice, of men who rather dared the current and the crash of contending floes than land where *they* were, seemed of evil augury. The little incident left a curiously sinister impression on the camp.

Even Mac was found agreeing with the others of his Trio that, since they had a grand, tough time in front of them, it was advisable to get through the black months ahead with as little wear and tear as possible. In spite of the Trio's superior talents, they built a small ramshackle cabin with a tumble-down fireplace, which served them so ill that they ultimately spent all their waking hours in the more comfortable quarters of the Colonel and the Boy. It had been agreed that these two, with the help, or, at all events, the advice, of the others, should build the bigger, better cabin, where the stores should be kept and the whole party should mess—a cabin with a solid outside chimney of stone and an open fireplace, generous of proportion and ancient of design, "just like down South."

The weather was growing steadily colder; the ice was solid now many feet out from each bank of the river. In the middle of the flood the clotted current still ran with floe-ice, but it was plain the river was settling down for its long sleep.

Not silently, not without stress and thunder. The handful of dwellers on the shore would be waked in the night by the shock and crash of colliding floes, the sound of the great winds rushing by, and—— "Hush! What's that?" Tired men would start up out of sleep and sit straight to listen. Down below, among the ice-packs, the noise as of an old-time battle going on—tumult and crashing and a boom! boom! like cannonading.

Then one morning they woke to find all still, the conflict over, the Yukon frozen from bank to bank. No sound from that day on; no more running water for a good seven months.

Winter had come.

While the work went forward they often spoke of the only two people they had thus far seen. Both Potts and O'Flynn had been heard to envy them.

Mac had happened to say that he believed the fellow in furs was an Englishman—a Canadian, at the very least. The Americans chaffed him, and said, "That accounts for it," in a tone not intended to flatter. Mac hadn't thought of it before, but he was prepared to swear now that if an Englishman—they were the hardiest pioneers on earth—or a Canadian was in favour of lighting out, "it must be for some good reason."

"Oh yes; we all know that reason."

The Americans laughed, and Mac, growing hot, was goaded into vaunting the Britisher and running down the Yankee.

"Yankee!" echoed the Kentuckian. "And up in Nova Scotia they let this man teach school! Doesn't know the difference yet between the little corner they call New England and all the rest of America."

"All the rest of America!" shouted Mac. "The cheeky way you people of the States have of gobbling the Continent (in *talk*), just as though the British part of it wasn't the bigger half!"

"Yes; but when you think *which* half, you ought to be obliged to any fellow for forgetting it." And then they referred to

9

effete monarchical institutions, and by the time they reached the question of the kind of king the Prince of Wales would make, Mac was hardly a safe man to argue with.

There was one bond between him and the Kentucky Colonel: they were both religious men; and although Mac was blue Presbyterian and an inveterate theologian, somehow, out here in the wilderness, it was more possible to forgive a man for illusions about the Apostolic Succession and mistaken views upon Church government. The Colonel, at all events, was not so lax but what he was ready to back up the Calvinist in an endeavour to keep the Sabbath (with a careful compromise between church and chapel) and help him to conduct a Saturday-night Bible-class.

But if the Boy attended the Bible-class with fervour and aired his heresies with uncommon gusto, if he took with equal geniality Colonel Warren's staid remonstrance and Mac's fiery objurgation, Sunday morning invariably found him more "agnostic" than ever, stoutly declining to recognise the necessity for "service." For this was an occasion when you couldn't argue or floor anybody, or hope to make Mac "hoppin' mad," or have the smallest kind of a shindy. The Colonel read the lessons, Mac prayed, and they all sang, particularly O'Flynn. Now, the Boy couldn't sing a note, so there was no fair division of entertainment, wherefore he would go off into the woods with his gun for company, and the Catholic O'Flynn, and even Potts, were in better odour than he "down in camp" on Sundays. So far you may travel, and yet not escape the tyranny of the "outworn creeds."

The Boy came back a full hour before service on the second Sunday with a couple of grouse and a beaming countenance. Mac, who was cook that week, was the only man left in the tent. He looked agreeably surprised at the apparition.

"Hello!" says he more pleasantly than his Sunday gloom usually permitted. "Back in time for service?"

"I've found a native," says the Boy, speaking as proudly as any Columbus. "He's hurt his foot, and he's only got one eye, but he's splendid. Told me no end of things. He's coming here as fast as his foot will let him—he and three other Indians—Esquimaux, I mean. They haven't had anything to eat but berries and roots for seven days."

The Boy was feverishly overhauling the provisions behind the stove.

"Look here," says Mac, "hold on there. I don't know that we've come all this way to feed a lot o' dirty savages."

"But they're starving." Then, seeing that that fact did not produce the desired impression: "My savage is an awfully good fellow. He—he's a converted savage, seems to be quite a Christian." Then, hastily following up his advantage: "He's been taught English by the Jesuits at the mission forty miles above us, on the river. He can give us a whole heap o' tips."

Mac was slowly bringing out a small panful of cold boiled beans.

"There are four of them," said the Boy—"big fellows, almost as big as our Colonel, and *awful* hungry."

Mac looked at the handful of beans and then at the small sheet-iron stove.

"There are more cooking," says he not over-cordially.

"The one that talks good English is the son of the chief. You can see he's different from the others. Knows a frightful lot. He's taught me some of his language already. The men with him said 'Kaiomi' to everything I asked, and that means 'No savvy.' Says he'll teach me—he'll teach all of us—how to snow-shoe."

"We know how to snow-shoe."

"Oh, I mean on those long narrow snow-shoes that make you go so fast you always trip up! He'll show us how to steer with a pole, and how to make fish-traps and—and everything."

Mac began measuring out some tea.

"He's got a team of Esquimaux dogs—calls 'em Mahlemeuts, and he's got a birch-bark canoe, and a skin kyak from the coast." Then with an inspiration: "His people are the sort of Royal Family down there," added the Boy, thinking to appeal to the Britisher's monarchical instincts.

Mac had meditatively laid his hand on a side of bacon, the Boy's eyes following.

"He's asked us—*all* of us, and we're five—up to visit him at Pymeut, the first village above us here." Mac took up a knife to cut the bacon. "And—good gracious! why, I forgot the grouse; they can have the grouse!"

"No, they can't," said Mac firmly; "they're lucky to get bacon."

The Boy's face darkened ominously. When he looked like that the elder men found it was "healthiest to give him his head." But the young face cleared as quickly as it had clouded. After all, the point wasn't worth fighting for, since grouse would take time to cook, and—here were the natives coming painfully along the shore.

The Boy ran out and shouted and waved his cap. The other men of the camp, who had gone in the opposite direction, across the river ice to look at an air-hole, came hurrying back and reached camp about the same time as the visitors.

"Thought you said they were big fellows!" commented Mac, who had come to the door for a glimpse of the Indians as they toiled up the slope.

"Well, so they are!"

"Why, the Colonel would make two of any one of them."

"The Colonel! Oh well, you can't expect anybody else to be quite as big as that. I was in a hurry, but I suppose what I meant was, they could eat as much as the Colonel."

"How do you know?"

"Well, just look how broad they are. It doesn't matter to your stomach whether you're big up and down, or big to and fro."

"It's their furs make 'em look like that. They're the most awful little runts I ever saw!"

"Well, I reckon *you'd* think they were big, too—big as Nova Scotia—if *you'd* found 'em—come on 'em suddenly like that in the woods——"

"Which is the. . .?"

"Oh, the son of the chief is in the middle, the one who is taking off his civilised fur-coat. He says his father's got a heap of pelts (you could get things for your collection, Mac), and he's got two reindeer-skin shirts with hoods—'parkis,' you know, like the others are wearing——"

They were quite near now.

"How do," said the foremost native affably.

"How do." The Boy came forward and shook hands as though he hadn't seen him for a month. "This," says he, turning first to Mac and then to the other white men, "this is Prince Nicholas of Pymeut. Walk right in, all of you, and have something to eat."

The visitors sat on the ground round the stove, as close as they could get without scorching, and the atmosphere was quickly heavy with their presence. When they slipped back their hoods it was seen that two of the men wore the "tartar tonsure," after the fashion of the coast.

"Where do you come from?" inquired the Colonel of the man nearest him, who simply blinked and was dumb.

"This is the one that talks English," said the Boy, indicating Nicholas, "and he lives at Pymeut, and he's been converted."

"How far is Pymeut?"

"We sleep Pymeut to-night," says Nicholas.

"Which way?"

The native jerked his head up the river.

"Many people there?"

He nodded.

"White men, too?"

He shook his head.

"How far to the nearest white men?"

Nicholas's mind wandered from the white man's catechism and fixed itself on his race's immemorial problem: how far it was to the nearest thing to eat.

"I thought you said he could speak English."

"So he can, first rate. He and I had a great pow-wow, didn't we, Nicholas?"

Nicholas smiled absently, and fixed his one eye on the bacon that Mac was cutting on the deal box into such delicate slices.

"He'll talk all right," said the Boy, "when he's had some breakfast."

Mac had finished the cutting, and now put the frying-pan on an open hole in the little stove.

"Cook him?" inquired Nicholas.

"Yes. Don't you cook him?"

"Take heap time, cook him."

"You couldn't eat it raw!"

Nicholas nodded emphatically.

Mac said "No," but the Boy was curious to see if they would really eat it uncooked.

"Let them have *some* of it raw while the rest is frying"; and he beckoned the visitors to the deal box. They made a dart forward, gathered up the fat bacon several slices at a time, and pushed it into their mouths.

"Ugh!" said the Colonel under his breath.

Mac quickly swept what was left into the frying-pan, and began to cut a fresh lot.

The Boy divided the cold beans, got out biscuits, and poured the tea, while silence and a strong smell of ancient fish and rancid seal pervaded the little tent.

O'Flynn put a question or two, but Nicholas had gone stone-deaf. There was no doubt about it, they had been starving.

After a good feed they sat stolidly by the fire, with no sign of consciousness, save the blinking of beady eyes, till the Colonel suggested a smoke. Then they all grinned broadly, and nodded with great vigour. Even those who had no other English understood "tobacco."

When he had puffed awhile, Nicholas took his pipe out of his mouth, and, looking at the Boy, said:

"You no savvy catch fish in winter?"

"Through the ice? No. How you do it?"

"Make hole—put down trap—heap fish all winter."

"You get enough to live on?" asked the Colonel.

"They must have dried fish, too, left over from the summer," said Mac.

Nicholas agreed. "And berries and flour. When snow begin get soft, Pymeuts all go off——" He motioned with his big head towards the hills.

"What do you get there?" Mac was becoming interested.

"Caribou, moose——"

"Any furs?"

"Yes; trap ermun, marten——"

"Lynx, too, I suppose, and fox?"

Nicholas nodded. "All kinds. Wolf—muskrat, otter—wolverine—all kinds."

"You got some skins now?" asked the Nova Scotian.

"Y-yes. More when snow get soft. You come Pymeut—me show."

"Where have ye been just now?" asked O'Flynn.

"St. Michael."

"How long since ye left there?"

"Twelve sleeps."

"He means thirteen days."

Nicholas nodded.

"They couldn't possibly walk that far in——"

"Oh yes," says the Boy; "they don't follow the windings of the river, they cut across the portage, you know."

"Snow come—no trail—big mountains—all get lost."

"What did you go to St. Michael's for?"

"Oh, me pilot. Me go all over. Me leave N. A. T. and T. boat St. Michael's last trip."

"Then you're in the employ of the great North American Trading and Transportation Company?"

Nicholas gave that funny little duck of the head that meant yes.

"That's how you learnt English," says the Colonel.

"No; me learn English at Holy Cross. Me been baptize."

"At that Jesuit mission up yonder?"

"Forty mile."

"Well," says Potts, "I guess you've had enough walking for one winter."

Nicholas seemed not to follow this observation. The Boy interpreted:

"You heap tired, eh? You no go any more long walk till ice go out, eh?"

Nicholas grinned.

"Me go Ikogimeut—all Pymeut go."

"What for?"

"Big feast."

"Oh, the Russian mission there gives a feast?"

"No. Big Innuit feast."

"When?"

"Pretty quick. Every year big feast down to Ikogimeut when Yukon ice get hard, so man go safe with dog-team."

"Do many people go?"

"All Innuit go, plenty Ingalik go."

"How far do they come?"

"All over; come from Koserefsky, come from Anvik—sometime Nulato."

"Why, Nulato's an awful distance from Ikogimeut."

"Three hundred and twenty miles," said the pilot, proud of his general information, and quite ready, since he had got a pipe between his teeth, to be friendly and communicative.

"What do you do at Ikogimeut when you have these——"

"Big fire—big feed—tell heap stories—big dance. Oh, heap big time!"

"Once every year, eh, down at Ikogimeut?"

"Three times ev' year. Ev' village, and"—he lowered his voice, not with any hit of reverence or awe, but with an air of making a sly and cheerful confidence—"and when man die."

"You make a feast and have a dance when a friend dies?"

"If no priests. Priests no like. Priests say, 'Man no dead;

15

man gone up.'" Nicholas pondered the strange saying, and slowly shook his head.

"In that the priests are right," said Mac grudgingly.

It was anything but politic, but for the life of him the Boy couldn't help chipping in:

"You think when man dead he stay dead, eh, and you might as well make a feast?"

Nicholas gave his quick nod.

"We got heap muskeetah, we cold, we hungry. We here heap long time. Dead man, he done. Why no big feast? Oh yes, heap big feast."

The Boy was enraptured. He would gladly have encouraged these pagan deliverances on the part of the converted Prince, but the Colonel was scandalised, and Mac, although in his heart of hearts not ill-satisfied at the evidence of the skin-deep Christianity of a man delivered over to the corrupt teaching of the Jesuits, found in this last fact all the stronger reason for the instant organisation of a good Protestant prayer-meeting. Nicholas of Pymeut must not be allowed to think it was only Jesuits who remembered the Sabbath day to keep it holy.

And the three "pore benighted heathen" along with him, if they didn't understand English words, they should have an object-lesson, and Mac would himself pray the prayers they couldn't utter for themselves. He jumped up, motioned the Boy to put on more wood, cleared away the granite-ware dishes, filled the bean-pot and set it back to simmer, while the Colonel got out Mac's Bible and his own Prayer-Book.

The Boy did his stoking gloomily, reading aright these portents. Almost eclipsed was joy in this "find" of his (for he regarded the precious Nicholas as his own special property). It was all going to end in his—the Boy's—being hooked in for service. As long as the Esquimaux were there *he* couldn't, of course, tear himself away. And here was the chance they'd all been waiting for. Here was a native chock-full of knowledge of the natural law and the immemorial gospel of the North, who would be gone soon—oh, very soon, if Mac and the Colonel went on like this—and they were going to choke off Nicholas's communicativeness with—a service!

"It's Sunday, you know," says the Colonel to the Prince, laying open his book, "and we were just going to have church. You are accustomed to going to church at Holy Cross, aren't you?"

"When me kid me go church."

"You haven't gone since you grew up? They still have church there, don't they?"

"Oh, Father Brachet, him have church."

"Why don't you go?"

Nicholas was vaguely conscious of threatened disapproval.

"Me. . .me must take up fish-traps."

"Can't you do that another day?"

It seemed not to have occurred to Nicholas before. He sat and considered the matter.

"Isn't Father Brachet," began the Colonel gravely—"he doesn't like it, does he, when you don't come to church?"

"He take care him church; him know me take care me fish-trap."

But Nicholas saw plainly out of his one eye that he was not growing in popularity. Suddenly that solitary organ gleamed with self-justification.

"Me bring fish to Father Brachet and to Mother Aloysius and the Sisters."

Mac and the Colonel exchanged dark glances.

"Do Mother Aloysius and the Sisters live where Father Brachet does?"

"Father Brachet, and Father Wills, and Brother Paul, and Brother Etienne, all here." The native put two fingers on the floor. "Big white cross in middle"—he laid down his pipe to personate the cross—"here"—indicating the other side—"here Mother Aloysius and the Sisters."

"I thought," says Mac, "we'd be hearing of a convent convenient."

"Me help Father Brachet," observed Nicholas proudly. "Me show him boys how make traps, show him girls how make muck-lucks."

"*What!*" gasps the horrified Mac, "Father Brachet has got a family?"

"Famly?" inquired Nicholas. "Kaiomi"; and he shook his head uncertainly.

"You say Father Brachet has got boys, and"—as though this were a yet deeper brand of iniquity—"*girls?*"

Nicholas, though greatly mystified, nodded firmly.

"I suppose he thinks away off up here nobody will ever know. Oh, these Jesuits!"

"How many children has this shameless priest?"

"Father Brachet, him got seventeen boys, and—me no savvy how much girl—twelve girl . . . twenty girl . . ."

The Boy, who had been splitting with inward laughter, exploded at this juncture.

"He keeps a native school, Mac."

"Yes," says Nicholas, "teach boy make table, chair, potatoes grow—all kinds. Sisters teach girl make dinner, wash—all kinds. Heap good people up at Holy Cross."

"Divil a doubt of it," says O'Flynn.

But this blind belauding of the children of Loyola only fired Mac the more to give the heathen a glimpse of the true light. In what darkness must they grope when a sly, intriguing Jesuit (it was well known they were all like that) was for them a type of the "heap good man"—a priest, forsooth, who winked at Sabbath-breaking because he and his neighbouring nuns shared in the spoil!

Well, they must try to have a truly impressive service. Mac and the Colonel telegraphed agreement on this head. Savages were said to be specially touched by music.

"I suppose when you were a kid the Jesuits taught you chants and so on," said the Colonel, kindly.

"Kaiomi," answered Nicholas after reflection.

"You can sing, can't you?" asks O'Flynn.

"Sing? No, me dance!"

The Boy roared with delight.

"Why, yes, I never thought of that. You fellows do the songs, and Nicholas and I'll do the dances."

Mac glowered angrily. "Look here: if you don't mind being blasphemous for yourself, don't demoralise the natives."

"Well, I like that! Didn't Miriam dance before the Lord? Why shouldn't Nicholas and me?"

The Colonel cleared his throat, and began to read the lessons for the day. The natives sat and watched him closely. They really behaved very well, and the Boy was enormously proud of his new friends. There was a great deal at stake. The Boy felt he must walk warily, and he already regretted those light expressions about dancing before the Lord. All the fun of the winter might depend on a friendly relation between Pymeut and the camp. It was essential that the Esquimaux should not only receive, but make, a good impression.

The singing "From Greenland's icy mountains to India's coral strand" seemed to please them; but when, after the Colonel's

"Here endeth the second lesson," Mac said, in sepulchral tones, "Let us pray," the visitors seemed to think it was time to go home.

"No," said Mac sternly, "they mustn't go in the middle of the meeting"; and he proceeded to kneel down.

But Nicholas was putting on his fur coat, and the others only waited to follow him out. The Boy, greatly concerned lest, after all, the visit should end badly, dropped on his knees to add the force of his own example, and through the opening phrases of Mac's prayer the agnostic was heard saying, in a loud stage-whisper, "Do like me—down! Look here! Suppose you ask us come big feast, and in the middle of your dance we all go home——.

"Oh no," remonstrated Nicholas.

"Very well. These friends o' mine no like man go home in the middle. They heap mad at me when I no stay. You savvy?"

"Me savvy," says Nicholas slowly and rather depressed.

"Kneel down, then," says the Boy. And first Nicholas, and then the others, went on their knees.

Alternately they looked in the Boy's corner where the grub was, and then over their shoulders at the droning Mac and back, catching the Boy's eye, and returning his reassuring nods and grins.

Mac, who had had no innings up to this point, was now embarked upon a most congenial occupation. Wrestling with the Lord on behalf of the heathen, he lost count of time. On and on the prayer wound its slow way; involution after involution, coil after coil, like a snake, the Boy thought, lazing in the sun. Unaccustomed knees grew sore.

"Hearken to the cry of them that walk in darkness, misled by wolves in sheep's clothing—*wolves, Lord, wearing the sign of the Holy Cross——*"

O'Flynn shuffled, and Mac pulled himself up. No light task this of conveying to the Creator, in covert terms, a due sense of the iniquity of the Jesuits, without, at the same time, stirring O'Flynn's bile, and seeing him get up and stalk out of meeting, as had happened once before.

O'Flynn was not deeply concerned about religious questions, but "there were limits." The problem was how to rouse the Lord without rousing O'Flynn—a piece of negotiation so delicate, calling for a skill in pious invective so infinitely absorbing to Mac's particular cast of mind, that he was quickly stone-blind and deaf to all things else.

"Not all the heathen are sunk in iniquity; but they are weak, tempted, and they weary, Lord!"

"Amen," said the Boy, discreetly.

"How long?" groaned Mac—"O Lord, how long?" But it was much longer than he realised. The Boy saw the visitors shifting from one knee to another, and feared the worst. But he sympathised deeply with their predicament. To ease his own legs, he changed his position, and dragged a corner of the sail-cloth down off the little pile of provisions, and doubled it under his knees.

The movement revealed the bag of dried apples within arm's length. Nicholas was surreptitiously reaching for his coat. No doubt about it, he had come to the conclusion that this was the fitting moment to depart. A look over his shoulder showed Mac absorbed, and taking fresh breath at "Sixthly, O Lord." The Boy put out a hand, and dragged the apple-bag slowly, softly towards him. The Prince dropped the sleeve of his coat, and fixed his one eye on his friend. The Boy undid the neck of the sack, thrust in his hand, and brought out a fist full. Another look at Mac—still hard at it, trying to spare O'Flynn's feelings without mincing matters with the Almighty.

The Boy winked at Nicholas, made a gesture, "Catch!" and fired a bit of dried apple at him, at the same time putting a piece in his own mouth to show him it was all right.

Nicholas followed suit, and seemed pleased with the result. He showed all his strong, white teeth, and ecstatically winked his one eye back at the Boy, who threw him another bit and then a piece to each of the others.

The Colonel had "caught on," and was making horrible frowns at the Boy. Potts and O'Flynn looked up, and in dumb-show demanded a share. No? Very well, they'd tell Mac. So the Boy had to feed them, too, to keep them quiet.

And still Mac prayed the Lord to catch up this slip he had made here on the Yukon with reference to the natives. In the midst of a powerful peroration, he happened to open his eyes a little, and they fell on the magnificent great sable collar of Prince Nicholas's coat.

Without any of the usual slowing down, without the accustomed warning of a gradual descent from the high themes of heaven to the things of common earth, Mac came down out of the clouds with a bump, and the sudden, business-like "Amen" startled all the apple-chewing congregation.

Mac stood up, and says he to Nicholas:

"Where did you get that coat?"

Nicholas, still on his knees, stared, and seemed in doubt if this were a part of the service.

"Where did you get that coat?" repeated Mac.

The Boy had jumped up nimbly. "I told you his father has a lot of furs."

"Like this?"

"No," says Nicholas; "this belong white man."

"Ha," says Mac excitedly, "I thought I'd seen it before. Tell us how you got it."

"Me leave St. Michael; me got ducks, reindeer meat—oh, *plenty* kow-kow!* Two sleeps away St. Michael me meet Indian. Heap hungry. Him got bully coat." Nicholas picked it up off the floor. "Him got no kow-kow. Him say, 'Give me duck, give me back-fat. You take coat, him too heavy.' Me say, 'Yes.'"

"But how did he get the coat?"

"Him say two white men came down river on big ice."

"Yes, yes——"

"Men sick." He tapped his forehead. "Man no sick, he no go down with the ice"; and Nicholas shuddered. "Before Ikogimeut, ice jam. Indian see men jump one big ice here, more big ice here, and one . . . go down. Indian"—Nicholas imitated throwing out a line—"man tie mahout round—but—big ice come——" Nicholas dashed his hands together, and then paused significantly. "Indian sleep there. Next day ice hard. Indian go little way out to see. Man dead. Him heap good coat," he wound up unemotionally, and proceeded to put it on.

"And the other white man—what became of him?"

Nicholas shrugged: "Kaiomi," though it was plain he knew well enough the other lay under the Yukon ice.

"And that —*that* was the end of the fellows who went by jeering at us!"

"We'd better not crow yet," said Mac. And they bade Princ Nicholas and his heathen retinue good-bye in a mood chastened not by prayer alone.

* Food.

CHAPTER II

HOUSE-WARMING

"There is a sort of moral climate in a household."—JOHN MORLEY.

NO idle ceremony this, but the great problem of the dwellers in the country of the Yukon.

The Colonel and the Boy made up their minds that, whatever else they had or had not, they would have a warm house to live in. And when they had got it, they would have a "Blow-out" to celebrate the achievement.

"We'll invite Nicholas," says the Boy. "I'll go to Pymeut myself, and let him know *we* are going to have 'big fire, big feed. Oh, heap big time!' "

If the truth were told, it had been a difficult enough matter to keep away from Pymeut since the hour Nicholas had vanished in that direction; but until winter quarters were made, and until they were proved to be warm, there was no time for the amenities of life.

The Big Cabin (as it was quite seriously called, in contradistinction to the hut of the Trio) consisted of a single room, measuring on the outside sixteen feet by eighteen feet.

The walls of cotton-wood logs soared upward to a level of six feet, and this height was magnificently increased in the middle by the angle of the mildly gable roof. But before the cabin was breast-high the Boy had begun to long for a window.

"Sorry we forgot the plate-glass," says Mac.

"Wudn't ye like a grrand-piana?" asks O'Flynn.

"What's the use of goin' all the way from Nova Scotia to Caribou," says the Boy to the Schoolmaster-Miner, "if you haven't learned the way to make a window like the Indians, out of transparent skin?"

Mac assumed an air of elevated contempt.

"I went to mine, not to learn Indian tricks."

"When the door's shut it'll be dark as the inside of a cocoa-nut."

"You ought to have thought of that before you left the sunny South," said Potts.

"It'll be dark all winter, window or no window," Mac reminded them.

"Never mind," said the Colonel, "when the candles give out we'll have the fire-light. Keep all the spruce knots, boys!"

But one of the boys was not pleased. The next day, looking for a monkey-wrench under the tarpaulin, he came across the wooden box a California friend had given him at parting, containing a dozen tall glass jars of preserved fruit. The others had growled at the extra bulk and weight, when the Boy put the box into the boat at St. Michael's, but they had now begun to look kindly on it and ask when it was to be opened. He had answered firmly:

"Not before Christmas," modifying this since Nicholas's visit to "Not before the House-Warming." But one morning the Boy was found pouring the fruit out of the jars into some empty cans.

"What you up to?"

"Wait an' see." He went to O'Flynn, who was dish-washer that week, got him to melt a couple of buckets of snow over the open-air camp-fire and wash the fruit-jars clean.

"Now, Colonel," says the Boy, "bring along that buck-saw o' yours and lend a hand."

They took off the top log from the south wall of the cabin, measured a two-foot space in the middle, and the Colonel sawed out the superfluous spruce intervening. While he went on doing the same for the other logs on that side, the Boy roughly chiselled a moderately flat sill. Then one after another he set up six of the tall glass jars in a row, and showed how, alternating with the other six bottles turned upside down, the thick belly of one accommodating itself to the thin neck of the other, the twelve made a very decent rectangle of glass. When they had hoisted up, and fixed in place, the logs on each side, and the big fellow that went all across on top; when they had filled the inconsiderable cracks between the bottles with some of the mud-mortar with which the logs were to be chinked, behold a double glass window fit for a king!

The Boy was immensely pleased.

"Oh, that's an old dodge," said Mac depreciatingly. "Why, they did that at Caribou!"

"Then, why in—— Why didn't you suggest it?"

"You wait till you know more about this kind o' life, and you won't go in for fancy touches."

Nevertheless, the man who had mined at Caribou seemed to feel that some contribution from him was necessary to offset the huge success of that window. He did not feel called upon to help to split logs for the roof of the Big Cabin, but he sat cutting and whittling away at a little shelf which he said was to be nailed up at the right of the Big Cabin door. Its use was not apparent, but no one dared call it a "fancy touch," for Mac was a miner, and had been to Caribou.

When the shelf was nailed up, its maker brought forth out of his medicine-chest a bottle of Perry Davis's Pain-killer.

"Now at Caribou," says he, "they haven't got any more thermometers kicking round than we have here, but they discovered that when Perry Davis congeals you must keep a sharp look-out for frost-bite, and when Perry Davis freezes solid, you'd better mind your eye and stay in your cabin, if you don't want to die on the trail." With which he tied a string round Perry Davis's neck, set the bottle up on the shelf, and secured it firmly in place. They all agreed it was a grand advantage to have been to Caribou!

But Mac knew things that he had probably not learned there, about trees, and rocks, and beasts, and their manners and customs and family names. If there were more than a half-truth in the significant lament of a very different man, "I should be a poet if only I knew the names of things," then, indeed, Samuel MacCann was equipped to make a mark in literature.

From the time he set foot on the volcanic shore of St. Michael's Island, Mac had begun his "collection."

Nowadays, when he would spend over "that truck of his" hours that might profitably (considering his talents) be employed in helping to fortify the camp against the Arctic winter, his companions felt it little use to remonstrate.

By themselves they got on rapidly with work on the roof, very much helped by three days' unexpectedly mild weather. When the split logs had been marshalled together on each side of the comb, they covered them with dried moss and spruce boughs. Over all they laid a thick blanket of the earth which had been dug out to make a level foundation. The cracks in the walls were chinked with moss and mud-mortar. The floor was the naked ground, "to be carpeted with skins by-and-by," so Mac said; but nobody believed Mac would put a skin to any such sensible use.

The unreasonable mildness of three or four days and the little surface thaw, came to an abrupt end in a cold rain that turned to sleet as it fell. Nobody felt like going far afield just then, even after game, but they had set the snare that Nicholas told the Boy about on that first encounter in the wood. Nicholas, it seemed, had given him a noose made of twisted sinew, and showed how it worked in a running loop. He had illustrated the virtue of this noose when attached to a pole balanced in the crotch of a tree, caught over a horizontal stick by means of a small wooden pin tied to the snare. A touch at the light end of the suspended pole (where the baited loop dangles) loosens the pin, and the heavy end of the pole falls, hanging ptarmigan or partridge in the air.

For some time after rigging this contrivance, whenever anyone reported "tracks," Mac and the Boy would hasten to the scene of action, and set a new snare, piling brush on each side of the track that the game had run in, so barring other ways, and presenting a line of least resistance straight through the loop.

In the early days Mac would come away from these preparations saying with dry pleasure:

"Now, with luck, we may get a *Xema Sabinii*," or some such fearful wild-fowl.

"Good to eat?" the Boy would ask, having had his disappointments ere now in moments of hunger for fresh meat, when Mac, with the nearest approach to enthusiasm he permitted himself, had brought in some miserable little hawk-owl or a three-toed woodpecker to add, not to the larder, but to the "collection."

"No, you don't *eat* Sabine gulls," Mac would answer pityingly.

But those snares never seemed to know what they were there for. The first one was set expressly to catch one of the commonest birds that fly—Mac's *Lagopus albus*, the beautiful white Arctic grouse, or at the very least a *Bonasa umbellus,* which, being interpreted, is ruffed ptarmigan. The tracks had been bird tracks, but the creature that swung in the air next day was a baby hare. The Schoolmaster looked upon the incident as being in the nature of a practical joke, and resented it. But the others were enchanted, and professed thereafter a rooted suspicion of the soundness of the Schoolmaster's Natural History, which nobody actually felt. For he had never yet pretended to know anything that he didn't know well; and when Potts would say something disparaging of Mac's learning behind his back (which was against the unwritten rules of the game) the Colonel invariably sat on Potts.

"Knows a darned sight too much? No, he *don't*, sir; that's just the remarkable thing about Mac. He isn't trying to carry any more than he can swing."

At the same time it is to be feared that none of his companions really appreciated the pedagogue's learning. Nor had anyone but the Boy sympathised with his resolution to make a Collection. What they wanted was eatable game, and they affected no intelligent interest in knowing the manners and customs of the particular species that was sending up appetising odours from the pot.

They even applauded the rudeness of the Boy, who one day responded to Mac's gravely jubilant "Look here! I've got the *Parus Hudsonicus!*"——

"Poor old man! What do you do for it?"

And when anybody after that was indisposed, they said he might be sickening for an attack of Parus Hudsonicus, and in that case it was a bad look-out.

Well for Mac that he wouldn't have cared a red cent to impress the greatest naturalist alive, let alone a lot of fellows who didn't know a titmouse from a disease.

Meanwhile work on the Big Cabin had gone steadily forward. From the outside it looked finished now, and distinctly imposing. From what were left of the precious planks out of the bottom of the best boat they had made the door—two by four, and opening directly in front of that masterpiece, the rock fireplace. The great stone chimney was the pride of the camp and the talk before the winter was done of all "the Lower River."

Spurred on partly by the increased intensity of the cold, partly by the Colonel's nonsense about the way they did it "down South," Mac roused himself, and turned out a better piece of masonry for the Big Cabin than he had thought necessary for his own. But everybody had a share in the glory of that fireplace. The Colonel, Potts, and the Boy selected the stone, and brought it on a rude litter out of a natural quarry from a place a mile or more away up on the bare mountain-side. O'Flynn mixed and handed up the mud-mortar, while Mac put in some brisk work with it before it stiffened in the increasing cold.

Everybody was looking forward to getting out of the tent and into the warm cabin, and the building of the fireplace stirred enthusiasm. It was two and a half feet deep, three and a half feet high, and four feet wide, and when furnished with ten-inch back logs, packed in glowing ashes and laid one above another, with a roaring good blaze in front of birch and spruce, that fire would take a lot of beating, as the Boy admitted, "even in the fat-pine Florida country."

But no fire on earth could prevent the cabin from being swept through, the moment the door was opened, by a fierce and icy air-current. The late autumnal gales revealed the fact that the sole means of ventilation had been so nicely contrived that whoever came in or went out admitted a hurricane of draught that nearly knocked him down. Potts said it took a good half-hour, after anyone had opened the door, to heat the place up again.

"What! You cold?" inquired the usual culprit. The Boy had come in to put an edge on his chopper. "It's stopped snowin', an' you better come along with me, Potts. Swing an axe for a couple of hours—that'll warm you."

"I've got rheumatism in my shoulder to-day," says Potts, hugging the huge fire closer.

"And you've got something wrong with your eyes, eh, Mac?"

Potts narrowed his and widened the great mouth; but he had turned his head so Mac couldn't see him.

The Nova Scotian only growled and refilled his pipe. Up in the woods the Boy repeated the conversation to the Colonel, who looked across at O'Flynn several yards away, and said: "Hush!"

"Why must I shut up? Mac's eyes *do* look rather queer and bloodshot. I should think he'd rather feel we lay it to his eyes than know we're afraid he's peterin' out altogether."

"I never said I was afraid——"

"No, you haven't *said* much."

"I haven't opened my head about it."

"No, but you've tried hard enough for five or six days to get Mac to the point where he would come out and show us how to whip-saw. You haven't *said* anything, but you've—you've got pretty dignified each time you failed, and we all know what that means."

"We ought to have begun sawing boards for our bunks and swing-shelf a week back, before this heavy snowfall. Besides, there's enough fire-wood now; we're only marking time until——"

"Until Mac's eyes get all right. I understand."

Again the Colonel had made a sound like "Sh!" and went on swinging his axe.

They worked without words till the Boy's tree came down. Then he stopped a moment, and wiped his face.

"It isn't so cold to-day, not by a long shot, for all Potts's howling about his rheumatics."

"It isn't cold that starts that kind of pain."

"No, siree. I'm not much of a doctor, but I can see Potts's rheumatism doesn't depend on the weather."

"Never you mind Potts."

"I don't mind Potts. I only mind Mac. What's the matter with Mac, anyway?"

"Oh, he's just got cold feet. Maybe he'll thaw out by-and-by."

"Did you ever think what Mac's like? With that square-cut jaw and sawed-off nose, everything about him goin' like this"— the Boy described a few quick blunt angles in the air—"well, sir, he's the livin' image of a monkey-wrench. I'm comin' to think he's as much like it inside as he is out. He can screw up for a prayer-meetin', or he can screw down for business—when he's a mind, but, as Jimmie over there says, 'the divil a different pace can you put him through.' I *like* monkey-wrenches! I'm only sayin' they aren't as limber as willa-trees."

No response from the Colonel, who was making the chips fly. It had cost his great body a good many aches and bruises, but he was a capital axeman now, and not such a bad carpenter, though when the Boy said as much he had answered:

"Carpenter! I'm just a sort of a well-meanin' wood-butcher"; and deeply he regretted that in all his young years on a big place in the country he had learnt so little about anything but horses and cattle.

On the way back to dinner they spoke again of this difficulty of the boards. O'Flynn whistled "Rory O'More" with his pleasant air of detachment.

"You and the others would take more interest in the subject," said the Boy a little hotly, "if we hadn't let you fellows use nearly all the boat-planks for *your* bunks, and now we haven't got any for our own."

"*Let* us use 'em! Faith! we had a right to 'm."

"To boards out of *our* boat!"

"And ye can have the loan o' the whip-saw to make more, whenever the fancy takes ye."

"Loan o' the whip-saw! Why, it's mine," says the Colonel.

"Divil a bit of it, man!" says O'Flynn serenely. "Everything we've got belongs to all of us, except a sack o' coffee, a medicine-chest, and a dimmi-john. And it's mesilf that's afraid the dimmi-john——"

"What's the use of my having bought a whip-saw?" interrupted the Colonel, hurriedly. "What's the good of it, if the only man that knows how to use it——"

"Is more taken up wid bein' a guardjin angel to his pardner's dimmi-john——"

The Colonel turned and frowned at the proprietor of the dimmi-john. The Boy had dropped behind to look at some marten tracks in the fresh-fallen snow.

"I'll follow that trail after dinner," says he, catching up the others in time to hear O'Flynn say:

"If it wusn't that ye think only a feller that's been to Caribou can teach ye annything it's Jimmie O'Flynn that 'ud show ye how to play a chune on that same whip-saw."

"Will you show us after dinner?"

"Sure I will."

And he was as good as his word.

This business of turning a tree into boards without the aid of a saw-mill is a thing many placer-miners have to learn; for, even if they are disposed to sleep on the floor, and to do without shelves, they can't do sluicing without sluice-boxes, and they can't make those long, narrow boxes without boards.

So every party that is well fitted out has a whip-saw.

"Furrst ye dig a pit," O'Flynn had said airily, stretched out before the fire after dinner. "Make it about four feet deep, and as long as ye'd like yer boards. When ye've done that I'll come and take a hand."

The little job was not half finished when the light failed. Two days more of soil-burning and shovelling saw it done.

"Now ye sling a couple o' saplings acrost the durrt ye've chucked out. R-right! Now ye roll yer saw-timber inter the middle. R-right! An' on each side ye want a log to stand on. See? Wid yer 'guide-man' on top sthradlin' yer timberr, watchin' the chalk-line and doin' the pull-up, and the otherr fellerr in the pit lookin' afther the haul-down, ye'll be able to play a chune wid that there whip-saw that'll make the serryphims sick o' plain harps." O'Flynn superintended it all, and even Potts had the curiosity to come out and see what they were up to. Mac was "kind o' dozin'" by the fire.

When the frame was finished O'Flynn helped to put the trial-log in place, having marked it off with charcoal to indicate inch and a quarter planks. Then the Colonel, down in the pit, and O'Flynn on top of the frame, took the great two-handled saw between them, and began laboriously, one drawing the big blade up, and the other down, vertically through the log along the charcoal line.

"An' *that's* how it's done, wid bits of yer arrums and yer back that have niver been called on to wurruk befure. An' whin ye've been at it an hour ye'll find it goes betther wid a little blasphemin';" and he gave his end of the saw to the reluctant Potts.

Potts was about this time as much of a problem to his pardners as was the ex-schoolmaster. If the bank clerk had surprised them all by his handiness on board ship, and by making a crane to swing the pots over the fire, he surprised them all still more in these days by an apparent eclipse of his talents. It was unaccountable. Potts's carpentering, Potts's all-round cleverness, was, like "payrock in a pocket," as the miners say, speedily worked out, and not a trace of it afterwards to be found.

But less and less was the defection of the Trio felt. The burly Kentucky stock-farmer was getting his hand in at "frontier" work, though he still couldn't get on without his "nigger," as the Boy said, slyly indicating that it was he who occupied this exalted post. These two soon had the bunks made out of the rough planks they had sawed with all a green-horn's pains. They put in a fragrant mattress of spring moss, and on that made up a bed of blankets and furs.

More boards were laboriously turned out to make the great swing-shelf to hang up high in the angle of the roof, where the provisions might be stored out of reach of possible marauders.

The days were very short now, bringing only about five hours of pallid light, so little of which struggled through the famous bottle-window that at all hours they depended chiefly on the blaze from the great fireplace. There was still a good deal of work to be done indoors, shelves to be put up on the left as you entered (whereon the granite-ware tea-service, etc., was kept), a dinner-table to be made, and three-legged stools. While these additions—"fancy touches," as the Trio called them—were being made, Potts and O'Flynn, although occasionally they went out for an hour or two, shot-gun on shoulder, seldom brought home anything, and for the most part were content with doing what they modestly considered their share of the cooking and washing. For the rest, they sat by the fire playing endless games of euchre, seven-up and bean poker, while Mac, more silent than ever, smoked and read Copps's "Mining Laws" and the magazines of the previous August.

Nobody heard much in those days of Caribou. The Colonel had gradually slipped into the position of Boss of the camp. The Trio were still just a trifle afraid of him, and he, on his side, never pressed a dangerous issue too far.

But this is a little to anticipate.

One bitter gray morning, that had reduced Perry Davis to a solid lump of ice, O'Flynn, the Colonel, and the Boy were bringing into the cabin the last of the whip-sawed boards. The Colonel halted and looked steadily up the river.

"Is that a beast or a human?" said he.

"It's a man," the Boy decided after a moment—"no, two men, single file, and—yes—Colonel, it's dogs. Hooray! a dog-team at last!"

They had simultaneously dropped the lumber. The Boy ran on to tell the cook to prepare more grub, and then pelted after O'Flynn and the Colonel, who had gone down to meet the new-comers—an Indian driving five dogs, which were hitched tandem to a low Esquimaux sled, with a pack and two pairs of web-foot snow-shoes lashed on it, and followed by a white man. The Indian was a fine fellow, younger than Prince Nicholas, and better off in the matter of eyes. The white man was a good deal older than either, with grizzled hair, a worn face, bright dark eyes, and a pleasant smile.

"I had heard some white men had camped hereabouts," says he. "I am glad to see we have such substantial neighbours." He was looking up at the stone chimney, conspicuous a long way off.

"We didn't know we had any white neighbours," said the Colonel in his most grand and gracious manner. "How far away are you, sir?"

"About forty miles above."

As he answered he happened to be glancing at the Boy, and observed his eagerness cloud slightly. Hadn't Nicholas said it was "about forty miles above" that the missionaries lived?

"But to be only forty miles away," the stranger went on,

misinterpreting the fading gladness, "is to be near neighbours in this country."

"We aren't quite fixed yet," said the Colonel, "but you must come in and have some dinner with us. We can promise you a good fire, anyhow."

"Thank you. You have chosen a fine site." And the bright eyes with the deep crow's-feet raying out from the corners scanned the country in so keen and knowing a fashion that the Boy, with hope reviving, ventured:

"Are—are you a prospector?"

"No. I am Father Wills from Holy Cross."

"Oh!" And the Boy presently caught up with the Indian, and walked on beside him, looking back every now and then to watch the dogs or examine the harness. The driver spoke English, and answered questions with a tolerable intelligence. "Are dogs often driven without reins?"

The Indian nodded.

The Colonel, after the stranger had introduced himself, was just a shade more reserved, but seemed determined not to be lacking in hospitality. O'Flynn was overflowing, or would have been had the Jesuit encouraged him. He told their story, or, more properly, his own, and how they had been wrecked.

"And so ye're the Father Superior up there?" says the Irishman, pausing to take breath.

"No. Our Superior is Father Brachet. That's a well-built cabin!"

The dogs halted, though they had at least five hundred yards still to travel before they would reach the well-built cabin.

"Mush!" shouted the Indian.

The dogs cleared the ice-reef, and went spinning along so briskly over the low hummocks that the driver had to run to keep up with them.

The Boy was flying after when the priest, having caught sight of his face, called out: "Here! Wait! Stop a moment!" and hurried forward.

He kicked through the ice-crust, gathered up a handful of snow, and began to rub it on the Boy's right cheek.

"What in the name of——" The Boy was drawing back angrily.

"Keep still," ordered the priest; "your cheek is frozen"; and he applied more snow and more friction. "You ought to watch one another in such weather as this. When a man turns dead-white like that, he's touched with frost-bite." After he had restored the circulation: "There now, don't go near the fire, or it will begin to hurt."

"Thank you," said the Boy, a little shame-faced. "It's all right now, I suppose?"

"I think so," said the priest. "You'll lose the skin, and you may be a little sore—nothing to speak of," with which he fell back to the Colonel's side.

The dogs had settled down into a jog-trot now, but were still well on in front.

"Is 'mush' their food?" asked the Boy.

"*Mush?* No, fish."

"Why does your Indian go on like that about mush, then?"

"Oh, that's the only word the dogs know, except—a—certain expressions we try to discourage the Indians from using. In the old days the dog-drivers used to say 'mahsh.' Now you never hear anything but swearing and 'mush,' a corruption of the French-Canadian *marche*." He turned to the Colonel: "You'll get over trying to wear cheechalko boots here—nothing like mucklucks with a wisp of straw inside for this country."

"I agree wid ye. I got me a pair in St. Michael's," says O'Flynn proudly, turning out his enormous feet. "Never wore anything so comf'table in me life."

"You ought to have drill parkis too, like this of mine, to keep out the wind."

They were going up the slope now, obliquely to the cabin, close behind the dogs, who were pulling spasmodically between their little rests.

Father Wills stooped and gathered up some moss that the wind had swept almost bare of snow. "You see that?" he said to O'Flynn, while the Boy stopped, and the Colonel hurried on. "Wherever you find that growing no man need starve."

The Colonel looked back before entering the cabin and saw that the Boy seemed to have forgotten not alone the Indian, but the dogs, and was walking behind with the Jesuit, face upturned, smiling, as friendly as you please.

Within a different picture.

Potts and Mac were having a row about something, and the Colonel struck in sharply on their growling comments upon each other's character and probable destination.

"Got plenty to eat? Two hungry men coming in. One's an Indian, and you know what that means, and the other's a Catholic priest." It was this bomb that he had hurried on to get exploded and done with before the said priest should appear on the scene.

"A *what?*" Mac raised his heavy eyes with fight in every wooden feature.

"A Jesuit priest is what I said."

"He won't eat his dinner here."

"That is exactly what he will do."

"Not by——" Whether it was the monstrous proposition that had unstrung Mac, he was obliged to steady himself against the table with a shaking hand. But he set those square features of his like iron, and, says he, "No Jesuit sits down to the same table with me."

"That means, then, that you'll eat alone."

"Not if I know it."

The Colonel slid in place the heavy wooden bar that had never before been requisitioned to secure the door, and he came and stood in the middle of the cabin, where he could let out all his inches. Just clearing the swing-shelf, he pulled his great figure up to its full height, and standing there like a second Goliath, he said quite softly in that lingo of his childhood that always came back to his tongue's tip in times of excitement: "Just as shuah as yo' bohn that priest will eat his dinner to-day in my cabin, sah; and if yo' going t' make any trouble, just say so now, and we'll get it ovah, and the place cleaned up again befoh our visitors arrive."

"Mind what you're about, Mac," growled Potts. "You know he could lick the stuffin' out o' you."

The ex-schoolmaster produced some sort of indignant sound in his throat and turned, as if he meant to go out. The Colonel came a little nearer. Mac flung up his head and squared for battle.

Potts, in a cold sweat, dropped a lot of tinware with a rattle, while the Colonel said, "No, no. We'll settle this after the people go, Mac." Then in a whisper: "Look here: I've been trying to shield you for ten days. Don't give yourself away now—before the first white neighbour that comes to see us. You call yourself a Christian. Just see if you can't behave like one, for an hour or two, to a fellow-creature that's cold and hungry. Come, *you're* the man we've always counted on! Do the honours, and take it out of me after our guests are gone."

Mac seemed in a haze. He sat down heavily on some bean-bags in the corner; and when the newcomers were brought in and introduced, he "did the honours" by glowering at them with red eyes, never breaking his surly silence.

"Well!" says Father Wills, looking about, "I must say you're very comfortable here. If more people made homes like this, there'd be fewer failures." They gave him the best place by the fire, and Potts dished up dinner. There were only two stools made yet. The Boy rolled his section of sawed spruce over near the priest, and prepared to dine at his side.

"No, no," said Father Wills firmly. "You shall sit as far away from this splendid blaze as you can get, or you will have trouble with that cheek." So the Boy had to yield his place to O'Flynn, and join Mac over on the bean-bags.

"Why didn't you get a parki when you were at St. Michael's?" said the priest as this change was being effected.

"We had just as much—more than we could carry. Besides, I thought we could buy furs up river; anyway, I'm warm enough."

"No you are not," returned the priest smiling. "You must get a parki with a hood."

"I've got an Arctic cap; it rolls down over my ears and goes all round my neck—just leaves a little place in front for my eyes."

"Yes; wear that if you go on the trail; but the good of the parki hood is, that it is trimmed all round with long wolf-hair. You see"—he picked his parki up off the floor and showed it to the company—"those long hairs standing out all round the face break the force of the wind. It is wonderful how the Esquimaux hood lessens the chance of frost-bite."

While the only object in the room that he didn't seem to see was Mac, he was most taken up with the fireplace.

The Colonel laid great stress on the enormous services of the delightful, accomplished master-mason over there on the bean-bags, who sat looking more than ever like a monkey-wrench incarnate.

But whether that Jesuit was as wily as the Calvinist thought, he had quite wit enough to overlook the great chimney-builder's wrathful silence.

He was not the least "professional," talked about the country and how to live here, saying incidentally that he had spent twelve years at the mission of the Holy Cross. The Yukon wasn't a bad place to live in, he told them, if men only took the trouble

35

to learn how to live here. While teaching the Indians, there was a great deal to learn from them as well.

"You must all come and see our schools," he wound up.

"We'd like to awfully," said the Boy, and all but Mac echoed him. "We were so afraid," he went on, "that we mightn't see anybody all winter long."

"Oh, you'll have more visitors than you want."

"Shall we, though?" Then, with a modified rapture: "Indians, I suppose, and—and missionaries."

"Traders, too, and miners, and this year cheechalkos as well. You are directly on the great highway of winter travel. Now that there's a good hard crust on the snow you will have dog-trains passing every week, and sometimes two or three."

It *was* good news!

"We've already had one visitor before you," said the Boy, looking wonderfully pleased at the prospect the priest had opened out. "You must know Nicholas of Pymeut, don't you?"

"Oh yes; we all know Nicholas"; and the priest smiled.

"We *like* him," returned the Boy as if some slighting criticism had been passed upon his friend.

"Of course you do; so do we all"; and still that look of quiet amusement on the worn face and a keener twinkle glinting in the eyes.

"We're afraid he's sick," the Boy began.

Before the priest could answer, "He was educated at Howly Cross, he *says,*" contributed O'Flynn.

"Oh, he's been to Holy Cross, among other places."

"What do you mean?"

"Well, Nicholas is a most impartial person. He was born at Pymeut, but his father, who is the richest and most intelligent man in his tribe, took Nicholas to Ikogimeut when the boy was only six. He was brought up in the Russian mission there, as the father had been before him, and was a Greek—in religion—till he was fourteen. There was a famine that year down yonder, so Nicholas turned Catholic and came up to us. He was at Holy Cross some years, when business called him to Anvik, where he turned Episcopalian. At Eagle City, I believe, he is regarded as a pattern Presbyterian. There are those that say, since he has been a pilot, Nicholas makes six changes a trip in his religious convictions."

Father Wills saw that the Colonel, to whom he most frequently addressed himself, took his pleasantry gravely. "Nicholas is not a bad fellow," he added. "He told me you had been kind to him."

"If you believe that about his insincerity," said the Colonel, "are you not afraid the others you spend your life teaching may turn out as little credit to you—to Christianity?"

The priest glanced at the listening Indian. "No," said he gravely; "I do not think *all* the natives are like Nicholas. Andrew here is a true son of the Church. But even if it were otherwise, *we,* you know"—the Jesuit rose from the table with that calm smile of his—"we simply do the work without question. The issue is not in our hands." He made the sign of the cross and set back his stool.

"Come, Andrew," he said; "we must push on."

The Indian repeated the priest's action, and went out to see to the dogs.

"Oh, are you going right away?" said the Colonel politely, and O'Flynn volubly protested.

"We thought," said the Boy, "you'd sit awhile and smoke and —at least, of course, I don't mean smoke exactly—but——"

The Father smiled and shook his head.

"Another time I would stay gladly."

"Where are you going now?"

"Andrew and I are on our way to the *Oklahoma,* the steamship frozen in the ice below here."

"How far?" asked the Boy.

"About seven miles below the Russian mission, and a mile or so up the Kuskoquim Slough."

"Wrecked there?"

"Oh no. Gone into winter quarters."

"In a slew?" for it was so Father Wills pronounced s-l-o-u-g-h.

"Oh, that's what they call a blind river up in this country. They come into the big streams every here and there, and cheechalkos are always mistaking them for the main channel. Sometimes they're wider and deeper for a mile or so than the river proper, but before you know it they land you in a marsh. This place I'm going to, a little way up the Kuskoquim, out of danger when the ice breaks up, has been chosen for a new station by the N. A. T. and T. Company—rival, you know, to the old-established Alaska Commercial, that inherited the Russian fur monopoly and controlled the seal and salmon trade so long. Well, the younger company runs the old one hard, and they've sent this steamer into winter quarters loaded with provisions, ready to start for Dawson the instant the ice goes out."

"Why, then, it's the very boat that'll be takin' us to the Klondyke."

"You just goin' down to have a look at her?" asked Potts enviously.

"No. I go to get relief for the Pymeuts."

"What's the matter with 'em?"

"Epidemic all summer, starvation now."

"Guess you won't find *any*body's got such a lot he wants to give it away to the Indians."

"Our Father Superior has given much," said the priest gently; "but we are not inexhaustible at Holy Cross. And the long winter is before us. Many of the supply steamers have failed to get in, and the country is flooded with gold-seekers. There'll be wide-spread want this year—terrible suffering all up and down the river."

"The more reason for people to hold on to what they've got. A white man's worth more 'n an Indian."

The priest's face showed no anger, not even coldness.

"White men have got a great deal out of Alaska and as yet done little but harm here. The government ought to help the natives, and we believe the Government will. All we ask of the captain of the *Oklahoma* is to sell us, on fair terms, a certain supply, we assuming part of the risk, and both of us looking to the Government to make it good."

"Reckon you'll find that steamer-load down in the ice is worth its weight in gold," said Potts.

"One must always try," replied the Father.

He left the doorpost, straightened his bowed back, and laid a hand on the wooden latch.

"But Nicholas—when you left Pymeut was he——" began the Boy.

"Oh, he is all right," the Father smiled and nodded. "Brother Paul has been looking after Nicholas's father. The old chief has enough food, but he has been very ill. By the way, have you any letters you want to send out?"

"Oh, if we'd only known!" was the general chorus; and Potts flew to close and stamp one he had hardly more than begun to the future Mrs. Potts.

The Boy had thoughtlessly opened the door to have a look at the dogs.

"Shut that da—— Don't keep the door open!" howled Potts, trying to hold his precious letter down on the table while he added "only two words." The Boy slammed the door behind him.

"With all our trouble, the cabin isn't really warm," said the Colonel apologetically. "In a wind like this, if the door is open, we have to hold fast to things to keep them from running down the Yukon. It's a trial to anybody's temper."

"Why don't you build a false wall?"

"Well, I don't know; we hadn't thought of it."

"You'd find it correct this draught"; and the priest explained his views on the subject while Potts's letter was being addressed. Andrew put his head in.

"Ready, Father!"

As the priest was pocketing the letter the Boy dashed in, put on the Arctic cap he set such store by, and a fur coat and mittens.

"Do you mind if I go a little way with you?" he said.

"Of course not," answered the priest. "I will send him back in half an hour," he said low to the Colonel. "It's a bitter day."

It was curious how already he had divined the relation of the elder man to the youngest of that odd household.

The moment they had gone Mac, with an obvious effort, pulled himself up out of his corner, and, coming towards the Colonel at the fireplace, he said thickly:

"You've put an insult upon me, Warren, and that's what I stand from no man. Come outside."

The Colonel looked at him.

"All right, Mac; but we've just eaten a rousing big dinner. Even Sullivan wouldn't accept that as the moment for a round. We'll both have forty winks, hey? and Potts shall call us, and O'Flynn shall be umpire. You can have the Boy's bunk."

Mac was in a haze again, and allowed himself to be insinuated into bed.

The others got rid of the dinner things, and "sat round" for an hour.

"Doubt if he sleeps long," says Potts a little before two; "that's what he's been doing all morning."

"We haven't had any fresh meat for a week," returns the Colonel significantly. "Why don't you and O'Flynn go down to meet the Boy, and come round by the woods? There'll be full moon up by four o'clock; you might get a brace of grouse or a rabbit or two."

O'Flynn was not very keen about it; but the Jesuit's visit had stirred him up, and he offered less opposition to the unusual call to activity than the Colonel expected.

When at last he was left alone with the sleeping man, the Kentuckian put on a couple more logs, and sat down to wait. At three he got up, swung the crane round so that the darting tongues of flame could lick the hot-water pot, and then he measured out some coffee. In a quarter of an hour the cabin was full of the fragrance of good Mocha.

The Colonel sat and waited. Presently he poured out a little coffee, and drank it slowly, blissfully, with half-closed eyes. But when he had set the granite cup down again, he stood up alert, like a man ready for business. Mac had been asleep nearly three hours. The others wouldn't be long now.

Well, if they came prematurely, they must go to the Little Cabin for awhile. The Colonel shot the bar across door and jamb for the second time that day. Mac stirred and lifted himself on his elbow, but he wasn't really awake.

"Potts," he said huskily.

The Colonel made no sound.

"Potts, measure me out two fingers, will you? Cabin's damn cold."

No answer.

Mac roused himself, muttering compliments for Potts. When he had bundled himself out over the side of the bunk, he saw the Colonel seemingly dozing by the fire.

He waited a moment. Then, very softly, he made his way to the farther end of the swing-shelf.

The Colonel opened one eye, shut it, and shuffled in a sleepy sort of way. Mac turned sharply back to the fire.

The Colonel opened his eyes and yawned.

"I made some cawfee a little while back. Have some?"

"No."

"Better; it's A 1."

"Where's Potts?"

"Gone out for a little. Back soon." He poured out some of the strong, black decoction, and presented it to his companion. "Just try it. Finest cawfee in the world, sir."

Mac poured it down without seeming to bother about tasting it.

40

They sat quite still after that, till the Colonel said meditatively:

"You and I had a little account to settle, didn't we?"

"I'm ready."

But neither moved for several moments.

"See here, Mac: you haven't been ill or anything like that, have you?"

"No." There was no uncertain note in the answer; if anything, there was in it more than the usual toneless decision. Mac's voice was machine-made—as innocent of modulation as a buzz-saw, and with the same uncompromising finality as the shooting of a bolt. "I'm ready to stand up against any man."

"Good!" interrupted the Colonel. "Glad o' that, for I'm just longing to see you stand up——"

Mac was on his feet in a flash.

"You had only to say so, if you wanted to see me stand up against any man alive. And when I sit down again it's my opinion one of us two won't be good-lookin' any more."

He pushed back the stools.

"I thought maybe it was only necessary to mention it," said the Colonel slowly. "I've been wanting for a fortnight to see you stand up"—Mac turned fiercely—"against Samuel David MacCann."

"Come on! I'm in no mood for monkeyin'!"

"Nor I. I realise, MacCann, we've come to a kind of a crisis. Things in this camp are either going a lot better, or a lot worse, after to-day."

"There's nothing wrong, if you quit asking dirty Jesuits to sit down with honest men."

"Yes; there's something worse out o' shape than that."

Mac waited warily.

"When we were stranded here, and saw what we'd let ourselves in for, there wasn't one of us that didn't think things looked pretty much like the last o' pea time. There was just one circumstance that kept us from throwing up the sponge; *we had a man in camp.*"

The Colonel paused.

Mac stood as expressionless as the wooden crane.

"A man we all believed in, who was going to help us pull through."

"That was you, I s'pose." Mac's hard voice chopped out the sarcasm.

41

"You know mighty well who it was. The Boy's all right, but he's young for this kind o' thing—young and heady. There isn't much wrong with me that I'm aware of, except that I don't know shucks. Potts's petering out wasn't altogether a surprise, and nobody expected anything from O'Flynn till we got to Dawson, when a lawyer and a fella with capital behind him may come in handy. But there was one man—who had a head on him, who had experience, and who"—he leaned over to emphasise the climax—"who had *character*. It was on that man's account that I joined this party."

Mac put his hands in his pockets and leaned against the wall. His face began to look a little more natural. The long sleep or the coffee had cleared his eyes.

"Shall I tell you what I heard about that man last night?" asked the Colonel gravely.

Mac looked up, but never opened his lips.

"You remember you wouldn't sit here——"

"The Boy was always in and out. The cabin was cold."

"I left the Boy and O'Flynn at supper-time and went down to the Little Cabin to——"

"To see what I was doin'—to spy on me."

"Well, all right—maybe I was spying, too. Incidentally I wanted to tell you the cabin was hot as blazes, and get you to come to supper. I met Potts hurrying up for his grub, and I said, 'Where's Mac? Isn't he coming?' and your pardner's answer was: 'Oh, let him alone. He's got a flask in his bunk, swillin' and gruntin'; he's just in hog-heaven.'"

"Damn that sneak!"

"The man he was talkin' about, Mac, was the man we had all built our hopes on."

"I'll teach Potts——"

"You can't, Mac. Potts has got to die and go to heaven—perhaps to hell, before he'll learn any good. But you're a different breed. Teach MacCann."

Mac suddenly sat down on the stool with his head in his hands.

"The Boy hasn't caught on," said the Colonel presently, "but he said something this morning to show he was wondering about the change that's come over you."

"That I don't split wood all day, I suppose, when we've got enough for a month. Potts doesn't either. Why don't you go for Potts?"

"As the Boy said, I don't care about Potts. It's Mac that matters."

"Did the Boy say that?" He looked up.

The Colonel nodded.

"After you had made that chimney, you know, you were a kind of hero in his eyes."

Mac looked away.

"The cabin's been cold," he muttered.

"We are going to remedy that."

"I didn't bring any liquor into camp. You must admit that I didn't intend——"

"I do admit it."

"And when O'Flynn said that about keeping his big demijohn out of the inventory and apart from the common stores, I sat on him."

"So you did."

"I knew it was safest to act on the 'medicinal purposes' principle."

"So it is."

"But I wasn't thinking so much of O'Flynn. I was thinking of . . . things that had happened before . . . for . . . I'd had experience. Drink was the curse of Caribou. It's something of a scourge up in Nova Scotia . . . I'd had experience."

"You did the very best thing possible under the circumstances." Mac was feeling about after his self-respect, and must be helped to get hold of it. "I realise, too, that the temptation is much greater in cold countries," said the Kentuckian unblushingly. "Italians and Greeks don't want fiery drinks half as much as Russians and Scandinavians—haven't the same craving as Nova Scotians and cold-country people generally, I suppose. But that only shows, temperance is of more vital importance in the North."

"That's right! It's not much in my line to shift blame, even when I don't deserve it; but you know so much you might as well know . . . it wasn't I who opened that demijohn first."

"But you don't mind being the one to shut it up—do you?"

"Shut it up?"

"Yes; let's get it down and——" The Colonel swung it off the shelf. It was nearly empty, and only the Boy's and the Colonel's single bottles stood unbroached. Even so, Mac's prolonged spree was something of a mystery to the Kentuckian. It must be that a very little was too much for Mac. The Colonel handed the demijohn to his companion, and lit the solitary candle standing on its little block of wood, held in place between three half-driven nails.

"What's that for?"

"Don't you want to seal it up?"

"I haven't got any wax."

"I have an inch or so." The Colonel produced out of his pocket the only piece in camp.

Mac picked up a billet of wood, and drove the cork in flush with the neck. Then, placing upright on the cork the helve of the hammer, he drove the cork down a quarter of an inch farther.

"Give me your wax. What's for a seal?" They looked about. Mac's eye fell on a metal button that hung by a thread from the old militia jacket he was wearing. He put his hand up to it, paused, glanced hurriedly at the Colonel, and let his fingers fall.

"Yes, yes," said the Kentuckian, "that'll make a capital seal."

"No; something of yours, I think, Colonel. The top of that tony pencil-case, hey?"

The Colonel produced his gold pencil, watched Mac heat the wax, drop it into the neck of the demipohn, and apply the initialled end of the Colonel's property. While Mac, without any further waste of words, was swinging the wicker-bound temptation up on the shelf again, they heard voices.

"They're coming back," says the Kentuckian hurriedly. "But we've settled our little account, haven't we, old man?"

Mac jerked his head in that automatic fashion that with him meant genial and whole-hearted agreement.

"And if Potts or O'Flynn want to break that seal——"

"I'll call 'em down," says Mac. And the Colonel knew the seal was safe.

* * * * *

"By-the-by, Colonel," said the Boy, just as he was turning in that night, "I—a—I've asked that Jesuit chap to the House-Warming.'

"Oh, you did, did you?"

"Yes."

"Well, you'd just better have a talk with Mac about it."

"Yes. I've been tryin' to think how I'd square Mac. Of course, I know I'll have to go easy on the raw."

"I reckon you just will."

"If Monkey-wrench screws down hard on me, you'll come to the rescue, won't you, Colonel?"

"No; I'll side with Mac on that subject.   Whatever he says, goes!"

"Humph! *that* Jesuit's all right."

Not a word out of the Colonel.

CHAPTER III

TWO NEW SPISSIMENS

Medwjedew (zu Luka). Sag' mal—wer bist du? Ich kenne dich nicht.

Luka. Kennst du denn sonst alle Leute?

Medwjedew. In meinem Revier muß ich jeden kennen—und dich kenn' ich nicht. . . .

Luka. Das kommt wohl daher Onkelchen, daß dein Revier nicht die ganze Erde umfaßt . . . 's ist da noch ein Endchen draußen geblieben. . . .

ONE of the curious results of what is called wild life, is a blessed release from many of the timidities that assail the easy liver in the centres of civilisation. Potts was the only one in the white camp who had doubts about the wisdom of having to do with the natives.

However, the agreeable necessity of going to Pymeut to invite Nicholas to the Blow-out was not forced upon the Boy. They were still hard at it, four days after the Jesuit had gone his way, surrounding the Big Cabin with a false wall, that final and effectual barrier against Boreas—finishing touch warranted to convert a cabin, so cold that it drove its inmates to drink, into a dwelling where practical people, without cracking a dreary joke, might fitly celebrate a House-Warming.

In spite of the shortness of the days, Father Wills's suggestion was being carried out with a gratifying success. Already manifest were the advantages of the stockade, running at a foot's distance round the cabin to the height of the eaves, made of spruce saplings not even lopped of their short bushy branches, but planted close together, after burning the ground cleared of snow. A second visitation of mild weather, and a further two days' thaw, made the Colonel determine to fill in the space between the spruce stockade and the cabin with "burnt-out" soil closely packed down and well tramped in. It was generally

46

conceded, as the winter wore on, that to this contrivance of the "earthwork" belonged a good half of the credit of the Big Cabin, and its renown as being the warmest spot on the lower river that terrible memorable year of the Klondyke Rush.

The evergreen wall with the big stone chimney shouldering itself up to look out upon the frozen highway, became a conspicuous feature in the landscape, welcome as the weeks went on to many an eye wearied with long looking for shelter, and blinded by the snow-whitened waste.

An exception to what became a rule was, of all men, Nicholas. When the stockade was half done, the Prince and an equerry appeared on the horizon, with the second team the camp had seen, the driver much concerned to steer clear of the softened snow and keep to that part of the river ice windswept and firm, if roughest of all. Nicholas regarded the stockade with a cold and beady eye.

No, he hadn't time to look at it. He had promised to "mush." He wasn't even hungry.

It did little credit to his heart, but he seemed more in haste to leave his new friends than the least friendly of them would have expected.

"Oh, wait a sec.," urged the deeply disappointed Boy. "I wanted awf'ly to see how your sled is made. It's better 'n Father Wills'."

"Humph!" grunted Nicholas scornfully; "him no got Innuit sled."

"Mac and I are goin' to try soon's the stockade's done——"

"Goo'-bye," interrupted Nicholas.

But the Boy paid no attention to the word of farewell. He knelt down in the snow and examined the sled carefully.

"Spruce runners," he called out to Mac, "and—jee! they're shod with ivory! *Jee!* fastened with sinew and wooden pegs. Hey?"—looking up incredulously at Nicholas—"not a nail in the whole shebang, eh?"

"Nail?" says Nicholas. "Huh, no *nail!*" as contemptuously as though the Boy had said "bread-crumbs."

"Well, she's a daisy! When you comin' back?"

"Comin' pretty quick; goin' pretty quick. Goo'-bye! *Mush!*" shouted Nicholas to his companion, and the dogs got up off their haunches.

But the Boy only laughed at Nicholas's struggles to get started. He hung on to the loaded sled, examining, praising, while the dogs, after the merest affectation of trying to make a start, looked round at him over their loose collars and grinned contentedly.

"Me got to mush. Show nex' time. Mush!"

"What's here?" the Boy shouted through the "mushing"; and he tugged at the goodly load, so neatly disposed under an old reindeer-skin sleeping-bag, and lashed down with raw hide.

That? Oh, that was fish.

"Fish! Got so much fish at starving Pymeut you can go hauling it down river? Well, sir, *we* want fish. We *must* have fish. Hey?" The Boy appealed to the others.

"Yes."

"R-right y'arre!"

"I reckon we just do!"

But Nicholas had other views.

"No, me take him——" He hitched his body in the direction of Ikogimeut.

"Bless my soul! you've got enough there for a regiment. You goin' to sell him? Hey?"

Nicholas shook his head.

"Oh, come off the roof!" advised the Boy genially.

"You ain't carryin' it about for your health, I suppose?" said Potts.

"The people down at Ikogimeut don't need it like us. We're white duffers, and can't get fish through the ice. You sell *some* of it to us." But Nicholas shook his head and shuffled along on his snow-shoes, beckoning the dog-driver to follow.

"Or trade some fur—fur tay," suggested O'Flynn.

"Or for sugar," said Mac.

"Or for tobacco," tempted the Colonel.

And before that last word Nicholas's resolve went down. Up at the cabin he unlashed the load, and it quickly became manifest that Nicholas was a dandy at driving a bargain. He kept on saying shamelessly:

"More—more shuhg. Hey? Oh yes, me give heap fish. No nuff shuhg."

If it hadn't been for Mac (his own clear-headed self again, and by no means to be humbugged by any Prince alive) the purchase of a portion of that load of frozen fish, corded up like so much wood, would have laid waste the commissariat.

But if the white men after this passage did not feel an absolute confidence in Nicholas's fairness of mind, no such unworthy suspicion of them found lodgment in the bosom of the Prince. With the exception of some tobacco, he left all his ill-gotten store to be kept for him by his new friends till he should return. When was that to be? In five sleeps he would be back.

"Good! We'll have the stockade done by then. What do you say to our big chimney, Nicholas?"

He emitted a scornful "Peeluck!"

"What! Our chimney no good?"

He shrugged: "Why you have so tall hole your house? How you cover him up?"

"We don't want to cover him up."

"Humph! winter fin' you tall hole. Winter come down—bring in snow—drive fire out." He shivered in anticipation of what was to happen. "Peeluck!"

The white men laughed.

"What you up to now? Where you going?"

Well, the fact was, Nicholas had been sent by his great ally, the Father Superior of Holy Cross, on a mission, very important, demanding despatch.

"Father Brachet—him know him heap better send Nicholas when him want man go God-damn quick. Me no stop—no—no stop."

He drew on his mittens proudly, unjarred by remembrance of how his good resolution had come to grief.

"Where you off to now?"

"Me ketchum Father Wills—me give letter." He tapped his deerskin-covered chest. "Ketchum *sure* 'fore him leave Ikogimeut."

"You come back with Father Wills?"

Nicholas nodded.

"Hooray! we'll all work like sixty!" shouted the Boy, "and by Saturday (that's five sleeps) we'll have the wall done and the house warm, and you and"—he caught himself up; not thus in public would he break the news to Mac—"you'll be back in time for the big Blow-Out." To clinch matters, he accompanied Nicholas from the cabin to the river trail, explaining: "You savvy? Big feast—all same Indian. Heap good grub. No prayer-meetin'—you savvy?—no church this time. Big fire, big feed. All kinds—apples, shuhg, bacon—no cook him, you no like," he added, basely truckling to the Prince's peculiar taste.

49

Nicholas rolled his single eye in joyful anticipation, and promised faithfully to grace the scene.

*   *   *   *   *

This was all very fine . . . but Father Wills! The last thing at night and the first thing in the morning the Boy looked the problem in the face, and devised now this, now that, adroit and disarming fashion of breaking the news to Mac.

But it was only when the daring giver of invitations was safely in bed, and Mac equally safe down in the Little Cabin, that it seemed possible to broach the subject. He devised scenes in which, airily and triumphantly, he introduced Father Wills, and brought Mac to the point of pining for Jesuit society; but these scenes were actable only under conditions of darkness and of solitude. The Colonel refused to have anything to do with the matter.

"Our first business, as I see it, is to keep peace in the camp, and hold fast to a good understanding with one another. It's just over little things like this that trouble begins. Mac's one of us; Father Wills is an outsider. I won't rile Mac for the sake of any Jesuit alive. No, sir; this is *your* funeral, and you're obliged to attend."

Before three of Nicholas's five sleeps were accomplished, the Boy began to curse the hour he had laid eyes on Father Wills. He began even to speculate desperately on the good priest's chances of tumbling into an air-hole, or being devoured by a timely wolf. But no, life was never so considerate as that. Yet he could neither face being the cause of the first serious row in camp, nor endure the thought of having *his* particular guest— drat him!—flouted, and the whole House-Warming turned to failure and humiliation.

Indeed, the case looked desperate. Only one day more now before he would appear—be flouted, insulted, and go off wounded, angry, leaving the Boy with an irreconcilable quarrel against Mac, and the House-Warming turned to chill recrimination and to wretchedness.

But until the last phantasmal hope went down before the logic of events it was impossible not to cling to the idea of melting Mac's Arctic heart. There was still one course untried.

Since there was so little left to do to the stockade, the Boy announced that he thought he'd go up over the hill for a tramp. Gun in hand and grub in pocket, he marched off to play his last trump-card. If he could bring home a queer enough bird or beast for the collection, there was still hope. To what lengths might Mac not go if one dangled before him the priceless bait of a golden-tipped emperor goose, dressed in imperial robes of rose-flecked snow? Or who, knowing Mac, would not trust a *Xema Sabinii* to play the part of a white-winged angel of peace? Failing some such heavenly messenger, there was nothing for it but that the Boy should face the ignominy of going forth to meet the Father on the morrow, and confess the humiliating truth. It wasn't fair to let him come expecting hospitality, and find—— Visions arose of Mac receiving the bent and wayworn missionary with the greeting: "There is no corner by the fire, no place in the camp for a pander to the Scarlet Woman." The thought lent impassioned fervour to the quest for goose or gull.

It was pretty late when he got back to camp, and the men were at supper. No, he hadn't shot anything.

"What's that bulging in your pocket?"

"Sort o' stone."

"Struck it rich?"

"Don't give me any chin-music, boys; give me tea. I'm dog-tired."

But when Mac got up first, as usual, to go down to the Little Cabin to "wood up" for the night, "I'll walk down with you," says the Boy, though it was plain he was dead-beat.

He helped to revive the failing fire, and then, dropping on the section of sawed wood that did duty for a chair, with some difficulty and a deal of tugging he pulled "the sort o' stone" out of the pocket of his duck shooting-jacket.

"See that?" He held the thing tightly clasped in his two red, chapped hands.

Mac bent down, shading his eyes from the faint flame flicker.

"What is it?"

"Piece o' tooth."

"By the Lord Harry! so it is." He took the thing nearer the faint light. "Fossil! Where'd you get it?"

"Over yonder—by a little frozen river."

"How far? Any more? Only this?"

The Boy didn't answer. He went outside, and returned instantly, lugging in something brown and whitish, weather-stained, unwieldy.

"I dropped this at the door as I came along home. Thought it might do for the collection."

Mac stared with all his eyes, and hurriedly lit a candle. The Boy dropped exhausted on a ragged bit of burlap by the bunks. Mac knelt down opposite, pouring liberal libation of candle-grease on the uncouth, bony mass between them.

"Part of the skull!" he rasped out, masking his ecstasy as well as he could.

"Mastodon?" inquired the Boy.

Mac shook his head.

"I'll bet my boots," says Mac, "it's an *Elephas primigenius;* and if I'm right, it's 'a find,' young man. Where'd you stumble on him?"

"Over yonder." The Boy leaned his head against the lower bunk.

"Where?"

"Across the divide. The bones have been dragged up on to some rocks. I saw the end of a tusk stickin' up out of the snow, and I scratched down till I found——" He indicated the trophy between them on the floor.

"Tusk? How long?"

"'Bout nine feet."

"We'll go and get it to-morrow."

No answer from the Boy.

"Early, hey?"

"Well—a—it's a good ways."

"What if it is?"

"Oh, I don't mind. I'd do more 'n that for you, Mac."

There was something unnatural in such devotion. Mac looked up. But the Boy was too tired to play the big fish any longer. "I wonder if you'll do something for me." He watched with a sinking heart Mac's sharp uprising from the worshipful attitude. It was not like any other mortal's gradual, many-jointed getting-up; it was more like the sudden springing out of the big blade of a clasp-knife.

"What's your game?"

"Oh, I ain't got any game," said the Boy desperately; "or, if I have, there's mighty little fun in it. However, I don't know as I want to walk ten hours again in this kind o' weather with an elephant on my back just for—for the poetry o' the thing." He laid his chapped hands on the side board of the bunk and pulled himself up on his legs.

"What's your game?" repeated Mac sternly, as the Boy reached the door.

"What's the good o' talkin'?" he answered; but he paused, turned, and leaned heavily against the rude lintel.

"Course, I know you'd be shot before you'd do it, but what I'd *like,* would be to hear you say you wouldn't kick up a hell of a row if Father Wills happens in to the House-Warmin'."

Mac jerked his set face, fire-reddened, towards the fossil-finder; and he, without waiting for more, simply opened the door, and heavily footed it back to the Big Cabin.

*   *   *   *

Next morning when Mac came to breakfast he heard that the Boy had had his grub half an hour before the usual time, and was gone off on some tramp again. Mac sat and mused.

O'Flynn came in with a dripping bucket, and sat down to breakfast shivering.

"Which way 'd he go?"

"The Boy? Down river."

"Sure he didn't go over the divide?"

O'Flynn was sure. He'd just been down to the water-hole, and in the faint light he'd seen the Boy far down on the river-trail "leppin' like a hare in the direction of the Roosian mission."

"Goin' to meet . . . a . . . Nicholas?"

"Reckon so," said the Colonel, a bit ruffled. "Don't believe he'll run like a hare very far with his feet all blistered."

"Did you know he'd discovered a fossil elephant?"

"No."

"Well, he has. I must light out, too, and have a look at it."

"Do; it'll be a cheerful sort of House-Warming with one of you off scouring the country for more blisters and chilblains, and another huntin' antediluvian elephants." The Colonel spoke with uncommon irascibility. The great feast-day had certainly not dawned propitiously.

When breakfast was done Mac left the Big Cabin without a word; but, instead of going over the divide across the treeless snow-waste to the little frozen river, where, turned up to the pale northern dawn, were lying the bones of a beast that had trampled tropic forests, in that other dawn of the Prime, the naturalist, turning his back on *Elephas primigenius,* followed in the track of the Boy down the great river towards Ikogimeut.

*   *   *   *

On the low left bank of the Yukon a little camp. On one side, a big rock hooded with snow. At right angles, drawn up one on top of the other, two sleds covered with reindeer-skins held down by stones. In the corner formed by the angle of rocks and sleds, a small A-tent, very stained and old. Burning before it on a hearth of greenwood, a little fire struggling with a veering wind.

Mac had seen from far off the faint blue banners of smoke blowing now right, now left, then tossed aloft in the pallid sunshine. He looked about sharply for the Boy, as he had been doing this two hours. There was the Jesuit bending over the fire, bettering the precarious position of a saucepan that insisted on sitting lop-sided, looking down into the heart of coals. Nicholas was holding up the tent-flap.

"Hello! How do!" he sang out, recognising Mac. The priest glanced up and nodded pleasantly. Two Indians, squatting on the other side of the fire, scrambled away as the shifting wind brought a cloud of stifling smoke into their faces.

"Where's the Boy?" demanded Mac, arresting the stampede.

Nicholas's dog-driver stared, winked, and wiped his weeping, smoke-reddened eyes.

"Is he in there?" Mac looked towards the tent.

Andrew nodded between coughs.

"What's he doing in there? Call him out," ordered Mac.

"He no walk."

Mac's hard face took on a look of cast-iron tragedy.

The wind, veering round again, had brought the last words to the priest on the other side of the fire.

"Oh, it'll be all right by-and-by," he said cheerfully.

"But knocking up like that just for blisters?"

"Blisters? No; cold and general weakness. That's why we delayed——"

Without waiting to hear more Mac strode over to the tent, and as he went in, Nicholas came out. No sign of the Boy—nobody, nothing. What? Down in the corner a small, yellow face lying in a nest of fur. Bright, dark eyes stared roundly, and as Mac glowered astonished at the apparition, a mouth full of gleaming teeth opened, smiling, to say in a very small voice:

"Farva!"

Astonished as Mac was, disappointed and relieved all at once, there was something arresting in the appeal.

"I'm not your father," he said stiffly. "Who're you? Hey? You speak English?"

The child stared at him fixedly, but suddenly, for no reason on earth, it smiled again. Mac stood looking down at it, seeming lost in thought. Presently the small object stirred, struggled about feebly under the encompassing furs, and, freeing itself, held out its arms. The mites of hands fluttered at his sleeve and made ineffectual clutches.

"What do you want?" To his own vast astonishment Mac lifted the little thing out of its warm nest. It was woefully thin, and seemed, even to his inexperience, to be insufficiently clothed, though the beaded moccasins on its tiny feet were new and good.

"Why, you're only about as big as a minute," he said gruffly. "What's the matter—sick?" It suddenly struck him as very extraordinary that he should have taken up the child, and how extremely embarrassing it would be if anyone came in and caught him. Clutching the small morsel awkwardly, he fumbled with the furs preparatory to getting rid, without delay, of the unusual burden. While he was straightening the things, Father Wills appeared at the flap, smoking saucepan in hand. The instant the cold air struck the child it began to cough.

"Oh, you mustn't do that!" said the priest to Mac with unexpected severity. "Kaviak must lie in bed and keep warm." Down on the floor went the saucepan. The child was caught away from the surprised Mac, and the furs so closely gathered round the small shrunken body that there was once more nothing visible but the wistful yellow face and gleaming eyes, still turned searchingly on its most recent acquaintance.

But the priest, without so much as a glance at the newcomer, proceeded to feed Kaviak out of the saucepan, blowing vigorously at each spoonful before administering.

"He's pretty hungry," commented Mac. "Where'd you find him?"

"In a little village up on the Kuskoquim. Kaviak's an Esquimaux from Norton Sound, aren't you, Kaviak?" But the child was wholly absorbed, it seemed, in swallowing and staring at Mac. "His family came up there from the coast in a bidarra only last summer—all dead now. Everybody else in the village —and there isn't but a handful—all ailing and all hungry. I was tramping across an igloo there a couple of days ago, and I heard a strange little muffled sound, more like a snared rabbit than anything else. But the Indian with me said no, everybody who had lived there was dead, and he was for hurrying on. They're superstitious, you know, about a place where people have died. But I crawled in, and found this little thing lying in a bundle of rags with its hands bound and dried grass stuffed in its mouth. It was too weak to stir or do more than occasionally to make that muffled noise that I'd heard coming up through the smoke-hole."

"What you goin' to do with him?"

"Well, I hardly know. The Sisters will look after him for a while, if I get him there alive."

"Why shouldn't you?"

Kaviak supplied the answer straightway by choking and falling into an appalling fit of coughing.

"I've got some stuff that'll be good for that," said Mac, thinking of his medicine-chest. "I'll give you some when we get back to camp."

The priest nodded, taking Mac's unheard of civility as a matter of course.

"The ice is very rough; the jolting makes him cough awfully."

The Jesuit had fastened his eyes on Mac's woollen muffler, which had been loosened during the ministering to Kaviak and had dropped on the ground. "Do you need that scarf?" he asked, as though he suspected Mac of wearing it for show. "Because if you didn't you could wrap it round Kaviak while I help the men strike camp." And without waiting to see how his suggestion was received, he caught up the saucepan, lifted the flap, and vanished.

"Farva," remarked Kaviak, fixing melancholy eyes on Mac.

"I ain't your father," muttered the gentleman so addressed. He picked up his scarf and hung it round his own neck.

"Farva!" insisted Kaviak. They looked at each other.

"You cold? That it, hey?" Mac knelt down and pulled away the furs. "God bless me! you only got this one rag on? God bless me!" He pulled off his muffler and wound the child in it mummy-wise, round and round, muttering the while in a surly way. When it was half done he stopped—thought profoundly with a furrow cutting deep into his square forehead between the straight brows. Slowly he pulled his gloves out of his pocket, and turned out from each beaver gauntlet an inner mitten of knitted wool. "Here," he said, and put both little moccasined feet into one of the capacious mittens. Much pleased with his ingenuity, he went on winding the long scarf until the yellow little Esquimaux bore a certain whimsical resemblance to one of the adorable Della Robbia infants. But Mac's sinewy

56

hands were exerting a greater pressure than he realized. The morsel made a remonstrant squeaking, and squirmed feebly.

"Oh, oh! Too tight? Beg your pardon," said Mac hastily, as though not only English, but punctilious manners were understanded of Kaviak. He relaxed the woollen bandage till the morsel lay contented again within its folds.

Nicholas came in for Kaviak, and for the furs, that he might pack them both in the Father's sled. Already the true son of the Church was undoing the ropes that lashed firm the canvas of the tent.

"Where's the Boy?" said Mac suddenly. "The young fellow that's with us. You know, the one that found you that first Sunday and brought you to camp. Where is he?"

Nicholas paused an instant with Kaviak on his shoulder.

"Kaiomi—no savvy."

"You not seen him to-day?"

"No. He no up——?" With the swaddled child he made a gesture up the river towards the white camp.

"No, he came down this morning to meet you."

Nicholas shook his head, and went on gathering up the furs. As he and Mac came out, Andrew was undoing the last fastening that held the canvas to the stakes. In ten minutes they were on the trail, Andrew leading, with Father Wills' dogs, Kaviak lying in the sled muffled to the eyes, still looking round out of the corners—no, strangely enough, the Kaviak eye had no corners, but fixedly he stared sideways at Mac. "Farva," seeming not to take the smallest notice, trudged along on one side of him, the priest on the other, and behind came Nicholas and the other Indians with the second sled. It was too windy to talk much even had they been inclined.

The only sounds were the *Mush! Mush!* of the drivers, the grate and swish of the runners over the ice, and Kaviak's coughing.

Mac turned once and frowned at him. It was curious that the child seemed not to mind these menacing looks, not in the smallest degree.

By-and-by the order of march was disturbed.

Kaviak's right runner, catching at some obstacle, swerved and sent the sled bumping along on its side, the small head of the passenger narrowly escaping the ice. Mac caught hold of the single-tree and brought the racing dogs to an abrupt halt. The priest and he righted the sled, and Mac straddling it, tucked in a loosened end of fur. When all was again in running order, Mac was on the same side as Father Wills. He still wore that look of dour ill-temper, and especially did he glower at the unfortunate Kaviak, seized with a fresh fit of coughing that filled the round eyes with tears.

"Don't you get kind o' tired listenin' to that noise? Suppose I was to carry—just for a bit——. This is the roughest place on the trail. Hi! Stop!" he called to Andrew. The priest had said nothing; but divining what Mac would be at, he helped him to undo the raw-hide lashing, and when Kaviak was withdrawn he wrapped one of the lighter fur things round him.

It was only when Mac had marched off, glowering still, and sternly refusing to meet Kaviak's tearful but grateful eyes—it was only then, bending over the sled and making fast the furs, that Father Wills, all to himself, smiled a little.

It wasn't until they were in sight of the smoke from the Little Cabin that Mac slackened his pace. He had never for a moment found the trail so smooth that he could return his burden to the sled. Now, however, he allowed Nicholas and the priest to catch up with him.

"You carry him the rest of the way," he commanded, and set his burden in Nicholas's arms. Kaviak was ill-pleased, but Mac, falling behind with the priest, stalked on with eyes upon the ground.

"I've got a boy of my own," he jerked out presently, with the air of a man who accounts confidentially for some weakness.

"Really!" returned the priest; "they didn't tell me."

"I haven't told them yet."

"Oh, all right."

"Why is he called that heathen name?"

"Kaviak? Oh, it's the name of his tribe. His people belong to that branch of the Innuits known as Kaviaks."

"Humph! Then he's only Kaviak as I'm MacCann. I suppose you've christened him?"

"Well, not yet—no. What shall we call him? What's your boy's name?"

"Robert Bruce." They went on in silence till Mac said, "It's on account of my boy I came up here."

"Oh!"

"It didn't use to matter if a man *was* poor and self-taught, but in these days of competition it's different. A boy must have chances if he's going to fight the battle on equal terms. Of course, some boys ain't worth botherin' about. But my boy—well, he seems to have something in him."

The priest listened silently, but with that look of brotherliness on his face that made it so easy to talk to him.

"It doesn't really matter to those other fellows." Mac jerked his hand towards the camp. "It's never so important to men—who stand alone—but I've *got* to strike it rich over yonder." He lifted his head, and frowned defiantly in the general direction of the Klondyke, thirteen hundred miles away. "It's my one chance," he added half to himself. "It means everything to Bob and me. Education, scientific education, costs like thunder."

"In the United States?"

"Oh, I mean to send my boy to the old country. I want Bob to be thorough."

The priest smiled, but almost imperceptibly.

"How old is he?"

"Oh, 'bout as old as this youngster." Mac spoke with calculated indifference.

"Six or thereabouts?"

"No; four and a half. But he's bigger——"

"Of course."

"And you can see already—he's got a lot in him."

Father Wills nodded with a conviction that brought Mac nearer confession than he had ever been in his life.

"You see," he said quite low, and as if the words were dragged out with pincers, "the fact is—my married life—didn't pan out very well. And I—ran away from home as a little chap—after a lickin'—and never went back. But there's one thing I mean to make a success of—that's my boy."

"Well, I believe you will, if you feel like that."

"Why, they've gone clean past the camp trail," said Mac sharply, "all but Nicholas—and what in thunder?—he's put the kid back on the sled——"

"Yes, I told my men we'd be getting on. But they were told to leave you the venison——"

"What! You goin' straight on? Nonsense!" Mac interrupted, and began to shout to the Indians.

"No; I *meant* to stop; just tell your friends so," said the unsuspecting Father; "but with a sick child——"

"What can you do for him that we can't? And to break the journey may make a big difference. We've got some condensed milk left—and——"

"Ah yes, but we are more accustomed to—it's hardly fair to burden a neighbour. No, we'll be getting on."

"If those fellers up there make a row about your bringing in a youngster"—he thrust out his jaw—"they can settle the account with me. I've got to do something for that cough before the kid goes on."

"Well," said the priest; and so wily are these Jesuits that he never once mentioned that he was himself a qualified doctor in full and regular practice. He kept his eyes on the finished stockade and the great chimney, wearing majestically its floating plume of smoke.

"Hi!" Mac called between his hands to the Indians, who had gone some distance ahead. "Hi!" He motioned them back up the hill trail.

O'Flynn had come out of the Little Cabin, and seemed to be laboriously trundling something along the footpath. He got so excited when he heard the noise and saw the party that, inadvertently, he let his burden slide down the icy slope, bumping and bouncing clumsily from one impediment to another.

"Faith, look at 'im! Sure, that fossle can't resthrain his j'y at seein' ye back. Mac, it's yer elephunt. I was takin' him in to the sate of honour be the foir. We thought it 'ud be a pleasant surprise fur ye. Sure, ye'r more surprised to see 'im leppin' down the hill to meet ye, like a rale Irish tarrier."

Mac was angry, and didn't conceal the fact. As he ran to stop the thing before it should be dashed to pieces, the priest happened to glance back, and saw coming slowly along the river trail a solitary figure that seemed to make its way with difficulty.

"It looks as though you'd have more than you bargained for at the House-Warming," he said.

O'Flynn came down the hill babbling like a brook.

"Good-day to ye, Father. The blessin's o' Heaven on ye fur not kapin' us starvin' anny longer. There's Potts been swearin', be this and be that, that yourself and the little divvle wudn't be at the Blow-Out at ahl, at ahl."

"You mean the Boy hasn't come back?" called out Mac. He leaned *Elephas primigenius* against a tuft of willow banked round with snow, and turned gloomily as if to go back down the river again.

"Who's this?" They all stood and watched the limping traveller.

"Why it's—of course. I didn't know him with that thing tied over his cap"; and Mac went to meet him.

The Boy bettered his pace.

"How did I miss you?" demanded Mac.

"Well," said the Boy, looking rather mischievous, "I can't think how it happened on the way down, unless you passed when I'd gone uphill a piece after some tracks. I was lyin' under the bluff a few miles down when you came back, and you—well, I kind o' thought you seemed to have your hands full." Mac looked rigid and don't-you-try-to-chaff-me-sir. "Besides," the Boy went on, "I couldn't cover the ground like you and Father Wills."

"What's the matter with you?"

"Oh, nothin' to howl about. But see here, Mac."

"Well?"

"Soon 's I can walk I'll go and get you the rest o' that elephant."

There was no more said till they got up to the others, who had waited for the Indians to come back, and had unpacked Kaviak to spare him the jolting uphill.

O'Flynn was screaming with excitement as he saw that the bundle Nicholas was carrying had a head and two round eyes.

"The saints in glory be among us! What's that? Man alive, what *is* it, be the Siven?"

"That," answered Mac with a proprietary air, "is a little Esquimaux boy, and I'm bringing him in to doctor his cold."

"Glory be! An Esquimer! And wid a cowld! Sure, he can have some o' my linnyeemint. Well, y'arre a boss collector, Mac! Faith, ye bang the Jews! And me thinkin' ye'd be satisfied wid yer elephunt. Not him, be the Siven! It's an Esquimer he must have to finish off his collection, wan wid the rale Arctic cowld in his head, and two eyes that goes snappin' through ye like black torpeders. Two spissimens in wan day! Yer growin' exthravagant, Mac. Why, musha, child, if I don't think yer the dandy Spissimen o' the lot!"

CHAPTER IV

THE BLOW-OUT

" How good it is to invite men to the pleasant feast."

COMFORTABLE as rock fireplace and stockade made the cabin now, the Colonel had been feeling all that morning that the official House-Warming was foredoomed to failure. Nevertheless, as he was cook that week, he could not bring himself to treat altogether lightly his office of Master of the Feast. There would probably be no guests. Even their own little company would likely be incomplete; but there was to be a spread that afternoon, "anyways."

Even had the Colonel needed any keeping up to the mark, the office would have been cheerfully undertaken by O'Flynn or by Potts, for whom interest in the gustatory aspect of the occasion was wholly undimmed by the threatened absence of Mac and the "little divvle."

"There'll be the more for us," said Potts enthusiastically.

O'Flynn's argument seemed to halt upon a reservation. He looked over the various contributions to the feast, set out on a board in front of the water-bucket, and, "It's mate I'm wishin' fur," says he.

"We've got fish."

"That's only mate on Fridays. We've had fish fur five days stiddy, an' befure that, bacon three times a day wid sivin days to the week, an' not enough bacon ayther, begob, whin all's said and done! Not enough to be fillin', and plenty to give us the scurrvy. May the divil dance on shorrt rations!"

"No scurvy in this camp for a while yet," said the Colonel, throwing some heavy objects into a pan and washing them vigorously round and round.

"Pitaties!" O'Flynn's eyes dwelt lovingly on the rare food. "Ye've hoarded 'em too long, man; they've sprouted."

"That won't prevent you hoggin' more'n your share, I'll bet," said Potts pleasantly.

"I don't somehow like wasting the sprouts," observed the Colonel anxiously. "It's such a wonderful sight—something growing." He had cut one pallid slip, and held it tenderly between knife and thumb.

"Waste 'em with scurvy staring us in the face? Should think not. Mix 'em with cold potaters in a salad."

"No. Make slumgullion," commanded O'Flynn.

"What's that?" quoth the Colonel.

"Be the Siven! I only wonder I didn't think of it befure. Arre ye listening, Kentucky? Ye take lots o' wathur, an' if ye want it rich, ye take the wathur ye've boiled pitaties or cabbage in—a vegetable stock, ye mind—and ye add a little flour, salt, and pepper, an' a tomater if ye're in New York or 'Frisco, and ye boil all that together with a few fish-bones or bacon-rin's to make it rale tasty."

"Yes—well?"

"Well, an' that's slumgullion."

"Don't sound heady enough for a 'Blow-Out,'" said the Colonel. "We'll sober up on slumgullion to-morrow."

"Anyhow, it's mate I'm wishin' fur," sighed O'Flynn, subsiding among the tin-ware. "What's the good o' the little divvle and his thramps, if he can't bring home a burrud, or so much as the scut iv a rabbit furr the soup?"

"Well, he's contributed a bottle of California apricots, and we'll have boiled rice."

"An' punch, glory be!"

"Y-yes," answered the Colonel. "I've been thinkin' a good deal about the punch."

"So's myself," said O'Flynn frankly; but Potts looked at the Colonel suspiciously through narrowed eyes.

"There's very little whiskey left, and I propose to brew a mild bowl——"

"To hell with your mild bowls!"

"A good enough punch, sah, but one that—that—a—well, that the whole kit and boodle of us can drink. Indians and everybody, you know . . . Nicholas and Andrew may turn up. I want you two fellas to suppoht me about this. There are reasons foh it, sah"—he had laid a hand on Potts' shoulder and fixed O'Flynn with his eye—"and"—speaking very solemnly—"yoh neither o' yoh gentlemen that need mo' said on the subject."

Whereupon, having cut the ground from under their feet,

he turned decisively, and stirred the mush-pot with a magnificent air and a newly-whittled birch stick.

To give the Big Cabin an aspect of solid luxury, they had spread the Boy's old buffalo "robe" on the floor, and as the morning wore on Potts and O'Flynn made one or two expeditions to the Little Cabin, bringing back selections out of Mac's hoard "to decorate the banquet-hall," as they said. On the last trip Potts refused to accompany his pardner—no, it was no good. Mac evidently wouldn't be back to see, and the laugh would be on them "takin' so much trouble for nothin'." And O'Flynn wasn't to be long either, for dinner had been absurdly postponed already.

When the door opened the next time, it was to admit Mac, Nicholas with Kaviak in his arms, O'Flynn gesticulating like a windmill, and, last of all, the Boy.

Kaviak was formally introduced, but instead of responding to his hosts' attentions, the only thing he seemed to care about, or even see, was something that in the hurly-burly everybody else overlooked—the decorations. Mac's stuffed birds and things made a remarkably good show, but the colossal success was reserved for the minute shrunken skin of the baby white hare set down in front of the great fire for a hearthrug. If the others failed to appreciate that joke, not so Kaviak. He gave a gurgling cry, struggled down out of Nicholas's arms, and folded the white hare to his breast.

"Where are the other Indians?" said Mac.

"Looking after the dogs," said Father Wills; and as the door opened, "Oh yes, give us that," he said to Andrew. " I thought"—he turned to the Colonel—"maybe you'd like to try some Yukon reindeer."

"Hooray!"

"Mate? Arre ye sayin' mate, or is an angel singin'?"

"Now I *know* that man's a Christian," soliloquised Potts.

"Look here: it'll take a little time to cook," said Mac, "and it's worth waitin' for. Can you let us have a pail o' hot water in the meantime?"

"Y-yes," said the Colonel, looking as if he had enough to think about already.

"Yes, we always wash them first of all," said Father Wills, noticing how Mac held the little heathen off at arm's length. "Nicholas used to help with that at Holy Cross." He gave the new order with the old authoritative gesture.

"And where's the liniment I lent you that you're so generous with?" Mac arraigned O'Flynn. "Go and get it."

Under Nicholas's hands Kaviak was forced to relinquish not only the baby hare, but his own elf locks. He was closely sheared, his moccasins put off, and his single garment dragged unceremoniously wrong side out over his head and bundled out of doors.

"Be the Siven! he's got as manny bones as a skeleton!"

"Poor little codger!" The Colonel stood an instant, skillet in hand staring.

"What's that he's got round his neck?" said the Boy, moving nearer.

Kaviak, seeing the keen look menacing his treasure, lifted a shrunken yellow hand and clasped tight the dirty shapeless object suspended from a raw-hide necklace.

Nicholas seemed to hesitate to divest him of this sole remaining possession.

"You must get him to give it up," said Father Wills, "and burn it."

Kaviak flatly declined to fall in with as much as he understood of this arrangement.

"What is it, anyway?" the Boy pursued.

"His amulet, I suppose." As Father Wills proceeded to enforce his order, and pulled the leather string over the child's head, Kaviak rent the air with shrieks and coughs. He seemed to say as well as he could, "I can do without my parki and my mucklucks, but I'll take my death without my amulet."

Mac insinuated himself brusquely between the victim and his persecutors. He took the dirty object away from the priest with scant ceremony, in spite of the whisper, "Infection!" and gave it back to the wrathful owner.

"You talk his language, don't you?" Mac demanded of Nicholas.

The Pymeut pilot nodded.

"Tell him, if he'll lend the thing to me to wash, he shall have it back."

Nicholas explained.

Kaviak, with streaming eyes and quivering lips, reluctantly handed it over, and watched Mac anxiously till overwhelmed by a yet greater misfortune in the shape of a bath for himself.

"How shall I clean this thing thoroughly?" Mac condescended to ask Father Wills. The priest shrugged.

"He'll have forgotten it to-morrow."

"He shall have it to-morrow," said Mac.

With his back to Kaviak, the Boy, O'Flynn, and Potts crowding round him, Mac ripped open the little bird-skin pouch, and took out three objects—an ivory mannikin, a crow's feather, and a thing that Father Wills said was a seal-blood plug.

"What's it for?"

"Same as the rest. It's an amulet; only as it's used to stop the flow of blood from the wound of a captive seal, it is supposed to be the best of all charms for anyone who spits blood."

"I'll clean 'em all after the Blow-Out," said Mac, and he went out, buried the charms in the snow, and stuck up a spruce twig to mark the spot.

Meanwhile, to poor Kaviak it was being plainly demonstrated what an awful fate descended on a person so unlucky as to part with his amulet. He stood straight up in the bucket like a champagne-bottle in a cooler, and he could not have resented his predicament more if he had been set in crushed ice instead of warm water. Under the remorseless hands of Nicholas he began to splutter and choke, to fizz, and finally explode with astonishment and wrath. It was quite clear Nicholas was trying to drown him. He took the treatment so to heart, that he kept on howling dismally for some time after he was taken out, and dried, and linimented and dosed by Mac, whose treachery about the amulet he seemed to forgive, since "Farva" had had the air of rescuing him from the horrors he had endured in that water-bucket, where, for all Kaviak knew, he might have stayed till he succumbed to death. The Boy contributed a shirt of his own, and helped Mac to put it on the incredibly thin little figure. The shirt came down to Kaviak's heels, and had to have the sleeves rolled up every two minutes. But by the time the reindeer-steak was nearly done Kaviak was done, too, and O'Flynn had said, "That Spissimen does ye credit, Mac."

Said Spissimen was now staring hungrily out of the Colonel's bunk, holding towards Mac an appealing hand, with half a yard of shirt-sleeve falling over it.

Mac pretended not to see, and drew up to the table the one remaining available thing to sit on, his back to his patient.

When the dogs had been fed, and the other Indians had come in, and squatted on the buffalo-skin with Nicholas, the first course was sent round in tin cups, a nondescript, but warming, "camp soup."

"Sorry we've got so few dishes, gentlemen," the Colonel had said. "We'll have to ask some of you to wait till others have finished."

"Farva," remarked Kaviak, leaning out of the bunk and sniffing the savoury steam.

"He takes you for a priest," said Potts, with the cheerful intention of stirring Mac's bile. But not even so damning a suspicion as that could cool the collector's kindness for his new Spissimen.

"You come here," he said. Kaviak didn't understand. The Boy got up, limped over to the bunk, lifted the child out, and brought him to Mac's side.

"Since there ain't enough cups," said Mac, in self-justification, and he put his own, half empty, to Kaviak's lips. The Spissimen imbibed greedily, audibly, and beamed. Mac, with unimpaired gravity, took no notice of the huge satisfaction this particular remedy was giving his patient, except to say solemnly, "Don't bubble in it."

The next course was fish à la Pymeut.

"You're lucky to be able to get it," said the Father, whether with suspicion or not no man could tell. "I had to send back for some by a trader and couldn't get enough."

"We didn't see any trader," said the Boy to divert the current.

"He may have gone by in the dusk; he was travelling hotfoot."

"Thought that steamship was chockful o' grub. What did you want o' fish?"

"Yes; they've got plenty of food, but——"

"They don't relish parting with it," suggested Potts.

"They haven't much to think about except what they eat; they wanted to try our fish, and were ready to exchange. I promised I would send a load back from Ikogimeut if they'd——" He seemed not to care to finish the sentence.

"So you didn't do much for the Pymeuts after all?"

"I did something," he said almost shortly. Then, with recovered serenity, he turned to the Boy: "I promised I'd bring back any news."

"Yes."

"Well?"

Everybody stopped eating and hung on the priest's words.

"Captain Rainey's heard there's a big new strike——"

"In the Klondyke?"

"On the American side this time."

"Hail Columbia!"

"Whereabouts?"

"At a place called Minóok."

"Where's that?"

"Up the river by the Ramparts."

"How far?"

"Oh, a little matter of six or seven hundred miles from here."

"Glory to God!"

"Might as well be six or seven thousand."

"And very probably isn't a *bonâ-fide* strike at all," said the priest, "but just a stampede—a very different matter."

"Well, I tell you straight: I got no use for a gold-mine in Minóok at this time o' year."

"Nop! Venison steak's more in my line than grub-stake just about now."

Potts had to bestir himself and wash dishes before he could indulge in his "line." When the grilled reindeer did appear, flanked by really-truly potatoes and the Colonel's hot Kentucky biscuit, there was no longer doubt in any man's mind but what this Blow-Out was being a success.

"Colonel's a daisy cook, ain't he?" the Boy appealed to Father Wills.

The Jesuit assented cordially.

"My family meant *me* for the army," he said. "Seen much service, Colonel?"

The Kentuckian laughed.

"Never wasted a day soldiering in my life."

"Oh!"

"Maybe you're wonderin'," said Potts, "why he's a Colonel!"

The Jesuit made a deprecatory gesture, politely disclaiming any such rude curiosity.

"He's from Kentucky, you see;" and the smile went round. "Beyond that, we can't tell you why he's a Colonel unless it's because he ain't a Judge;" and the boss of the camp laughed with the rest, for the Denver man had scored.

By the time they got to the California apricots and boiled rice everybody was feeling pretty comfortable. When, at last,

68

the table was cleared, except for the granite-ware basin full of punch, and when all available cups were mustered and tobacco-pouches came out, a remarkably genial spirit pervaded the company—with three exceptions.

Potts and O'Flynn waited anxiously to sample the punch before giving way to complete satisfaction, and Kaviak was impervious to considerations either of punch or conviviality, being wrapped in slumber on a corner of the buffalo-skin, between Mac's stool and the natives, who also occupied places on the floor.

Upon O'Flynn's first draught he turned to his next neighbour:

"Potts, me bhoy, 'tain't s' bad."

"I'll bet five dollars it won't make yer any happier."

"Begob, I'm happy enough! Gentlemen, wud ye like I should sing ye a song?"

"Yes."

"Yes," and the Colonel thumped the table for order, infinitely relieved that the dinner was done, and the punch not likely to turn into a *casus belli*. O'Flynn began a ditty about the Widdy Malone that woke up Kaviak and made him rub his round eyes with astonishment. He sat up, and hung on to the back of Mac's coat to make sure he had some anchorage in the strange new waters he had so suddenly been called on to navigate.

The song ended, the Colonel, as toast-master, proposed the health of— he was going to say Father Wills, but felt it discreeter to name no names. Standing up in the middle of the cabin, where he didn't have to stoop, he lifted his cup till it knocked against the swing-shelf, and called out, "Here's to Our Visitors, Neighbours, and Friends!" Whereupon he made a stately circular bow, which ended by his offering Kaviak his hand, in the manner of one who executes a figure in an old-fashioned dance. The smallest of "Our Visitors," still keeping hold of Mac, presented the Colonel with the disengaged half-yard of flannel undershirt on the other side, and the speech went on, very flowery, very hospitable, very Kentuckian.

When the Colonel sat down there was much applause, and O'Flynn, who had lent his cup to Nicholas, and didn't feel he could wait till it came back, began to drink punch out of the dipper between shouts of:

"Hooray! Brayvo! Here's to the Kurrnul! God bless him! That's rale oratry, Kurrnul! Here's to Kentucky—and ould Ireland."

Father Wills stood up, smiling, to reply.

"*Friends*" (the Boy thought the keen eyes rested a fraction of a moment longer on Mac than on the rest),—"*I think in some ways this is the pleasantest House-Warming I ever went to. I won't take up time thanking the Colonel for the friendly sentiments he's expressed, though I return them heartily. I must use these moments you are good enough to give me in telling you something of what I feel is implied in the founding of this camp of yours.*

"*Gentlemen, the few white dwellers in the Yukon country have not looked forward*" (his eyes twinkled almost wickedly) "*with that pleasure you might expect in exiles, to the influx of people brought up here by the great Gold Discovery. We knew what that sort of craze leads to. We knew that in a barren land like this, more and more denuded of wild game every year, more and more the prey of epidemic disease—we knew that into this sorely tried and hungry world would come a horde of men, all of them ignorant of the conditions up here, most of them ill-provided with proper food and clothing, many of them (I can say it without offence in this company)—many of them men whom the older, richer communities were glad to get rid of. Gentlemen, I have ventured to take you into our confidence so far, because I want to take you still farther—to tell you a little of the intense satisfaction with which we recognise that good fortune has sent us in you just the sort of neighbours we had not dared to hope for. It means more to us than you realise. When I heard a few weeks ago that, in addition to the boat-loads that had already got some distance up the river beyond Holy Cross——*" .

"Going to Dawson?"

"Oh, yes, Klondyke mad——"

"They'll be there before us, boys!"

"Anyways, they'll get to Minóok."

The Jesuit shook his head. "It isn't so certain. They probably made only a couple of hundred miles or so before the Yukon went to sleep."

"Then if grub gives out they'll be comin' back here?" suggested Potts.

"*Small doubt of it,*" agreed the priest. "*And when I heard there were parties of the same sort stranded at intervals all along the Lower River——*"

"You sure?"

He nodded.

"*And when Father Orloff of the Russian mission told us that he was already having trouble with the two big rival parties frozen in the ice below Ikogimeut——*"

"Gosh! Wonder if any of 'em were on our ship?"

"*Well, gentlemen, I do not disguise from you that, when I heard of the large amount of whiskey, the small amount of food, and the low type of manners brought in by these gold-seekers, I felt my fears justified. Such men don't work, don't contribute anything to the decent social life of the community, don't build cabins like this. When I came down on the ice the first time after you'd camped, and I looked up and saw your solid stone chimney*" (he glanced at Mac), "*I didn't know what a House-Warming it would make; but already, from far off across the ice and snow, that chimney warmed my heart. Gentlemen, the fame of it has gone up the river and down the river. Father Orloff is coming to see it next week, and so are the white traders from Anvik and Andreiefsky, for they've heard there's nothing like it in the Yukon. Of course, I know that you gentlemen have not come to settle permanently. I know that when the Great White Silence, as they call the long winter up here, is broken by the thunder of the ice rushing down to the sea, you, like the rest, will exchange the snow-fields for the gold-fields, and pass out of our ken. Now, I'm not usually prone to try my hand at prophecy; but I am tempted to say, even on our short acquaintance, that I am tolerably sure that, while we shall be willing enough to spare most of the new-comers to the Klondyke, we shall grudge to the gold-fields the men who built this camp and warmed this cabin.*" (His eye rested reflectively on Mac.) "*I don't wish to sit down leaving an impression of speaking with entire lack of sympathy of the impulse that brings men up here for gold. I believe that, even with the sort in the two camps below Ikogimeut—drinking, quarrelling, and making trouble with the natives at the Russian mission—I believe that even with them, the gold they came up here for is a symbol—a fetich, some of us may think. When such men have it in their hands, they feel dimly that they are laying tangible hold at last on some elusive vision of happiness that has hitherto escaped them. Be-*

hind each man braving the Arctic winter up here, is some hope, not all ignoble; some devotion, not all unsanctified. Behind most of these men I seem to see a wife or child, a parent, or some dear dream that gives that man his share in the Eternal Hope. Friends, we call that thing we look for by different names; but we are all seekers after treasure, all here have turned our backs on home and comfort, hunting for the Great Reward—each man a new Columbus looking for the New World. Some of us looking north, some south, some"—he hesitated the briefest moment, and then with a faint smile, half sad, half triumphant, made a little motion of his head—*"some of us . . . looking upwards."*

But quickly, as though conscious that, if he had raised the moral tone of the company, he had not raised its spirits, he hurried on:

"Before I sit down, gentlemen, just one word more. I must congratulate you on having found out so soon, not only the wisdom, but the pleasure of looking at this Arctic world with intelligent eyes, and learning some of her wonderful lessons. It is so that, now the hardest work is finished, you will keep up your spirits and avoid the disease that attacks all new-comers who simply eat, sleep, and wait for the ice to go out. When I hear cheechalkos complaining of boredom up here in this world of daily miracles, I think of the native boy in the history-class, who, called on to describe the progress of civilisation, said: 'In those days men had as many wives as they liked, and that was called polygamy. Now they have only one wife, and that's called monotony.'"

While O'Flynn howled with delight, the priest wound up:

"Gentlemen, if we find monotony up here, it's not the country's fault, but a defect in our own civilisation." Wherewith he sat down amid cheers.

"Now, Colonel, is Mac goin' to recite some Border ballads?" inquired the Boy, "or will he make a speech, or do a Highland fling?"

The Colonel called formally upon Mr. MacCann.

Mac was no sooner on his legs than Kaviak, determined not to lose his grasp of the situation, climbed upon the three-legged stool just vacated, and resumed his former relations with the friendly coat-tail.

Everybody laughed but Mac, who pretended not to know what was going on behind his back.

"Gentlemen," he began harshly, with the air of one about to launch a heavy indictment, "there's one element largely represented here by numbers and by interests"—he turned round suddenly toward the natives, and almost swung Kaviak off into space—"one element not explicitly referred to in the speeches, either of welcome or of thanks. But, gentlemen, I submit that these hitherto unrecognised Natives are our real hosts, and a word about them won't be out of place. I've been told to-day that, whether in Alaska, Greenland, or British America, they call themselves *Innuits*, which means human beings. They believed, no doubt, that they were the only ones in the world. I've been thinking a great deal about these Esquimaux of late——"

"Hear, hear!"

"About their origin and their destiny." (Mac was beginning to enjoy himself. The Boy was beginning to be bored and to drum softly with his fingers.) "Now, gentlemen, Buffon says that the poles were the first portions of the earth's crust to cool. While the equator, and even the tropics of Cancer and of Capricorn, were still too boiling hot to support life, up here in the Arctic regions there was a carboniferous era goin' on——"

"Where's the coal, then?" sneered Potts.

"It's bein' discovered . . . all over . . . ask him" (indicating Father Wills, who smiled assent). "Tropical forests grew where there are glayshers now, and elephants and mastodons began life here."

"Jimminy Christmas!" interrupted the Boy, sitting up very straight. "Is that Buffer you quoted a good authority?"

"First-rate," Mac snapped out defiantly.

"Good Lord! then the Garden o' Eden was up here."

"Hey?"

"Course! *This* was the cradle o' the human race. Blow the Ganges! Blow the Nile! It was our Yukon that saw the first people, 'cause of course the first people lived in the first place got ready for 'em."

"That don't follow. Read your Bible."

"If I'm not right, how did it happen there were men here when the North was first discovered?"

"Sh!"

"Mac's got the floor."

"Shut up!"

But the Boy thumped the table with one hand and arraigned the schoolmaster with the other.

"Now, Mac, I put it to you as a man o' science: if the race had got a foothold in any other part o' the world, what in Sam Hill could make 'em come up here?"

"*We're* here."

"Yes, tomfools after gold. They never dreamed there was gold. No, Sir*ee!* the only thing on earth that could make men stay here, would be that they were born here, and didn't know any better. Don't the primitive man cling to his home, no matter what kind o' hole it is? He's *afraid* to leave it. And these first men up here, why, it's plain as day—they just hung on, things gettin' worse and worse, and colder and colder, and some said, as the old men we laugh at say at home, 'The climate ain't what it was when I was a boy,' and nobody believed 'em, but everybody began to dress warmer and eat fat, and——"

"All that Buffon says is——"

"Yes—and they invented one thing after another to meet the new conditions—kaiaks and bidarras and ivory-tipped harpoons"—he was pouring out his new notions at the fastest express rate—"and the animals that couldn't stand it emigrated, and those that stayed behind got changed——"

"Dry up."

"One at a time."

"Buffon——"

"Yes, yes, Mac, and the hares got white, and the men, playin' a losin' game for centuries, got dull in their heads and stunted in their legs—always cramped up in a kaiak like those fellas at St. Michael's. And, why, it's clear as crystal—they're survivals! The Esquimaux are the oldest race in the world."

"Who's makin' this speech?"

"Order!"

"Order!"

"Well, see here: *do* you admit it, Mac? Don't you see there were just a few enterprisin' ones who cleared out, or, maybe, got carried away in a current, and found better countries and got rich and civilised, and became our forefathers? Hey, boys, ain't I right?"

"You sit down."

"You'll get chucked out."

"Buffon——"

Everybody was talking at once.

"Why, it goes on still," the Boy roared above the din. "People who stick at home, and are patient, and put up with things, they're doomed. But look at the fellas that come out o' starvin' attics and stinkin' pigsties to America. They live like lords, and they look at life like men."

Mac was saying a great deal about the Ice Age and the first and second periods of glaciation, but nobody could hear what.

"*Prince* Nicholas? Well, I should smile. He belongs to the oldest family in the world. Hoop-la!" The Boy jumped up on his stool and cracked his head against the roof; but he only ducked, rubbed his wild, long hair till it stood out wilder than ever, and went on: "Nicholas's forefathers were kings before Cæsar; they were here before the Pyramids——"

The Colonel came round and hauled the Boy down. Potts was egging the miscreant on. O'Flynn, poorly disguising his delight in a scrimmage, had been shouting: "Ye'll spoil the Blow-Out, ye meddlin' jackass! Can't ye let Mac make his spache? No; ye must ahlways be huntin' round fur harrum to be doin' or throuble to make."

In the turmoil and the contending of many voices Nicholas began to explain to his friends that it wasn't a real fight, as it had every appearance of being, and the visitors were in no immediate danger of their lives. But Kaviak feared the worst, and began to weep forlornly.

"The world is dyin' at top and bottom!" screamed the Boy, writhing under the Colonel's clutch. "The ice will spread, the beasts will turn white, and we'll turn yella, and we'll all dress in skins and eat fat and be exactly like Kaviak, and the last man'll be found tryin' to warm his hands at the Equator, his feet on an iceberg and his nose in a snowstorm. Your old Buffer's got a long head, Mac. Here's to Buffer!" Whereupon he subsided and drank freely of punch.

"Well," said the Colonel, severely, "*you've* had a Blow-Out if nobody else has!"

"Feel better?" inquired Potts, tenderly.

"Now, Mac, you shall have a fair field," said the Colonel, "and if the Boy opens his trap again——"

"I'll punch 'im," promised O'Flynn, replenishing the disturber's cup.

But Mac wouldn't be drawn. Besides, he was feeding Kaviak. So the Colonel filled in the breach with "My old

Kentucky Home," which he sang with much feeling, if not great art.

This performance restored harmony and a gentle reflectiveness.

Father Wills told about his journey up here ten years before and of a further expedition he'd once made far north to the Koyukuk.

"But Nicholas knows more about the native life and legends than anyone I ever met, except, of course, Yagorsha."

"Who's Yag——?" began the Boy.

"Oh, that's the Village Story-teller." He was about to speak of something else, but, lifting his eyes, he caught Mac's sudden glance of grudging attention. The priest looked away, and went on: "There's a story-teller in every settlement. He has always been a great figure in the native life, I believe, but now more than ever."

"Why's that?"

"Oh, battles are over and blood-feuds are done, but the need for a story-teller abides. In most villages he is a bigger man than the chief—they're all 'ol' chiefs,' the few that are left—and when they die there will be no more. So the tribal story-teller comes to be the most important character"—the Jesuit smiled in that shrewd and gentle way of his—"that is, of course, after the Shamán, as the Russians call him, the medicine-man, who is a teller of stories, too, in his more circumscribed fashion. But it's the Story-teller who helps his people through the long winter—helps them to face the terrible new enemies, epidemic disease and famine. He has always been their best defence against that age-old dread they all have of the dark. Yes, no one better able to send such foes flying than Yagorsha of Pymeut. Still, Nicholas is a good second."

The Prince of Pymeut shook his head.

"Tell them 'The White Crow's Last Flight,'" urged the priest.

But Nicholas was not in the vein, and when they all urged him overmuch, he, in self-defence, pulled a knife out of his pocket and a bit of walrus ivory about the size of his thumb, and fell to carving.

"What you makin'?"

"Button," says Nicholas; "me heap hurry get him done."

"It looks more like a bird than a button," remarked the Boy.

"Him bird—him button," replied the imperturbable one.

THE BLOW-OUT

"Half the folk-lore of the North has to do with the crow (or raven)," the priest went on. "Seeing Kaviak's feather reminded me of a native cradle-song that's a kind of a story, too. It's been roughly translated."

"Can you say it?"

"I used to know how it went."

He began in a deep voice:

"'The wind blows over the Yukon.
My husband hunts deer on the Koyukun mountains.
Ahmi, ahmi, sleep, little one.

There is no wood for the fire,
The stone-axe is broken, my husband carries the other.
Where is the soul of the sun? Hid in the dam of the beaver, waiting the
    spring-time.
Ahmi, ahmi, sleep little one, wake not!

Look not for ukali, old woman.
Long since the cache was emptied, the crow lights no more on the ridge
    pole.
Long since, my husband departed. Why does he wait in the mountains?
Ahmi, ahmi, sleep little one, softly.

Where, where, where is my own?
Does he lie starving on the hillside? Why does he linger?
Comes he not soon I must seek him among the mountains.
Ahmi, ahmi, little one, sleep sound.

Hush! hush! hush! The crow cometh laughing.
Red is his beak, his eyes glisten, the false one!
"Thanks for a good meal to Kuskokala the Shaman—
On the far mountain quietly lieth your husband."
Ahmi, ahmi, sleep little one, wake not.

"Twenty deers' tongues tied to the pack on his shoulders;
Not a tongue in his mouth to call to his wife with.
Wolves, foxes, and ravens are tearing and fighting for morsels.
Tough and hard are the sinews; not so the child in your bosom."
Ahmi, ahmi, sleep little one, wake not!

Over the mountain slowly staggers the hunter.
Two bucks' thighs on his shoulders.
Twenty deers' tongues in his belt.
"Go, gather wood, kindle a fire, old woman!"
Off flew the crow—liar, cheat and deceiver.
Wake, oh sleeper, awake! welcome your father!

He brings you back fat, marrow, venison fresh from the mountain
Tired and worn, yet he's carved you a toy of the deer's horn,
While he was sitting and waiting long for the deer on the hillside.
Wake! see the crow! hiding himself from the arrow;
Wake, little one, wake! here is your father safe home.'"

"Who's 'Kuskokala the Shamán'?" the Boy inquired.
"Ah, better ask Nicholas," answered the priest.
But Nicholas was absorbed in his carving.
Again Mr. O'Flynn obliged, roaring with great satisfaction:

> "'I'm a stout rovin' blade, and what matther my name,
> For I ahlways was wild, an' I'll niver be tame;
> An' I'll kiss putty gurrls wheriver I go,
> An' what's that to annyone whether or no.

> *Chorus.*

> "'Ogedashin, den thashin, come, boys! let us drink;
> 'Tis madness to sorra, 'tis folly to think.
> For we're ahl jolly fellows wheriver we go—
> Ogedashin, den thashin, na boneen sheen lo!"

Potts was called on. No, he couldn't sing, but he could show them a trick or two. And with his grimy euchre-deck he kept his word, showing that he was not the mere handy-man, but the magician of the party. The natives, who know the cards as we know our A B C's, were enthralled, and began to look upon Potts as a creature of more than mortal skill.

Again the Boy pressed Nicholas to dance.

"No, no;" and under his breath: "You come Pymeut."

Meanwhile, O'Flynn, hugging the pleasant consciousness that he had distinguished himself—his pardner, too—complained loudly that the only contribution Mac or the Boy had made was to kick up a row. What steps were they going to take to retrieve their characters and minister to the public entertainment?

"I've supplied the decorations," said Mac in a final tone.

"Well, and the Bhoy? What good arre ye, annyway?"

"Hard to say," said the person addressed; but, thinking hard: "Would you like to see me wag my ears?" Some languid interest was manifested in this accomplishment, but it fell rather flat after Potts' splendid achievements with the euchre-deck.

"No, ye ain't good fur much as an enthertainer," said O'Flynn frankly.

Kaviak had begun to cry for more punch, and Mac was evidently growing a good deal perplexed as to the further treatment for his patient.

"Did ye be tellin' some wan, Father, that when ye found that Esquimer he had grass stuffed in his mouth? Sure, he'll be missin' that grass. Ram somethin' down his throat."

"Was it done to shorten his sufferings?" the Colonel asked in an undertone.

"No," answered the priest in the same low voice; "if they listen long to the dying, the cry gets fixed in their imagination, and they hear it after the death, and think the spirit haunts the place. Their fear and horror of the dead is beyond belief. They'll turn a dying man out of his own house, and not by the door, but through a hole in the roof. Or they pull out a log to make an opening, closing it up quick, so the spirit won't find his way back."

Kaviak continued to lament.

"Sorry we can't offer you some blubber, Kaviak."

" 'Tain't that he's missin'; he's got an inexhaustible store of his own. His mistake is offerin' it to us."

"I know what's the matter with that little shaver," said the Boy. "He hasn't got any stool, and you keep him standin' on those legs of his like matches."

"Let him sit on the buffalo-skin there," said Mac gruffly.

"Don't you s'pose he's thought o' the buffalo-skin? But he'd hate it. A little fella likes to be up where he can see what's goin' on. He'd feel as lost 'way down there on the buffalo as a puppy in a corn-brake."

The Boy was standing up, looking round.

"I know. Elephas! come along, Jimmie!" In spite of remonstrance, they rushed to the door and dragged in the "fossle." When Nicholas and his friends realised what was happening, they got up grunting and protesting. "Lend a hand, Andrew," the Boy called to the man nearest.

"No—no!" objected the true son of the Church, with uncommon fervour.

"You, then, Nicholas."

"*Oo*, ha, *oo!* No touch! No touch!"

"What's up? You don't know what this is."

"Huh! Nicholas know plenty well. Nicholas no touch bones of dead devils."

This view of the "fossle" so delighted the company that, acting on a sudden impulse, they pushed the punch-bowl out of the way, and, with a whoop, hoisted the huge thing on the table. Then the Boy seized the whimpering Kaviak, and set him high on the throne. So surprised was the topmost Spissimen that he was as quiet for a moment as the one underneath him, staring about, blinking. Then, looking down at Mac's punch-cup, he remembered his grievance, and took up the wail where he had left it off.

"Nuh, nuh! don't you do that," said the Boy with startling suddenness. "If you make that noise, I'll have to make a worse one. If you cry, Kaviak, I'll have to sing. Hmt, hmt! don't you do it." And as Kaviak, in spite of instructions, began to bawl, the Boy began to do a plantation jig, crooning monotonously:

> " 'Grashoppah sett'n on de swee' p'tater vine,
> Swee' p'tater vine, swee' p'tater vine ;
> Grasshoppah——' "

He stopped as suddenly as he'd begun. "*Now,* will you be good?"

Kaviak drew a breath with a catch in it, looked round, and began as firmly as ever:

"Weh!—eh!—eh!"

"Sh—sh!" The Boy clapped his hands, and lugubriously intoned:

> " 'Dey's de badger and de bah,
> En de funny lil hah,
> En de active lil flea,
> En de lil armadillah
> Dat sleeps widouter pillah,
> An dey all gottah mate but me—ee—eel' '

Weh—eh—eh!" and he joined in Kaviak's lament. This was intrusive of the Boy, and Kaviak was offended. He sat stiffly on his throne, looking most disgusted, albeit silenced, for the moment.

"Farva!" Kaviak gasped.

"Say, do a nigger breakdown," solicited Potts.

"Ain't room; besides, I can't do it with blisters."

They did the impossible—they made room, and turned back the buffalo-skin. Only the big Colonel, who was most in the way of all, sat, not stirring, staring in the fire. Such a look on the absent, tender face as the great masters, the divinest poets cannot often summon, but which comes at the call of some foolish old nursery jingle, some fragment of half-forgotten folk-lore, heard when the world was young—when all hearing was music, when all sight was "pictures," when every sense brought marvels that seemed the everyday way of the wonderful, wonderful world.

THE BLOW-OUT

For an obvious reason it is not through the utterances of the greatest that the child receives his first intimations of the beauty and the mystery of things. These come in lowly guise with familiar everyday voices, but their eloquence has the incommunicable grace of infancy, the promise of the first dawn, the menace of the first night.

"Do you remember the thing about the screech-owl and the weather signs?" said the Colonel, roused at last by the jig on his toes and the rattle of improvised "bones" almost in his face.

"Reckon I do, honey," said the Boy, his feet still flying and flapping on the hard earthen floor.

> " 'W'en de screech-owl light on de gable en'
> En holler, Who-oo! oh-oh!' "

He danced up and hooted in Kaviak's face.

> " 'Den yo' bettah keep yo eyeball peel,
> Kase 'e bring bad luck t' yo'.
> Oh-oh! oh-oh!' "

Then, sinking his voice, dancing slowly, and glancing anxiously under the table:

> " 'W'en de ole black cat widdee yalla eyes
> Slink round like she atterah mouse,
> Den yo' bettah take keer yo'self en frien's,
> Kase deys sholy a witch en de house.' "

An awful pause, a shiver, and a quick change of scene, indicated by a gurgling whoop, ending in a quacking:

> " 'W'en de puddle-duck 'e leave de pon',
> En start t' comb e fedder,
> Den yo' bettah take yo' omberel,
> Kase deys gwine tubbee wet wedder.' "

"Now comes the speckly rooster," the Colonel prompted. The Boy crowed long and loud:

> " 'Effer ole wite rooster widder speckly tail
> Commer crowin' befoh de do',
> En yo got some comp'ny a'ready,
> Yo's gwinter have some mo'.' "

Then he grunted, and went on all fours. "Kaviak!" he called, "you take warnin'——

> " 'W'en yo' see a pig agoin' along——' "

81

Look here: Kaviak's *never* seen a pig! I call it a shame.

> " 'W'en yo' see a pig agoin' along
> Widder straw en de sider 'is mouf,
> It'll be a tuhble winter,
> En yo' bettuh move down Souf.' "

He jumped up and dashed into a breakdown, clattering the bones, and screeching:

> " 'Squirl he got a bushy tail,
> Possum's tail am bah,
> Raccoon's tail am ringed all roun'—
> Touch him ef yo' dah!
> Rabbit got no tail at all,
> Cep a little bit o' bunch o' hah.' "

The group on the floor, undoubtedly, liked that part of the entertainment that involved the breakdown, infinitely the best of all, but simultaneously, at its wildest moment, they all turned their heads to the door. Mac noticed the movement, listened, and then got up, lifted the latch, and cautiously looked out. The Boy caught a glimpse of the sky over Mac's shoulder.

"Jimminy Christmas!" He stopped, nearly breathless. "It can't be a fire. Say, boys! they're havin' a Blow-Out up in heaven."

The company crowded out. The sky was full of a palpitant light. An Indian appeared from round the stockade; he was still staring up at the stone chimney.

"Are we on fire?"

"How-do." He handed Father Wills a piece of dirty paper.

"Hah! Yes. All right. Andrew!"

Andrew needed no more. He bustled away to harness the dogs. The white men were staring up at the sky.

"What's goin' on in heaven, Father? S'pose you call this the Aurora Borealis—hey?"

"Yes," said the priest; "and finer than we often get it. We are not far enough north for the great displays."

He went in to put on his parki.

Mac, after looking out, had shut the door and stayed behind with Kaviak.

On Father Will's return Farva, speaking apparently less to the priest than to the floor, muttered: "Better let him stop where he is till his cold's better."

The Colonel came in.

"Leave the child here!" ejaculated the priest.

"——till he's better able to travel."

"Why not?" said the Colonel promptly.

"Well, it would be a kindness to keep him a few days. I'll *have* to travel fast to-night."

"Then it's settled." Mac bundled Kaviak into the Boy's bunk.

When the others were ready to go out again, Farva caught up his fur coat and went along with them.

The dogs were not quite ready. The priest was standing a little absent-mindedly, looking up. The pale green streamers were fringed with the tenderest rose colour, and from the corona uniting them at the zenith, they shot out across the heavens, with a rapid circular and lateral motion, paling one moment, flaring up again the next.

"Wonder what makes it," said the Colonel.

"Electricity," Mac snapped out promptly.

The priest smiled.

"One mystery for another."

He turned to the Boy, and they went on together, preceding the others, a little, on the way down the trail towards the river.

"I think you must come and see us at Holy Cross—eh? Come soon;" and then, without waiting for an answer: "The Indians think these flitting lights are the souls of the dead at play. But Yagorsha says that long ago a great chief lived in the North who was a mighty hunter. It was always summer up here then, and the big chief chased the big game from one end of the year to another, from mountain to mountain and from river to sea. He killed the biggest moose with a blow of his fist, and caught whales with his crooked thumb for a hook. One long day in summer he'd had a tremendous chase after a wonderful bird, and he came home without it, dead-beat and out of temper. He lay down to rest, but the sunlight never winked, and the unending glare maddened him. He rolled, and tossed, and roared, as only the Yukon roars when the ice rushes down to the sea. But he couldn't sleep. Then in an awful fury he got up, seized the day in his great hands, tore it into little bits, and tossed them high in the air. So it was dark. And winter fell on the world for the first time. During months and months, just to punish this great crime, there was no bright sunshine; but often in the long night, while the chief was wearying for summer to come again, he'd be tantalised by these little bits of the broken day that flickered in the sky. Coming, Andrew?" he called back.

The others trooped down-hill, dogs, sleds, and all. There was a great hand-shaking and good-byeing.

Nicholas whispered:

"You come Pymeut?"

"I should just pretty nearly think I would."

"You dance heap good. Buttons no all done." He put four little ivory crows into the Boy's hands. They were rudely but cleverly carved, with eyes outlined in ink, and supplied under the breast with a neat inward-cut shank.

"Mighty fine!" The Boy examined them by the strange glow that brightened in the sky.

"You keep."

"Oh no, can't do that."

"*Yes!*" Nicholas spoke peremptorily. "Yukon men have big feast, must bring present. Me no got reindeer, me got button." He grinned. "Goo'-bye." And the last of the guests went his way.

*　　*　　*　　*　　*　　*　　*

It was only habit that kept the Colonel toasting by the fire before he turned in, for the cabin was as warm to-night as the South in mid-summer.

　　　　"'Grasshoppah sett'n on a swee' p'tater vine,'"

the Boy droned sleepily as he untied the leathern thongs that kept up his muckluck legs—

　　　　"'Swee' p'tater vine, swee' p'ta——'"

"All those othahs"—the Colonel waved a hand in the direction of Pymeut—"I think we dreamed 'em, Boy. You and me playing the Big Game with Fohtune. Foolishness! Klondyke? Yoh crazy. Tell me the river's hard as iron and the snow's up to the windah? Don' b'lieve a wo'd of it. We're on some plantation, Boy, down South, in the niggah quawtaws."

The Boy was turning back the covers, and balancing a moment on the side of the bunk.

　　　　"'Sett'n on a swee' p'tater vine, swee' p'ta——'"

"Great Cæsar's ghost!" He jumped up, and stood staring down at the sleeping Kaviak.

"Ah—a—didn't you know? He's been left behind for a few days."

"Yes, I can see he's left behind. No, Colonel, I reckon we're in the Arctic regions all right when it comes to catchin' Esquimers in your bed!"

He pulled the furs over Kaviak and himself, and curled down to sleep.

CHAPTER V

THE SHAMÁN.

"For my part, I have ever believed and do now know, that there are witches."—*Religio Medici.*

THE Boy had hoped to go to Pymeut the next day, but his feet refused to carry him. Mac took a diagram and special directions, and went after the rest of elephas, conveying the few clumsy relics home, bit by bit, with a devotion worthy of a pious pilgrim.

For three days the Boy growled and played games with Kaviak, going about at first chiefly on hands and knees.

On the fifth day after the Blow-Out, "You comin' long to Pymeut this mornin'?" he asked the Colonel.

"What's the rush?"

"*Rush!* Good Lord! it's 'most a week since they were here. And it's stopped snowin', and hasn't thought of sleetin' yet or anything else rambunksious. Come on, Colonel."

But Father Wills had shown the Colonel the piece of dirty paper the Indian had brought on the night of the Blow-Out.

"*Trouble threatened. Pymeuts think old chief dying not of consumption, but of a devil. They've sent a dog-team to bring the Shamán down over the ice. Come quickly.—*PAUL."

"Reckon we'd better hold our horses till we hear from Holy Cross."

"Hear what?"

The Colonel didn't answer, but the Boy didn't wait to listen. He swallowed his coffee scalding hot, rolled up some food and stuff for trading, in a light reindeer-skin blanket, lashed it packwise on his back, shouldered his gun, and made off before the Trio came in to breakfast.

The first sign that he was nearing a settlement, was the appearance of what looked like sections of rude wicker fencing, set up here and there in the river and frozen fast in the ice.

High on the bank lay one of the long cornucopia-shaped basket fish-traps, and presently he caught sight of something in the bleak Arctic landscape that made his heart jump, something that to Florida eyes looked familiar.

"Why, if it doesn't make me think of John Fox's cabin on Cypress Creek!" he said to himself, formulating an impression that had vaguely haunted him on the Lower River in September; wondering if the Yukon flooded like the Caloosahatchee, and if the water could reach as far up as all that.

He stopped to have a good look at this first one of the Pymeut caches, for this modest edifice, like a Noah's Ark on four legs, was not a habitation, but a storehouse, and was perched so high, not for fear of floods, but for fear of dogs and mice. This was manifest from the fact that there were fish-racks and even ighloos much nearer the river.

The Boy stopped and hesitated; it was a sore temptation to climb up and see what they had in that cache. There was an inviting plank all ready, with sticks nailed on it transversely to prevent the feet from slipping. But the Boy stopped at the rude ladder's foot, deciding that this particular mark of interest on the part of a stranger might be misinterpreted. It would, perhaps, be prudent to find Nicholas first of all. But where was Nicholas?—where was anybody?

The scattered, half-buried huts were more like earth-mounds, snow-encrusted, some with drift-logs propped against the front face looking riverwards.

While he was cogitating how to effect an entrance to one of these, or to make his presence known, he saw, to his relief, the back of a solitary Indian going in the direction of an ighloo farther up the river.

"Hi, hi!" he shouted, and as the figure turned he made signs. It stopped.

"How-do?" the Boy called out when he got nearer. "You talk English?"

The native laughed. A flash of fine teeth and sparkling eyes lit up a young, good-looking face. This boy seemed promising.

"How d'ye do? You know Nicholas?"

"Yes."

The laugh was even gayer. It seemed to be a capital joke to know Nicholas.

"Where is he?"

The figure turned and pointed, and then: "Come. I show you."

This was a more highly educated person than Nicholas, thought the visitor, remarking the use of the nominative scorned of the Prince.

They walked on to the biggest of the underground dwellings.

"Is this where the King hangs out? Nicholas' father lives here?"

"No. This is the Kazhga."

"Oh, the Kachime. Ain't you comin' in?"

"Oh no."

"Why?"

His guide had a fit of laughter, and then turned to go.

"Say, what's your name?"

The answer sounded like "Muckluck."

And just then Nicholas crawled out of the tunnel-like opening leading into the council-house. He jumped up, beaming at the sight of his friend.

"Say, Nicholas, who's this fella that's always laughing, no matter what you say? Calls himself 'Muckluck.'"

The individual referred to gave way to another spasm of merriment, which infected Nicholas.

"My sister—this one," he explained.

"Oh-h!" The Boy joined in the laugh, and pulled off his Arctic cap with a bow borrowed straight from the Colonel.

"Princess Muckluck, I'm proud to know you."

"Name no Muckluck," began Nicholas; "name Mahk——"

"Mac? Nonsense! Mac's a man's name—she's Princess Muckluck. Only, how's a fella to tell, when you dress her like a man?"

The Princess still giggled, while her brother explained.

"No like man. See?" He showed how the skirt of her deerskin parki, reaching, like her brother's, a little below the knee, was shaped round in front, and Nicholas's own— all men's parkis were cut straight across.

"I see. How's your father?"

Nicholas looked grave; even Princess Muckluck stopped laughing.

"Come," said Nicholas, and the Boy followed him on all fours into the Kachime.

Entering on his stomach, he found himself in a room about sixteen by twenty feet, two-thirds underground, log-walls chinked with moss, a roof of poles sloping upwards, tent-like, but leaving an opening in the middle for a smoke-hole some three feet square, and covered at present by a piece of thin, translucent skin. With the sole exception of the smoke-hole, the whole thing was so covered with earth, and capped with snow, that, expecting a mere cave, one was surprised at the wood-lining within. The Boy was still more surprised at the concentration, there, of malignant smells.

He gasped, and was for getting out again as fast as possible, when the bearskin flap fell behind him over the Kachime end of the entrance-tunnel.

Through the tobacco-smoke and the stifling air he saw, vaguely, a grave gathering of bucks sitting, or, rather, lounging and squatting, on the outer edge of the wide sleeping-bench that ran all round the room, about a foot and a half from the hewn-log floor.

Their solemn, intent faces were lit grotesquely by the uncertain glow of two seal-oil lamps, mounted on two posts, planted one in front of the right sleeping-bench, the other on the left.

The Boy hesitated. Was it possible he could get used to the atmosphere? Certainly it was warm in here, though there was no fire that he could see. Nicholas was talking away very rapidly to the half-dozen grave and reverend signiors, they punctuating his discourse with occasional grunts and a well-nigh continuous coughing. Nicholas wound up in English.

"Me tell you: he heap good friend. You ketch um tobacco?" he inquired suddenly of his guest. Fortunately, the Boy had remembered to "ketch" that essential, and his little offering was laid before the council-men. More grunts, and room made for the visitor on the sleeping-bench next the post that supported one of the lamps, a clay saucer half-full of seal-oil, in which a burning wick of twisted moss gave forth a powerful odour, a fair amount of smoke, and a faint light.

The Boy sat down, still staring about him, taking note of the well-hewn logs, and of the neat attachment of the timbers by a saddle-joint at the four corners of the roof. .

"Who built this?" he inquired of Nicholas.

"Ol' father, an' . . . heap ol' men gone dead."

"Gee! Well, whoever did it was on to his job," he said. "I don't seen a nail in the whole sheebang."

"No, no nail."

The Boy remembered Nicholas's sled, and, looking again at the disproportionately small hands of the men about him, corrected his first impression that they were too feminine to be good for much.

A dirty old fellow, weak and sickly in appearance, began to talk querulously. All the others listened with respect, smoking and making inarticulate noises now and then. When that discourse was finished, a fresh one was begun by yet another coughing councillor.

"What's it all about?" the Boy asked.

"Ol' Chief heap sick," said the buck on the Boy's right.

"Ol' Chief, ol' father, b'long me," Nicholas observed with pride.

"Yes; but aren't the Holy Cross people nursing him?"

"Brother Paul gone; white medicine no good."

They all shook their heads and coughed despairingly.

"Then try s'm' other—some yella-brown, Esquimaux kind," hazarded the Boy lightly, hardly noticing what he was saying till he found nearly all the eyes of the company fixed intently upon him. Nicholas was translating, and it was clear the Boy had created a sensation.

"Father Wills no like," said one buck doubtfully. "He make cross-eyes when Shamán come."

"Oh yes, medicine-man," said the Boy, following the narrative eagerly.

"Shamán go way," volunteered an old fellow who hitherto had held his peace; "all get sick"—he coughed painfully—"heap Pymeuts die."

"Father Wills come." Nicholas took up the tale afresh. "Shamán come. Father Wills heap mad. He no let Shamán stay."

"No; him say, "Go! plenty quick, plenty far. Hey, you! *Mush!*"

They smoked awhile in silence broken only by coughs.

"Shamán say, "Yukon Inua plenty mad.""

"Who is Yukon Inua? Where does he live?"

"Unner Yukon ice," whispered Nicholas.

"Oh, the river spirit? . . . Of course."

"Him heap strong. Long time"—he motioned back into the ages with one slim brown hand—"fore Holy Cross here, Yukon Inua take good care Pymeuts."

"No tell Father Wills?"

"No."

Then in a low guttural voice: "Shamán come again."

"Gracious! When?"

"To-night."

"Jiminny Christmas!"

They sat and smoked and coughed. By-and-by, as if wishing thoroughly to justify their action, Nicholas resumed:

"You savvy, ol' father try white medicine—four winter, four summer. No good. Ol' father say, 'Me well man? Good friend Holy Cross, good friend Russian mission. Me ol'? me sick? Send for Shamán.'"

The entire company grunted in unison.

"You no tell?" Nicholas added with recurrent anxiety.

"No, no; they shan't hear through me. I'm safe."

Presently they all got up, and began removing and setting back the hewn logs that formed the middle of the floor. It then appeared that, underneath, was an excavation about two feet deep. In the centre, within a circle of stones, were the charred remains of a fire, and here they proceeded to make another.

As soon as it began to blaze, Yagorsha the Story-teller took the cover off the smoke-hole, so the company was not quite stifled.

A further diversion was created by several women crawling in, bringing food for the men-folk, in old lard-cans or native wooden kantaks. These vessels they deposited by the fire, and with an exchange of grunts went out as they had come.

Nicholas wouldn't let the Boy undo his pack.

"No, we come back," he said, adding something in his own tongue to the company, and then crawled out, followed by the Boy. Their progress was slow, for the Boy's "Canadian web-feet" had been left in the Kachime, and he sank in the snow at every step. Twice in the dusk he stumbled over an ighloo, or a sled, or some sign of humanity, and asked of the now silent, preoccupied Nicholas, "Who lives here?" The answer had been, "Nobody; all dead."

The Boy was glad to see approaching, at last, a human figure. It came shambling through the snow, with bent head and swaying, jerking gait, looked up suddenly and sheered off, flitting uncertainly onward, in the dim light, like a frightened ghost.

"Who is that?"

"Shamán. Him see in dark all same owl. Him know you white man."

The Boy stared after him. The bent figure of the Shamán looked like a huge bat flying low, hovering, disappearing into the night.

"Those your dogs howling?" the visitor asked, thinking that for sheer dismalness Pymeut would be hard to beat.

Nicholas stopped suddenly and dropped down; the ground seemed to open and swallow him. The Boy stooped and saw his friend's feet disappearing in a hole. He seized one of them.

"Hold on; wait for me!"

Nicholas kicked, but to no purpose; he could make only such progress as his guest permitted.

Presently a gleam. Nicholas had thrust away the flap at the tunnel's end, and they stood in the house of the Chief of the Pymeuts, that native of whom Father Wills had said, "He is the richest and most intelligent man of his tribe."

The single room seemed very small after the spaciousness of the Kachime, but it was the biggest ighloo in the settlement.

A fire burnt brightly in the middle of the earthen floor, and over it was bending Princess Muckluck, cooking the evening meal. She nodded, and her white teeth shone in the blaze. Over in the corner, wrapped in skins, lay a man on the floor groaning faintly. The salmon, toasting on sticks over wood coals, smelt very appetising.

"Why, your fish are whole. Don't you clean 'em first?" asked the visitor, surprised out of his manners.

"No," said Nicholas; "him better no cut."

They sat down by the fire, and the Princess waited on them. The Boy discovered that it was perfectly true. Yukon salmon broiled in their skins over a birch fire are the finest eating in the world, and any "other way" involves a loss of flavour.

He was introduced for the first time to the delights of reindeer "back-fat," and found even that not so bad.

"You are lucky, Nicholas, to have a sister—such a nice one, too"—(the Princess giggled)—"to keep house for you."

Nicholas understood, at least, that politeness was being offered, and he grinned.

"I've got a sister myself. I'll show you her picture some day. I care about her a lot. I've come up here to make a pile so that we can buy back our old place in Florida."

He said this chiefly to the Princess, for she evidently had profited more by her schooling, and understood things quite like a Christian.

"Did you ever eat an orange, Princess?" he continued.

"Kind o' fish?"

"No, fruit; a yella ball that grows on a tree."

"Me know," said Nicholas; "me see him in boxes St. Michael's. Him bully."

"Yes. Well, we had a lot of trees all full of those yella balls, and we used to eat as many as we liked. We don't have much winter down where I live—summer pretty nearly all the time."

"I'd like go there," said the girl.

"Well, will you come and see us, Muckluck? When I've found a gold-mine and have bought back the Orange Grove, my sister and me are goin' to live together, like you and Nicholas."

"She look like you?"

"No; and it's funny, too, 'cause we're twins."

"Twins! What's twins?"

"Two people born at the same time."

"No!" ejaculated Nicholas.

"Why, yes, and they always care a heap about each other when they're twins."

But Muckluck stared incredulously.

"*Two* at the same time!" she exclaimed. "It's like that, then, in your country?"

The Boy saw not astonishment alone, but something akin to disgust in the face of the Princess. He felt, vaguely, he must justify his twinship.

"Of course; there's nothing strange about it; it happens quite often."

"*Often?*"

"Yes; people are very much pleased. Once in a while there are even three——"

"All at the same time!" Her horror turned into shrieks of laughter. "Why, your women are like our dogs! Human beings and seals never have more than one at a time!"

The old man in the corner began to moan and mutter feverishly. Nicholas went to him, bent down, and apparently tried to soothe him. Muckluck gathered up the supper-things and set them aside.

"You were at the Holy Cross school?" asked the Boy.

"Six years—with Mother Aloysius and the Sisters. They very good."

"So you're a Catholic, then?"

"Oh yes."

"You speak the best English I've heard from a native."

"I love Sister Winifred. I want to go back—unless"—she regarded the Boy with a speculative eye—"unless I go your country."

The sick man began to talk deliriously, and lifted up a terrible old face with fever-bright eyes glaring through wisps of straight gray hair. No voice but his was heard for some time in the ighloo, then, "I fraid," said Muckluck, crouching near the fire, but with head turned over shoulder, staring at the sick man.

"No wonder," said the Boy, thinking such an apparition enough to frighten anybody.

"Nicholas 'fraid, too," she whispered, "when the devil talks."

"The devil?"

"Yes. Sh! You hear?"

The delirious chatter went on, rising to a scream. Nicholas came hurrying back to the fire with a look of terror in his face.

"Me go get Shamán."

"No; he come soon." Muckluck clung to him.

They both crouched down by the fire.

"You 'fraid he'll die before the Shamán gets here?"

"Oh no," said Muckluck soothingly, but her face belied her words.

The sick man called hoarsely. Nicholas got him some water, and propped him up to drink. He glared over the cup with wild eyes, his teeth chattering against the tin. The Boy, himself, felt a creep go down his spine.

Muckluck moved closer to him.

"Mustn't say he die," she whispered. "If Nicholas think he die, he drag him out—leave him in the snow."

"Never!"

"Sh!" she made him a sign to be quiet. The rambling fever-talk went on, Nicholas listening fascinated. "No Pymeut," she whispered, "like live in ighloo any more if man die there."

"You mean, if they know a person's dying they haul him out o' doors—and *leave* him a night like this?"

"If not, how get him out . . . after?"

"Why, carry him out."

"*Touch* him? Touch *dead* man?" She shuddered. "Oh, no. Bad, bad! I no think he die," she resumed, raising her voice. But Nicholas rejoined them, silent, looking very grave. Was he contemplating turning the poor old fellow out? The Boy sat devising schemes to prevent the barbarism should it come to that. The wind had risen; it was evidently going to be a rough night.

With imagination full of sick people turned out to perish, the Boy started up as a long wail came, muffled, but keen still with anguish, down through the snow and the earth, by way of the smoke-hole, into the dim little room.

"Oh, Nicholas! what was that?"

"What?"

"Wait! Listen! There, that! Why, it's a child crying."

"No, him Chèe."

"Let's go and bring him in."

"Bring dog in here?"

"Dog! That's no dog."

"Yes, him dog; him my Chèe."

"Making a human noise like that?"

Nicholas nodded. The only sounds for some time were the doleful lamenting of the Mahlemeut without, and the ravings of the Pymeut Chief within.

The Boy was conscious of a queer, dream-like feeling. All this had been going on up here for ages. It had been like this when Columbus came over the sea. All the world had changed since then, except the steadfast North. The Boy sat up suddenly, and rubbed his eyes. With that faculty on the part of the unlearned that one is tempted to call "American," a faculty for assimilating the grave conclusions of the doctors, and importing them light-heartedly into personal experience, he realised that what met his eyes here in Nicholas' house was one of the oldest pictures humanity has presented. This was what was going on by the Yukon, when King John, beside that other river, was yielding Magna Charta to the barons. While the Cæsars were building Rome the Pymeut forefathers were building just such ighloos as this. While Pheidias wrought his marbles, the men up here carved walrus-ivory, and, in lieu of Homer, recited "The Crow's Last Flight" and "The Legend of the Northern Lights."

Nicholas had risen again, his mouth set hard, his small hands shaking. He unrolled an old reindeer-skin full of holes, and examined it. At this the girl, who had been about to make up the fire, threw down the bit of driftwood and hid her face.

The sick man babbled on.

Faint under the desolate sound another—sibilant, clearer, uncannily human. Nicholas had heard, too, for he threw down the tattered deerskin, and went to the other side of the fire. Voices in the tunnel. Nicholas held back the flap and gravely waited there, till one Pymeut after another crawled in. They were the men the Boy had seen at the Kachime, with one exception—a vicious-looking old fellow, thin, wiry, with a face like a smoked chimpanzee and eyes of unearthly brightness. He was given the best place by the fire, and held his brown claws over the red coals while the others were finding their places.

The Boy, feeling he would need an interpreter, signed to Muckluck to come and sit by him. Grave as a judge she got up, and did as she was bid.

"That the Shamán?" whispered the Boy.

She nodded. It was plain that this apparition, however hideous, had given her great satisfaction.

"Any more people coming?"

"Got no more now in Pymeut."

"Where is everybody?"

"Some sick, some dead."

The old Chief rambled on, but not so noisily.

"See," whispered Muckluck, "devil 'fraid already. He begin to speak small."

The Shamán never once looked towards the sufferer till he himself was thoroughly warm. Even then he withdrew from the genial glow, only to sit back, humped together, blinking, silent. The Boy began to feel that, if he did finally say something it would be as surprising as to hear an aged monkey break into articulate speech.

Nicholas edged towards the Shamán, presenting something in a birch-bark dish.

"What's that?"

"A deer's tongue," whispered Muckluck.

The Boy remembered the Koyukun song, "Thanks for a good meal to Kuskokala, the Shamán."

Nicholas seemed to be haranguing the Shamán deferentially, but with spirit. He pulled out from the bottom of his father's bed three fine marten-skins, shook them, and dangled them before the Shamán. They produced no effect. He then took a box of matches and a plug of the Boy's tobacco out of his pocket, and held the lot towards the Shamán, seeming to say that to save his life he couldn't rake up another earthly thing to tempt his Shamánship. Although the Shamán took the offerings his little black eyes glittered none the less rapaciously, as they flew swiftly round the room, falling at last with a vicious snap and gleam upon the Boy. Then it was that for the first time he spoke.

"Nuh! nuh!" interrupted Muckluck, chattering volubly, and evidently commending the Boy to the Shamán. Several of the old bucks laughed.

"He say Yukon Inua no like you."

"He think white men bring plague, bring devils."

"Got some money?" whispered Muckluck.

"Not here."

The Boy saw the moment when he would be turned out. He plunged his hands down into his trousers pockets and fished up a knife, his second-best one, fortunately.

"Tell him I'm all right, and he can give this to Yukon Inua with my respects."

Muckluck explained and held up the shining object, blades open, corkscrew curling attractively before the covetous eyes of the Shamán. When he could endure the temptation no longer his two black claws shot out, but Nicholas intercepted the much-envied object, while, as it seemed, he drove a more advantageous bargain. Terms finally settled, the Shamán seized the knife, shut it, secreted it with a final grunt, and stood up.

Everyone made way for him. He jerked his loosely-jointed body over to the sick man, lifted the seal-oil lamp with his shaky old hands, and looked at the patient long and steadily. When he had set the lamp down again, with a grunt, he put his black thumb on the wick and squeezed out the light. When he came back to the fire, which had burnt low, he pulled open his parki and drew out an ivory wand, and a long eagle's feather with a fluffy white tuft of some sort at the end. He deposited these solemnly, side by side, on the ground, about two feet apart.

Turning round to the dying fire, he took a stick, and with Nicholas's help gathered the ashes up and laid them over the smouldering brands.

The ighloo was practically dark. No one dared speak save the yet unabashed devil in the sick man, who muttered angrily. It was curious to see how the coughing of the others, which in the Kachime had been practically constant, was here almost silenced. Whether this was achieved through awe and respect for the Shamán, or through nervous absorption in the task he had undertaken, who shall say?

The Boy felt rather than saw that the Shamán had lain down between the ivory wand and the eagle's feather. Each man sat as still as death, listening, staring, waiting.

Presently a little jet of flame sprang up out of the ashes. The Shamán lifted his head angrily, saw it was no human hand that had dared turn on the light, growled, and pulled something else from under his inexhaustible parki. The Boy peered curiously. The Shamán seemed to be shutting out the offensive light by wrapping himself up in something, head and all.

"What's he doing now?" the Boy ventured to whisper under cover of the devil's sudden loud remonstrance, the sick man at this point breaking into ghastly groans.

"He puts on the Kamlayka. Sh!"

The Shamán, still enveloped head and body, began to beat softly, keeping time with the eagle's feather. You could follow the faint gleam of the ivory wand, but on what it fell with that hollow sound no eye could see. Now, at intervals, he uttered a cry, a deep bass danger-note, singularly unnerving. Someone answered in a higher key, and they kept this up in a kind of rude, sharply-timed duet, till one by one the whole group of natives was gathered into the swing of it, swept along involuntarily, it would seem, by some magnetic attraction of the rhythm.

"Ung hi yah! ah-ha-yah! yah-yah-yah!" was the chorus to that deep, recurrent cry of the Shamán. Its accompanying drum-note was muffled like far-off thunder, conjured out of the earth by the ivory wand.

Presently a scream of terror from the bundle of skins and bones in the corner.

"Ha!" Muckluck clasped her hands and rocked back and forth.

"They'll frighten the old man to death if he's conscious," said the Boy, half rising.

She pulled him down.

"No, no; frighten devil." She was shaking with excitement and with ecstacy.

The sick man cried aloud. A frenzy seemed to seize the Shamán. He raised his voice in a series of blood-curdling shrieks, then dropped it, moaning, whining, then bursting suddenly into diabolic laughter, bellowing, whispering, ventriloquising, with quite extraordinary skill. The dim and fœtid cave might indeed be full of devils.

If the hideous outcry slackened, but an instant, you heard the sick man raving with the preternatural strength of delirium, or of mad resentment. For some time it seemed a serious question as to who would come out ahead. Just as you began to feel that the old Chief was at the end of his tether, and ready to give up the ghost, the Shamán, rising suddenly with a demoniac yell, flung himself down on the floor in a convulsion. His body writhed horribly; he kicked and snapped and quivered.

The Boy was for shielding Muckluck from the crazy flinging out of legs and arms; but she leaned over, breathless, to catch what words might escape the Shamán during the fit, for these were omens of deep significance.

When at last the convulsive movements quieted, and the Shamán lay like one dead, except for an occasional faint twitch, the Boy realised for the first time that the sick man, too, was dumb. Dead? The only sound now was the wind up in the world above. Even the dog was still.

The silence was more horrible than the hell-let-loose of a few minutes before.

The dim group sat there, motionless, under the spell of the stillness even more than they had been under the spell of the noise. At last a queer, indescribable scratching and scraping came up out of the bowels of the earth.

How does the old devil manage to do that? thought the Boy. But the plain truth was that his heart was in his mouth, for the sound came from the opposite direction, behind the Boy, and not near the Shamán at all. It grew louder, came nearer, more inexplicable, more awful. He felt he could not bear it another minute, sprang up, and stood there, tense, waiting for what might befall. Were *all* the others dead, then?

Not a sound in the place, only that indescribable stirring of something in the solid earth under his feet.

The Shamán had his knife. A ghastly sensation of stifling

came over the Boy as he thought of a struggle down there under the earth and the snow.

On came the horrible underground thing. Desperately the Boy stirred the almost extinct embers with his foot, and a faint glow fell on the terror-frozen faces of the natives, fell on the bear-skin flap. *It moved!* A huge hand came stealing round. A hand? The skeleton of a hand—white, ghastly, with fingers unimaginably long. No mortal in Pymeut had a hand like that—no mortal in all the world!

A crisp, smart sound, and a match blazed. A tall, lean figure rose up from behind the bear-skin and received the sudden brightness full in his face, pale and beautiful, but angry as an avenging angel's. For an instant the Boy still thought it a spectre, the delusion of a bewildered brain, till the girl cried out, "Brother Paul!" and fell forward on the floor, hiding her face in her hands.

"Light! make a light!" he commanded. Nicholas got up, dazed but obedient, and lit the seal-oil lamp.

The voice of the white man, the call for light, reached the Shamán. He seemed to shiver and shrink under the folds of the Kamlayka. But instead of getting up and looking his enemy in the face, he wriggled along on his belly, still under cover of the Kamlayka, till he got to the bear-skin, pushed it aside with a motion of the hooded head, and crawled out like some snaky symbol of darkness and superstition fleeing before the light.

"Brother Paul!" sobbed the girl, "don't, *don't* tell Sister Winifred."

He took no notice of her, bending down over the motionless bundle in the corner.

"You've killed him, I suppose?"

"Brother Paul——" began Nicholas, faltering.

"Oh, I heard the pandemonium. He lifted his thin white face to the smoke-hole. "It's all useless, useless. I might as well go and leave you to your abominations. But instead, go *you,* all of you—go!" He flung out his long arms, and the group broke and scuttled, huddling near the bear-skin, fighting like rats to get out faster than the narrow passage permitted.

The Boy turned from watching the instantaneous flight, the scuffle, and the disappearance, to find the burning eyes of the Jesuit fixed fascinated on his face. If Brother Paul had appeared as a spectre in the ighloo, it was plain that he looked upon the white face present at the diabolic rite as dream or devil. The Boy stood up. The lay-brother started, and crossed himself.

"In Christ's name, what—who are you?"

"I—a—I come from the white camp ten miles below."

"And you were *here*—you allowed this? Ah-h!" He flung up his arms, the pale lips moved convulsively, but no sound came forth.

"I—you think I ought to have interfered?" began the Boy.

"I think——" the Brother began bitterly, checked himself, knelt down, and felt the old man's pulse.

Nicholas at the bear-skin was making the Boy signs to come.

The girl was sobbing with her face on the ground. Again Nicholas beckoned, and then disappeared. There seemed to be nothing to do but to follow his host. When the bear-skin had dropped behind the Boy, and he crawled after Nicholas along the dark passage, he heard the muffled voice of the girl praying: "Oh, Mary, Mother of God, don't let him tell Sister Winifred."

CHAPTER VI

A PENITENTIAL JOURNEY

"... Certain London parishes still receive £12 per annum for fagots to burn heretics."—JOHN RICHARD GREEN.

THE Boy slept that night in the Kachime beside a very moody, restless host. Yagorsha dispensed with the formality of going to bed, and seemed bent on doing what he could to keep other people awake. He sat monologuing under the seal lamp till the Boy longed to throw the dish of smouldering oil at his head. But strangely enough, when, through sheer fatigue, his voice failed and his chin fell on his broad chest, a lad of fourteen or so, who had also had difficulty to keep awake, would jog Yagorsha's arm, repeating interrogatively the last phrase used, whereon the old Story-Teller would rouse himself and begin afresh, with an iteration of the previous statement. If the lad failed to keep him going, one or other of the natives would stir uneasily, lift a head from under his deerskin, and remonstrate. Yagorsha, opening his eyes with a guilty start, would go on with the yarn. When morning came, and the others waked, Yagorsha and the lad slept.

Nicholas and all the rest who shared the bench at night, and the fire in the morning, seemed desperately depressed and glum. A heavy cloud hung over Pymeut, for Pymeut was in disgrace.

About sunset the women came in with the kantaks and the lard-cans. Yagorsha sat up and rubbed his eyes. He listened eagerly, while the others questioned the women. The old Chief wasn't dead at all. No, he was much better. Brother Paul had been about to all the house-bound sick people, and given everybody medicine, and flour, and a terrible scolding. Oh yes, he was angrier than anybody had ever been before. Some natives from the school at Holy Cross were coming for him to-morrow, and they were all going down river and across the southern portage to the branch mission at Kuskoquim.

"Down river? Sure?"

Yes, sure. Brother Paul had not waited to come with those others, being so anxious to bring medicine and things to Ol' Chief quick; and this was how he was welcomed back to the scene of his labours. A Devil's Dance was going on! That was what he called it.

"You savvy?" said Nicholas to his guest. "Brother Paul go plenty soon. You wait."

I'll have company back to camp, was the Boy's first thought, and then—would there be any fun in that after all? It was plain Brother Paul was no such genial companion as Father Wills.

And so it was that he did not desert Nicholas, although Brother Paul's companions failed to put in an appearance on the following morning. However, on the third day after the incident of the Shamán (who seemed to have vanished into thin air), Brother Paul shook the snow of Pymeut from his feet, and with three Indians from the Holy Cross school and a dog-team, he disappeared from the scene. Not till he had been gone some time did Nicholas venture to return to the parental roof.

They found Muckluck subdued but smiling, and the old man astonishingly better. It looked almost as if he had turned the corner, and was getting well.

There was certainly something very like magic in such a recovery, but it was quickly apparent that this aspect of the case was not what occupied Nicholas, as he sat regarding his parent with a keen and speculative eye. He asked him some question, and they discussed the point volubly, Muckluck following the argument with close attention. Presently it seemed that father and son were taking the guest into consideration. Muckluck also turned to him now and then, and by-and-by she said: "I think he go."

"Go where?"

"Holy Cross," said the old man eagerly.

"Brother Paul," Nicholas explained. "He go *down* river. We get Holy Cross—more quick."

"I see. Before he can get back. But why do you want to go?"

"See Father Brachet."

"Sister Winifred say: 'Always tell Father Brachet; then everything all right,'" contributed Muckluck.

"You tell Pymeut belly solly," the old Chief said.

"Nicholas know he not able tell all like white man," Muckluck continued. "Nicholas say you good—hey? you good?"

"Well—a—pretty tollable, thank you."

"You go with Nicholas; you make Father Brachet unnerstan'—forgive. Tell Sister Winifred——" She stopped, perplexed, vaguely distrustful at the Boy's chuckling.

"You think we can explain it all away, hey?" He made a gesture of happy clearance. "Shamán and everything, hey?"

"Me no can," returned Nicholas, with engaging modesty. "*You*——" He conveyed a limitless confidence.

"Well, I'll be jiggered if I don't try. How far is it?"

"Go slow—one sleep."

"Well, we won't go slow. We've got to do penance. When shall we start?"

"Too late now. Tomalla," said the Ol' Chief.

* * * * * * *

They got up very early—it seemed to the Boy like the middle of the night—stole out of the dark Kachime, and hurried over the hard crust that had formed on the last fall of snow, down the bleak, dim slope to the Ol' Chief's, where they were to breakfast.

Not only Muckluck was up and doing, but the Ol' Chief seemed galvanised into unwonted activity. He was doddering about between his bed and the fire, laying out the most imposing parkis and fox-skins, fur blankets, and a pair of sealskin mittens, all of which, apparently, he had had secreted under his bed, or between it and the wall.

They made a sumptuous breakfast of tea, the last of the bacon the Boy had brought, and slapjacks.

The Boy kept looking from time to time at the display of furs. Father Wills was right; he ought to buy a parki with a hood, but he had meant to have the priest's advice, or Mac's, at least, before investing. Ol' Chief watching him surreptitiously, and seeing he was no nearer making an offer, felt he should have some encouragement. He picked up the seal-skin mittens and held them out.

"Present," said Ol' Chief. "You tell Father Brachet us belly solly."

"Oh, I'll handle him without gloves," said the Boy, giving

back the mittens. But Ol' Chief wouldn't take them. He was holding up the smaller of the two parkis.

"You no like?"

"Oh, very nice."

"You no buy?"

"You go sleep on trail," said Nicholas, rising briskly. "You die, no parki."

The Boy laughed and shook his head, but still Ol' Chief held out the deer-skin shirt, and caressed the wolf-fringe of the hood.

"Him cheap."

"How cheap?"

"Twenty-fi' dollah."

"Don't know as I call that cheap."

"Yes," said Nicholas. "St. Michael, him fifty dollah."

The Boy looked doubtful.

"I saw a parki there at the A. C. Store about like this for twenty."

"A. C. parki, peeluck," Nicholas said contemptuously. Then patting the one his father held out, "You wear *him* fifty winter."

"Lord forbid! Anyhow, I've only got about twenty dollars' worth of tobacco and stuff along with me."

"Me come white camp," Nicholas volunteered. "Me get more fi' dollah."

"Oh, will you? Now, that's very kind of you." But Nicholas, impervious to irony, held out the parki. The Boy laughed, and took it. Nicholas stooped, picked up the fur mittens, and, laying them on the Boy's arm, reiterated his father's "Present!" and then departed to the Kachime to bring down the Boy's pack.

The Princess meanwhile had withdrawn to her own special corner, where in the daytime appeared only a roll of plaited mats, and a little, cheap, old hat-box, which she evidently prized most of all she had in the world.

"You see? Lock!"

The Boy expressed surprise and admiration.

"No! Really! I call that fine."

"I got present for Father Brachet"; and turning over the rags and nondescript rubbish of the hat-box, she produced an object whose use was not immediately manifest. A section of walrus ivory about six inches long had been cut in two.

One of these curved halves had been mounted on four ivory legs. In the upper flat side had been stuck, at equal distances from the two ends and from each other, two delicate branches of notched ivory, standing up like horns. Between these sat an ivory mannikin, about three inches long, with a woeful countenance and with arms held out like one beseeching mercy.

"It's fine," said the Boy, "but—a—what's it for? Just look pretty?"

"Wait, I show you." She dived into the hat-box, and fished up a bit of battered pencil. With an air of pride, she placed the pencil across the outstretched hands of the ivory suppliant, asking the Boy in dumb-show, was not this a pen-rest that might be trusted to melt the heart of the Holy Father?

"This way, too." She illustrated how anyone embarrassed by the possession of more than one pencil could range them in tiers on the ivory horns above the head of the Woeful One.

"I call that scrumptious! And he looks as if he was saying he was sorry all the time."

She nodded, delighted that the Boy comprehended the subtle symbolism.

"One more!" she said, showing her dazzling teeth. Like a child playing a game, she half shut the hat-box and hugged it lovingly. Then with eyes sparkling, slowly the small hand crept in—was thrust down the side and drew out with a rapturous "Ha!" a gaudy advertisement card, setting forth the advantages of smoking "Kentucky Leaf." She looked at it fondly. Then slowly, regretfully, all the fun gone now, she passed it to the Boy.

"For Sister Winifred!" she said, like one who braces herself to make some huge renunciation. "You tell her I send with my love, and I always say my prayers. I very good. Hey? You tell Sister Winifred?"

"*Sure,*" said the Boy.

The Ol' Chief was pulling the other parki over his head. Nicholas reappeared with the visitor's effects. Under the Boy's eyes, he calmly confiscated all the tea and tobacco. But nothing had been touched in the owner's absence.

"Look here: just leave me enough tea to last till I get home. I'll make it up to you."

Nicholas, after some reflection, agreed. Then he bustled

about, gathered together an armful of things, and handed the Boy a tea-kettle and an axe.

"You bring—dogs all ready. Mush!" and he was gone.

To the Boy's surprise, while he and Muckluck were getting the food and presents together, the lively Ol' Chief—so lately dying—made off, in a fine new parki, on all fours, curious, no doubt, to watch the preparations without.

But not a bit of it. The Ol' Chief's was a more intimate concern in the expedition. When the Boy joined him, there he was sitting up in Nicholas's sled, appallingly emaciated, but brisk as you please, ordering the disposition of the axe and rifle along either side, the tea-kettle and grub between his feet, showing how the deer-skin blankets should be wrapped, and especially was he dictatorial about the lashing of the mahout.

"How far's he comin'?" asked the Boy, astonished.

"All the way," said Muckluck. "He want to be *sure*."

Several bucks came running down from the Kachime, and stood about, coughed and spat, and offered assistance or advice. When at last Ol' Chief was satisfied with the way the raw walrus-hide was laced and lashed, Nicholas cracked his whip and shouted, "Mush! God-damn! Mush!"

"Good-bye, Princess. We'll take care your father, though I'm sure he oughtn't to go."

"Oh yes," answered Muckluck confidently; then lower, "Shamán make all well quick. Hey? Goo'-bye."

"Good-bye."

"Don't forget tell Sister Winifred I say my p——" But the Boy had to run to keep up with the sled.

For some time he kept watching the Ol' Chief with unabated astonishment, wondering if he'd die on the way. But, after all, the open-air cure was tried for his trouble in various other parts of the world—why not here?

There was no doubt about it, Nicholas had a capital team of dogs, and knew how to drive them. Two-legged folk often had to trot pretty briskly to keep up. Pymeut was soon out of sight.

"Nicholas, what'll you take for a couple o' your dogs?"

"No sell."

"Pay you a good long price."

"No sell."

"Well, will you help me to get a couple?"

"Me try"; but he spoke dubiously.

"What do they cost?"

"Good leader cost hunder and fifty in St. Michael."

"You don't mean dollahs?"

"Mean dollahs."

"Come off the roof!"

But Nicholas seemed to think there was no need.

"You mean that if I offer you a hundred and fifty dollahs for your leader, straight off, this minute, you won't take it?"

"No, no take," said the Prince, stolidly.

And his friend reflected. Nicholas without a dog-team would be practically a prisoner for eight months of the year, and not only that, but a prisoner in danger of starving to death. After all, perhaps a dog-team in such a country *was* priceless, and the Ol' Chief was travelling in truly royal style.

However, it was stinging cold, and running after those expensive dogs was an occupation that palled. By-and-by, "How much is your sled worth?" he asked Ol' Chief.

"Six sables," said the monarch.

*   *   *   *   *

It was a comfort to sight a settlement off there on the point.

"What's this place?"

"Fish-town."

"Pymeuts there?"

"No, all gone. Come back when salmon run."

Not a creature there, as Nicholas had foretold—a place built wilfully on the most exposed point possible, bleak beyond belief. If you open your mouth at this place on the Yukon, you have to swallow a hurricane. The Boy choked, turned his back to spit out the throttling blast, and when he could catch his breath inquired:

"This a good place for a village?"

"Bully. Wind come, blow muskeetah——"

Nicholas signified a remote destination with his whip.

"B'lieve you! This kind o' thing would discourage even a mosquito."

In the teeth of the blast they went past the Pymeut Summer Resort. Unlike Pymeut proper, its cabins were built entirely above ground, of logs unchinked, its roofs of watertight birch-bark.

A couple of hours farther on Nicholas permitted a halt on the edge of a struggling little grove of dwarfed cotton-wood.

The kettle and things being withdrawn from various portions of the Ol' Chief's person, he, once more warmly tucked up and tightly lashed down, drew the edge of the outer coverlid up till it met the wolf-skin fringe of his parki hood, and relapsed into slumber.

Nicholas chopped down enough green wood to make a hearth.

"What! bang on the snow?"

Nicholas nodded, laid the logs side by side, and on them built a fire of the seasoned wood the Boy had gathered. They boiled the kettle, made tea, and cooked some fish.

Ol' Chief waked up just in time to get his share. The Boy, who had kept hanging about the dogs with unabated interest, had got up from the fire to carry them the scraps, when Nicholas called out quite angrily, "No! no feed dogs," and waved the Boy off.

"What! It's only some of my fish. Fish is what they eat, ain't it?"

"No feed now; wait till night."

"What for? They're hungry."

"You give fish—dogs no go any more."

Peremptorily he waved the Boy off, and fell to work at packing up. Not understanding Nicholas's wisdom, the Boy was feeling a little sulky and didn't help. He finished up the fish himself, then sat on his heels by the fire, scorching his face while his back froze, or wheeling round and singeing his new parki while his hands grew stiff in spite of seal-skin mittens.

No, it was no fun camping with the temperature at thirty degrees below zero—better to be trotting after those expensive and dinnerless dogs; and he was glad when they started again.

But once beyond the scant shelter of the cottonwood, it was evident the wind had risen. It was blowing straight out of the north and into their faces. There were times when you could lean your whole weight against the blast.

After sunset the air began to fill with particles of frozen snow. They did not seem to fall, but continually to whirl about, and present stinging points to the travellers' faces. Talking wasn't possible even if you were in the humour, and the dead, blank silence of all nature, unbroken hour after hour, became as nerve-wearing as the cold and stinging wind. The Boy fell behind a little. Those places on his heels that had been so badly galled had begun to be troublesome again. Well, it wouldn't do any good to holla about it—the only thing to do was to harden one's foolish feet. But in his heart he felt that all the time-honoured conditions of a penitential journey were being complied with, except on the part of the arch sinner. Ol' Chief seemed to be getting on first-rate.

The dogs, hardly yet broken in to the winter's work, were growing discouraged, travelling so long in the eye of the wind. And Nicholas, in the kind of stolid depression that had taken possession of him, seemed to have forgotten even to shout "Mush!" for a very long time.

"By-and-by Ol' Chief called out sharply, and Nicholas seemed to wake up. He stopped, looked back, and beckoned to his companion.

The Boy came slowly on.

"Why you no push?"

"Push what?"

"Handle-bar."

He went to the sled and illustrated, laying his hands on the arrangement at the back that stood out like the handle behind a baby's perambulator. The Boy remembered. Of course, there were usually two men with each sled. One ran ahead and broke trail with snow-shoes, but that wasn't necessary to-day, for the crust bore. But the other man's business was to guide the sled from behind and keep it on the trail.

"Me gottah drive, you gottah push. Dogs heap tired."

Nicholas spoke severely. The Boy stared a moment at what he mentally called "the nerve of the fella," laughed, and took hold, swallowing Nicholas's intimation that he, after all, was far more considerate of the dogs than the person merely sentimental, who had been willing to share his dinner with them.

"How much farther?"

"Oh, pretty quick now."

The driver cracked his whip, called out to the dogs, and suddenly turned off from the river course. Unerringly he followed an invisible trail, turning sharply up a slough, and went zig-zagging on without apparent plan. It was better going when they got to a frozen lake, and the dogs seemed not to need so much encouragement. It would appear an impossible task to steer accurately with so little light; but once on the other side of the lake it was found that Nicholas had hit a well-beaten track as neatly as a thread finds the needle's eye.

Far off, out of the dimness, came a sound—welcome because it was something to break the silence but hardly cheerful in itself.

"Hear that, Nicholas?"

"Mission dogs."

Their own had already thrown up their noses and bettered the pace.

The barking of the dogs had not only announced the mission to the travellers, but to the mission a stranger at the gates.

Before anything could be seen of the settlement, clumsy, fur-clad figures had come running down the slope and across the ice, greeting Nicholas with hilarity.

Indian or Esquimaux boys they seemed to be, who talked some jargon understanded of the Pymeut pilot. The Boy, lifting tired eyes, saw something white glimmering high in the air up on the right river bank. In this light it refused to form part of any conceivable plan, but hung there in the air detached, enigmatic, spectral. Below it, more on humanity's level, could be dimly distinguished, now, the Mission Buildings, apparently in two groups with an open space in the middle. Where are the white people? wondered the Boy, childishly impatient. Won't they come and welcome us? He followed the Esquimaux and Indians from the river up to the left group of buildings. With the heathen jargon beating on his ears, he looked up suddenly, and realized what the white thing was that had shone out so far. In the middle of the open space a wooden cross stood up, encrusted with frost crystals, and lifting gleaming arms out of the gloom twenty feet or so above the heads of the people.

"Funny thing for an Agnostic," he admitted to himself, "but I'm right glad to see a Christian sign." And as he knocked at the door of the big two-story log-house on the left he defended himself. "It's the swing-back of the pendulum after a big dose of Pymeut and heathen tricks. I welcome it as a mark of the white man." He looked over his shoulder a little defiantly at the Holy Cross. Recognition of what the high white apparition was had given him a queer jolt, stirring unsuspected things in imagination and in memory. He had been accustomed to see that symbol all his life, and it had never spoken to him before. Up here it cried aloud and dominated the scene. "Humph!" he said to himself, "to look at you a body'd think

'The Origin' had never been written, and Spencer and Huxley had never been born.' He knocked again, and again turned about to scan the cross.

"Just as much a superstition, just as much a fetich as Kaviak's seal-plug or the Shamán's eagle feather. With long looking at a couple of crossed sticks men grow as dazed, as hypnotized, as Pymeuts watching a Shamán's ivory wand. All the same, I'm not sure that faith in 'First Principles' would build a house like this in the Arctic Regions, and it's convenient to find it here—if only they'd open the door."

He gave another thundering knock, and then nearly fell backwards into the snow, for Brother Paul stood on the threshold holding up a lamp.

"I—a—oh! How do you do? Can I come in?"

Brother Paul, still with the look of the Avenging Angel on his pale, young face, held the door open to let the Boy come in. Then, leaning out into the night and lifting the lamp high, "Is that Nicholas?" he said sternly.

But the Pymeuts and the school-boys had vanished. He came in and set down the lamp.

"We—a—we heard you were going down river," said the Boy, tamely, for he had not yet recovered himself after such an unexpected blow.

"Are you cold? Are you wet?" demanded Brother Paul, standing erect, unwelcoming, by the table that held the lamp.

The Boy pulled himself together.

"Look here"—he turned away from the comforting stove and confronted the Jesuit—"those Pymeuts are not only cold and wet and sick too, but they're sorry. They've come to ask forgiveness."

"It's easily done."

Such scorn you would hardly expect from a follower of the meek Galilean.

"No, *not* easily done, a penance like this. I know, for I've just travelled that thirty miles with 'em over the ice from Pymeut."

"You? Yes, it amuses you."

The sombre eyes shone with a cold, disconcerting light.

"Well, to tell you the truth, I've been better amused."

The Boy looked down at his weary, wounded feet. And the others—where were his fellow pilgrims? It struck him as comic that the upshot of the journey should be that he was doing penance for the Pymeuts, but he couldn't smile with that offended archangel in front of him.

"Thirty miles over the ice, in the face of a norther, hasn't been so 'easy' even for me. And I'm not old, nor sick—no, nor frightened, Brother Paul."

He flung up his head, but his heart failed him even while he made the boast. Silently, for a moment, they confronted each other.

"Where are you bound for?"

"I—a——" The Boy had a moment of wondering if he was expected to answer "Hell," and he hesitated.

"Are you on your way up the river?"

"No—I" (was the man not going to let them rest their wicked bones there a single night?)—"a—I——"

The frozen river and the wind-racked wood were as hospitable as the beautiful face of the brother. Involuntarily the Boy shivered.

"I came to see the Father Superior."

He dropped back into a chair.

"The Father Superior is busy."

"I'll wait."

"And very tired."

"So'm I."

"——worn out with the long raging of the plague. I have waited till he is less harassed to tell him about the Pymeuts' deliberate depravity. Nicholas, too!—one of our own people, one of the first pupils of the school, a communicant in the church; distinguished by a thousand kindnesses. And this the return!"

"The return is that he takes his backsliding so to heart, he can't rest without coming to confess and to beg the Father Superior——"

"I shall tell the Father Superior what I heard and saw. He will agree that, for the sake of others who are trying to resist temptation, an example should be made of Nicholas and of his father."

"And yet you nursed the old man and were kind to him, I believe, after the offense."

"I—I thought you had killed him. But even you must see that we cannot have a man received here as Nicholas was—the most favoured child of the mission—who helps to perpetuate the degrading blasphemies of his unhappy race. It's nothing to you; you even encourage——"

"'Pon my soul——" But Brother Paul struck in with an impassioned earnestness:

"We spend a life-time making Christians of these people; and such as you come here, and in a week undo the work of years."

"I—*I?*"

"It's only eighteen months since I myself came, but already I've seen——" The torrent poured out with never a pause. "Last summer some white prospectors bribed our best native teacher to leave us and become a guide. He's a drunken wreck now somewhere up on the Yukon Flats. You take our boys for pilots, you entice our girls away with trinkets——"

"Great Cæsar! *I* don't."

But vain was protest. For Brother Paul the visitor was not a particular individual. He stood there for the type of the vicious white adventurer.

The sunken eyes of the lay-brother, burning, impersonal, saw not a particular young man and a case compounded of mixed elements, but—The Enemy! against whom night and day he waged incessant warfare.

"The Fathers and Sisters wear out their lives to save these people. We teach them with incredible pains the fundamental rules of civilization; we teach them how to save their souls alive." The Boy had jumped up and laid his hand on the door-knob. "*You* come. You teach them to smoke——"

The Boy wheeled round.

"I don't smoke."

" . . . and to gamble."

"Nicholas taught *me* to gamble. Brother Paul, I swear——"

"Yes, and to swear and get drunk, and so find the shortest way to hell."

"Father Brachet! Father Wills!" a voice called without.

The door-knob turned under the Boy's hand, and before he could more than draw back, a whiff of winter blew into the room, and a creature stood there such as no man looks to find on his way to an Arctic gold camp. A girl of twenty odd, with the face of a saint, dressed in the black habit of the Order of St. Anne.

"Oh, Brother Paul! you are wanted—wanted quickly. I think Catherine is worse; don't wait, or she'll die without——"

And as suddenly as she came the vision vanished, carrying Brother Paul in the wake of her streaming veil.

The Boy sat down by the stove, cogitating how he should best set about finding Nicholas to explain the failure of their mission. . . . What was that? Voices from the other side. The opposite door opened and a man appeared, with Nicholas and his father close behind, looking anything but cast down or decently penitential.

"How do you do?" The white man's English had a strong French accent. He shook hands with great cordiality. "We have heard of you from Father Wills also. These Pymeut friends of ours say you have something to tell me."

He spoke as though this something were expected to be highly gratifying, and, indeed, the cheerfulness of Nicholas and his father would indicate as much.

As the Boy, hesitating, did not accept the chair offered, smiling, the Jesuit went on:

"Will you talk of zis matter—whatever it is—first, or will you first go up and wash, and have our conference after supper?"

"No, thank you—a—— Are you the Father Superior?"

He bowed a little ceremoniously, but still smiling.

"I am Father Brachet."

"Oh, well, Nicholas is right. The first thing to do is to explain why we're here."

Was it the heat of the stove after the long hours of cold that made him feel a little dizzy? He put up his hand to his head.

"I have told zem to take hot water upstairs," the Father was saying, "and I zink a glass of toddy would be a good sing for you." He slightly emphasised the "you," and turned as if to supplement the original order.

"No, no!" the Boy called after him, choking a little, half with suppressed merriment, half with nervous fatigue. "Father Brachet, if you're kind to us, Brother Paul will never forgive you. We're all in disgrace."

"Hein! What?"

"Yes, we're all desperately wicked."

"No, no," objected Nicholas, ready to go back on so tactless an advocate.

"And Brother Paul has just been saying——"

"What is it, what is it?"

The Father Superior spoke a little sharply, and himself sat

down in the wooden armchair he before had placed for his white guest.

The three culprits stood in front of him on a dead level of iniquity.

"You see, Father Brachet, Ol' Chief has been very ill——"

"I know. Much as we needed him here, Paul insisted on hurrying back to Pymeut"—he interrupted himself as readily as he had interrupted the Boy—"but ze Ol' Chief looks lively enough."

"Yes; he—a—his spirits have been raised by—a—what you will think an unwarrantable and wicked means."

Nicholas understood, at least, that objectionable word "wicked" cropping up again, and he was not prepared to stand it from the Boy.

He grunted with displeasure, and said something low to his father.

"Brother Paul found them—found *us* having a séance with the Shamán."

Father Brachet turned sharply to the natives.

"Ha! you go back to zat."

Nicholas came a step forward, twisting his mittens and rolling his eye excitedly.

"Us no wicked. Shamán say he gottah scare off——" He waved his arm against an invisible army. Then, as it were, stung into plain speaking: "Shamán say *white man* bring sickness—bring devils——"

"Maybe the old Orang Outang's right."

The Boy drew a tired breath, and sat down without bidding in one of the wooden chairs. What an idiot he'd been not to take the hot grog and the hot bath, and leave these people to fight their foolishness out among themselves! It didn't concern him. And here was Nicholas talking away comfortably in his own tongue, and the Father was answering. A native opened the door and peeped in cautiously.

Nicholas paused.

"Hein!" said Father Brachet, "what is it!"

The Indian came in with two cups of hot tea and a cracker in each saucer. He stopped at the priest's side.

"You get sick, too. Please take. Supper little late." He nodded to Nicholas, and gave the white stranger the second cup. As he was going out: "Same man here in July. You know"—he tapped himself on the left side—"man with sore heart."

"Yansey?" said the priest quickly. "Well, what about Yansey?"

"He is here."

"But no! Wiz zose ozzers?"

"No, I think they took the dogs and deserted him. He's just been brought in by our boys; they are back with the moose-meat. Sore heart worse. He will die."

"Who's looking after him?"

"Brother Paul;" and he padded out of the room in his soft native shoes.

"Then Brother Paul has polished off Catherine," thought the Boy, "and he won't waste much time over a sore heart. It behoves us to hurry up with our penitence." This seemed to be Nicholas's view as well. He was beginning again in his own tongue.

"You know we like best for you to practise your English," said the priest gently; "I expect you speak very well after working so long on ze John J. Healy."

"Yes," Nicholas straightened himself. "Me talk all same white man now." (He gleamed at the Boy: "Don't suppose I need you and your perfidious tongue.") "No; us Pymeuts no wicked!"

Again he turned away from the priest, and challenged the Boy to repeat the slander. Then with an insinuating air, "Shamán no say you wicked," he reassured the Father. "Shamán say Holy Cross all right. Cheechalko no good; Cheechalko bring devils; Cheechalko all same *him*," he wound up, flinging subterfuge to the winds, and openly indicating his faithless ambassador.

"Strikes me I'm gettin' the worst of this argument all round. Brother Paul's been sailing into me on pretty much the same tack."

"No," said Nicholas, firmly; "Brother Paul no unnerstan'. *You* unnerstan'." He came still nearer to the Father, speaking in a friendly, confidential tone. "You savvy! Plague come on steamboat up from St. Michael. One white man, he got coast sickness. Sun shining. Salmon run big. Yukon full o' boats. Two days: no canoe on river. Men all sit in tent like so." He let his mittens fall on the floor, crouched on his heels, and rocked his head in his hands. Springing up, he went on with slow, sorrowful emphasis: "*Men begin die——*"

"Zen we come," said the Father, "wiz nurses and proper medicine——"

Nicholas gave the ghost of a shrug, adding the damaging fact: "Sickness come to Holy Cross."

The Father nodded.

"We've had to turn ze schools into wards for our patients," he explained to the stranger. "We do little now but nurse ze sick and prepare ze dying. Ze Muzzer Superieure has broken down after heroic labours. Paul, I fear, is sickening too. Yes, it's true: ze disease came to us from Pymeut."

In the Father's mind was the thought of contagion courageously faced in order to succour "the least of these my brethren." In Nicholas's mind was the perplexing fact that these white men could bring sickness, but not stay it. Even the heap good people at Holy Cross were not saved by their deaf and impotent God.

"Fathers sick, eight Sisters sick, boy die in school, three girl die. Holy Cross people kind——" Again he made that almost French motion of the shoulders. "Shamán say, '*Peeluck!*' No good be kind to devils; scare 'em—make 'em *run*."

"Nicholas," the priest spoke wearily, "I am ashamed of you. I sought you had learned better. Zat old Shamán—he is a rare old rogue. What did you give him?"

Nicholas' mental processes may not have been flattering, but their clearness was unmistakable. If Father Brachet was jealous of the rival holy man's revenue, it was time to bring out the presents.

Ol' Chief had a fine lynx-skin over his arm. He advanced at a word from Nicholas, and laid it down before the Father.

"No!" said Father Brachet, with startling suddenness; "take it away and try to understand."

Nicholas approached trembling, but no doubt remembering how necessary it had been to add to the Shamán's offering before he would consent to listen with favour to Pymeut prayers, he pulled out of their respective hiding-places about his person a carved ivory spoon and an embroidered bird-skin pouch, advanced boldly under the fire of the Superior's keen eyes and sharp words, and laid the further offering on the lynx-skin at his feet.

"Take zem away," said the priest, interrupting his brief

homily and standing up. "Don't you understand yet zat we are your friends wizzout money and wizzout price? We do not want zese sings. Shamán takes ivories from ze poor, furs from ze shivering, and food from zem zat starve. And he gives nossing in return—nossing! Take zese sings away; no one wants zem at Holy Cross."

Ol' Chief wiped his eyes pathetically. Nicholas, the picture of despair, turned in a speechless appeal to his despised ambassador. Before anyone could speak, the door-knob rattled rudely, and the big bullet-head of a white man was put in.

"Pardon, mon Père; cet homme qui vient de Minóok—faudrait le coucher de suite—mais où, mon Dieu, où?"

While the Superior cogitated, "How-do, Brother Etienne?" said Nicholas, and they nodded.

Brother Etienne brought the rest of his heavy body half inside the door. He wore aged, weather-beaten breeches, and a black sweater over an old hickory shirt.

"Ses compagnons l'ont laissé, là, je crois. Mais ça ne durera pas longtemps."

"Faudra bien qu'il reste ici—je ne vois pas d'autre moyen," said the Father. "Enfin—on verra. Attendez quelques instants."

"C'est bien." Brother Etienne went out.

Ol' Chief was pulling the Boy's sleeve during the little colloquy, and saying, "You tell." But the Boy got up like one who means to make an end.

"You haven't any time or strength for this——"

"Oh yes," said Father Brachet, smiling, and arresting the impetuous movement. "Ziz is—part of it."

"Well," said the Boy, still hesitating, "they *are* sorry, you know, *really* sorry."

"You sink so?" The question rang a little sceptically.

"Yes, I do, and I'm in a position to know. You'd forgive them if you'd seen, as I did, how miserable and overwhelmed they were when Brother Paul—when—— I'm not saying it's the highest kind of religion that they're so almighty afraid of losing your good opinion, but it—it gives you a hold, doesn't it?" And then, as the Superior said nothing, only kept intent eyes on the young face, the Boy wound up a little angrily: "Unless, of course, you're like Brother Paul, ready to throw away the power you've gained——"

"Paul serves a great and noble purpose—but—zese questions

are—a—not in his province." Still he bored into the young face with those kind gimlets, his good little eyes, and—

"You are—one of us?" he asked, "of ze Church?"

"No, I—I'm afraid I'm not of any Church."

"Ah!"

"And I ought to take back 'afraid.' But I'm telling you the truth when I say there never were honester penitents than the Pymeuts. The whole Kachime's miserable. Even the girl, Ol' Chief's daughter she cried like anything when she thought Sister——"

"Winifred?"

"Sister Winifred would be disappointed in her."

"Ah, yes; Sister Winifred has zem——" he held out his hand, spread the fingers apart, and slowly, gently closed them. "Comme ça."

"But what's the good of it if Brother Paul——"

"Ah, it is not just zere Paul comes in. But I tell you, my son, Paul does a work here no ozzer man has done so well."

"He is a flint—a fanatic."

"Fanatique!" He flung out an expressive hand. "It is a name, my son. It often means no more but zat a man is in earnest. Out of such a 'flint' we strike sparks, and many a generous fire is set alight. We all do what we can here at Holy Cross, but Paul will do what we cannot."

"Well, give *me*——" He was on the point of saying "Father Wills," but changed it to "a man who is tolerant."

"Tolerant? Zere are plenty to be tolerant, my son. Ze world is full. But when you find a man zat can *care,* zat can be 'fanatique'—ah! It is"—he came a little nearer—"it is but as if I would look at you and say, 'He has earnest eyes! He will go far *whatever* road he follow.'" He drew off, smiling shrewdly. "You may live, my son, to be yourself called 'fanatique.' Zen you will know how little——"

"I!" the Boy broke in. "You are pretty wide of the mark this time."

"Ah, perhaps! But zere are more trails zan ze Yukon for a fanatique. You have zere somesing to show me?"

"I promised the girl that cried so—I promised her to bring the Sister this." He had pulled out the picture. In spite of the careful wrapping, it had got rather crumpled. The Father looked at it, and then a swift glance passed between him and the Boy.

"You could see it was like pulling out teeth to part with it. Can it go up there till the Sister sends for it?"

Father Brachet nodded, and the gorgeous worldling, counselling all men to "Smoke Kentucky Leaf!" was set up in the high place of honour on the mantel-shelf, beside a print of the Madonna and the Holy Child. Nicholas cheered up at this, and Ol' Chief stopped wiping his eyes. While the Boy stood at the mantel with his back to Father Brachet, acting on a sudden impulse, he pulled the ivory pen-rest out of his shirt, and stuck its various parts together, saying as he did so, "She sent an offering to you, too. If the Ol' Chief an' I fail to convince you of our penitence, we're all willin' to let this gentleman plead for us." Whereupon he wheeled round and held up the Woeful One before the Father's eyes.

The priest grasped the offering with an almost convulsive joy, and instantly turned his back that the Pymeuts might not see the laugh that twisted up his humorous old features. The penitents looked at each other, and telegraphed in Pymeut that after all the Boy had come up to time. The Father had refused the valuable lynx-skin and Nicholas' superior spoon, but was ready, it appeared, to look with favour on anything the Boy offered.

But very seriously the priest turned round upon the Pymeuts. "I will just say a word to you before we wash and go in to supper." With a kindly gravity he pronounced a few simple sentences about the gentleness of Christ with the ignorant, but how offended the Heavenly Father was when those who knew the true God descended to idolatrous practices, and how entirely He could be depended upon to punish wicked people.

Ol' Chief nodded vigorously and with sudden excitement. "Me jus' like God."

"Hein?"

"Oh, yes. Me no stan' wicked people. When me young me kill two ol' squaws—*witches!*" With an outward gesture of his lean claws he swept these wicked ones off the face of the earth, like a besom of the Lord.

A sudden change had passed over the tired face of the priest. "Go, go!" he called out, driving the Pymeuts forth as one shoos chickens out of a garden. "Go to ze schoolhouse and get fed, for it's all you seem able to get zere."

But the perplexed flight of the Pymeuts was arrested.

Brother Paul and Brother Etienne blocked the way with a stretcher. They all stood back to let the little procession come in. Nobody noticed them further, but the Pymeuts scuttled away the instant they could get by. The Boy, equally forgotten, sat down in a corner, while the three priests conferred in low-voiced French over the prostrate figure.

"Father Brachet," a weak voice came up from the floor.

Brother Paul hurried out, calling Brother Etienne softly from the door.

"I am here." The Superior came from the foot of the pallet, and knelt down near the head.

"You—remember what you said last July?"

"About——"

"About making restitution."

"Yes."

"Well, I can do it now."

"I am glad."

"I've brought you the papers. That's why—I—*had* to come. Will you—take them—out of my——"

The priest unbuckled a travel-stained buckskin miner's belt and laid it on the floor. All the many pockets were empty save the long one in the middle. He unbuttoned the flap and took out some soiled, worn-looking papers. "Are zese in proper form?" he asked, but the man seemed to have dropped into unconsciousness. Hurriedly the priest added: "Zere is no time to read zem. Ah! Mr. —— will you come and witness zis last will and testament?"

The Boy got up and stood near. The man from Minóok opened his eyes.

"Here!" The priest had got writing materials, and put a pen into the slack hand, with a block of letter-paper under it.

"I—I'm no lawyer," said the faint voice, "but I think it's all—in shape. Anyhow—you write—and I'll sign." He half closed his eyes, and the paper slipped from under his hand. The Boy caught it, and set down the faint words:—"will and bequeath to John M. Berg, Kansas City, my right and title to claim No. 11 Above, Little Minóok, Yukon Ramparts——" And the voice fell away into silence. They waited a moment, and the Superior whispered:

"Can you sign it?"

The dull eyes opened. "Didn't I——?"

Father Brachet held him up; the Boy gave him the pen and

steadied the paper. "Thank you, Father. Obliged to you, too." He turned his dimming eyes upon the Boy, who wrote his name in witness. "You—going to Minóok?"

"I hope so."

The Father went to the writing-table, where he tied up and sealed the packet.

"Anybody that's going to Minóok will have to hustle." The slang of everyday energy sounded strangely from dying lips—almost a whisper, and yet like a far-off bugle calling a captive to battle.

The Boy leaned down to catch the words, yet fainter:

"Good claims going like hot cakes."

"How much," the Boy asked, breathless, "did you get out of yours?"

"Waiting till summer. Nex' summer——" The eyelids fell.

"So it isn't a fake after all." The Boy stood up. "The camp's all right!"

"You'll see. It will out-boom the Klondyke."

"Ha! How long have you been making the trip?"

"Since August."

The wild flame of enterprise sunk in the heart of the hearer. "Since *August?*"

"No cash for steamers; we had a canoe. She went to pieces up by——" The weak voice fell down into that deep gulf that yawns waiting for man's last word.

"But there *is* gold at Minóok, you're sure? You've seen it?"

The Father Superior locked away the packet and stood up. But the Boy was bending down fascinated, listening at the white lips. "There is gold there?" he repeated.

Out of the gulf came faintly back like an echo:

"Plenty o' gold there—plenty o' gold."

"Jee-rusalem!" He stood up and found himself opposite the comtemplative face of the priest.

"We have neglected you, my son. Come upstairs to my room."

They went out, the old head bent, and full of thought; the young head high, and full of dreams. Oh, to reach this Minóok, where there was "plenty of gold, plenty of gold," before the spring floods brought thousands. What did any risk matter? Think of the Pymeuts doing their sixty miles over the ice just to apologise to Father Brachet for being Pymeuts. This other, this white man's penance might, would involve a greater mortification of the flesh. What then? The reward was proportionate—"plenty of gold." The faint whisper filled the air.

A little more hardship, and the long process of fortune-building is shortened to a few months. No more office grind. No more anxiety for those one loves.

Gold, plenty of gold, while one is young and can spend it gaily—gold to buy back the Orange Grove, to buy freedom and power, to buy wings, and to buy happiness!

On the stairs they passed Brother Paul and the native.

"Supper in five minutes, Father."

The Superior nodded.

"There is a great deal to do," the native went on hurriedly to Paul. "We've got to bury Catherine to-morrow——"

"And this man from Minóok," agreed Paul, pausing with his hand on the door.

CHAPTER VII

KAVIAK'S CRIME

"My little son, who look'd from thoughtful eyes,
And moved and spoke in quiet grown-up wise,
Having my law the seventh time disobey'd,
I struck him, and dismiss'd
With hard words and unkiss'd. . . ."

EVEN with the plague and Brother Paul raging at the mission—even with everyone preoccupied by the claims of dead and dying, the Boy would have been glad to prolong his stay had it not been for "nagging" thoughts of the Colonel. As it was, with the mercury rapidly rising and the wind fallen, he got the Pymeuts on the trail next day at noon, spent what was left of the night at the Kachime, and set off for camp early the following day. He arrived something of a wreck, and with an enormous respect for the Yukon trail.

It did him good to sight the big chimney, and still more to see the big Colonel putting on his snow-shoes near the bottom of the hill, where the cabin trail met the river trail. When the Boss o' the camp looked up and saw the prodigal coming along, rather groggy on his legs, he just stood still a moment. Then he kicked off his web-feet, turned back a few paces uphill, and sat down on a spruce stump, folded his arms, and waited. Was it the knapsack on his back that bowed him so?

"Hello, Kentucky!"

But the Colonel didn't look up till the Boy got quite near, chanting in his tuneless voice:

"'Grasshoppah sett'n on a swee' p'tater vine,
Swee' p'tater vine, swee' p'tater vine——'"

"What's the matter, hey, Colonel? Sorry as all that to see me back?"

"Reckon it's the kind o' sorrah I can bear," said the Colonel. "We thought you were dead."

"You ought t' known me better. Were you just sendin' out a rescue-party of one?"

The Colonel nodded. "That party would have started before, but I cut my foot with the axe the day you left. Where have you been, in the name o' the nation?"

"Pymeut an' Holy Cross."

"Holy Cross? Holy Moses! *You?*"

"Yes; and do you know, one thing I saw there gave me a serious nervous shock."

"That don't surprise me. What was it?"

"Sheets. When I came to go to bed—a real bed, Colonel, on legs—I found I was expected to sleep between sheets, and I just about fainted."

"That the only shock you had?"

"No, I had several. I saw an angel. I tell you straight, Colonel—you can bank on what I'm sayin'—that Jesuit outfit's all right."

"Oh, you think so?" The rejoinder came a little sharply.

"Yes, sir, I just do. I think I'd be bigoted not to admit it."

"So, you'll be thick as peas in a pod with the priests now?"

"Well, I'm the one that can afford to be. They won't convert *me!* And, from my point o' view, it don't matter what a man is s' long's he's a decent fella."

The Colonel's only answer was to plunge obliquely uphill.

"Say, Boss, wait for me."

The Colonel looked back. The Boy was holding on to a scrub willow that put up wiry twigs above the snow.

"Feel as if I'd never get up the last rungs o' this darn ice-ladder!"

"Tired? H'm! Something of a walk to Holy Cross even on a nice mild day like this." The Colonel made the reflection with obvious satisfaction, took off his knapsack, and sat down again. The Boy did the same. "The very day you lit out Father Orloff came up from the Russian mission."

"What's he like?"

"Oh, little fella in petticoats, with a beard an' a high pot-hat, like a Russian. And that same afternoon we had a half-breed trader fella here, with two white men. Since that day we haven't seen a human creature. We bought some furs of the trader. Where'd you get yours?"

"Pymeut. Any news about the strike?"

"Well, the trader fella was sure it was all gammon, and told us stories of men who'd sacrificed everything and joined a stampede, and got sold—sold badly. But the two crazy whites with him—miners from Dakotah—they were on fire about Minóok. Kept on bragging they hadn't cold feet, and swore they'd get near to the diggins as their dogs'd take 'em. The half-breed said they might do a hundred miles more, but probably wouldn't get beyond Anvik."

"Crazy fools! I tell you, to travel even thirty miles on the Yukon in winter, even with a bully team and old Nick to drive 'em, and not an extra ounce on your back—I tell you, Colonel, it's no joke."

"B'lieve you, sonny."

It wasn't thirty seconds before sonny was adding: "Did that half-breed think it was any use our trying to get dogs?"

"Ain't to be had now for love or money."

"Lord, Colonel, if we had a team——"

"Yes, I know. We'll probably owe our lives to the fact that we haven't."

It suddenly occurred to the Boy that, although he had just done a pretty good tramp and felt he'd rather die than go fifty feet further, it was the Colonel who was most tired.

"How's everybody?"

"Oh, I s'pose we might all of us be worse off."

"What's the matter?"

He was so long answering that the Boy's eyes turned to follow the serious outward gaze of the older man, even before he lifted one hand and swept it down the hill and out across the dim, grey prospect.

"This," said the Colonel.

Their eyes had dropped down that last stretch of the steep snow slope, across the two miles of frozen river, and ran half round the wide horizon-line, like creatures in a cage. Whether they liked it or whether they didn't, for them there was no way out.

"It's the awful stillness." The Colonel arraigned the distant ice-plains.

They sat there looking, listening, as if they hoped their protest might bring some signal of relenting. No creature, not even a crystal-coated willow-twig, nothing on all the ice-bound earth stirred by as much as a hair; no mark of man past or present broke the grey monotony; no sound but their two voices disturbed the stillness of the world.

It was a quiet that penetrated, that pricked to vague alarm. Already both knew the sting of it well.

"It's the kind of thing that gets on a fella's nerves," said the Colonel. "I don't know as I ever felt helpless in any part of the world before. But a man counts for precious little up here. Do you notice how you come to listen to the silence?"

"Oh, yes, I've noticed."

"Stop." Again he lifted his hand, and they strained their ears. "I've done that by the hour since you left and the daft gold-diggers went up trail after you. The other fellas feel it, too. Don't know what we'd have done without Kaviak. Think we ought to keep that kid, you know."

"I could get on without Kaviak if only we had some light. It's this villainous twilight that gets into my head. All the same, you know"—he stood up suddenly—"we came expecting to stand a lot, didn't we?"

The elder man nodded. "Big game, big stakes. It's all right."

Eventless enough after this, except for the passing of an Indian or two, the days crawled by.

The Boy would get up first in the morning, rake out the dead ashes, put on a couple of back-logs, bank them with ashes, and then build the fire in front. He broke the ice in the water-bucket, and washed; filled coffee-pot and mush-kettle with water (or ice), and swung them over the fire; then he mixed the corn-bread, put it in the Dutch oven, covered it with coals, and left it to get on with its baking. Sometimes this part of the programme was varied by his mixing a hoe-cake on a board, and setting it up "to do" in front of the fire. Then he would call the Colonel—

> " 'Wake up Massa,
> De day am breakin';
> Peas in de pot, en de
> Hoe-cake bakin' ' "—

for it was the Colonel's affair to take up proceedings at this point—make the coffee and the mush and keep it from burning, fry the bacon, and serve up breakfast.

Saturday brought a slight variation in the early morning routine. The others came straggling in, as usual, but once a week Mac was sure to be first, for he had to get Kaviak up. Mac's view of his whole duty to man seemed to centre in the

Saturday scrubbing of Kaviak. Vainly had the Esquimer stood out against compliance with this most repulsive of foreign customs. He seemed to be always ready with some deep-laid scheme for turning the edge of Mac's iron resolution. He tried hiding at the bottom of the bed. It didn't work. The next time he crouched far back under the lower bunk. He was dragged out. Another Saturday he embedded himself, like a moth, in a bundle of old clothes. Mac shook him out. He had been very sanguine the day he hid in the library. This was a wooden box nailed to the wall on the right of the door. Most of the bigger books — Byron, Wordsworth, Dana's "Mineralogy," and two Bibles—he had taken out and concealed in the lower bunk very skilfully, far back behind the Colonel's feet. Copps's "Mining" and the two works on "Parliamentary Law" piled at the end of the box served as a pillow. After climbing in and folding himself up into an incredibly small space, Kaviak managed with superhuman skill to cover himself neatly with a patchwork quilt of *Munsey, Scribner, Century, Strand,* and *Overland* for August, '97. No one would suspect, glancing into that library, that underneath the usual top layer of light reading, was matter less august than Law, Poetry, Science, and Revelation.

It was the base Byron, tipping the wink to Mac out of the back of the bunk, that betrayed Kaviak.

It became evident that "Farva" began to take a dour pride in the Kid's perseverance. One morning he even pointed out to the camp the strong likeness between Kaviak and Robert Bruce.

"No, sah; the Scottish chief had to have an object-lesson, but Kaviak—Lawd!—Kaviak could give points to any spider livin'!"

This was on the morning that the Esquimer thought to escape scrubbing, even at the peril of his life, by getting up on to the swing-shelf—how, no man ever knew. But there he sat in terror, like a very young monkey in a wind-rocked tree, hardly daring to breathe, his arms clasped tight round the demijohn; but having Mac to deal with, the end of it was that he always got washed, and equally always he seemed to register a vow that, s'help him, Heaven! it should never happen again.

After breakfast came the clearing up. It should have been done (under this régime) by the Little Cabin men, but it seldom was. O'Flynn was expected to keep the well-hole in the river chopped open and to bring up water every day. This didn't always happen either, though to drink snow-water was to invite scurvy, Father Wills said. There was also a daily need, if the Colonel could be believed, for everybody to chop firewood.

"We got enough," was Potts' invariable opinion.

"For how long? S'pose we get scurvy and can't work; we'd freeze to death in a fortnight."

"Never saw a fireplace swalla logs whole an' never blink like this one."

"But you got no objection to sittin' by while the log-swaller' goes on."

The Colonel or the Boy cooked the eternal beans, bacon and mush dinner, after whatever desultory work was done; as a matter of fact, there was extraordinarily little to occupy five able-bodied men. The fun of snow-shoeing, mitigated by frostbite, quickly degenerated from a sport into a mere means of locomotion. One or two of the party went hunting, now and then, for the scarce squirrel and the shy ptarmigan. They tried, with signal lack of success, to catch fish, Indian fashion, through a hole in the ice.

But, for the most part, as winter darkened round them, they lounged from morning till night about the big fireplace, and smoked, and growled, and played cards, and lived as men do, finding out a deal about each other's characters, something about each other's opinions, and little or nothing about each other's history.

In the appalling stillness of the long Arctic night, any passer-by was hailed with enthusiasm, and although the food-supply in the Big Cabin was plainly going to run short before spring, no traveller—white, Indian, or Esquimaux—was allowed to go by without being warmed and fed, and made to tell where he came from and whither he was bound—questions to tax the sage. Their unfailing hospitality was not in the least unexpected or unusual, being a virtue practised even by scoundrels in the great North-west; but it strained the resources of the little camp, a fourth of whose outfit lay under the Yukon ice.

In the state of lowered vitality to which the poor, ill-cooked food, the cold and lack of exercise, was slowly reducing them, they talked to one another less and less as time went on, and more and more—silently and each against his will—grew hyper-sensitive to the shortcomings and even to the innocent "ways" of the other fellow.

Not Mac's inertia alone, but his trick of sticking out his jaw became an offence, his rasping voice a torture. The Boy's occasional ebullition of spirits was an outrage, the Colonel's mere size intolerable. O'Flynn's brogue, which had amused them, grew to be just part of the hardship and barbarism that had overtaken them like an evil dream, coercing, subduing all the forces of life. Only Kaviak seemed likely to come unscathed through the ordeal of the winter's captivity; only he could take the best place at the fire, the best morsel at dinner, and not stir angry passions; only he dared rouse Mac when the Nova Scotian fell into one of his bear-with-a-sore-head moods. Kaviak put a stop to his staring angrily by the hour into the fire, and set him to whittling out boats and a top, thereby providing occupation for the morrow, since it was one man's work to break Kaviak of spinning the one on the table during mealtime, and sailing the other in the drinking-water bucket at all times when older eyes weren't watching. The Colonel wrote up his journal, and read the midsummer magazines and Byron, in the face of Mac's "I do not like Byron's thought; I do not consider him healthy or instructive." In one of his more energetic moods the Colonel made a four-footed cricket for Kaviak, who preferred it to the high stool, and always sat on it except at meals.

Once in a while, when for hours no word had been spoken except some broken reference to a royal flush or a jack-pot, or O'Flynn had said, "Bedad! I'll go it alone," or Potts had inquired anxiously, "Got the joker? Guess I'm euchred, then," the Boy in desperation would catch up Kaviak, balance the child on his head, or execute some other gymnastic, soothing the solemn little heathen's ruffled feelings, afterwards, by crooning out a monotonous plantation song. It was that kind of addition to the general gloom that, at first, would fire O'Flynn to raise his own spirits, at least, by roaring out an Irish ditty. But this was seldomer as time went on. Even Jimmie's brogue suffered, and grew less robust.

In a depressed sort of way Mac was openly teaching Kaviak his letters, and surreptitiously, down in the Little Cabin, his prayers. He was very angry when Potts and O'Flynn eavesdropped and roared at Kaviak's struggles with "Ow Farva." In fact, Kaviak did not shine as a student of civilisation, though that told less against him with O'Flynn, than the fact that he wasn't "jolly and jump about, like white children." Moreover, Jimmie, swore there was something "bogey" about the boy's intermittent knowledge of English. Often for days he would utter nothing but "Farva" or "Maw" when he wanted his plate replenished, then suddenly he would say something that nobody could remember having taught him or even said in his presence.

It was not to be denied that Kaviak loved sugar mightily, and stole it when he could. Mac lectured him and slapped his minute yellow hands, and Kaviak stole it all the same. When he was bad—that is, when he had eaten his daily fill of the camp's scanty store (in such a little place it was not easy to hide from such a hunter as Kaviak)—he was taken down to the Little Cabin, smacked, and made to say "Ow Farva." Nobody could discover that he minded much, though he learnt to try to shorten the ceremony by saying "I solly" all the way to the cabin.

As a rule he was strangely undemonstrative; but in his own grave little fashion he conducted life with no small intelligence, and learned, with an almost uncanny quickness, each man's uses from the Kaviak point of view. The only person he wasn't sworn friends with was the handy-man, and there came to be a legend current in the camp, that Kaviak's first attempt at spontaneously stringing a sentence under that roof was, "Me got no use for Potts."

The best thing about Kaviak was that his was no craven soul. He was obliged to steal the sugar because he lived with white people who were bigger than he, and who always took it away when they caught him. But once the sugar was safe under his shirt, he owned up without the smallest hesitation, and took his smacking like a man. For the rest, he flourished, filled out, and got as fat as a seal, but never a whit less solemn.

One morning the Colonel announced that now the days had grown so short, and the Trio were so late coming to breakfast, and nobody did any work to speak of, it would be a good plan to have only two meals a day.

The motion was excessively unpopular, but it was carried by a plain, and somewhat alarming, exposition of the state of supplies.

"We oughtn't to need as much food when we lazy round the

fire all day," said the Colonel. But Potts retorted that they'd need a lot more if they went on adoptin' the aborigines.

They knocked off supper, and all but the aborigine knew what it meant sometimes to go hungry to bed.

Towards the end of dinner one day late in December, when everybody else had finished except for coffee and pipe, the aborigine held up his empty plate.

"Haven't you had enough?" asked the Colonel mildly, surprised at Kaviak's bottomless capacity.

"Maw." Still the plate was extended.

"There isn't a drop of syrup left," said Potts, who had drained the can, and even wiped it out carefully with halves of hot biscuit.

"He don't really want it."

"Mustn't open a fresh can till to-morrow."

"No, sir*ee*. We've only got——"

"Besides, he'll bust."

Kaviak meanwhile, during this paltry discussion, had stood up on the high stool "Farva" had made for him, and personally inspected the big mush-pot. Then he turned to Mac, and, pointing a finger like a straw (nothing could fatten those infinitesimal hands), he said gravely and fluently:

"Maw in de plenty-bowl."

"Yes, maw mush, but no maw syrup."

The round eyes travelled to the store corner.

"We'll have to open a fresh can some time—what's the odds?"

Mac got up, and not only Kaviak watched him—for syrup was a luxury not expected every day—every neck had craned, every pair of eyes had followed anxiously to that row of rapidly diminishing tins, all that was left of the things they all liked best, and they still this side of Christmas!

"What you rubber-neckin' about?" Mac snapped at the Boy as he came back with the fresh supply. This unprovoked attack was ample evidence that Mac was uneasy under the eyes of the camp—angry at his own weakness, and therefore the readier to dare anybody to find fault with him.

"How can I help watchin' you?" said the Boy. Mac lifted his eyes fiercely. "I'm fascinated by your winnin' ways; we're all like that."

Kaviak had meanwhile made a prosperous voyage to the plenty-bowl, and returned to Mac's side—an absurd little fig-

ure in a strange priest-like cassock buttoned from top to bottom (a waistcoat of Mac's), and a jacket of the Boy's, which
was usually falling off (and trailed on the ground when it
wasn't), and whose sleeves were rolled up in inconvenient
muffs. Still, with a gravity that did not seem impaired by
these details, he stood clutching his plate anxiously with both
hands, while down upon the corn-mush descended a slender
golden thread, manipulated with a fine skill to make the most
of its sweetness. It curled and spiralled, and described the
kind of involved and long-looped flourishes which the grave
and reverend of a hundred years ago wrote jauntily underneath the most sober names.

Lovingly the dark eyes watched the engrossing process. Even
when the attenuated thread was broken, and the golden rain
descended in slow, infrequent drops, Kaviak stood waiting, always for just one drop more.

"That's enough, greedy."

"Now go away and gobble."

But Kaviak daintily skimmed off the syrupy top, and left his
mush almost as high a hill as before.

It wasn't long after the dinner-things had been washed up,
and the Colonel settled down to the magazines—he was reading the advertisements now—that Potts drew out his watch.

"Golly! do you fellers know what o'clock it is?" He held
the open timepiece up to Mac. "Hardly middle o' the afternoon. All these hours before bedtime, and nothin' to eat till
to-morrow!"

"Why, you've just finished——"

"But look at the *time!*"

The Colonel said nothing. Maybe he had been a little previous with dinner to-day; it was such a relief to get it out of
the way. Oppressive as the silence was, the sound of Potts's
voice was worse, and as he kept on about how many hours it
would be till breakfast, the Colonel said to the Boy:

" 'Johnny, get your gun,' and we'll go out."

In these December days, before the watery sun had set, the
great, rich-coloured moon arose, having now in her resplendent
fulness quite the air of snuffing out the sun. The pale and
heavy-eyed day was put to shame by this brilliant night-lamp,
that could cast such heavy shadows, and by which men might
read.

The instant the Big Cabin door was opened Kaviak darted

out between the Colonel's legs, threw up his head like a Siwash dog, sniffed at the frosty air and the big orange moon, flung up his heels, and tore down to the forbidden, the fascinating fish-hole. If he hadn't got snared in his trailing coat he would have won that race. When the two hunters had captured Kaviak, and shut him indoors, they acted on his implied suggestion that the fish-trap ought to be examined. They chopped away the fresh-formed ice. Empty, as usual.

It had been very nice, and neighbourly, of Nicholas, as long ago as the 1st of December, to bring the big, new, cornucopia-shaped trap down on his sled on the way to the Ikogimeut festival. It had taken a long time to cut through the thick ice, to drive in the poles, and fasten the slight fencing, in such relation to the mouth of the sunken trap, that all well-conducted fish ought easily to find their way thither. As a matter of fact, they didn't. Potts said it was because the Boy was always hauling out the trap "to see"; but what good would it be to have it full of fish and not know?

They had been out about an hour when the Colonel brought down a ptarmigan, and said he was ready to go home. The Boy hesitated.

"Going to give in, and cook that bird for supper?"

It was a tempting proposition, but the Colonel said, rather sharply: "No, sir. Got to keep him for a Christmas turkey."

"Well, I'll just see if I can make it a brace."

The Colonel went home, hung his trophy outside to freeze, and found the Trio had decamped to the Little Cabin. He glanced up anxiously to see if the demijohn was on the shelf. Yes, and Kaviak sound asleep in the bottom bunk. The Colonel would climb up and have forty winks in the top one before the Boy got in for their game of chess. He didn't know how long he had slept when a faint scratching pricked through the veil of slumber, and he said to himself, "Kaviak's on a raid again," but he was too sodden with sleep to investigate. Just before he dropped off again, however, opening a heavy eye, he saw Potts go by the bunk, stop at the door and listen. Then he passed the bunk again, and the faint noise recommenced. The Colonel dropped back into the gulf of sleep, never even woke for his chess, and in the morning the incident had passed out of his mind.

Just before dinner the next day the Boy called out:

"See here! who's spilt the syrup?"

"Spilt it?"

"Syrup?"

"No; it don't seem to be spilt, either." He patted the ground with his hand.

"You don't mean that new can——"

"Not a drop in it." He turned it upside down.

Every eye went to Kaviak. He was sitting on his cricket by the fire waiting for dinner. He returned the accusing looks of the company with self-possession.

"Come here." He got up and trotted over to "Farva."

"Have you been to the syrup?"

Kaviak shook his head.

"You *must* have been."

"No."

"You sure?"

He nodded.

"How did it go—all away—do you know?"

Again the silent denial. Kaviak looked over his shoulder at the dinner preparations, and then went back to his cricket. It was the best place from which to keep a strict eye on the cook.

"The gintlemin don't feel conversaytional wid a pint o' surrup in his inside."

"I tell you he'd be currled up with colic if he——"

"Well," said O'Flynn hopefully, "bide a bit. He ain't lookin' very brash."

"Come here."

Kaviak got up a second time, but with less alacrity.

"Have you got a pain?"

He stared.

"Does it hurt you there?" Kaviak doubled up suddenly.

"He's awful ticklish," said the Boy.

Mac frowned with perplexity, and Kaviak retired to the cricket.

"Does the can leak anywhere?"

"That excuse won't hold water 'cause the can will." The Colonel had just applied the test.

"Besides, it would have leaked on to something," Mac agreed.

"Oh, well, let's mosy along with our dinner," said Potts.

"It's gettin' pretty serious," remarked the Colonel. "We can't afford to lose a pint o' syrup."

"No, *Siree,* we can't; but there's one thing about Kaviak," said the Boy, "he always owns up. Look here, Kiddie: don't say no; don't shake your head till you've thought. Now, think *hard*."

Kaviak's air of profound meditation seemed to fill every requirement.

"Did you take the awful good syrup and eat it up?"

Kaviak was in the middle of a head-shake when he stopped abruptly. The Boy had said he wasn't to do that. Nobody had seemed pleased when he said "No."

"I b'lieve we're on the right track. He's remembering. Think again. You are a tip-top man at finding sugar, aren't you?"

"Yes, fin' shugh." Kaviak modestly admitted his prowess in that direction.

"And you get hungry in the early morning?"

Yes, he would go so far as to admit that he did.

"You go skylarkin' about, and you remember—the syrup can! And you get hold of it—didn't you?"

"To-malla."

"You mean yesterday—this morning?"

"N——"

"Sh!"

Kaviak blinked.

"Wait and think. Yesterday this was full. You remember Mac opened it for you?"

Kaviak nodded.

"And now, you see"—he turned the can bottom side up— "all gone!"

"Oh-h!" murmured Kaviak with an accent of polite regret. Then, with recovered cheerfulness, he pointed to the store corner: "Maw!"

Potts laughed in his irritating way, and Mac's face got red. Things began to look black for Kaviak.

"Say, fellas, see here!" The Boy hammered the lid on the can with his fist, and then held it out. "It was put away shut up, for I shut it, and even one of us can't get that lid off without a knife or something to pry it."

The company looked at the small hands doubtfully. They were none too little for many a forbidden feat. How had he got on the swing-shelf? How——

"Ye see, crayther, it must uv been yersilf, becuz there isn't annybuddy else."

"Look here," said the Colonel, "we'll forgive you this time if you'll own up. Just tell us——"

"Kaviak!" Again that journey from the cricket to the judgment-seat.

"Show us"—Mac had taken the shut tin, and now held it out—"show us how you got the lid off."

But Kaviak turned away. Mac seized him by the shoulder and jerked him round.

Everyone felt it to be suspicious that Kaviak was unwilling even to try to open the all too attractive can. Was he really cunning, and did he want not to give himself away? Wasn't he said to be much older than he looked? and didn't he sometimes look a hundred, and wise for his years?

"See here: I haven't caught you in a lie yet, but if I do——"

Kaviak stared, drew a long breath, and seemed to retire within himself.

"You'd better attend to me, for I mean business."

Kaviak, recalled from internal communing, studied "Farva" a moment, and then retreated to the cricket, as to a haven now, hastily and with misgiving, tripping over his trailing coat. Mac stood up.

"Wait, old man." The Colonel stooped his big body till he was on a level with the staring round eyes. "Yo' see, child, yo' can't have any dinnah till we find out who took the syrup."

The little yellow face was very serious. He turned and looked at the still smoking plenty-bowl.

"Are yoh hungry?"

He nodded, got up briskly, held up his train, and dragged his high stool to the table, scrambled up, and established himself.

"Look at that!" said the Colonel triumphantly. "That youngster hasn't just eaten a pint o' syrup."

Mac was coming slowly up behind Kaviak with a face that nobody liked looking at.

"Oh, let the brat alone, and let's get to our grub!" said Potts, with an extreme nervous irritation.

Mac swept Kaviak off the stool. "You come with me!"

Only one person spoke after that till the meal was nearly done. That one had said, "Yes, Farva," and followed Mac, dinnerless, out to the Little Cabin.

The Colonel set aside a plateful for each of the two absent

ones, and cleared away the things. Potts stirred the fire in a shower of sparks, picked up a book and flung it down, searched through the sewing-kit for something that wasn't lost, and then went to the door to look at the weather—so he said. O'Flynn sat dozing by the fire. He was in the way of the washing-up.

"Stir your stumps, Jimmie," said the Colonel, "and get us a bucket of water." Sleepily O'Flynn gave it as his opinion that he'd be damned if he did.

With unheard-of alacrity, "I'll go," said Potts.

The Colonel stared at him, and, by some trick of the brain, he had a vision of Potts listening at the door the night before, and then resuming that clinking, scratching sound in the corner—the store corner.

"Hand me over my parki, will you?" Potts said to the Boy. He pulled it over his head, picked up the bucket, and went out.

"Seems kind o' restless, don't he?"

"Yes. Colonel——"

"Hey?"

"Nothin'."

Ten minutes—a quarter of an hour went by.

"Funny Mac don't come for his dinner, isn't it? S'pose I go and look 'em up?"

"S'pose you do."

Not far from the door he met Mac coming in.

"Well?" said the Boy, meaning, Where's the kid?

"Well?" Mac echoed defiantly. "I lammed him, as I'd have lammed Robert Bruce if he'd lied to me."

The Boy stared at this sudden incursion into history, but all he said was: "Your dinner's waitin'."

The minute Mac got inside he looked round hungrily for the child. Not seeing him, he went over and scrutinised the tumbled contents of the bunks.

"Where's Kaviak?"

"P'raps you'll tell us."

"You mean he isn't here?" Mac wheeled round sharply. "*Here?*"

"He didn't come back here for his dinner?"

"Haven't seen him since you took him out." Mac made for the door. The Boy followed.

"Kaviak!" each called in turn. It was quite light enough to see if he were anywhere about, although the watery sun had sunk full half an hour before. The fantastically huge full-moon hung like a copper shield on a steel-blue wall.

"Do you see anything?" whispered Mac.

"No."

"Who's that yonder?"

"Potts gettin' water."

The Boy was bending down looking for tracks. Mac looked, too, but ineffectually, feverishly.

"Isn't Potts calling?"

"I knew he would if he saw us. He's never carried a bucket uphill yet without help. See, there are the Kid's tracks going. We must find some turned the other way."

They were near the Little Cabin now.

"Here!" shouted the Boy; "and . . . yes, here again!" And so it was. Clean and neatly printed in the last light snow-fall showed the little footprints. "We're on the right trail now. Kaviak!"

Through his parki the Boy felt a hand close vise-like on his shoulder, and a voice, not like MacCann's:

"Goin' straight down to the fish-trap hole!"

The two dashed forward, down the steep hill, the Boy saying breathless as they went: "And Potts—where's Potts?"

He had vanished, but there was no time to consider how or where.

"Kaviak!"

"Kaviak!" And as they got to the river:

"Think I hear——"

"So do I——"

"Coming! coming! Hold on tight! Coming, Kaviak!"

They made straight for the big open fish-hole. Farther away from the Little Cabin, and nearer the bank, was the small well-hole. Between the two they noticed, as they raced by, the water-bucket hung on that heavy piece of driftwood that had frozen aslant in the river. Mac saw that the bucket-rope was taut, and that it ran along the ice and disappeared behind the big funnel of the fish-trap.

The sound was unmistakable now—a faint, choked voice calling out of the hole, "Help!"

"Coming!"

"Hold tight!"

"Half a minute!"

And how it was done or who did it nobody quite knew,

but Potts, still clinging by one hand to the bucket-rope, was hauled out and laid on the ice before it was discovered that he had Kaviak under his arm—Kaviak, stark and unconscious, with the round eyes rolled back till one saw the whites and nothing more.

Mac picked the body up and held it head downwards; laid it flat again, and, stripping off the great sodden jacket, already beginning to freeze, fell to putting Kaviak through the action of artificial breathing.

"We must get them up to the cabin first thing," said the Boy.

But Mac seemed not to hear.

"Don't you see Kaviak's face is freezing?"

Still Mac paid no heed. Potts lifted a stiff, uncertain hand, and, with a groan, let it fall heavily on his own cheek.

"Come on; I'll help you in, anyhow, Potts."

"Can't walk in this damned wet fur."

With some difficulty having dragged off Potts' soaked parki, already stiffening unmanageably, the Boy tried to get him on his feet.

"Once you're in the cabin you're all right."

But the benumbed and miserable Potts kept his eyes on Kaviak, as if hypnotised by the strange new death-look in the little face.

"Well, I can't carry you up," said the Boy; and after a second he began to rub Potts furiously, glancing over now and then to see if Kaviak was coming to, while Mac, dumb and tense, laboured on without success. Potts, under the Boy's ministering, showed himself restored enough to swear feebly.

"H'ray! my man's comin' round. How's yours?" No answer, but he could see that the sweat poured off Mac's face as he worked unceasingly over the child. The Boy pulled Potts into a sitting posture. It was then that Mac, without looking up, said:

"Run and get whiskey. Run like hell!"

When he got back with the Colonel and the whiskey, O'Flynn floundering in the distance, Potts was feebly striking his breast with his arms, and Mac still bent above the motionless little body.

They tried to get some of the spirit down the child's throat, but the tight-clenched teeth seemed to let little or nothing pass. The stuff ran down towards his ears and into his neck. But

Mac persisted, and went on pouring, drop by drop, whenever he stopped trying to restore the action of the lungs. O'Flynn just barely managed to get "a swig" for Potts in the interval, though they all began to feel that Mac was working to bring back something that had gone for ever. The Boy went and bent his face down close over the rigid mouth to feel for the breath. When he got up he turned away sharply, and stood looking through tears into the fish-hole, saying to himself, "Yukon Inua has taken him."

"He was in too long." Potts' teeth were chattering, and he looked unspeakably wretched. "When my arm got numb I couldn't keep his head up;" and he swallowed more whiskey. "You fellers oughtn't to have left that damn trap up!"

"What's that got to do with it?" said the Boy guiltily.

"Kaviak knew it ought to be catchin' fish. When I came down he was cryin' and pullin' the trap backwards towards the hole. Then he slipped."

"Come, Mac," said the Colonel quietly, "let's carry the little man to the cabin."

"No, no, not yet; stuffy heat isn't what he wants;" and he worked on.

They got Potts up on his feet.

"I called out to you fellers. Didn't you hear me?"

"Y-yes, but we didn't understand."

"Well, you'd better have come. It's too late now." O'Flynn half dragged, half carried him up to the cabin, for he seemed unable to walk in his frozen trousers. The Colonel and the Boy by a common impulse went a little way in the opposite direction across the ice.

"What can we do, Colonel?"

"Nothing. It's not a bit o' use." They turned to go back.

"Well, the duckin' will be good for Potts' parki, anyhow," said the Boy in an angry and unsteady voice.

"What do you mean?"

"When he asked me to hand it to him I nearly stuck fast to it. It's all over syrup; and we don't wear furs at our meals."

"Tchah!" The Colonel stopped with a face of loathing.

"Yes, he was the only one of us that didn't bully the kid to-day."

"Couldn't go *that* far, but couldn't own up."

"Potts is a cur."

"Yes, sah." Then, after an instant's reflection: "But he's

a cur that can risk his life to save a kid he don't care a damn for."

They went back to Mac, and found him pretty well worn out. The Colonel took his place, but was soon pushed away. Mac understood better, he said; had once brought a chap round that everybody said was . . . dead. He wasn't dead. The great thing was not to give in.

A few minutes after, Kaviak's eyelids fluttered, and came down over the upturned eyeballs. Mac, with a cry that brought a lump to the Colonel's throat, gathered the child up in his arms and ran with him up the hill to the cabin.

* * * * * * *

Three hours later, when they were all sitting round the fire, Kaviak dosed, and warm, and asleep in the lower bunk, the door opened, and in walked a white man followed by an Indian.

"I'm George Benham." They had all heard of the Anvik trader, a man of some wealth and influence, and they made him welcome.

The Indian was his guide, he said, and he had a team outside of seven dogs. He was going to the steamship *Oklahoma* on some business, and promised Father Wills of Holy Cross that he'd stop on the way, and deliver a letter to Mr. MacCann.

"Stop on the way! I should think so."

"We were goin' to have supper to-night, anyhow, and you'll stay and sleep here."

All Mac's old suspicions of the Jesuits seemed to return with the advent of that letter.

"I'll read it presently." He laid it on the mantel-shelf, between the sewing-kit and the tobacco-can, and he looked at it, angrily, every now and then, while he helped to skin Mr. Benham. That gentleman had thrown back his hood, pulled off his great moose-skin gauntlets and his beaver-lined cap, and now, with a little help, dragged the drill parki over his head, and after that the fine lynx-bordered deer-skin, standing revealed at last as a well-built fellow, of thirty-eight or so, in a suit of mackinaws, standing six feet two in his heelless salmon-skin snow-boots.

"Bring in my traps, will you?" he said to the Indian, and then relapsed into silence. The Indian reappeared with his arms full.

"Fine lot o' pelts you have there," said the Colonel.

Benham didn't answer. He seemed to be a close-mouthed kind of a chap. As the Indian sorted and piled the stuff in the corner, Potts said:

"Got any furs you want to sell?"

"No."

"Where you takin' 'em?"

"Down to the *Oklahoma*."

"All this stuff for Cap'n Rainey?"

Benham nodded.

"I reckon there's a mistake about the name, and he's Cap'n Tom Thumb or Commodore Nutt." The Boy had picked up a little parki made carefully of some very soft dark fur and trimmed with white rabbit, the small hood bordered with white fox.

"That's a neat piece of work," said the Colonel.

Benham nodded. "One of the Shageluk squaws can do that sort of thing."

"What's the fur?"

"Musk-rat." And they talked of the weather—how the mercury last week had been solid in the trading-post thermometer, so it was "over forty degrees, anyhow."

"What's the market price of a coat like that?" Mac said suddenly.

"That isn't a 'market' coat. It's for a kid of Rainey's back in the States."

Still Mac eyed it enviously.

"What part of the world are you from, sir?" said the Colonel when they had drawn up to the supper table.

"San Francisco. Used to teach numskulls Latin and mathematics in the Las Palmas High School."

"What's the value of a coat like that little one?" interrupted Mac.

"Oh, about twenty dollars."

"The Shageluks ask that much?"

Benham laughed. "If *you* asked the Shageluks, they'd say forty."

"You've been some time in this part of the world, I understand," said the Colonel.

"Twelve years."

"Without going home?"

"Been home twice. Only stayed a month. Couldn't stand it."

"I'll give you twenty-two dollars for that coat," said Mac.

"I've only got that one, and as I think I said——"

"I'll give you twenty-four."

"It's an order, you see. Rainey——"

"I'll give you twenty-six."

Benham shook his head.

"Sorry. Yes, it's queer about the hold this country gets on you. The first year is hell, the second is purgatory, with glimpses . . . of something else. The third—well, more and more, forever after, you realise the North's taken away any taste you ever had for civilisation. That's when you've got the hang of things up here, when you've learned not to stay in your cabin all the time, and how to take care of yourself on the trail. But as for going back to the boredom of cities—no, thank you."

Mac couldn't keep his eyes off the little coat. Finally, to enable him to forget it, as it seemed, he got up and opened Father Wills' letter, devoured its contents in silence, and flung it down on the table. The Colonel took it up, and read aloud the Father's thanks for all the white camp's kindness to Kaviak, and now that the sickness was about gone from Holy Cross, how the Fathers felt that they must relieve their neighbours of further trouble with the little native.

"I've said I'd take him back with me when I come up river about Christmas."

"We'd be kind o' lost, now, without the little beggar," said the Boy, glancing sideways at Mac.

"There's nothin' to be got by luggin' him off to Holy Cross," answered that gentleman severely.

"Unless it's clo'es," said Potts.

"He's all right in the clo'es he's got," said Mac, with the air of one who closes an argument. He stood up, worn and tired, and looked at his watch.

"You ain't goin' to bed this early?" said Potts, quite lively and recovered from his cold bath. That was the worst of sleeping in the Little Cabin. Bedtime broke the circle; you left interesting visitors behind, and sometimes the talk was better as the night wore on.

"Well, someone ought to wood up down yonder. O'Flynn, will you go?"

O'Flynn was in the act of declining the honour. But Benham, who had been saying, "It takes a year in the Yukon for a man to get on to himself," interrupted his favourite theme to ask: "Your other cabin like this?"

Whereon, O'Flynn, shameless of the contrast in cabins, jumped up, and said: "Come and see, while I wood up."

"You're very well fixed here," said Benham, rising and looking round with condescension; "but men like you oughtn't to try to live without real bread. No one can live and work on baking-powder."

There was a general movement to the door, of which Benham was the centre.

"I tell you a lump of sour dough, kept over to raise the next batch, is worth more in this country than a pocket full of gold."

"I'll give you twenty-eight for that musk-rat coat," said Mac.

Benham turned, stared back at him a moment, and then laughed.

"Oh, well, I suppose I can get another made for Rainey before the first boat goes down."

"Then is it on account o' the bread," the Colonel was saying, "that the old-timer calls himself a Sour-dough?"

"All on account o' the bread."

They crowded out after Benham.

"Coming?" The Boy, who was last, held the door open. Mac shook his head.

It wasn't one of the bitter nights; they'd get down yonder, and talk by the fire, till he went in and disturbed them. That was all he had wanted. For Mac was the only one who had noticed that Kaviak had waked up. He was lying as still as a mouse.

Alone with him at last, Mac kept his eyes religiously turned away, sat down by the fire, and watched the sparks. By-and-by a head was put up over the board of the lower bunk. Mac saw it, but sat quite still.

"Farva."

He meant to answer the appeal, half cleared his throat, but his voice felt rusty; it wouldn't turn out a word.

Kaviak climbed timidly, shakily out, and stood in the middle of the floor in his bare feet.

"Farva!"

He came a little nearer till the small feet sank into the rough brown curls of the buffalo. The child stooped to pick up his wooden cricket, wavered, and was about to fall. Mac shot out a hand, steadied him an instant without looking, and then set the cricket in front of the fire. He thereupon averted his face, and sat as before with folded arms. He hadn't deliberately meant to make Kaviak be the first to "show his hand" after all that had happened, but something had taken hold of him and made him behave as he hadn't dreamed of behaving. It was, perhaps, a fear of playing the fool as much as a determination to see how much ground he'd lost with the youngster.

The child was observing him with an almost feverish intensity. With eyes fixed upon the wooden face to find out how far he might venture, shakily he dragged the cricket from where Mac placed it, closer, closer, and as no terrible change in the unmoved face warned him to desist, he pulled it into its usual evening position between Mac's right foot and the fireplace. He sank down with a sigh of relief, as one who finishes a journey long and perilous. The fire crackled and the sparks flew gaily. Kaviak sat there in the red glow, dressed only in a shirt, staring with incredulous, mournful eyes at the Farva who had——

Then, as Mac made no sign, he sighed again, and held out two little shaky hands to the blaze.

Mac gave out a sound between a cough and a snort, and wiped his eyes on the back of his hand.

Kaviak had started nervously.

"You cold?" asked Mac.

Kaviak nodded

"Hungry?"

He nodded again, and fell to coughing.

Mac got up and brought the newly purchased coat to the fire.

"It's for you," he said, as the child's big eyes grew bigger with admiration.

"Me? Me own coat?" He stood up, and his bare feet fluttered up and down feebly, but with huge delight.

As the parki was held ready the child tumbled dizzily into it, and Mac held him fast an instant.

In less than five minutes Kaviak was once more seated on the cricket, but very magnificent now in his musk-rat coat, so close up to Mac that he could lean against his arm, and eating out of a plenty-bowl on his knees a discreet spoonful of mush drowned in golden syrup—a supper for a Sultan if only there had been more!

When he had finished, he set the bowl down, and, as a

puppy might, he pushed at Mac's arm till he found a way in, laid his head down on "Farva's" knee with a contented sigh, and closed his heavy eyes.

Mac put his hand on the cropped head and began:

"About that empty syrup-can——"

Kaviak started up, shaking from head to foot. Was the obscure nightmare coming down to crush him again?

Mac tried to soothe him. But Kaviak, casting about for charms to disarm the awful fury of the white man—able to endure with dignity any reverse save that of having his syrup spilt—cried out:

"I solly—solly. Our Farva——"

"I'm sorry, too, Kaviak," Mac interrupted, gathering the child up to him; "and we won't either of us do it any more."

CHAPTER VIII

CHRISTMAS

"Himlen morkner, mens Jordens Trakt
Straaler lys som i Stjernedragt.
Himlen er bleven Jordens Gjæst
Snart er det Julens sode Fest."

IT had been moved, seconded, and carried by acclamation that they should celebrate Christmas, not so much by a feast of reason as by a flow of soul and a bang-up dinner, to be followed by speeches and some sort of cheerful entertainment.

"We're goin' to lay ourselves out on this entertainment," said the Boy, with painful misgivings as to the "bang-up dinner."

Every time the banquet was mentioned somebody was sure to say, "Well, anyhow, there's Potts's cake," and that reflection never failed to raise the tone of expectation, for Potts's cake was a beauty, evidently very rich and fruity, and fitted by Nature to play the noble part of plum-pudding. But, in making out the bill of fare, facts had to be faced. "We've got our everyday little rations of beans and bacon, and we've got Potts's cake, and we've got one skinny ptarmigan to make a banquet for six hungry people!"

"But we'll have a high old time, and if the bill o' fare is a little . . . restricted, there's nothin' to prevent our programme of toasts, songs, and miscellaneous contributions from bein' rich and varied."

"And one thing we can get, even up here"—the Colonel was looking at Kaviak—"and that's a little Christmas-tree."

"Y-yes," said Potts, "you can get a little tree, but you can't get the smallest kind of a little thing to hang on it."

"Sh!" said the Boy, "it must be a surprise."

And he took steps that it should be, for he began stealing away Kaviak's few cherished possessions—his amulet, his top from under the bunk, his boats from out the water-bucket, wherewith to mitigate the barrenness of the Yukon tree, and

149

to provide a pleasant surprise for the Esquimer who mourned his playthings as gone for ever. Of an evening now, after sleep had settled on Kaviak's watchful eyes, the Boy worked at a pair of little snow-shoes, helped out by a ball of sinew he had got from Nicholas. Mac bethought him of the valuable combination of zoological and biblical instruction that might be conveyed by means of a Noah's Ark. He sat up late the last nights before the 25th, whittling, chipping, pegging in legs, sharpening beaks, and inking eyes, that the more important animals might be ready for the Deluge by Christmas.

The Colonel made the ark, and O'Flynn took up a collection to defray the expense of the little new mucklucks he had ordered from Nicholas. They were to come "*sure* by Christmas Eve," and O'Flynn was in what he called "a froightful fanteeg" as the short day of the 24th wore towards night, and never a sign of the one-eyed Pymeut. Half a dozen times O'Flynn had gone beyond the stockade to find out if he wasn't in sight, and finally came back looking intensely disgusted, bringing a couple of white travellers who had arrived from the opposite direction; very cold, one of them deaf, and with frost-bitten feet, and both so tired they could hardly speak. Of course, they were made as comfortable as was possible, the frozen one rubbed with snow and bandaged, and both given bacon and corn-bread and hot tea.

"You oughtn't to let yourself get into a state like this," said Mac, thinking ruefully of these strangers' obvious inability to travel for a day or two, and of the Christmas dinner, to which Benham alone had been bidden, by a great stretch of hospitality.

"That's all very well," said the stranger, who shouted when he talked at all, "but how's a man to know his feet are going to freeze?"

"Ye see, sorr," O'Flynn explained absent-mindedly, "Misther MacCann didn't know yer pardner was deaf."

This point of view seemed to thaw some of the frost out of the two wayfarers. They confided that they were Salmon P. Hardy and Bill Schiff, fellow-passengers in the *Merwin,* "locked in the ice down below," and they'd mined side by side back in the States at Cripple Creek. "Yes, sir, and sailed for the Klondyke from Seattle last July." And now at Christmas they were hoping that, with luck, they might reach the new Minóok Diggings, seven hundred miles this side of the Klondyke, before the spring rush. During this recital O'Flynn kept rolling his eyes absently.

"Theyse a quare noise without."

"It's the wind knockin' down yer chimbly," says Mr. Hardy encouragingly.

"It don't sound like Nich'las, annyhow. May the divil burrn him in tarment and ile fur disappoyntin' th' kid."

A rattle at the latch, and the Pymeut opened the door.

"Lorrd love ye! ye're a jool, Nich'las!" screamed O'Flynn; and the mucklucks passed from one to the other so surreptitiously that for all Kaviak's wide-eyed watchfulness he detected nothing.

Nicholas supped with his white friends, and seemed bent on passing the night with them. He had to be bribed with tobacco and a new half-dollar to go home and keep Christmas in the bosom of his family. And still, at the door, he hesitated, drew back, and laid the silver coin on the table.

"No. It nights."

"But it isn't really dark."

"Pretty soon heap dark."

"Why, I thought you natives could find your way day or night?"

"Yes. Find way."

"Then what's the matter?"

"Pymeut no like dark;" and it was not until Mac put on his own snow-shoes and offered to go part of the way with him that Nicholas was at last induced to return home.

The moment Kaviak was ascertained to be asleep, O'Flynn displayed the mucklucks. No mistake, they were dandies! The Boy hung one of them up, by its long leg, near the child's head at the side of the bunk, and then conferred with O'Flynn.

"The Colonel's made some little kind o' sweet-cake things for the tree. I could spare you one or two."

"Divil a doubt Kaviak 'll take it kindly, but furr mesilf I'm thinkin' a pitaty's a dale tastier."

There was just one left in camp. It had rolled behind the flour-sack, and O'Flynn had seized on it with rapture. Where everybody was in such need of vegetable food, nobody underestimated the magnificence of O'Flynn's offering, as he pushed the pitaty down into the toe of the muckluck.

"Sure, the little haythen 'll have a foine Christian Christmas wid that same to roast in the coals, begorra!" and they all went to bed save Mac, who had not returned, and the Boy, who put on his furs, and went up the hill to the place where he kept the Christmas-tree lodged in a cotton-wood.

He shook the snow off its branches, brought it down to the cabin, decorated it, and carried it back.

*   *   *   *   *   *   *

Mac, Salmon P. Hardy, and the frost-bitten Schiff were waked, bright and early Christmas morning, by the Boy's screaming with laughter.

The Colonel looked down over the bunk's side, and the men on the buffalo-skin looked up, and they all saw Kaviak sitting in bed, holding in one hand an empty muckluck by the toe, and in the other a half-eaten raw potato.

"Keep the rest of it to roast, anyhow, or O'Flynn's heart will be broken."

So they deprived Kaviak of the gnawed fragment, and consoled him by helping him to put on his new boots.

When the Little Cabin contingent came in to breakfast, "Hello! what you got up on the roof?" says Potts.

"Foot of earth and three feet o' snow!"

"But what's in the bundle!"

"Bundle?" echoes the Boy.

"If *you* put a bundle on the roof, I s'pose you know what's in it," says the Colonel severely.

The occupants of the two cabins eyed each other with good-humoured suspicion.

"Thank you," says the Boy, "but we're not takin' any bundles to-day."

"Call next door," advised the Colonel.

"You think we're tryin' to jolly you, but just go out and see for yourself——"

"No, sir, you've waked the wrong passenger!"

"They're tryin' it on *us*," said Potts, and subsided into his place at the breakfast-table.

During the later morning, while the Colonel wrestled with the dinner problem, the Boy went through the thick-falling snow to see if the tree was all right, and the dogs had not appropriated the presents. Half-way up to the cotton-wood, he glanced back to make sure Kaviak wasn't following, and there, sure enough, just as the Little Cabin men had said—there below him on the broad-eaved roof was a bundle packed round and nearly covered over with snow. He went back eyeing it suspiciously.

Whatever it was, it seemed to be done up in sacking, for a

bit stuck out at the corner where the wind struck keen. The Boy walked round the cabin looking, listening. Nobody had followed him, or nothing would have induced him to risk the derision of the camp. As it was, he would climb up very softly and lightly, and nobody but himself would be the wiser even if it was a josh. He brushed away the snow, touching the thing with a mittened hand and a creepy feeling at his spine. It was precious heavy, and hard as iron. He tugged at the sacking. "Jee! if I don't b'lieve it's meat." The lid of an old cardboard box was bound round the frozen mass with a string, and on the cardboard was written: "Moose and Christmas Greeting from Kaviak's friends at Holy Cross to Kaviak's friends by the Big Chimney."

"H'ray! h'ray! Come out, you fellas! Hip! hip! hurrah!" and the Boy danced a breakdown on the roof till the others had come out, and then he hurled the moose-meat down over the stockade, and sent the placard flying after. They all gathered round Mac and read it.

"Be the Siven!"

"Well, I swan!"

"Don't forget, Boy, you're not takin' any."

"Just remember, if it hadn't been for me it might have stayed up there till spring."

"You run in, Kaviak, or you'll have no ears."

But that gentleman pulled up his hood and stood his ground.

"How did it get on the roof, in the name o' the nation?" asked the Colonel, stamping his feet.

"Never hear of Santa Claus? Didn't I tell you, Kaviak, he drove his reindeer team over the roofs?"

"Did you hear any dogs go by in the night?"

"I didn't; Nicholas brought it, I s'pose, and was told to cache it up there. Maybe that's why he came late to give us a surprise."

"Don't believe it; we'd have heard him. Somebody from the mission came by in the night and didn't want to wake us, and saw there were dogs——"

"It's froze too hard to cut," interrupted Salmon P. Hardy, who had been trying his jack-knife on one end; "it's too big to go in any mortal pot."

"And it'll take a month to thaw!"

They tried chopping it, but you could more easily chop a bolt of linen sheeting. The axe laboriously chewed out little bits and scattered shreds.

"Stop! We'll lose a lot that way."

While they were lamenting this fact, and wondering what to do, the dogs set up a racket, and were answered by some others. Benham was coming along at a rattling pace, his dogs very angry to find other dogs there, putting on airs of possession.

"We got all this moose-meat," says Potts, when Benham arrived on the scene, "but we can't cut it."

"Of course not. Where's your hand-saw?"

The Boy brought it, and Mr. Benham triumphantly sawed off two fine large steaks. Kaviak scraped up the meat saw-dust and ate it with grave satisfaction. With a huge steak in each hand, the Colonel, beaming, led the procession back to the cabin. The Boy and Mac cached the rest of the moose on the roof and followed.

"Fine team, that one o' yours," said Salmon P. Hardy to the trader. *"You'll* get to Minóok, anyhow."

"Not me."

"Hey?"

"I'm not going that way."

"Mean to skip the country? Got cold feet?"

"No. I'm satisfied enough with the country," said the trader quietly, and acknowledged the introduction to Mr. Schiff, sitting in bandages by the fire.

Benham turned back and called out something to his guide.

"I thought maybe you'd like some oysters for your Christmas dinner," he said to the Colonel when he came in again, "so I got a couple o' cans from the A. C. man down below;" and a mighty whoop went up.

The great rapture of that moment did not, however, prevent O'Flynn's saying under his breath:

"Did ye be chanct, now, think of bringin' a dtrop o'—hey?"

"No," says Benham a little shortly.

"Huh! Ye say that like's if ye wuz a taytotlerr?"

"Not me. But I find it no good to drink whiskey on the trail."

"Ah!" says Salmon P. with interest, "you prefer brandy?"

"No," says Benham, "I prefer tea."

"Lorrd, now! look at that!"

"Drink spirit, and it's all very fine and reviving for a few minutes; but a man can't work on it."

"It's the wan thing, sorr," says O'Flynn with solemnity—

"it's the wan thing on the top o' God's futstool that makes me feel I cud wurruk."

"Not in this climate; and you're safe to take cold in the reaction."

"Cowld is ut? Faith, ye'll be tellin' us Mr. Schiff got his toes froze wid settin' too clost be the foire."

"You don't seriously mean you go on the trail without any alcohol?" asks the Colonel.

"No, I don't go without, but I keep it on the outside of me, unless I have an accident."

Salmon P. studied the trader with curiosity. A man with seven magnificent dogs and a native servant, and the finest furs he'd ever seen—here was either a capitalist from the outside or a man who had struck it rich "on the inside."

"Been in long?"

"Crossed the Chilcoot in June, '85."

"What! twelve year ago?"

Benham nodded.

"Gosh! then you've been in the Klondyke?"

"Not since the gold was found."

"And got a team like that 'n outside, and not even goin' to Minóok?"

"Guess not!"

What made the feller so damn satisfied? Only one explanation was possible: he'd found a mine without going even as far as Minóok. He was a man to keep your eye on.

A goodly aroma of steaming oysters and of grilling moose arose in the air. The Boy set up the amended bill of fare, lit the Christmas candles—one at the top, one at the bottom of the board—and the Colonel announced the first course, though it wasn't one o'clock, and they usually dined at four.

The soup was too absorbingly delicious to admit of conversation. The moose-steaks had vanished like the "snaw-wreath in the thaw" before anything much was said, save:

"Nothin' th' matter with moose, hey?"

"Nop! Bet your life."

The "Salmi of ptarmigan" appeared as a great wash of gravy in which portions of the much cut-up bird swam in vain for their lives. But the high flat rim of the dish was plentifully garnished by fingers of corn-bread, and the gravy was "galopp-shus," so Potts said.

Salmon P., having appeased the pangs of hunger, returned to his perplexed study of Benham.

"Did I understand you to say you came into this country to *prospect?*"

"Came down the Never-Know-What and prospected a whole summer at Forty Mile."

"What river did you come by?"

"Same as you go by—the Yukon. Indians up yonder call it the Never-Know-What, and the more you find out about it, the better you think the name."

"Did you do any good at Forty Mile?"

"Not enough to turn my head, so I tried the Koyukuk—and other diggins too."

"Hear that, Schiff?" he roared at his bandaged friend. "Never say die! This gen'l'man's been at it twelve years—tried more 'n one camp, but now—well, he's so well fixed he don't care a cuss about the Klondyke."

Schiff lit up and pulled hard at the cutty.

O'Flynn had taken Kaviak to the fire, and was showing him how to roast half a petaty in wood ashes; but he was listening to the story and putting in "Be the Siven!" at appropriate moments.

Schiff poured out a cloud of rank smoke.

"Gen'lemen," he said, "the best Klondyke claims 'll be potted. Minóok's the camp o' the future. You'd better come along with us."

"Got no dogs," sighed the Boy; but the two strangers looked hard at the man who hadn't that excuse.

Benham sat and idly watched preparations for the next course.

"Say, a nabob like you might give us a tip. How did you do the trick?"

"Well, I'd been playing your game for three years, and no galley slave ever worked half as hard——"

"That's it! work like the devil for a couple o' years and then live like a lord for ever after."

"Yes; well, when the time came for me to go into the Lord business I had just forty-two dollars and sixty cents to set up on."

"What had you done with the rest?"

"I'd spent the five thousand dollars my father left me, and I'd cleaned up just forty-two dollars sixty cents in my three years' mining."

The announcement fell chill on the company.

"I was dead broke and I had no credit. I went home."

"But"—Mac roused himself—"you didn't stay——"

"No, you don't stay—as a rule;"—Mac remembered Caribou—"get used to this kind o' thing, and miss it. Miss it so you——"

"You came back," says Salmon P., impatient of generalities.

"And won this time," whispered Schiff.

For that is how every story must end. The popular taste in fiction is universal.

"A friend at home grub-staked me, and I came in again—came down on the high water in June. Prospected as long as my stuff lasted, and then—well, I didn't care about starving, I became an A. C. Trader."

A long pause. This was no climax; everybody waited.

"And now I'm on my own. I often make more money in a day trading with the Indians in furs, fish, and cord-wood, than I made in my whole experience as a prospector and miner."

A frost had fallen on the genial company.

"But even if _you_ hadn't any luck," the Boy suggested, "you must have seen others——"

"Oh, I saw some washing gravel that kept body and soul together, and I saw some . . . that didn't."

In the pause he added, remorseless:

"I helped to bury some of them."

"Your experience was unusual, or why do men come back year after year?"

"Did you ever hear of a thing called Hope?"

They moved uneasily on their stools, and some rubbed stubbly chins with perplexed, uncertain fingers, and they all glowered at the speaker. He was uncomfortable, this fellow.

"Well, there mayn't be as much gold up here as men think, but there's more hope than anywhere on earth."

"To hell with hope; give me certainty," says Salmon P.

"Exactly. So you shuffle the cards, and laugh down the five-cent limit. You'll play one last big game, and it'll be for life this time as well as fortune."

"Cheerful cuss, ain't he?" whispered Schiff.

"They say we're a nation of gamblers. Well, sir, the biggest game we play is the game that goes on near the Arctic Circle."

"What's the matter with Wall Street?"

" 'Tisn't such a pretty game, and they don't play for their

lives. I tell you it's love of gambling brings men here, and it's the splendid stiff game they find going on that keeps them. There's nothing like it on earth."

His belated enthusiasm deceived nobody.

"It don't seem to have excited you much," said Mac.

"Oh, I've had my turn at it. And just by luck I found I could play another—a safer game, and not bad fun either." He sat up straight and shot his hands down deep in the pockets of his mackinaws. "I've got a good thing, and I'm willing to stay with it."

The company looked at him coldly.

"Well," drawled Potts, "you can look after the fur trade; give me a modest little claim in the Klondyke."

"Oh, Klondyke! Klondyke!" Benham got up and stepped over Kaviak on his way to the fire. He lit a short briarwood with a flaming stick and turned about. "Shall I tell you fellows a little secret about the Klondyke?" He held up the burning brand in the dim room with telling emphasis. The smoke and flame blew black and orange across his face as he said:

"Every dollar that's taken out of the Klondyke in gold-dust will cost three dollars in coin."

A sense of distinct dislike to Benham had spread through the company—a fellow who called American enterprise love of gambling, for whom heroism was foolhardy, and hope insane. Where was a pioneer so bold he could get up now and toast the Klondyke? Who, now, without grim misgiving, could forecast a rosy future for each man at the board? And that, in brief, had been the programme.

"Oh, help the puddin', Colonel," said the Boy like one who starts up from an evil dream.

But they sat chilled and moody, eating plum-pudding as if it had been so much beans and bacon. Mac felt Robert Bruce's expensive education slipping out of reach. Potts saw his girl, tired of waiting, taking up with another fellow. The Boy's Orange Grove was farther off than Florida. Schiff and Hardy wondered, for a moment, who was the gainer for all their killing hardship? Not they, at present, although there was the prospect—the hope—oh, damn the Trader!

The Colonel made the punch. O'Flynn drained his cup without waiting for the mockery of that first toast—*To our Enterprise*—although no one had taken more interest in the programme than O'Flynn. Benham talked about the Anvik saw-mill, and the money made in wood camps along the river. Nobody listened, though everyone else sat silent, smoking and sulkily drinking his punch.

Kaviak's demand for some of the beverage reminded the Boy of the Christmas-tree. It had been intended as a climax to wind up the entertainment, but to produce it now might save the situation. He got up and pulled on his parki.

"Back 'n a minute." But he was gone a long time.

Benham looked down the toast-list and smiled inwardly, for it was Klondyked from top to bottom. The others, too, stole uneasy glances at that programme, staring them in the face, unabashed, covertly ironic—nay, openly jeering. They actually hadn't noticed the fact before, but every blessed speech was aimed straight at the wonderful gold camp across the line—not the Klondyke of Benham's croaking, but the Klondyke of their dreams.

Even the death's head at the feast regretted the long postponement of so spirited a programme, interspersed, as it promised to be, with songs, dances, and "tricks," and winding up with an original poem, "He won't be happy till he gets it."

Benham's Indian had got up and gone out. Kaviak had tried to go too, but the door was slammed in his face. He stood there with his nose to the crack exactly as a dog does. Suddenly he ran back to Mac and tugged at his arm. Even the dull white men could hear an ominous snarling among the Mahlemeuts.

Out of the distance a faint answering howl of derision from some enemy, advancing or at bay. It was often like this when two teams put up at the Big Chimney Camp.

"Reckon our dogs are gettin' into trouble," said Salmon P. anxiously to his deaf and crippled partner.

"It's nothing," says the Trader. "A Siwash dog of any spirit is always trailing his coat"; and Salmon P. subsided.

Not so Kaviak. Back to the door, head up, he listened. They had observed the oddity before. The melancholy note of the Mahlemeut never yet had failed to stir his sombre little soul. He was standing now looking up at the latch, high, and made for white men, eager, breathing fast, listening to that dismal sound that is like nothing else in nature—listening as might an exiled Scot to the skirl of bagpipes; listening as a Tyrolese who hears yodelling on foreign hills, or as the dweller in a distant land to the sound of the dear home speech.

The noise outside grew louder, the air was rent with howls of rage and defiance.

"Sounds as if there's 'bout a million mad dogs on your front stoop," says Schiff, knowing there must be a great deal going on if any of it reached his ears.

"You set still." His pardner pushed him down on his stool. "Mr. Benham and I'll see what's up."

The Trader leisurely opened the door, Salmon P. keeping modestly behind, while Kaviak darted forward only to be caught back by Mac. An avalanche of sound swept in—a mighty howling and snarling and cracking of whips, and underneath the higher clamour, human voices—and in dashes the Boy, powdered with snow, laughing and balancing carefully in his mittened hands a little Yukon spruce, every needle diamond-pointed, every sturdy branch white with frost crystals and soft woolly snow, and bearing its little harvest of curious fruit—sweet-cake rings and stars and two gingerbread men hanging by pack-thread from the white and green branches, the Noah's Ark lodged in one crotch, the very amateur snow-shoes in another, and the lost toys wrapped up, transfigured in tobacco-foil, dangling merrily before Kaviak's incredulous eyes.

"There's your Christmas-tree!" and the bringer, who had carried the tree so that no little puff of snow or delicate crystal should fall off, having made a successful entrance and dazzled the child, gave way to the strong excitement that shot light out of his eyes and brought scarlet into his cheeks. "Here, take it!" He dashed the tree down in front of Kaviak, and a sudden storm agitated its sturdy branches; it snowed about the floor, and the strange fruit whirled and spun in the blast. Kaviak clutched it, far too dazed to do more than stare. The Boy stamped the snow off his mucklucks on the threshold, and dashed his cap against the lintel, calling out:

"Come in! come in! let the dogs fight it out." Behind him, between the snow-walls at the entrance, had appeared two faces—weather-beaten men, crowding in the narrow space, craning to see the reception of the Christmas-tree and the inside of the famous Big Chimney Cabin.

"These gentlemen," says the Boy, shaking with excitement as he ushered them in, "are Mr. John Dillon and General Lighter. They've just done the six hundred and twenty-five miles from Minóok with dogs over the ice! They've been forty days on the trail, and they're as fit as fiddles. An' no wonder, for Little Minóok has made big millionaires o' both o' them!"

Millionaires or not, they'll never, either of them, create a greater sensation than they did that Christmas Day, in the Big Chimney Cabin, on the bleak hillside, up above the Never-Know-What. Here was Certainty at last! Here was Justification!

Precious symbols of success, they were taken by both hands, they were shaken and wildly welcomed, "peeled," set down by the fire, given punch, asked ten thousand questions all in a breath, rejoiced over, and looked up to as glorious dispellers of doubt, blessed saviours from despair.

Schiff had tottered forward on bandaged feet, hand round ear, mouth open, as if to swallow whole whatever he couldn't hear. The Colonel kept on bowing magnificently at intervals and pressing refreshment, O'Flynn slapping his thigh and reiterating, "Be the Siven!" Potts not only widened his mouth from ear to ear, but, as O'Flynn said after, "stretched it clane round his head and tyed it up furr jy in a nate knot behind." Benham took a back seat, and when anybody remembered him for the next hour it was openly to gloat over his discomfiture.

John Dillon was one of those frontiersmen rightly called typically American. You see him again and again—as a cowboy in Texas, as a miner or herdsman all through the Far West; you see him cutting lumber along the Columbia, or throwing the diamond hitch as he goes from camp to camp for gold and freedom. He takes risks cheerfully, and he never works for wages when he can go "on his own."

John Dillon was like the majority, tall, lean, muscular, not an ounce of superfluous flesh on his bones, a face almost gaunt in its clearness of cut, a thin straight nose, chin not heavy but well curved out, the eye orbit arched and deep, a frown fixed between thick eyebrows, and few words in his firm, rather grim-looking mouth. He was perhaps thirty-six, had been "in" ten years, and had mined before that in Idaho. Under his striped parki he was dressed in spotted deer-skin, wore white deer-skin mucklucks, Arctic cap, and moose mittens. Pinned on his inner shirt was the badge of the Yukon Order of Pioneers—a foot-rule bent like the letter A above a scroll of leaves, and in the angle two linked O's over Y. P.

It was the other man—the western towns are full of General Lighters—who did the talking. An attorney from Seattle, he had come up in the July rush with very little but boundless assurance, fell in with an old miner who had been grubstaked by Captain Rainey out of the *Oklahoma's* supplies, and got to Minóok before the river went to sleep.

"No, we're not pardners exactly," he said, glancing good-humouredly at Dillon; "we've worked separate, but we're going home two by two like animals into the Ark. We've got this in common. We've both 'struck ile'—haven't we, Dillon?"

Dillon nodded.

"Little Minóok's as rich a camp as Dawson, and the gold's of higher grade—isn't it, Dillon?"

"That's right."

"One of the many great advantages of Minóok is that it's the *nearest* place on the river where they've struck pay dirt." says the General. "And another great advantage is that it's on the American side of the line."

"What advantage is that?" Mac grated out.

"Just the advantage of not having all your hard earnings taken away by an iniquitous tax."

"Look out! this fella's a Britisher——"

"Don't care if he is, and no disrespect to you, sir. The Canadians in the Klondyke are the first to say the tax is nothing short of highway robbery. You'll see! The minute they hear of gold across the line there'll be a stampede out of Dawson. I can put you in the way of getting a claim for eight thousand dollars that you can take eighty thousand out of next August, with no inspector coming round to check your clean-up, and no Government grabbing at your royalties."

"Why aren't you taking out that eighty thousand yourself?" asked Mac bluntly.

"Got more 'n one man can handle," answered the General. "Reckon we've earned a holiday."

Dillon backed him up.

"Then it isn't shortage in provisions that takes you outside," said the Boy.

"Not much."

"Plenty of food at Rampart City; that's the name o' the town where the Little Minóok meets the Yukon."

"Food at gold-craze prices, I suppose."

"No. Just about the same they quote you in Seattle."

"How is that possible when it's been carried four thousand miles?"

"Because the A. C. and N. A. T. and T. boats got frozen in this side of Dawson. They know by the time they get there in June a lot of stuff will have come in by the short route through the lakes, and the town will be overstocked. So there's flour and bacon to burn when you get up as far as Minóok. It's only along the Lower River there's any real scarcity."

The Big Chimney men exchanged significant looks.

"And there are more supply-boats wintering up at Fort Yukon and at Circle City," the General went on. "I tell you on the Upper River there's food to burn."

Again the Big Chimney men looked at one another. The General kept helping himself to punch, and as he tossed it off he would say, "Minóok's the camp for me!" When he had given vent to this conviction three times, Benham, who hadn't spoken since their entrance, said quietly:

"And you're going away from it as hard as you can pelt."

The General turned moist eyes upon him.

"Are you a man of family, sir?"

"No."

"Then I cannot expect you to understand." His eyes brimmed at some thought too fine and moving for public utterance.

Each member of the camp sat deeply cogitating. Not only gold at Minóok, but food! In the inner vision of every eye was a ship-load of provisions "frozen in" hard by a placer claim; in every heart a fervid prayer for a dog-team.

The Boy jumped up, and ran his fingers through his long wild hair. He panted softly like a hound straining at a leash. Then, with an obvious effort to throw off the magic of Minóok, he turned suddenly about, and "Poor old Kaviak!" says he, looking round and speaking in quite an everyday sort of voice.

The child was leaning against the door clasping the forgotten Christmas-tree so tight against the musk-rat coat that the branches hid his face. From time to time with reverent finger he touched silver boat and red-foil top, and watched, fascinated, how they swung. A white child in a tenth of the time would have eaten the cakes, torn off the transfiguring tinfoil, tired of the tree, and forgotten it. The Boy felt some compunction at the sight of Kaviak's steadfast fidelity.

"Look here, we'll set the tree up where you can see it better." He put an empty bucket on the table, and with Mac's help, wedged the spruce in it firmly, between some blocks of wood and books of the law.

The cabin was very crowded. Little Mr. Schiff was sitting on the cricket. Kaviak retired to his old seat on Elephas beyond the bunks, where he still had a good view of the wonderful tree, agreeably lit by what was left of the two candles.

"Those things are good to eat, you know," said the Colonel kindly.

Mac cut down a gingerbread man and gave it into the tiny hands.

"What wind blew that thing into your cabin?" asked the General, squinting up his snow-blinded eyes at the dim corner where Kaviak sat.

There wasn't a man in the camp who didn't resent the millionaire's tone.

"This is a great friend of ours—ain't you, Kaviak?" said the Boy. "He's got a soul above gold-mines, haven't you? He sees other fellas helping themselves to his cricket and his high chair—too polite to object—just goes and sits like a philosopher on the bones of dead devils and looks on. Other fellas sittin' in his place talkin' about gold and drinkin' punch—never offerin' him a drop——"

Several cups were held out, but Mac motioned them back.

"I don't think," says John Dillon slyly—"don't think *this* punch will hurt the gentleman."

And a roar went up at the Colonel's expense. General Lighter pulled himself to his feet, saying there was a little good Old Rye left outside, and he could stock up again when he got to the *Oklahoma*.

"Oh, and it's yersilf that don't shoy off from a dthrop o' the craythur whin yer thravellin' the thrail."

Everybody looked at Benham. He got up and began to put on his furs; his dog-driver, squatting by the door, took the hint, and went out to see after the team.

"Oh, well," said the General to O'Flynn, "it's Christmas, you know"; and he picked his way among the closely-packed company to the door.

"We ought to be movin', too," said Dillon, straightening up. The General halted, depressed at the reminder. "You know we swore we wouldn't stop again unless——"

"Look here, didn't you hear me saying it was Christmas?"

"You been sayin' that for twenty-four hours. Been keepin' Christmas right straight along since yesterday mornin'." But the General had gone out to unpack the whisky. "He knocked up the mission folks, bright and early yesterday, to tell 'em about the Glad News Tidin's—Diggin's, I mean."

"What did they say?"

"Weren't as good an audience as the General's used to; that's why we pushed on. We'd heard about your camp, and the General felt a call to preach the Gospel accordin' to Minóok down this way."

"He don't seem to be standin' the racket as well as you," said Schiff.

"Well, sir, this is the first time I've found him wantin' to hang round after he's thoroughly rubbed in the news."

Dillon moved away from the fire; the crowded cabin was getting hot.

Nevertheless the Colonel put on more wood, explaining to Salmon P. and the others, who also moved back, that it was for illuminating purposes—those two candles burning down low, each between three nails in a little slab of wood—those two had been kept for Christmas, and were the last they had.

In the general movement from the fire, Benham, putting on his cap and gloves, had got next to Dillon.

"Look here," said the Trader, under cover of the talk about candles, "what sort of a trip have you had?"

The Yukon pioneer looked at him a moment, and then took his pipe out of his mouth to say:

"Rank."

"No fun, hey?"

"That's right." He restored the pipe, and drew gently.

"And yet to hear the General chirp——"

"He's got plenty o' grit, the General has."

"Has he got gold?"

Dillon nodded. "Or will have."

"Out of Minóok?"

"Out of Minóok."

"In a sort of a kind of a way. I think I understand." Benham wagged his head. "He's talkin' for a market."

Dillon smoked.

"Goin' out to stir up a boom, and sell his claim to some sucker."

The General reappeared with the whisky, stamping the snow off his feet before he joined the group at the table, where the Christmas-tree was seasonably cheek by jowl with the punch-bowl between the low-burnt candles. Mixing the new brew did not interrupt the General's ecstatic references to Minóok.

"Look here!" he shouted across to Mac, "I'll give you a lay on my best claim for two thousand down and a small royalty."

Mac stuck out his jaw.

"I'd like to take a look at the country before I deal."

"Well, see here. When will you go?"

"We got no dogs."

"*We* have!" exclaimed Salmon P. and Schiff with one voice.

"Well, I can offer you fellows——"

"How many miles did you travel a day?"

"Sixty," said the General promptly.

"Oh Lord!" ejaculated Benham, and hurriedly he made his good-byes.

"What's the matter with *you?*" demanded the General with dignity.

"I'm only surprised to hear Minóok's twenty-four hundred miles away."

"More like six hundred," says the Colonel.

"And you've been forty days coming, and you cover sixty miles a day—— Good-bye," he laughed, and was gone.

"Well—a——" The General looked round.

"Travelin' depends on the weather." Dillon helped him out.

"Exactly. Depends on the weather," echoed the General. "You don't get an old Sour-dough like Dillon to travel at forty degrees."

"How are you to know?" whispered Schiff.

"Tie a little bottle o' quick to your sled," answered Dillon.

"Bottle o' what?" asked the Boy.

"Quicksilver—mercury," interpreted the General.

"No dog-puncher who knows what he's about travels when his quick goes dead."

"If the stuff's like lead in your bottle——" The General stopped to sample the new brew. In the pause, from the far side of the cabin Dillon spat straight and clean into the heart of the coals.

"Well, what do you do when the mercury freezes?" asked the Boy.

"Camp," said Dillon impassively, resuming his pipe.

"I suppose," the Boy went on wistfully—"I suppose you met men all the way making straight for Minóok?"

"Only on this last lap."

"They don't get far, most of 'em."

"But . . . but it's worth trying!" the Boy hurried to bridge the chasm.

The General lifted his right arm in the attitude of the orator about to make a telling hit, but he was hampered by having a mug at his lips. In the pause, as he stood commanding attention, at the same time that he swallowed half a pint of liquor, he gave Dillon time leisurely to get up, knock the ashes out of his pipe stick it in his belt, put a slow hand behind him towards his pistol pocket, and bring out his buckskin gold sack. Now, only Mac of the other men had ever seen a miner's purse before, but every one of the four cheechalkos knew instinctively what it was that Dillon held so carelessly. In that long, narrow bag, like the leg of a child's stocking, was the stuff they had all come seeking.

The General smacked his lips, and set down the granite cup. "*That's* the argument," he said. "Got a noospaper?"

The Colonel looked about in a flustered way for the tattered San Francisco *Examiner;* Potts and the Boy hustled the punchbowl on to the bucket board, recklessly spilling some of the precious contents. O'Flynn and Salmon P. whisked the Christmas tree into the corner, and not even the Boy remonstrated when a gingerbread man broke his neck, and was trampled under foot.

"Quick! the candles are going out!" shouted the Boy, and in truth each wick lay languishing in a little island of grease, now flaring bravely, now flickering to dusk. It took some time to find in the San Francisco *Examiner* of August 7 a foot square space that was whole. But as quickly as possible the best bit was spread in the middle of the table. Dillon, in the breathless silence having slowly untied the thongs, held his sack aslant between the two lights, and poured out a stream—nuggets and coarse bright gold.

The crowd about the table drew audible breath. Nobody actually spoke at first, except O'Flynn, who said reverently: "Be—the Siven! Howly Pipers!—that danced at me—gran'-mother's weddin'—when the divvle—called the chune!" Even the swimming wicks flared up, and seemed to reach out, each a hungry tongue of flame to touch and taste the glittering heap, before they went into the dark. Low exclamations, hands thrust out to feel, and drawn back in a sort of superstitious awe.

Here it was, this wonderful stuff they'd come for! Each one knew by the wild excitement in his own breast, how in secret he had been brought to doubt its being here. But here it was lying in a heap on the Big Cabin table! and—now it was gone.

The right candle had given out, and O'Flynn, blowing with impatience like a walrus, had simultaneously extinguished the other.

For an instant a group of men with strained and dazzled eyes still bent above the blackness on the boards.

"Stir the fire," called the Colonel, and flew to do it himself.

"I'll light a piece of fat pine," shouted the Boy, catching up a stick, and thrusting it into the coals.

"Where's your bitch?" said Dillon calmly.

"Bitch?"

"Haven't you got a condensed milk can with some bacon grease in it, and a rag wick? Makes a good enough light."

But the fire had been poked up, and the cabin was full of dancing lights and shadows. Besides that, the Boy was holding a resinous stick alight over the table, and they all bent down as before.

"It was passin' a bank in 'Frisco wid a windy full o' that stuff that brought me up here," said O'Flynn.

"It was hearin' about that winder brought *me*," added Potts.

Everyone longed to touch and feel about in the glittering pile, but no one as yet had dared to lay a finger on the smallest grain in the hoard. An electrical shock flashed through the company when the General picked up one of the biggest nuggets and threw it down with a rich, full-bodied thud. "That one is four ounces."

He took up another.

"This is worth about sixty dollars."

"More like forty," said Dillon.

They were of every conceivable shape and shapelessness, most of them flattened; some of them, the greenhorn would swear, were fashioned by man into roughly embossed hearts, or shells, or polished discs like rude, defaced coins. One was a perfect staple, another the letter "L," another like an axe-head, and one like a peasant's sabot. Some were almost black with iron stains, and some were set with "jewels" of quartz, but for the most part they were formless fragments of a rich and brassy yellow.

"Lots of the little fellas are like melon-seeds"; and the Boy pointed a shaking finger, longing and still not daring to touch the treasure.

Each man had a dim feeling in the back of his head that, after all, the hillock of gold was an illusion, and his own hand upon the dazzling pile would clutch the empty air.

"Where's your dust?" asked the Boy.

Dillon stared.

"Why, here."

"This is all nuggets and grains."

"Well, what more do you want?"

"Oh, it'd do well enough for me, but it ain't dust."

"It's what we call dust."

"As coarse as this?"

The Sour-dough nodded, and Lighter laughed.

"There's a fox's mask," said the Colonel at the bottom of the table, pointing a triangular bit out.

"Let me look at it a minute," begged the Boy.

"Hand it round," whispered Schiff.

It was real. It was gold. Their fingers tingled under the first contact. This was the beginning.

The rude bit of metal bred a glorious confidence. Under the magic of its touch Robert Bruce's expensive education became a simple certainty. In Potts's hand the nugget gave birth to a mighty progeny. He saw himself pouring out sackfuls before his enraptured girl.

The Boy lifted his flaring torch with a victorious sense of having just bought back the Orange Grove; and Salmon P. passed the nugget to his partner with a blissful sigh.

"Well, I'm glad we didn't get cold feet," says he.

"Yes," whispered Schiff; "it looks like we goin' to the right place."

The sheen of the heap of yellow treasure was trying even to the nerves of the Colonel.

"Put it away," he said quite solemnly, laying the nugget on the paper—"put it all away before the firelight dies down."

Dillon leisurely gathered it up and dropped the nuggets, with an absent-minded air, into the pouch which Lighter held.

But the San Francisco *Examiner* had been worn to the softness of an old rag and the thinness of tissue. Under Dillon's sinewy fingers pinching up the gold the paper gave way.

"Oh!" exclaimed more than one voice, as at some grave mishap.

Dillon improvised a scoop out of a dirty envelope. Nobody spoke and everybody watched, and when, finally, with his hand, he brushed the remaining grains off the torn paper into the envelope, poured them into the gaping sack-mouth, and lazily pulled at the buckskin draw-string, everybody sat wondering how much, if any, of the precious metal had escaped through the tear, and how soon Dillon would come out of his brown study, remember, and recover the loss. But a spell seemed to have fallen on the company. No one spoke, till Dillon, with that lazy motion, hoisting one square shoulder and half turning his body round, was in the act of returning the sack to his hip-pocket.

"Wait!" said Mac, with the explosiveness of a firearm, and O'Flynn jumped.

"You ain't got it all," whispered Schiff hurriedly.

"Oh, I'm leavin' the fox-face for luck," Dillon nodded at the Colonel.

But Schiff pointed reverently at the tear in the paper, as Dillon only went on pushing his sack deep down in his pocket, while Mac lifted the *Examiner*. All but the two millionaires bent forward and scrutinised the table. O'Flynn impulsively ran one lone hand over the place where the gold-heap had lain, his other hand held ready at the table's edge to catch any sweepings. None! But the result of O'Flynn's action was that those particles of gold that that fallen through the paper were driven into the cracks and inequalities of the board.

"There! See?"

"Now look what you've done!"

Mac pointed out a rough knot-hole, too, that slyly held back a pinch of gold.

"Oh, *that!*"

Dillon slapped his hip, and settled into his place. But the men nearest the crack and the knot-hole fell to digging out the renegade grains, and piously offering them to their lawful owner.

"That ain't worth botherin' about," laughed Dillon; "you always reckon to lose a little each time, even if you got a China soup-plate."

"Plenty more where that came from," said the General, easily.

Such indifference was felt to be magnificent indeed. The little incident said more for the richness of Minóok than all the General's blowing; they forgot that what was lost would amount to less than fifty cents. The fact that it was gold—Minóok gold—gave it a symbolic value not to be computed in coin.

"How do you go?" asked the Colonel, as the two millionaires began putting on their things.

"We cut across to Kuskoquim. Take on an Indian guide there to Nushagak, and from there with dogs across the ocean-ice to Kadiak."

"Oh! the way the letters go out."

"When they *do*," smiled Dillon. "Yes, it's the old Russian Post Trail, I believe. South of Kadiak Island the sea is said to be open as early as the 1st of March. We'll get a steamer to Sitka, and from Sitka, of course, the boats run regular."

"Seattle by the middle of March!" says the General. "Come along, Dillon; the sooner you get to Seattle, and blow in a couple o' hundred thousand, the sooner you'll get back to Minóok."

Dillon went out and roused up the dogs, asleep in the snow, with their bushy tails sheltering their sharp noses.

"See you later?"

"Yes, 'outside.'"

"Outside? No, sir! *Inside.*"

Dillon swore a blood-curdling string of curses and cracked his whip over the leader.

"Why, you comin' back?"

"Bet your life!"

And nobody who looked at the face of the Yukon pioneer could doubt he meant what he said.

They went indoors. The cabin wore an unwonted and a rakish air. The stools seemed to have tried to dance the lancers and have fallen out about the figure. Two were overturned. The unwashed dishes were tossed helter-skelter. A tipsy Christmas-tree leaned in drunken fashion against the wall, and under its boughs lay a forgotten child asleep. On the other side of the cabin an empty whisky bottle caught a ray of light from the fire, and glinted feebly back. Among the ashes on the hearth was a screw of paper, charred at one end, and thrown there after lighting someone's pipe. The Boy opened it. The famous programme of the Yukon Symposium!

"It's been a different sort of Christmas from what we planned," observed the Colonel, not quite as gaily as you might expect.

"Begob!" says O'Flynn, stretching out his interminable legs; "ye can't say we haven't hearrd Glad Tidings of gr-reat j'y——"

"Colonel," interrupts the Boy, throwing the Programme in the fire, "let's look at your nugget again."

And they all took turns. Except Potts. He was busy digging the remaining gold-grains out of the crack and the knot-hole.

CHAPTER IX

A CHRISTIAN AGNOSTIC

> "——giver mig Rum!
> Himlen har Stjerner Natten er stum."

IT was a good many days before they got the dazzle of that gold out of their eyes. They found their tongues again, and talked "Minóok" from morning till night among themselves, and with the rare passer up or down the trail.

Mac began to think they might get dogs at Anvik, or at one of the Ingalik villages, a little further on. The balance of opinion in the camp was against this view. But he had Potts on his side. When the New Year opened, the trail was in capital condition. On the 2nd of January two lots of Indians passed, one with dogs hauling flour and bacon for Benham, and the other lot without dogs, dragging light hand-sleds. Potts said restlessly:

"After all, *they* can do it."

"So can we if we've a mind to," said Mac.

"Come on, then."

The camp tried hard to dissuade them. Naturally neither listened. They packed the Boy's sled and set off on the morning of the third, to Kaviak's unbounded surprise and disgust, his view of life being that, wherever Mac went, he was bound to follow. And he did follow—made off as hard as his swift little feet could carry him, straight up the Yukon trail, and Farva lost a good half of that first morning bringing him home.

Just eight days later the two men walked into the Cabin and sat down—Potts with a heart-rending groan, Mac with his jaw almost dislocated in his cast-iron attempt to set his face against defeat; their lips were cracked with the cold, their faces raw from frostbite, their eyes inflamed. The weather—they called it the weather—had been too much for them. It was obvious they hadn't brought back any dogs, but——

"What did you think of Anvik?" says the Boy.

"*Anvik?* You don't suppose we got to Anvik in weather like this!"

"How far *did* you get?"

Mac didn't answer. Potts only groaned. He had frozen his cheek and his right hand.

They were doctored and put to bed.

"Did you see my friends at Holy Cross?" the Boy asked Potts when he brought him a bowl of hot bean-soup.

"You don't suppose we got as far as Holy Cross, with the wind——"

"Well, where *did* you get to? Where you been?"

"Second native village above."

"Why, that isn't more'n sixteen miles."

"Sixteen miles too far."

Potts breathed long and deep between hot and comforting swallows.

"Where's the Boy's sled?" said the Colonel, coming in hurriedly.

"We cached it," answered Potts feebly.

"Couldn't even bring his sled home! *Where've* you cached it?"

"It's all right—only a few miles back."

Potts relinquished the empty soup-bowl, and closed his eyes.

* * * * * * *

When he opened them again late in the evening it was to say:

"Found some o' those suckers who were goin' so slick to Minóok; some o' *them* down at the second village, and the rest are winterin' in Anvik, so the Indians say. Not a single son of a gun will see the diggins till the ice goes out."

"Then, badly off as we are here," says the Colonel to the Boy, "it's lucky for us we didn't join the procession."

When Mac and the Boy brought the sled home a couple of days later, it was found that a portion of its cargo consisted of a toy kyak and two bottles of hootchino, the maddening drink concocted by the natives out of fermented dough and sugar.

Apart from the question of drinking raised again by the "hootch," it is perhaps possible that, having so little else to do, they were ready to eat the more; it is also true that, busy or idle, the human body requires more nourishment in the North than it does in the South.

Certainly the men of the little Yukon camp began to find their rations horribly short commons, and to suffer a continual hunger, never wholly appeased. It is conditions like these that bring out the brute latent in all men. The day came to mean three scant meals. Each meal came to mean a silent struggle in each man's soul not to let his stomach get the better of his head and heart. At first they joked and laughed about their hunger and the scarcity. By-and-by it became too serious, the jest was wry-faced and rang false. They had, in the beginning, each helped himself from common dishes set in the middle of the rough plank table. Later, each found how, without meaning to—hating himself for it—he watched food on its way to others' plates with an evil eye. When it came to his turn, he had an ever-recurrent struggle with himself not to take the lion's share. There were ironical comments now and then, and ill-concealed bitterness. No one of the five would have believed he could feel so towards a human being about a morsel of food, but those who think they would be above it, have not wintered in the Arctic regions or fought in the Boer War. The difficulty was frankly faced at last, and it was ordained in council that the Colonel should be dispenser of the food.

"Can't say I like the office," quoth he, "but here goes!" and he cut the bacon with an anxious hand, and spooned out the beans solemnly as if he weighed each "go." And the Trio presently retired to the Little Cabin to discuss whether the Colonel didn't show favouritism to the Boy, and, when Mac was asleep, how they could get rid of Kaviak.

So presently another council was called, and the Colonel resigned his office, stipulating that each man in turn should hold it for a week, and learn how ungrateful it was. Moreover, that whoever was, for the nonce, occupying the painful post, should be loyally upheld by all the others, which arrangement was in force to the end.

And still, on grounds political, religious, social, trivial, the disaffection grew. Two of the Trio sided against the odd man, Potts, and turned him out of the Little Cabin one night during a furious snowstorm, that had already lasted two days, had more than half buried the hut, and nearly snowed up the little doorway. The Colonel and the Boy had been shovelling nearly all the day before to keep free the entrance to the Big Cabin and the precious "bottle" window, as well as their half of the path between the two dwellings. O'Flynn and Potts had played poker and quarrelled as usual.

The morning after the ejection of Potts, and his unwilling

reception at the Big Cabin, Mac and O'Flynn failed to appear for breakfast.

"Guess they're huffy," says Potts, stretching out his feet, very comfortable in their straw-lined mucklucks, before the big blaze. "Bring on the coffee, Kaviak."

"No," says the Colonel, "we won't begin without the other fellows."

"By the living Jingo, *I* will then!" says Potts, and helps himself under the Colonel's angry eyes.

The other two conferred a moment, then drew on their parkis and mittens, and with great difficulty, in spite of yesterday's work, got the door open. It was pretty dark, but there was no doubt about it, the Little Cabin had disappeared.

"Look! isn't that a curl of smoke?" said the Boy.

"Yes, by George! they're snowed under!"

"Serve 'em right!"

A heavy sigh from the Colonel. "Yes, but *we'll* have to dig 'em out!"

"Look here, Colonel"—the Boy spoke with touching solemnity—"*not before breakfast!*"

"Right you are!" laughed the Colonel; and they went in.

It was that day, after the others had been released and fed, that the Boy fell out with Potts concerning who had lost the hatchet—and they came to blows. A black eye and a bloody nose might not seem an illuminating contribution to the question, but no more was said about the hatchet after the Colonel had dragged the Boy off the prostrate form of his adversary.

But the Colonel himself lost his temper two days later when O'Flynn broached the seal set months before on the nearly empty demijohn. For those famous "temperance punches" the Colonel had drawn on his own small stock. He saw his blunder when O'Flynn, possessing himself of the demijohn, roared out:

"It's my whisky, I tell you! I bought it and paid furr it, and but for me it would be at the bottom o' the Yukon now."

"Yes, and you'd be at the bottom of the Yukon yourself if you hadn't been dragged out by the scruff o' your neck. And you'd be in a pretty fix now, if we left you alone with your whisky, which is about all you've got."

"We agreed," Potts chipped in, "that it should be kept for medicinal purposes only."

Sullenly O'Flynn sipped at his grog. Potts had "hogged most of the hootch."

* * * * * * *

"Look here, Boy," said Mac at supper, "I said I wouldn't eat off this plate again."

"Oh, dry up! One tin plate's like another tin plate."

"Are you reflecting on the washer-up, Mr. MacCann?" asked Potts.

"I'm saying what I've said before—that I've scratched my name on my plate, and I won't eat off this rusty, battered kettle-lid."

He held it up as if to shy it at the Boy. The young fellow turned with a flash in his eye and stood taut. Then in the pause he said quite low:

"Let her fly, MacCann."

But MacCann thought better of it. He threw the plate down on the table with a clatter. The Colonel jumped up and bent over the mush-pot at the fire, beside the Boy, whispering to him.

"Oh, all right."

When the Boy turned back to the table, with the smoking kettle, the cloud had gone from his face. MacCann had got up to hang a blanket over the door. While his back was turned the Boy brought a tin plate, still in good condition, set it down at Mac's place, planted a nail on end in the middle, and with three blows from a hammer fastened the plate firmly to the board.

"Maybe you can't hand it up for more as often as you like, but you'll always find it there," he said when McCann came back. And the laugh went against the dainty pioneer, who to the end of the chapter ate from a plate nailed fast to the table.

"I begin to understand," says the Colonel to the Boy, under cover of the others' talk, "why it's said to be such a devil of a test of a fellow's decency to winter in this infernal country."

"They say it's always a man's pardner he comes to hate most," returned the Boy, laughing good-humouredly at the Colonel.

"Naturally. Look at the row in the Little Cabin."

"That hasn't been the only row," the Boy went on more thoughtfully. "I say, Colonel"—he lowered his voice—"do you know there'll have to be a new system of rations? I've been afraid—now I'm *sure*—the grub won't last till the ice goes out."

"I know it," said the Colonel very gravely.

"Was there a miscalculation?"

"I hope it was that—or else," speaking still lower, "the stores have been tampered with, and not by Kaviak either. There'll be a hell of a row." He looked up, and saw Potts watching them suspiciously. It had come to this: if two men talked low the others pricked their ears. "But lack of grub," resumed the Colonel in his usual voice, as though he had not noticed, "is only one of our difficulties. Lack of work is just about as bad. It breeds a thousand devils. We're a pack o' fools. Here we are, all of us, hard hit, some of us pretty well cleaned out o' ready cash, and here's dollars and dollars all round us, and we sit over the fire like a lot of God-forsaken natives."

"Dollars! Where?"

"Growin' on the trees, boys; a forest full."

"Oh, timber." Enthusiasm cooled.

"Look at what they say about those fellows up at Anvik, what they made last year."

"They've got a saw-mill."

"*Now* they have. But they cut and sold cord-wood to the steamers two years before they got a mill, and next summer will be the biggest season yet. We ought to have set to, as soon as the cabins were built, and cut wood for the summer traffic. But since there are five of us, we can make a good thing of it yet."

The Colonel finally carried the day. They went at it next morning, and, as the projector of the work had privately predicted, a better spirit prevailed in the camp for some time. But here were five men, only one of whom had had any of the steadying grace of stiff discipline in his life, men of haphazard education, who had "chucked" more or less easy berths in a land of many creature comforts . . . for this—to fell and haul birch and fir trees in an Arctic climate on half-rations! It began to be apparent that the same spirit was invading the forest that had possession of the camp; two, or at most three, did the work, and the rest shirked, got snow-blindness and rheumatism, and let the others do his share, counting securely, nevertheless, on his fifth of the proceeds, just as he counted (no matter what proportion he had contributed) on his full share of the common stock of food.

A CHRISTIAN AGNOSTIC

"I came out here a Communist——" said the Boy one day to the Colonel.

"And an agnostic," smiled the older man.

"Oh, I'm an agnostic all right, now and for ever. But this winter has cured my faith in Communism."

Early February brought not only lengthening daylight, but a radical change in the weather. The woodsmen worked in their shirt-sleeves, perspired freely, and said in the innocence of their hearts, "If winter comes early up here, spring does the same." The whole hillside was one slush, and the snow melting on the ill-made Little Cabin roof brought a shower-bath into the upper bunk.

Few things in nature so surely stir the pulse of man as the untimely coming of a few spring days, that have lost their way in the calendar, and wandered into winter. No trouble now to get the Big Chimney men away from the fireside. They held up their bloodless faces in the faint sunshine, and their eyes, with the pupils enlarged by the long reign of night, blinked feebly, like an owl's forced to face the morning.

There were none of those signs in the animal world outside, of premature stir and cheerful awaking, that in other lands help the illusion that winter lies behind, but there was that even more stimulating sweet air abroad, that subtle mixture of sun and yielding frost, that softened wind that comes blowing across the snow, still keen to the cheek, but subtly reviving to the sensitive nostril, and caressing to the eyes. The Big Chimney men drew deep breaths, and said in their hearts the battle was over and won.

Kaviak, for ever following at Mac's heels "like a rale Irish tarrier," found his allegiance waver in these stirring, blissful days, if ever Farva so belied character and custom as to swing an axe for any length of time. Plainly out of patience, Kaviak would throw off the musk-rat coat, and run about in wet mucklucks and a single garment—uphill, downhill, on important errands which he confided to no man.

It is part of the sorcery of such days that men's thoughts, like birds', turn to other places, impatient of the haven that gave them shelter in rough weather overpast. The Big Chimney men leaned on their axes and looked north, south, east, west.

Then the Colonel would give a little start, turn about, lift his double-bitter, and swing it frontier fashion, first over one shoulder, then over the other, striking cleanly home each time,

179

working with a kind of splendid rhythm more harmonious, more beautiful to look at, than most of the works of men. This was, perhaps, the view of his comrades, for they did a good deal of looking at the Colonel. He said he was a modest man and didn't like it, and Mac, turning a little rusty under the gibe, answered:

"Haven't you got the sense to see we've cut all the good timber just round here?" and again he turned his eyes to the horizon line.

"Mac's right," said the Boy; and even the Colonel stood still a moment, and they all looked away to that land at the end of the world where the best materials are for the building of castles—it's the same country so plainly pointed out by the Rainbow's End, and never so much as in the springtime does it lure men with its ancient promise.

"Come along, Colonel; let's go and look for real timber——"

"And let's find it nearer water-level—where the steamers can see it right away."

"What about the kid?"

"Me come," said Kaviak, with a highly obliging air.

"No; you stay at home."

"No; go too."

"Go too, thou babbler! Kaviak's a better trail man than some I could mention."

"We'll have to carry him home," objected Potts.

"Now don't tell us you'll do any of the carryin', or we'll lose confidence in you, Potts."

The trail was something awful, but on their Canadian snow-shoes they got as far as an island, six miles off. One end of it was better wooded than any easily accessible place they had seen.

"Why, this is quite like real spruce," said the Boy, and O'Flynn admitted that even in California "these here would be called 'trees' wid no intintion o' bein' sarcastic."

So they cut holes in the ice, and sounded for the channel.

"Yes, sir, the steamers can make a landin' here, and here's where we'll have our wood-rack."

They went home in better spirits than they had been in since that welter of gold had lain on the Big Cabin table.

*   *   *   *   *   *   *

But a few days sufficed to wear the novelty off the new wood camp for most of the party. Potts and O'Flynn set out in the opposite direction one morning with a hand-sled, and provisions to last several days. They were sick of bacon and beans, and were "goin' huntin'." No one could deny that a moose or even a grouse—anything in the shape of fresh meat—was sufficiently needed. But Potts and O'Flynn were really sick and sore from their recent slight attack of wood-felling. They were after bigger game, too, as well as grouse, and a few days "off." It had turned just enough colder to glaze the trail and put it in fine condition. They went down the river to the *Oklahoma,* were generously entertained by Captain Rainey, and learned that, with earlier contracts on his hands, he did not want more wood from them than they had already corded. They returned to the camp without game, but with plenty of whisky, and information that freed them from the yoke of labour, and from the lash of ironic comment. In vain the Colonel urged that the *Oklahoma* was not the only steamer plying the Yukon, that with the big rush of the coming season the traffic would be enormous, and a wood-pile as good as a gold mine. The cause was lost.

"You won't get us to make galley-slaves of ourselves on the off-chance of selling. Rainey says that wood camps have sprung up like mushrooms all along the river. The price of wood will go down to——"

"All along the river! There isn't one between us and Andreievsky, nor between here and Holy Cross."

But it was no use. The travellers pledged each other in *Oklahoma* whisky, and making a common cause once more, the original Trio put in a night of it. The Boy and the Colonel turned into their bunks at eleven o'clock. They were roused in the small hours, by Kaviak's frightened crying, and the noise of angry voices.

"You let the kid alone."

"Well, it's mesilf that'll take the liberty o' mintionin' that I ain't goin' to stand furr another minyit an Esquimer's cuttin' down *my* rations. Sure it's a fool I've been!"

"You can't help that," Mac chopped out.

"Say Mac," said Potts in a drunken voice, "I'm talkin' to you like a friend. You want to get a move on that kid."

"Kaviak's goin' won't make any more difference than a fly's."

The other two grumbled incoherently.

"But I tell you what *would* make a difference: if you two would quit eatin' on the sly—out o' meal-times."

"Be the Siven!"

"You lie!" A movement, a stool overturned, and the two men in the bunks were struck broad awake by the smart concussion of a gun-shot. Nobody was hurt, and between them they disarmed Potts, and turned the Irishman out to cool off in his own cabin. It was all over in a minute. Kaviak, reassured, curled down to sleep again. Mac and Potts stretched themselves on the buffalo-robe half under the table, and speedily fell to snoring. The Boy put on some logs. He and the Colonel sat and watched the sparks.

"It's a bad business."

"It can't go on," says the Colonel; "but Mac's right: Kaviak's being here isn't to blame. They—we, too—are like a lot of powder-cans."

The Boy nodded. "Any day a spark, and *biff!* some of us are in a blaze, and wh-tt! bang! and some of us are in Kingdom Come."

"I begin to be afraid to open my lips," said the Colonel. "We all are; don't you notice?"

"Yes. I wonder why we came."

"*You* had no excuse," said the elder man almost angrily.

"Same excuse as you."

The Colonel shook his head.

"Exactly," maintained the Boy. "Tired of towns and desk-work, and—and——" The Boy shifted about on his wooden stool, and held up his hands to the reviving blaze. "Life owes us steady fellows one year of freedom, anyhow—one year to make ducks and drakes of. Besides, we've all come to make our fortunes. Doesn't every mother's son of us mean to find a gold-mine in the spring when we get to the Klondyke—eh?" And he laughed again, and presently he yawned, and tumbled back into his bunk. But he put his head out in a moment. "Aren't you going to bed?"

"Yes." The Colonel stood up.

"Did you know Father Wills went by, last night, when those fellows began to row about getting out the whisky?"

"No."

"He says there's another stampede on."

"Where to?"

"Koyukuk this time."

"Why didn't he come in?"

"Awful hurry to get to somebody that sent for him. Funny

fellas these Jesuits. They *believe* all those odd things they teach."

"So do other men," said the Colonel, curtly.

"Well, I've lived in a Christian country all my life, but I don't know that I ever saw Christianity *practised* till I went up the Yukon to Holy Cross."

"I must say you're complimentary to the few other Christians scattered about the world."

"Don't get mifft, Colonel. I've known plenty of people straight as a die, and capital good fellows. I've seen them do very decent things now and then. But with these Jesuit missionaries—Lord! there's no let up to it."

No answer from the Protestant Colonel. Presently the Boy in a sleepy voice added elegantly:

"No Siree! The Jesuits go the whole hog!"

*　　*　　*　　*　　*　　*　　*

Winter was down on the camp again. The whole world was hard as iron. The men kept close to the Big Chimney all day long, and sat there far into the small hours of the morning, saying little, heavy-eyed and sullen. The dreaded insomnia of the Arctic had laid hold on all but the Colonel. Even his usually unbroken repose was again disturbed one night about a week later. Some vague sort of sound or movement in the room—Kaviak on a raid?—or—wasn't that the closing of a door?

"Kaviak!" He put his hand down and felt the straight hair of the Esquimaux in the under bunk. "Potts! Who's there?" He half sat up. "Boy! Did you hear that, Boy?"

He leaned far down over the side and saw distinctly by the fire-light there was nobody but Kaviak in the under bunk.

The Colonel was on his legs in a flash, putting his head through his parki and drawing on his mucklucks. He didn't wait to cross and tie the thongs. A presentiment of evil was strong upon him. Outside in the faint star-light he thought a dim shape was passing down towards the river.

"Who's that? Hi, there! Stop, or I'll shoot!" He hadn't brought his gun, but the ruse worked.

"Don't shoot!" came back the voice of the Boy.

The Colonel stumbled down the bank in the snow, and soon stood by the shape. The Boy was dressed for a journey. His Arctic cap was drawn down over his ears and neck. The wolf-skin fringe of his parki hood stood out fiercely round the defiant young face. Wound about one of his seal-skin mittens was the rope of the new hand-sled he'd been fashioning so busily of nights by the camp fire. His two blankets were strapped on the sled, Indian fashion, along with a gunny sack and his rifle.

The two men stood looking angrily at each other a moment, and then the Colonel politely inquired:

"What in hell are you doing?"

"Goin' to Minóok."

"The devil you are!"

"Yes, the devil I am!"

They stood measuring each other in the dim light, till the Colonel's eyes fell on the loaded sled. The Boy's followed.

"I've only taken short rations for two weeks. I left a statement in the cabin; it's about a fifth of what's my share, so there's no need of a row."

"What are you goin' for?"

"Why, to be first in the field, and stake a gold-mine, of course."

The Colonel laid a rough hand on the Boy's shoulder. He shook it off impatiently, and before the older man could speak:

"Look here, let's talk sense. Somebody's got to go, or there'll be trouble. Potts says Kaviak. But what difference would Kaviak make? I've been afraid you'd get ahead of me. I've watched you for a week like a hawk watches a chicken. But it's clear I'm the one to go."

He pulled up the rope of the sled, and his little cargo lurched towards him. The Colonel stepped in front of him.

"Boy——" he began, but something was the matter with his voice; he got no further.

"I'm the youngest," boasted the other, "and I'm the strongest, and—I'm the hungriest."

The Colonel found a perturbed and husky voice in which to say:

"I didn't know you were such a Christian."

"Nothin' o' the sort."

"What's this but——"

"Why, it's just—just my little scheme."

"You're no fool. You know as well as I do you've got the devil's own job in hand."

"Somebody's got to go," he repeated doggedly.

"Look here," said the Colonel, "you haven't impressed me as being tired of life."

"Tired of life!" The young eyes flashed in that weird aureole of long wolf-hair. "Tired of life! Well, I should just pretty nearly think I wasn't."

"H'm! Then if it isn't Christianity, it must be because you're young."

"Golly, man! it's because I'm hungry—HUNGRY! Great Jehosaphat! I could eat an ox!"

"And you leave your grub behind, to be eaten by a lot of——"

"I can't stand here argyfying with the thermometer down to——" The Boy began to drag the sled over the snow.

"Come back into the cabin."

"No."

"Come with me, I say; I've got something to propose." Again the Colonel stood in front, barring the way. "Look here," he went on gently, "are you a friend of mine?"

"Oh, so-so," growled the Boy. But after looking about him for an angry second or two, he flung down the rope of his sled, walked sulkily uphill, and kicked off his snow-shoes at the door of the cabin, all with the air of one who waits, but is not baulked of his purpose. They went in and stripped off their furs.

"Now see here: if you've made up your mind to light out, I'm not going to oppose you."

"Why didn't you say anything as sensible as that out yonder?"

"Because I won't be ready to go along till to-morrow."

"You?"

"Yep."

There was a little silence.

"I wish you wouldn't, Colonel."

"It's dangerous alone—not for two."

"Yes, it IS dangerous, and you know it."

"I'm goin' along, laddie." Seeing the Boy look precious grave and harassed: "What's the matter?"

"I'd hate awfully for anything to happen to you."

The Colonel laughed. "Much obliged, but it matters uncommon little if I do drop in my tracks."

"You be blowed!"

"You see I've got a pretty bad kind of a complaint, anyhow."

The Boy leaned over in the firelight and scanned the Colonel's face.

"What's wrong?"

The Colonel smiled a queer little one-sided smile. "I've been out o' kelter nearly ten years."

"Oh, *that's* all right. You'll go on for another thirty if you stay where you are till the ice goes out."

The Colonel bent his head, and stared at the smooth-trodden floor at the edge of the buffalo-skin. "To tell the truth, I'll be glad to go, not only because of——" He hitched his shoulders towards the corner whence came the hoarse and muffled breathing of the Denver clerk. "I'll be glad to have something to tire me out, so I'll sleep—sleep too sound to dream. That's what I came for, not to sit idle in a God-damn cabin and think—think——" He got up suddenly and strode the tiny space from fire to door, a man transformed, with hands clenching and dark face almost evil. "They say the men who winter up here either take to drink or go mad. I begin to see it is so. It's no place to do any forgetting in." He stopped suddenly before the Boy with glittering eyes. "It's the country where your conscience finds you out."

"That religion of yours is makin' you morbid, Colonel." The Boy spoke with the detached and soothing air of a sage.

"You don't know what you're talking about." He turned sharply away. The Boy relapsed into silence. The Colonel in his renewed prowling brought up against the wooden crane. He stood looking down into the fire. Loud and regular sounded the sleeping man's breathing in the quiet little room.

"I did a wrong once to a woman—ten years ago," said the Colonel, speaking to the back-log—"although I loved her." He raised a hand to his eyes with a queer choking sound. "I loved her," he repeated, still with his back to the Boy. "By-and-by I could have righted it, but she—she wasn't the kind to hang about and wait on a man's better nature when once he'd shown himself a coward. She skipped the country." He leaned his head against the end of the shelf over the fire, and said no more.

"Go back in the spring, find out where she is, and——"

"I've spent every spring and every summer, every fall and every winter till this one, trying to do just that thing."

"You can't find her?"

"Nobody can find her."

"She's dead——"

"She's *not* dead!"

The Boy involuntarily shrank back; the Colonel looked ready to smash him. The action recalled the older man to himself.

"I feel sure she isn't dead," he said more quietly, but still trembling. "No, no; she isn't dead. She had some money of her own, and she went abroad. I followed her. I heard of her in Paris, in Rome. I saw her once in a droshky in Vienna; there I lost the trail. Her people said she'd gone to Japan. *I* went to Japan. I'm sure she wasn't in the islands. I've spent my life since trying to find her—writing her letters that always come back—trying——" His voice went out like a candle-wick suddenly dying in the socket. Only the sleeper was audible for full five minutes. Then, as though he had paused only a comma's space, the Colonel went on: "I've been trying to put the memory of her behind me, as a sane man should. But some women leave an arrow sticking in your flesh that you can never pull out. You can only jar against it, and cringe under the agony of the reminder all your life long. . . . Bah! Go out, Boy, and bring in your sled."

And the Boy obeyed without a word.

Two days after, three men with a child stood in front of the larger cabin, saying good-bye to their two comrades who were starting out on snow-shoes to do a little matter of 625 miles of Arctic travelling, with two weeks' scant provisioning, some tea and things for trading, bedding, two rifles, and a kettle, all packed on one little hand-sled.

There had been some unexpected feeling, and even some real generosity shown at the last, on the part of the three who were to profit by the exodus—falling heir thereby to a bigger, warmer cabin and more food.

O'Flynn was moved to make several touching remonstrances. It was a sign of unwonted emotion on Mac's part that he gave up arguing (sacrificing all the delight of a set debate), and simply begged and prayed them not to be fools, not to fly in the face of Providence.

But Potts was made of sterner stuff. Besides, the thing was too good to be true. O'Flynn, when he found they were not to be dissuaded, solemnly presented each with a little bottle of whisky. Nobody would have believed O'Flynn would go so far as that. Nor could anyone have anticipated that close-fisted

Mac would give the Boy his valuable aneroid barometer and compass, or that Potts would be so generous with his best Virginia straight-cut, filling the Colonel's big pouch without so much as a word.

"It's a crazy scheme," says he, shaking the giant Kentuckian by the hand, "and you won't get thirty miles before you find it out."

"Call it an expedition to Anvik," urged Mac. "Load up there with reindeer meat, and come back. If we don't get some fresh meat soon, we'll be having scurvy."

"What you're furr doin'," says O'Flynn for the twentieth time, "has niver been done, not ayven be Indians. The prastes ahl say so."

"So do the Sour-doughs," said Mac. "It isn't as if you had dogs."

"Good-bye," said the Colonel, and the men grasped hands.

Potts shook hands with the Boy as heartily as though that same hand had never half throttled him in the cause of a missing hatchet.

"Good-bye, Kiddie. I bequeath you my share o' syrup."

"Good-bye; meet you in the Klondyke!"

"Good-bye. Hooray for the Klondyke in June!"

"Klondyke in June! Hoop-la!"

The two travellers looked back, laughing and nodding, as jolly as you please. The Boy stooped, made a snow-ball, and fired it at Kaviak. The child ducked, chuckling, and returned as good as he got. His loosely packed ball broke in a splash on the back of the Boy's parki, and Kaviak was loudly cheered.

Still, as they went forward, they looked back. The Big Chimney wore an air wondrous friendly, and the wide, white world looked coldly at them, with small pretence of welcome or reward.

"I don't believe I ever really knew how awful jolly the Big Chimney was—till this minute."

The Colonel smiled. "Hardly like myself, to think whatever else I see, I'll never see that again."

"Better not boast."

The Colonel went on in front, breaking trail in the new-fallen snow, the Boy pulling the sled behind him as lightly as if its double burden were a feather.

"They look as if they thought it'd be a picnic," says Mac, grimly.

"I wonder be the Siven Howly Pipers! will we iver see ayther of 'em again."

"If they only stay a couple o' nights at Anvik," said Potts, with gloomy foreboding, "they could get back here inside a week."

"No," answered Mac, following the two figures with serious eyes, "they may be dead inside a week, but they won't be back here."

And Potts felt his anxiety eased. A man who had mined at Caribou ought to know.

CHAPTER X

"We all went to Tibbals to see the Kinge, who used my mother and my aunt very gratiouslie; but we all saw a great chaunge betweene the fashion of the Court as it was now, and of y in yᵉ Queene's, for we were all lowzy by sittinge in Sʳ Thomas Erskin's chamber."

Memoir: Anne Countess of Dorset, 1603.

IT was the 26th of February, that first day that they "hit the Long Trail."

Temperature only about twenty degrees, the Colonel thought, and so little wind it had the effect of being warmer. Trail in fair condition, weather gray and steady. Never men in better spirits. To have left the wrangling and the smouldering danger of the camp behind, that alone, as the Boy said, was "worth the price of admission." Exhilarating, too, to men of their temperament, to have cut the Gordian knot of the difficulty by risking themselves on this unprecedented quest for peace and food. Gold, too? Oh, yes—with a smile to see how far that main object had drifted into the background—they added, "and for gold."

They believed they had hearkened well to the counsel that bade them "travel light." "Remember, every added ounce is against you." "Nobody in the North owns anything that's heavy," had been said in one fashion or another so often that it lost its ironic sound in the ears of men who had come so far to carry away one of the heaviest things under the sun.

The Colonel and the Boy took no tent, no stove, not even a miner's pick and pan. These last, General Lighter had said, could be obtained at Minóok; and "there isn't a cabin on the trail," Dillon had added, "without 'em."

For the rest, the carefully-selected pack on the sled contained the marmot-skin, woollen blankets, a change of flannels apiece, a couple of sweaters, a Norfolk jacket, and several changes of foot-gear. This last item was dwelt on earnestly by all. "Keep your feet dry," John Dillon had said, "and leave the rest to God Almighty." They were taking barely two weeks' rations, and a certain amount of stuff to trade with the up-river Indians, when their supplies should be gone. They carried a kettle, an axe, some quinine, a box of the carbolic ointment all miners use for foot-soreness, O'Flynn's whisky, and two rifles and ammunition. In spite of having eliminated many things that most travellers would count essential, they found their load came to a little over two hundred pounds. But every day would lessen it, they told each other with a laugh, and with an inward misgiving, lest the lightening should come all too quickly.

They had seen in camp that winter so much of the frailty of human temper that, although full of faith by now in each other's native sense and fairness, they left nothing to a haphazard division of labour. They parcelled out the work of the day with absolute impartiality. To each man so many hours of going ahead to break trail, if the snow was soft, while the other dragged the sled; or else while one pulled in front, the other pushed from behind, in regular shifts by the watch, turn and turn about. The Colonel had cooked all winter, so it was the Boy's turn at that—the Colonel's to decide the best place to camp, because it was his affair to find seasoned wood for fuel, his to build the fire in the snow on green logs laid close together —his to chop enough wood to cook breakfast the next morning. All this they had arranged before they left the Big Chimney.

That they did not cover more ground that first day was a pure chance, not likely to recur, due to an unavoidable loss of time at Pymeut.

Knowing the fascination that place exercised over his companion, the Colonel called a halt about seven miles off from the Big Chimney, that they might quickly despatch a little cold luncheon they carried in their pockets, and push on without a break till supper.

"We've got no time to waste at Pymeut," observes the Colonel significantly.

"I ain't achin' to stop at Pymeut," says his pardner with a superior air, standing up, as he swallowed his last mouthful of cold bacon and corn-bread, and cheerfully surveyed the waste. "Who says it's cold, even if the wind is up? And the track's bully. But see here, Colonel, you mustn't go thinkin' it's smooth glare-ice, like this, all the way."

"Oh, I was figurin' that it would be." But the Boy paid no heed to the irony.

"And it's a custom o' the country to get the wind in your face, as a rule, whichever way you go."

"Well, I'm not complainin' as yet."

"Reckon you needn't if you're blown like dandelion-down all the way to Minóok. Gee! the wind's stronger! Say, Colonel, let's rig a sail."

"Foolishness."

"No, sir. We'll go by Pymeut in an ice-boat, lickety split. And it'll be a good excuse for not stopping, though I think we ought to say good-bye to Nicholas."

This view inclined the Colonel to think better of an ice-boat. He had once crossed the Bay of Toronto in that fashion, and began to wonder if such a mode of progression applied to sleds might not aid largely in solving the Minóok problem.

While he was wondering the Boy unlashed the sled-load, and pulled off the canvas cover as the Colonel came back with his mast. Between them, with no better tools than axe, jack-knives, and a rope, and with fingers freezing in the south wind, they rigged the sail.

The fact that they had this increasingly favourable wind on their very first day showed that they were specially smiled on by the great natural forces. The superstitious feeling that only slumbers in most breasts, that Mother Nature is still a mysterious being, who has her favourites whom she guards, her born enemies whom she baulks, pursues, and finally overwhelms, the age-old childishness stirred pleasantly in both men, and in the younger came forth unabashed in speech:

"I tell you the omens are good! This expedition's goin' to get there." Then, with the involuntary misgiving that follows hard upon such boasting, he laughed uneasily and added, "I mean to sacrifice the first deer's tongue I don't want myself, to Yukon Inua; but here's to the south wind!" He turned some corn-bread crumbs out of his pocket, and saw, delighted, how the gale, grown keener, snatched eagerly at them and hurried them up the trail. The ice-boat careened and strained eagerly to sail away. The two gold-seekers, laughing like schoolboys, sat astride the pack; the Colonel shook out the canvas, and they scudded off up the river like mad. The great difficulty was the steering; but it was rip-roaring fun, the Boy said, and very soon there were natives running down to the river, to stare open-mouthed at the astounding apparition, to point and shout something unintelligible that sounded like "Muchtaravik!"

"Why, it's the Pymeuts! Pardner, we'll be in Minóok by supper-ti——"

The words hadn't left his lips when he saw, a few yards in front of them, a faint cloud of steam rising up from the ice—that dim danger-signal that flies above an air-hole. The Colonel, never noticing, was heading straight for the ghastly trap.

"God, Colonel! Blow-hole!" gasped the Boy.

The Colonel simply rolled off the pack, turning over and over on the ice, but keeping hold of the rope.

The sled swerved, turned on her side, and slid along with a sound of snapping and tearing.

While they were still headed straight for the hole, the Boy had gathered himself for a clear jump to the right, but the sled's sudden swerve to the left broke his angle sharply. He was flung forward on the new impetus, spun over the smooth surface, swept across the verge and under the cloud, clutching wildly at the ragged edge of ice as he went down.

All Pymeut had come rushing pell-mell.

The Colonel was gathering himself up and looking round in a dazed kind of way as Nicholas flashed by. Just beyond, in that yawning hole, fully ten feet wide by fifteen long, the Boy's head appeared an instant, and then was lost like something seen in a dream. Some of the Pymeuts with quick knives were cutting the canvas loose. One end was passed to Nicholas; he knotted it to his belt, and went swiftly, but gingerly, forward nearer the perilous edge. He had flung himself down on his stomach just as the Boy rose again. Nicholas lurched his body over the brink, his arms outstretched, straining farther, farther yet, till it seemed as if only the counterweight of the rest of the population at the other end of the canvas prevented his joining the Boy in the hole. But Nicholas had got a grip of him, and while two of the Pymeuts hung on to the half-stunned Colonel to prevent his adding to the complication, Nicholas, with a good deal of trouble in spite of Yagorsha's help, hauled the Boy out of the hole and dragged him up on the ice-edge. The others applied themselves lustily to their end of the canvas, and soon they were all at a safe distance from the yawning danger.

The Boy's predominant feeling had been one of intense surprise. He looked round, and a hideous misgiving seized him.

"Anything the matter with you, Colonel?" His tone was so angry that, as they stared at each other, they both fell to laughing.

"Well, I rather thought that was what *I* was going to say"; and Kentucky heaved a deep sigh of relief.

The Boy's teeth began to chatter, and his clothes were soon freezing on him. They got him up off the ice, and Nicholas and the sturdy old Pymeut story-teller, Yagorsha, walked him, or ran him rather, the rest of the way to Pymeut, for they were not so near the village as the travellers had supposed on seeing nearly the whole male population. The Colonel was not far behind, and several of the bucks were bringing the disabled sled. Before reaching the Kachime, they were joined by the women and children, Muckluck much concerned at the sight of her friend glazed in ice from head to heel. Nicholas and Yagorsha half dragged, half pulled him into the Kachime. The entire escort followed, even two or three very dirty little boys—everybody, except the handful of women and girls left at the mouth of the underground entrance and the two men who had run on to make a fire. It was already smoking viciously as though the seal-lamps weren't doing enough in that line, when Yagorsha and Nicholas laid the half-frozen traveller on the sleeping-bench.

The Pymeuts knew that the great thing was to get the ice-stiffened clothes off as quickly as might be, and that is to be done expeditiously only by cutting them off. In vain the Boy protested. Recklessly they sawed and cut and stripped him, rubbed him and wrapped him in a rabbit-blanket, the fur turned inside, and a wolverine skin over that. The Colonel at intervals poured small doses of O'Flynn's whisky down the Boy's throat in spite of his unbecoming behaviour, for he was both belligerent and ungrateful, complaining loudly of the ruin of his clothes with only such intermission as the teeth-chattering, swallowing, and rude handling necessitated.

"I didn't like—bein' in—that blow-hole. (Do you know— it was so cold—it burnt!) But I'd rather—be—in a blow-hole—than—br-r-r! Blow-hole isn't so s-s-melly as these s-s-kins!'

"You better be glad you've got a whole skin of your own and ain't smellin' brimstone," said the Colonel, pouring a little more whisky down the unthankful throat. "Pretty sort o' Klondyker you are—go and get nearly drowned first day out!"

Several Pymeut women came in presently and joined the men at the fire, chattering low and staring at the Colonel and the Boy.

"I can't go—to the Klondyke—naked—no, nor wrapped in a rabbit-skin—like Baby Bunting——"

Nicholas was conferring with the Colonel and offering to take him to Ol' Chief's.

"Oh, yes; Ol' Chief got two clo'es. You come. Me show"; and they crawled out one after the other.

"You pretty near dead that time," said one of the younger women conversationally.

"That's right. Who are you, anyway?"

"Me Anna—Yagorsha's daughter."

"Oh, yes, I thought I'd seen you before." She seemed to be only a little older than Muckluck, but less attractive, chiefly on account of her fat and her look of ill-temper. She was on specially bad terms with a buck they called Joe, and they seemed to pass all their time abusing one another.

The Boy craned his neck and looked round. Except just where he was lying, the Pymeut men and women were crowded together, on that side of the Kachime, at his head and at his feet, thick as herrings on a thwart. They all leaned forward and regarded him with a beady-eyed sympathy. He had never been so impressed by the fact before, but all these native people, even in their gentlest moods, frowned in a chronic perplexity and wore their wide mouths open. He reflected that he had never seen one that didn't, except Muckluck.

Here she was, crawling in with a tin can.

"Got something there to eat?"

The rescued one craned his head as far as he could.

"Too soon," she said, showing her brilliant teeth in the fire-light. She set the tin down, looked round, a little embarrassed, and stirred the fire, which didn't need it.

"Well"—he put his chin down under the rabbit-skin once more—"how goes the world, Princess?"

She flashed her quick smile again and nodded reassuringly. "You stay here now?"

"No; goin' up river."

"What for?" She spoke disapprovingly.

"Want to get an Orange Grove."

"Find him up river?"

"Hope so."

"I think I go, too"; and all the grave folk, sitting so close on the sleeping-bench, stretched their wide mouths wider still, smiling good-humouredly.

"You better wait till summer."

"Oh!" She lifted her head from the fire as one who takes careful note of instructions. "Nex' summer?"

"Well, summer's the time for squaws to travel."

"I come nex' summer," she said.

By-and-by Nicholas returned with a new parki and a pair of wonderful buckskin breeches—not like anything worn by the Lower River natives, or by the coast-men either: well cut, well made, and handsomely fringed down the outside of the leg where an officer's gold stripe goes.

"Chaparejos!" screamed the Boy. "Where'd you get 'em?"

"Ol' Chief—he ketch um."

"They're *bully!*" said the Boy, holding the despised rabbit-skin under his chin with both hands, and craning excitedly over it. He felt that his fortunes were looking up. Talk about a tide in the affairs of men! Why, a tide that washes up to a wayfarer's feet a pair o' chaparejos like that—well! legs so habited would simply *have* to carry a fella on to fortune. He lay back on the sleeping-bench with dancing eyes, while the raw whisky hummed in his head. In the dim light of seal-lamps vague visions visited him of stern and noble chiefs out of the Leather Stocking Stories of his childhood—men of daring, whose legs were invariably cased in buck-skin with dangling fringes. But the dashing race was not all Indian, nor all dead. Famous cowboys reared before him on bucking bronchos, their leg-fringes streaming on the blast, and desperate chaps who held up coaches and potted Wells Fargo guards. Anybody must needs be a devil of a fellow who went about in "shaps," as his California cousins called chaparejos. Even a peaceable fella like himself, not out after gore at all, but after an Orange Grove—even he, once he put on—— He laughed out loud at his childishness, and then grew grave. "Say, Nicholas, what's the tax?"

"Hey?"

"How much?"

"Oh, your pardner—he pay."

"Humph! I s'pose I'll know the worst on settlin'-day."

Then, after a few moments, making a final clutch at economy before the warmth and the whisky subdued him altogether:

"Say, Nicholas, have you got—hasn't the Ol' Chief got any
—less glorious breeches than those?"

"Hey?"

"Anything little cheaper?"

"Nuh," says Nicholas.

The Boy closed his eyes, relieved on the whole. Fate had a
mind to see him in chaparejos. Let her look to the sequel,
then!

When consciousness came back it brought the sound of
Yagorsha's yarning by the fire, and the occasional laugh or
grunt punctuating the eternal "Story."

The Colonel was sitting there among them, solacing himself
by adding to the smoke that thickened the stifling air.

Presently the Story-teller made some shrewd hit, that shook
the Pymeut community into louder grunts of applause and a
general chuckling. The Colonel turned his head slowly, and
blew out a fresh cloud: "Good joke?"

In the pause that fell thereafter, Yagorsha, imperturbable,
the only one who had not laughed, smoothed his lank, iron-
gray locks down on either side of his wide face, and went on
renewing the sinew open-work in his snow-shoe.

"When Ol' Chief's father die——"

All the Pymeuts chuckled afresh. The Boy listened eagerly.
Usually Yagorsha's stories were tragic, or, at least, of serious
interest, ranging from bereaved parents who turned into wol-
verines, all the way to the machinations of the Horrid Dwarf
and the Cannibal Old Woman.

The Colonel looked at Nicholas. He seemed as entertained
as the rest, but quite willing to leave his family history in professional hands.

"Ol' Chief's father, Glovotsky, him Russian," Yagorsha began again, laying down his sinew-thread a moment and accept-
ing some of the Colonel's tobacco.

"I didn't know you had any white blood in you," interrupted
the Colonel, offering his pouch to Nicholas. "I might have
suspected Muckluck——"

"Heap got Russian blood," interrupted Joe.

As the Story-teller seemed to be about to repeat the enliven-
ing tradition concerning the almost mythical youth of Ol'
Chief's father, that subject of the great Katharine's, whose
blood was flowing still in Pymeut veins, just then in came
Yagorsha's daughter with some message to her father. He

grunted acquiescence, and she turned to go. Joe called something after her, and she snapped back. He jumped up to bar
her exit. She gave him a smart cuff across the eyes, which surprised him almost into the fire, and while he was recovering his
equilibrium she fled. Yagorsha and all the Pymeuts laughed
delightedly at Joe's discomfiture.

The Boy had been obliged to sit up to watch this spirited
encounter. The only notice the Colonel took of him was to
set the kettle on the fire. While he was dining his pardner
gathered up the blankets and crawled out.

"Comin' in half a minute," the Boy called after him. The
answer was swallowed by the tunnel.

"Him go say goo'-bye Ol' Chief," said Nicholas, observing
how the Colonel's pardner was scalding himself in his haste to
despatch a second cup of tea.

But the Boy bolted the last of his meal, gathered up the kettle, mug, and frying-pan, which had served him for plate as
well, and wormed his way out as fast as he could. There was
the sled nearly packed for the journey, and watching over it,
keeping the dogs at bay, was an indescribably dirty little boy
in a torn and greasy denim parki over rags of reindeer-skin.
Nobody else in sight but Yagorsha's daughter down at the
water-hole.

"Where's my pardner gone?" The child only stared, having
no English apparently.

While the Boy packed the rest of the things, and made the
tattered canvas fast under the lashing, Joe came out of the
Kachime. He stood studying the prospect a moment, and his
dull eyes suddenly gleamed. Anna was coming up from the
river with her dripping pail. He set off with an affectation of
leisurely indifference, but he made straight for his enemy. She
seemed not to see him till he was quite near, then she sheered
off sharply. Joe hardly quickened his pace, but seemed to gain.
She set down her bucket, and turned back towards the river.

"Idiot!" ejaculated the Boy; "she could have reached her
own ighloo." The dirty child grinned, and tore off towards the
river to watch the fun. Anna was hidden now by a pile of drift-
wood. The Boy ran down a few yards to bring her within
range again. For all his affectation of leisureliness and her
obvious fluster, no doubt about it, Joe was gaining on her.
She dropped her hurried walk and frankly took to her heels,
Joe doing the same; but as she was nearly as fleet of foot as

Muckluck, in spite of her fat, she still kept a lessening distance between herself and her pursuer.

The ragged child had climbed upon the pile of drift-wood, and stood hunched with the cold, his shoulders up to his ears, his hands withdrawn in his parki sleeves, but he was grinning still. The Boy, a little concerned as to possible reprisals upon so impudent a young woman, had gone on and on, watching the race down to the river, and even across the ice a little way. He stood still an instant staring as Joe, going now as hard as he could, caught up with her at last. He took hold of the daughter of the highly-respected Yagorsha, and fell to shaking and cuffing her. The Boy started off full tilt to the rescue. Before he could reach them Joe had thrown her down on the ice. She half got up, but her enemy, advancing upon her again, dealt her a blow that made her howl and sent her flat once more.

"Stop that! You hear? *Stop* it!" the Boy called out.

But Joe seemed not to hear. Anna had fallen face downward on the ice this time, and lay there as if stunned. Her enemy caught hold of her, pulled her up, and dragged her along in spite of her struggles and cries.

"Let her alone!" the Boy shouted. He was nearly up to them now. But Joe's attention was wholly occupied in hauling Anna back to the village, maltreating her at intervals by the way. Now the girl was putting up one arm piteously to shield her bleeding face from his fists. "Don't you hit her again, or it'll be the worse for you." But again Joe's hand was lifted. The Boy plunged forward, caught the blow as it descended, and flung the arm aside, wrenched the girl free, and as Joe came on again, looking as if he meant business, the Boy planted a sounding lick on his jaw. The Pymeut staggered, and drew off a little way, looking angry enough, but, to the Boy's surprise, showing no fight.

It occurred to him that the girl, her lip bleeding, her parki torn, seemed more surprised than grateful; and when he said, "You come back with me; he shan't touch you," she did not show the pleased alacrity that you would expect. But she was no doubt still dazed. They all stood looking rather sheepish, and like actors "stuck" who cannot think of the next line, till Joe turned on the girl with some mumbled question. She answered angrily. He made another grab at her. She screamed, and got behind the Boy. Very resolutely he widened his bold buck-skin legs, and dared Joe to touch the poor frightened creature cowering behind her protector. Again silence.

"What's the trouble between you two?"

They looked at each other, and then away. Joe turned unexpectedly, and shambled off in the direction of the village. Not a word out of Anna as she returned by the side of her protector, but every now and then she looked at him sideways. The Boy felt her inexpressive gratitude, and was glad his journey had been delayed, or else, poor devil——

Joe had stopped to speak to——

"Who on earth's that white woman?"

"Nicholas' sister."

"Not Muckluck?"

She nodded.

"What's she dressed like that for?"

"Often like that in summer. Me, too—me got Holy Cross clo'es."

Muckluck went slowly up towards the Kachime with Joe. When the others got to the water-hole, Anna turned and left the Boy without a word to go and recover her pail. The Boy stood a moment, looking for some sign of the Colonel, and then went along the river bank to Ol' Chief's. No, the Colonel had gone back to the Kachime.

The Boy came out again, and to his almost incredulous astonishment, there was Joe dragging the unfortunate Anna towards an ighloo. As he looked back, to steer straight for the entrance-hole, he caught sight of the Boy, dropped his prey, and disappeared with some precipitancy into the ground. When Anna had gathered herself up, the Boy was standing in front of her.

"You don't seem to be able to take very good care o' yourself." She pushed her tousled hair out of her eyes. "I don't wonder your own people give it up if you have to be rescued every half-hour. What's the matter with you and Joe?" She kept looking down. "What have you done to make him like this?" She looked up suddenly and laughed, and then her eyes fell.

"Done nothin'."

"Why should he want to kill you, then?"

"No *kill*," she said, smiling, a little rueful and embarrassed again, with her eyes on the ground. Then, as the Boy still stood there waiting, "Joe," she whispered, glancing over her shoulder—"Joe want me be he squaw."

The Boy fell back an astonished step.

"Jee-rusalem! He's got a pretty way o' sayin' so. Why don't you tell your father?"

"Tell—father?" It seemed never to have occurred to her.

"Yes; can't Yagorsha protect you?"

She looked about doubtfully and then over her shoulder.

"That Joe's ighloo," she said.

He pictured to himself the horror that must assail her blood at the sight. Yes, he was glad to have saved any woman from so dreadful a fate. Did it happen often? and did nobody interfere? Muckluck was coming down from the direction of the Kachime. The Boy went to meet her, throwing over his shoulder, "You'd better stick to me, Anna, as long as I'm here. I don't know, I'm sure, *what'll* happen to you when I'm gone." Anna followed a few paces, and then sat down on the snow to pull up and tie her disorganized leg-gear.

Muckluck was standing still, looking at the Boy with none of the kindness a woman ought to show to one who had just befriended her sex.

"Did you see that?"

She nodded. "See that any day."

The Boy stopped, appalled at the thought of woman in a perpetual state of siege.

"Brute! hound!" he flung out towards Joe's ighloo.

"No," says Muckluck firmly; "Joe all right."

"You say that, after what's happened this morning?" Muckluck declined to take the verdict back. "Did you see him strike her?"

"No *hurt*."

"Oh, didn't it? He threw her down, as hard as he could, on the ice."

"She get up again."

He despised Muckluck in that moment.

"You weren't sorry to see another girl treated so?"

She smiled.

"What if it had been you?"

"Oh, he not do that to *me*."

"Why not? You can't tell."

"Oh, yes." She spoke with unruffled serenity.

"It will very likely be you the next time." The Boy took a brutal pleasure in presenting the hideous probability.

"No," she returned unmoved. "Joe savvy I no marry Pymeut."

The Boy stared, mystified by the lack of sequence. "Poor Anna doesn't want to marry *that* Pymeut."

Muckluck nodded.

The Boy gave her up. Perversity was not confined to the civilized of her sex. He walked on to find the Colonel. Muckluck followed, but the Boy wouldn't speak to her, wouldn't look at her.

"You like my Holy Cross clo'es?" she inquired. "Me—I look like your kind of girls now, huh?" No answer, but she kept up with him. "See?" She held up proudly a medallion, or coin of some sort, hung on a narrow strip of raw-hide.

He meant not to look at it at all, and he jerked his head away after the merest glance that showed him the ornament was tarnished silver, a little bigger than an American dollar, and bore no device familiar to his eyes. He quickened his pace, and walked on with face averted. The Colonel appeared just below the Kachime.

"Well, aren't you *ever* comin'?" he called out.

"I've been ready this half-hour—hangin' about waitin' for you. That devil Joe," he went on, lowering his voice as he came up and speaking hurriedly, "has been trying to drag Yagorsha's girl into his ighloo. They've just had a fight out yonder on the ice. I got her away, but not before he'd thrown her down and given her a bloody face. We ought to tell old Yagorsha, hey?"

Muckluck chuckled. The Boy turned on her angrily, and saw her staring back at Joe's ighloo. There, sauntering calmly past the abhorred trap, was the story-teller's daughter. Past it? No. She actually halted and busied herself with her legging thong.

"That girl must be an imbecile!" Or was it the apparition of her father, up at the Kachime entrance, that inspired such temerity?

The Boy had gone a few paces towards her, and then turned. "Yagorsha!" he called up the slope. Yagorsha stood stock-still, although the Boy waved unmistakable danger-signals towards Joe's ighloo. Suddenly an arm flashed out of the tunnel, caught Anna by the ankle, and in a twinkling she lay sprawling on her back. Two hands shot out, seized her by the heels, and dragged the wretched girl into the brute's lair. It was all over in a flash. A moment's paralysis of astonishment, and the involuntary rush forward was arrested by Muckluck, who fastened herself on to the rescuer's parki-tail and refused to be detached. "Yagorsha!" shouted the Boy. But it was only the Colonel who hastened towards them at the summons. The poor girl's own father stood calmly smoking, up there, by the Kachime, one foot propped comfortably on the travellers' loaded sled. "Yagorsha!" he shouted again, and then, with a jerk to free himself from Muckluck, the Boy turned sharply towards the ighloo, seeming in a bewildered way to be, himself, about to transact this paternal business for the cowardly old loafer. But Muckluck clung to his arm, laughing.

"Yagorsha know. Joe give him nice mitts—sealskin—*new* mitts."

"Hear that, Colonel? For a pair of mitts he sells his daughter to that ruffian."

Without definite plan, quite vaguely and instinctively, he shook himself free from Muckluck, and rushed down to the scene of the tragedy. Muffled screams and yells issued with the smoke. Muckluck turned sharply to the Colonel, who was following, and said something that sent him headlong after the Boy. He seized the doughty champion by the feet just as he was disappearing in the tunnel, and hauled him out.

"What in thunder—— All right, you go first, then. *Quick!* as more screams rent the still air.

"Don't be a fool. You've been interruptin' the weddin' ceremonies."

Muckluck had caught up with them, and Yagorsha was advancing leisurely across the snow.

"She no want *you*," whispered Muckluck to the Boy. "She *like* Joe—like him best of all." Then, as the Boy gaped incredulously: "She tell me heap long time ago she want Joe."

"That's just part of the weddin' festivity," says the Colonel, as renewed shrieks issued from under the snow. "You've been an officious interferer, and I think the sooner I get you out o' Pymeut the healthier it'll be for you."

The Boy was too flabbergasted to reply, but he was far from convinced. The Colonel turned back to apologise to Yagorsha.

"No like this in your country?" inquired Muckluck of the crestfallen champion.

"N-no—not exactly."

"When you like girl—what you do?"

"Tell her so," muttered the Boy mechanically.

"Well—Joe been tellin' Anna—all winter."

"And she hated him."

"No. She like Joe—best of any."

"What did she go on like that for, then?"

"Oh-h! She know Joe savvy."

The Boy felt painfully small at his own lack of *savoir,* but no less angry.

"When you marry"—he turned to her incredulously—"will it be"—again the shrieks—"like this?"

"I no marry Pymeut."

Glancing riverwards, he saw the dirty imp, who had been so wildly entertained by the encounter on the ice, still huddled on his drift-wood observatory, presenting as little surface to the cold as possible, but grinning still with rapture at the spirited last act of the winter-long drama. As the Boy, with an exclamation of "Well, I give it up," walked slowly across the slope after the Colonel and Yagorsha, Muckluck lingered at his side.

"In your country when girl marry—she no scream?"

"Well, no; not usually, I believe."

"She go quiet? Like—like she *want*——" Muckluck stood still with astonishment and outraged modesty.

"They agree," he answered irritably. "They don't go on like wild beasts."

Muckluck pondered deeply this matter of supreme importance.

"When you—get you squaw, you no *make* her come?"

The Boy shook his head, and turned away to cut short these excursions into comparative ethnology.

But Muckluck was athirst for the strange new knowledge. "What you do?"

He declined to betray his plan of action.

"When you—all same Joe? Hey?"

Still no answer.

"When you *know*—girl like you best—you no drag her home?"

"No. Be quiet."

"*No?* How you marry you self, then?"

The conversation would be still more embarrassing before the Colonel, so he stopped, and said shortly: "In our country nobody beats a woman because he likes her."

"How she know, then?"

"They *agree*, I tell you."

"Oh—an' girl—just come—when he call? Oh-h!" She dropped her jaw, and stared. "No fight a *little?*" she gasped. "No scream quite *small?*"

"*No*, I tell you." He ran on and joined the Colonel. Muckluck stood several moments rooted in amazement.

Yagorsha had called the rest of the Pymeuts out, for these queer guests of theirs were evidently going at last.

They all said "Goo'-bye" with great goodwill. Only Muckluck in her chilly "Holy Cross clo'es" stood sorrowful and silent, swinging her medal slowly back and forth.

Nicholas warned them that the Pymeut air-hole was not the only one.

"No," Yagorsha called down the slope; "better no play tricks with *him.*" He nodded towards the river as the travellers looked back. "Him no like. Him got heap plenty mouths—chew you up." And all Pymeut chuckled, delighted at their story-teller's wit.

Suddenly Muckluck broke away from the group, and ran briskly down to the river trail.

"I will pray for you—hard." She caught hold of the Boy's hand, and shook it warmly. "Sister Winifred says the Good Father——"

"Fact is, Muckluck," answered the Boy, disengaging himself with embarrassment, "my pardner here can hold up that end. Don't you think you'd better square Yukon Inua? Don't b'lieve he likes me."

And they left her, shivering in her "Holy Cross clo'es," staring after them, and sadly swinging her medal on its walrus-string.

"I don't mind sayin' I'm glad to leave Pymeut behind," said the Colonel.

"Same here."

"You're safe to get into a muss if you mix up with anything that has to do with women. That Muckluck o' yours is a minx."

"She ain't my Muckluck, and I don't believe she's a minx, not a little bit."

Not wishing to be too hard on his pardner, the Colonel added:

"I lay it all to the chaparejos myself." Then, observing his friend's marked absence of hilarity, "You're very gay in your fine fringes."

"Been a little too gay the last two or three hours."

"Well, now, I'm glad to hear you say that. I think myself we've had adventures enough right here at the start."

"I b'lieve you. But there's something in that idea o' yours. Other fellas have noticed the same tendency in chaparejos."

"Well, if the worst comes to the worst," drawled the Colonel, "we'll change breeches."

The suggestion roused no enthusiasm.

"B'lieve I'd have a cammin' influence. Yes, sir, I reckon I could keep those fringes out o' kinks."

"Oh, I think they'll go straight enough after this"; and the Boy's good spirits returned before they passed the summer village.

It came on to snow again, about six o'clock, that second day out, and continued steadily all the night. What did it matter? They were used to snow, and they were as jolly as clams at high-tide.

The Colonel called a halt in the shelter of a frozen slough, between two banks, sparsely timbered, but promising all the wood they needed, old as well as new. He made his camp fire on the snow, and the Boy soon had the beef-tea ready— always the first course so long as Liebig lasted.

Thereafter, while the bacon was frying and the tea brewing, the Colonel stuck up in the snow behind the fire some sticks on which to dry their foot-gear. When he pulled off his mucklucks his stockinged feet smoked in the frosty air. The hint was all that was needed, that first night on the trail, for the Boy to follow suit and make the change into dry things. The smoky background was presently ornamented with German socks, and Arctic socks (a kind of felt slipper), and mucklucks, each with a stick run through them to the toe, all neatly planted in a row, like monstrous products of a snow-garden. With dry feet, burning faces and chilly backs, they hugged the fire, ate supper, laughed and talked, and said that life on the trail wasn't half bad. Afterwards they rolled themselves in their blankets, and went to sleep on their spruce-bough spring mattresses spread near the fire on the snow.

After about half an hour of oblivion the Boy started up with the drowsy impression that a flying spark from the dying fire had set their stuff ablaze. No. But surely the fire had been made up again—and—he rubbed the sleep out of his incredulous eyes—yes, Muckluck was standing there!

"What in thunder!" he began. "Wh-what is it?"

"It is me."

"I can see that much. But what brings you here?"

Shivering with cold, she crouched close to the fire, dressed, as he could see now, in her native clothes again, and it was her parki that had scorched—was scorching still.

"Me—I——" Smiling, she drew a stiff hand out of its mitten and held it over the reviving blaze, glancing towards the Colonel. He seemed to be sleeping very sound, powdered over already with soft wet snow; but she whispered her next remark.

"I think I come help you find that Onge Grove."

"I think you'll do nothing of the kind." He also spoke with a deliberate lowering of the note. His great desire not to wake the Colonel gave an unintentional softness to his tone.

"You think winter bad time for squaws to travel?" She shook her head, and showed her beautiful teeth an instant in the faint light. Then, rising, half shy, but very firm, "I no wait till summer."

He was so appalled for the moment, at the thought of having her on their hands, all this way from Pymeut, on a snowy night, that words failed him. As she watched him she, too, grew grave.

"You say me nice girl."

"When did I say that?" He clutched his head in despair.

"When you first come. When Shamán make Ol' Chief all well."

"I don't remember it."

"Yes."

"I think you misunderstood me, Muckluck."

"Heh?" Her countenance fell, but more puzzled than wounded.

"That is—oh, yes—of course—you're a nice girl."

"I think—Anna, too—you like me best." She helped out the white man's bashfulness. But as her interlocutor, appalled, laid no claim to the sentiment, she lifted the mittened hand to her eyes, and from under it scanned the white face through the lightly falling snow. The other hand, still held out to the comfort of the smoke, was trembling a little, perhaps not altogether with the cold.

"The Colonel 'll have to take over the breeches," said the Boy, with the air of one wandering in his head. Then, desperately: "What *am* I to do? What am I to *say*?"

"Say? You say you no like girl scream, no like her fight like Anna. Heh? So, me—I come like your girls—quite, quite good. . . . Heh?"

"You don't understand, Muckluck. I—you see, I could never find that Orange Grove if you came along."

"Why?"

"Well—a—no woman ever goes to help to find an Orange Grove. Th-there's a law against it."

"Heh? Law?"

Alas! she knew too little to be impressed by the Majesty invoked.

"You see, women, they—they come by-and-by—when the Orange Grove's all—all ready for 'em. No man *ever* takes a woman on that kind of hunt."

Her saddened face was very grave. The Boy took heart.

"Now, the Pymeuts are going in a week or two, Nicholas said, to hunt caribou in the hills."

"Yes."

"But they won't take you to hunt caribou. No; they leave you at home. It's exactly the same with Orange Groves. No nice girl *ever* goes hunting."

Her lip trembled.

"Me—I can fish."

"Course you can." His spirits were reviving. "You can do anything—except hunt." As she lifted her head with an air of sudden protest he quashed her. "From the beginning there's been a law against that. Squaws must stay at home and let the men do the huntin'."

"Me . . . I can cook"—she was crying now—"while you hunt. Good supper all ready when you come home."

He shook his head solemnly.

"Perhaps you don't know"—she flashed a moment's hope through her tears—"me learn sew up at Holy Cross. Sew up your socks for you when they open their mouths." But she could see that not even this grand new accomplishment availed.

"Can help pull sled," she suggested, looking round a little wildly as if instantly to illustrate. "Never tired," she added, sobbing, and putting her hands up to her face.

"Sh! sh! Don't wake the Colonel." He got up hastily and stood beside her at the smouldering fire. He patted her on the shoulder. "Of course you're a nice girl. The nicest girl in the Yukon"—he caught himself up as she dropped her hands from her face—"that is, you will be, if you go home quietly."

Again she hid her eyes.

Go home? How could he send her home all that way at this time of night? It *was* a bothering business!

Again her hands fell from the wet unhappy face. She shivered a little when she met his frowning looks, and turned away. He stooped and picked up her mitten. Why, you couldn't turn a dog away on a night like this——

Plague take the Pymeuts, root and branch! She had shuffled her feet into her snow-shoe straps, and moved off in the dimness. But for the sound of sobbing, he could not have told just where, in the softly-falling snow, Muckluck's figure was fading into the dusk. He hurried after her, conscience-stricken, but most unwilling.

"Look here," he said, when he had caught up with her, "I'm sorry you came all this way in the cold—very sorry." Her sobs burst out afresh, and louder now, away from the Colonel's restraining presence. "But, see here: I can't send you off like this. You might die on the trail."

"Yes, I think me die," she agreed.

"No, don't do that. Come back, and we'll tell the Colonel you're going to stay by the fire till morning, and then go home."

She walked steadily on. "No, I go now."

"But you can't, Muckluck. You can't find the trail."

"I tell you before, I not like your girls. I can go in winter as good as summer. I *can* hunt!" She turned on him fiercely. "Once I hunt a owel. Ketch him, too!" She sniffed back her tears. "I can do all kinds."

"No, you can't hunt Orange Groves," he said, with a severity that might seem excessive. "But I can't let you go off in this snowstorm——"

"He soon stop. Goo'-bye."

Never word of sweeter import in his ears than that. But he was far from satisfied with his conduct all the same. It was quite possible that the Pymeuts, discovering her absence, would think he had lured her away, and there might be complications. So it was with small fervour that he said: "Muckluck, I wish you'd come back and wait till morning."

"No, I go now." She was in the act of darting forward on those snow-shoes, that she used so skillfully, when some sudden thought cried halt. She even stopped crying. "I no like go near blow-hole by night. I keep to trail——"

"But how the devil do you do it?"

She paid no heed to the interruption, seeming busy in taking something over her head from round her neck.

"To-morrow," she said, lowering her tear-harshened voice, "you find blow-hole. You give this to Yukon Inua—say I send it. He will not hate you any more." She burst into a fresh flood of tears. In a moment the dim sight of her, the faint trail of crying left in her wake, had so wholly vanished that, but for the bit of string, as it seemed to be, left in his half-frozen hands, he could almost have convinced himself he had dreamt the unwelcome visit.

The half-shut eye of the camp fire gleamed cheerfully, as he ran back, and crouched down where poor little Muckluck had knelt, so sure of a welcome. Muckluck, cogitated the Boy, will believe more firmly than ever that, if a man doesn't beat a girl, he doesn't mean business. What was it he had wound round one hand? What was it dangling in the acrid smoke? *That*, then—her trinket, the crowning ornament of her Holy Cross holiday attire, that was what she was offering the old ogre of the Yukon—for his unworthy sake. He stirred up the dying fire to see it better. A woman's face—some Catholic saint? He held the medal lower to catch the fitful blaze. "*D. G. Autocratrix Russorum.*" The Great Katharine! Only a little crown on her high-rolled hair, and her splendid chest all uncovered to the Arctic cold.

Her Yukon subjects must have wondered that she wore no parki—this lady who had claimed sole right to all the finest sables found in her new American dominions. On the other side of the medal, Minerva, with a Gorgon-furnished shield and a beautiful bone-tipped harpoon, as it looked, with a throwing-stick and all complete. But she, too, would strike the Yukon eye as lamentably chilly about the legs. How had these ladies out of Russia and Olympus come to lodge in Ol' Chief's ighloo? Had Glovotsky won this guerdon at Great Katharine's hands? Had he brought it on that last long journey of his to Russian America, and left it to his Pymeut children with his bones? Well, Yukon Inua should not have it yet. The Boy thrust the medal into a pocket of his chaparejos, and crawled into his snow-covered bed.

CHAPTER XI

HOLY CROSS

"Raise the stone, and ye shall find me; cleave the wood, and there am I."

THE stars were shining frostily, in a clear sky, when the Boy crawled out from under his snow-drift in the morning. He built up the fire, quaking in the bitter air, and bustled the breakfast.

"You seem to be in something of a hurry," said the Colonel, with a yawn stifled in a shiver.

"We haven't come on this trip to lie abed in the morning," his pardner returned with some solemnity. "I don't care how soon I begin caperin' ahead with that load again."

"Well, it'll be warmin', anyway," returned the Colonel, "and I can't say as much for your fire."

It was luck that the first forty miles of the trail had already been traversed by the Boy. He kept recognising this and that in the landscape, with an effect of good cheer on both of them. It postponed a little the realization of their daring in launching themselves upon the Arctic waste, without a guide or even a map that was of the smallest use.

Half an hour after setting off, they struck into the portage. Even with a snow-blurred trail, the Boy's vivid remembrance of the other journey gave them the sustaining sense that they were going right. The Colonel was working off the surprising stiffness with which he had wakened, and they were both warm now; but the Colonel's footsoreness was considerable, an affliction, besides, bound to be worse before it was better.

The Boy spoke with the old-timer's superiority, of his own experience, and was so puffed up, at the bare thought of having hardened his feet, that he concealed without a qualm the fact of a brand-new blister on his heel. A mere nothing that, not worth mentioning to anyone who remembered the state he was in at the end of that awful journey of penitence.

It was well on in the afternoon before it began to snow

again, and they had reached the frozen lake. The days were lengthening, and they still had good light by which to find the well-beaten trail on the other side.

"Now in a minute we'll hear the mission dogs. What did I tell you?" Out of the little wood, a couple of teams were coming, at a good round pace. They were pulled up at the water-hole, and the mission natives ran on to meet the new arrivals. They recognised the Boy, and insisted on making the Colonel, who was walking very lame, ride to the mission in the strongest sled, and they took turns helping the dogs by pushing from behind. The snow was falling heavily again, and one of the Indians, Henry, looking up with squinted eyes, said, "There'll be nothing left of that walrus-tusk."

"Hey?" inquired the Boy, straining at his sled-rope and bending before the blast. "What's that?"

"Don't you know what makes snow?" said Henry.

"No. What does?"

"Ivory whittlings. When they get to their carving up yonder then we have snow."

What was happening to the Colonel?

The mere physical comfort of riding, instead of serving as packhorse, great as it was, not even that could so instantly spirit away the weariness, and light up the curious, solemn radiance that shone on the Colonel's face. It struck the Boy that good old Kentucky would look like that when he met his dearest at the Gate of Heaven—if there was such a place.

The Colonel was aware of the sidelong wonder of his comrade's glance, for the sleds, abreast, had come to a momentary halt. But still he stared in front of him, just as a sailor in a storm dares not look away from the beacon-light an instant, knowing all the waste about him abounds in rocks and eddies and in death, and all the world of hope and safe returning is narrowed to that little point of light.

After the moment's speculation the Boy turned his eyes to follow the Colonel's gaze into space.

"The Cross! the Cross!" said the man on the sled. "Don't you see it?"

"Oh, that? Yes."

At the Boy's tone the Colonel, for the first time, turned his eyes away from the Great White Symbol.

"Don't know what you're made of, if, seeing that . . . you needn't be a Church member, but only a man, I should think, to—to——" He blew out his breath in impotent clouds, and then went on. "We Americans think a good deal o' the Stars and Stripes, but that up yonder—that's the mightier symbol."

"Huh!" says the Boy.

"Stars and Stripes tell of an ideal of united states. That up there tells of an ideal of United Mankind. It's the great Brotherhood Mark. There isn't any other standard that men would follow just to build a hospice in a place like this."

At an upper window, in a building on the far side of the white symbol, the travellers caught a glimpse, through the slanting snow, of one of the Sisters of St. Ann shutting in the bright light with thick curtains.

"*Glass!*" ejaculated the Colonel.

One of the Indians had run on to announce them, and as they drew up at the door—that the Boy remembered as a frame for Brother Paul, with his lamp, to search out iniquity, and his face of denunciation—out came Father Brachet, brisk, almost running, his two hands outstretched, his face a network of welcoming wrinkles. No long waiting, this time, in the reception-room. Straight upstairs to hot baths and mild, reviving drinks, and then, refreshed and already rested, down to supper.

With a shade of anxiety the Boy looked about for Brother Paul. But Father Wills was here anyhow, and the Boy greeted him, joyfully, as a tried friend and a man to be depended on. There was Brother Etienne, and there were two strange faces.

Father Brachet put the Colonel on his right and the Boy on his left, introducing: "Fazzer Richmond, my predecessor as ze head of all ze Alaskan missions," calmly eliminating Greek, Episcopalian, and other heretic establishments. "Fazzer Richmond you must have heard much of. He is ze great ausority up here. He is now ze Travelling Priest. You can ask him all. He knows everysing."

In no wise abashed by this flourish, Father Richmond shook hands with the Big Chimney men, smiling, and with a pleasant ease that communicated itself to the entire company.

It was instantly manifest that the scene of this Jesuit's labours had not been chiefly, or long, beyond the borders of civilisation. In the plain bare room where, for all its hospitality and good cheer, reigned an air of rude simplicity and austerity of life—into this somewhat rarefied atmosphere

Father Richmond brought a whiff from another world. As he greeted the two strangers, and said simply that he had just arrived, himself, by way of the Anvik portage, the Colonel felt that he must have meant from New York or from Paris instead of the words he added, "from St. Michael's."

He claimed instant kinship with the Colonel on the strength of their both being Southerners.

"I'm a Baltimore man," he said, with an accent no Marylander can purge of pride.

"How long since you've been home?"

"Oh, I go back every year."

"He goes all over ze world, to tell ze people——"

"——something of the work being done here by Father Brachet—and all of them." He included the other priests and lay-brothers in a slight circular movement of the grizzled head.

And to collect funds! the Colonel rightly divined, little guessing how triumphantly he achieved that end.

"Alaska is so remote," said the Travelling Priest, as if in apology for popular ignorance, "and people think of it so . . . inadequately, shall we say? In trying to explain the conditions up here, I have my chief difficulty in making them realise the great distances we have to cover. You tell them that in the Indian tongue Alaska means "the great country," they smile, and think condescendingly of savage imagery. It is vain to say we have an area of six hundred thousand square miles. We talk much in these days of education; but few men and no women can count! Our Eastern friends get some idea of what we mean, when we tell them Alaska is bigger than all the Atlantic States from Maine to Louisiana with half of great Texas thrown in. With a coast-line of twenty-six thousand miles, this Alaska of ours turns to the sea a greater frontage than all the shores of all the United States combined. It extends so far out towards Asia that it carries the dominions of the Great Republic as far west of San Francisco as New York is east of it, making California a central State. I try to give Europeans some idea of it by saying that if you add England, Ireland, and Scotland together, and to that add France, and to that add Italy, you still lack enough to make a country the size of Alaska. I do not speak of our mountains, seventeen, eighteen, nineteen thousand feet high, and our Yukon, flowing for more than two thousand miles through a country almost virgin still."

"You travel about up here a good deal?"

"He travels *all* ze time. He will not rest," said Father Brachet as one airing an ancient grievance.

"Yes, I will rest now—a little. I have been eight hundred miles over the ice, with dogs, since January 1."

The Boy looked at him with something very like reverence. Here was a man who could give you tips!

"You have travelled abroad, too," the Colonel rather stated than asked.

"I spent a good deal of my youth in France and Germany."

"Educated over there?"

"Well, I am a Johns Hopkins man, but I may say I found my education in Rome. Speaking of education"—he turned to the other priests—"I have greatly advanced my grammar since we parted." Father Brachet answered with animation in French, and the conversation went forward for some minutes in that tongue. The discussion was interrupted to introduce the other new face, at the bottom of the table, to the Big Chimney men: "Resident Fazzer Roget of ze Kuskoquim mission."

"That is the best man on snow-shoes in Central Alaska," said Father Richmond low to the Colonel, nodding at the Kuskoquim priest.

"And he knows more of two of ze native dialects here zan anyone else," added the Father Superior.

"You must forgive our speaking much of the Indian tongues," said Father Richmond. "We are all making dictionaries and grammars; we have still to translate much of our religious instruction, and the great variety in dialect of the scattered tribes keeps us busy with linguistic studies."

"To-morrow you must see our schools," said Father Brachet. But the Boy answered quickly that they could not afford the time. He was surprised at the Colonel's silence; but the Boy didn't know what the Colonel's feet felt like.

Kentucky ain't sorry, he said to himself, to have a back to his chair, and to eat off china again. Kentucky's a voluptuary! I'll have to drag him away by main force; and the Boy allowed Father Richmond to help him yet more abundantly to the potatoes and cabbage grown last summer in the mission garden!

It was especially the vegetables that lent an element of luxury to the simple meal. The warm room, the excellent food, better cooked than any they had had for seven months, produced a gentle somnolence. The thought of the inviting look of the white-covered bed upstairs lay like a balm on the spirits of men not born to roughing it. As the travellers said an early and grateful good-night, the Boy added sleepily something about the start at dawn.

Father Brachet answered, "Morning will bring counsel, my son. I sink ze bleezzar-r will not let us lose you so soon."

They overslept themselves, and they knew it, in that way the would-be early riser does, before ever he looks into the accusing face of his watch. The Boy leapt out of bed.

"Hear that?" The wind was booming among the settlement buildings. "Sounds as if there was weather outside." A glance between the curtains showed the great gale at its height. The snow blew level in sheets and darkened the air.

"Well," said the Colonel, splashing mightily in the ice-cold water, "I don't know as I mind giving my feet twenty-four hours' time to come to their senses."

A hurried toilet and they went downstairs, sharp-set for breakfast after the long, refreshing sleep.

Father Richmond was writing on his knee by the stove in the reception-room.

"Good-morning—good-morning." He rang the bell. "Well, what did we tell you? I don't think you'll get far to-day. Let these gentlemen know when breakfast is ready," he said, as Christopher put his head in. He looked at his watch. "I hope you will find everything you need," he said; and, continuing to talk about the gale and some damage it had done to one of the outbuildings, he went into the entry, just beyond the reception-room door, and began to put on his furs.

"*You* are not going out in such weather!" the Colonel called after him incredulously.

"Only as far as the church."

"Oh, is there church to-day?" inquired the Boy more cheerfully than one might expect.

The Colonel started and made a signal for discretion.

"Blest if it isn't Sunday!" he said under his breath.

"He doesn't seem dead-set on our observing it," whispered the Boy.

The Colonel warmed himself luxuriously at the stove, and seemed to listen for that summons from the entry that never came. Was Father Richmond out there still, or had he gone?

"Do they think we are heathens because we are not Jesuits?"

he said under his breath, suddenly throwing out his great chest.

"Perhaps we ought to. . . . Hey? They've been awfully considerate of *us*——"

The Colonel went to the door. Father Richmond was struggling with his snow-boots.

"With your permission, sir," says the Colonel in his most magnificent manner, "we will accompany you, or follow if you are in haste."

"With all my heart. Come," said the priest, "if you will wait and breakfast with us after Mass."

It was agreed, and the immediate order was countermanded. The sound of a bell came, muffled, through the storm.

With thoughts turning reluctantly from breakfast, "What's that?" asked the Boy.

"That is our church bell." The Father had helped the Colonel to find his parki.

"Oh—a—of course——"

"A fine tone, don't you think? But you can't tell so well in this storm. We are fond of our bell. It is the first that ever rang out in the Yukon valley. Listen!"

They stood still a moment before opening the front door. The Boy, seeing the very look of a certain high-shouldered gray stone "St. Andrew's" far away, and himself trotting along beside that figure, inseparable from first memories, was dimly aware again, as he stood at the Jesuit's door, in these different days, of the old Sunday feeling invading, permeating his consciousness, half reluctant, half amused.

The Colonel sat in a rural church and looked at the averted face of a woman.

Only to the priest was the sound all music.

"That language," he said, "speaks to men whatever tongue they call their own. The natives hear it for miles up the river, and down the river, and over the white hills, and far across the tundra. They come many miles to Mass——"

He opened the door, and the gale rushed in.

"I do not mean on days like this," he wound up, smiling, and out they went into the whirling snow.

The church was a building of logs like the others, except that it was of one story. Father Brachet was already there, with Father Wills and Brother Etienne; and, after a moment, in came Brother Paul, looking more waxen and aloof than ever, at the head of the school, the rear brought up by Brother Vincent and Henry.

In a moment the little Mother Superior appeared, followed by two nuns, heading a procession of native women and girls. They took their places on the other side of the church and bowed their heads.

"Beautiful creature!" ejaculated the Colonel under his breath, glancing back.

His companion turned his head sharply just in time to see Sister Winifred come last into the church, holding by either hand a little child. Both men watched her as she knelt down. Between the children's sallow, screwed-up, squinting little visages the calm, unconscious face of the nun shone white like a flower.

The strangers glanced discreetly about the rude little church, with its pictures and its modest attempt at stained glass.

"No wonder all this impresses the ignorant native," whispered the Colonel, catching himself up suddenly from sharing in that weakness.

Without, the wild March storm swept the white world; within another climate reigned—something of summer and the far-off South, of Italy herself, transplanted to this little island of civilisation anchored in the Northern waste.

"S'pose you've seen all the big cathedrals, eh?"

"Good many."

There was still a subdued rustling in the church, and outside, still the clanging bell contended with the storm.

"And this—makes you smile?"

"N-no," returned the older man with a kind of reluctance. "I've seen many a worse church; America's full of 'em."

"Hey?"

"So far as—dignity goes——" The Colonel was wrestling with some vague impression difficult for him to formulate. "You see, you can't build anything with wood that's better than a log-cabin. For looks—just *looks*—it beats all your fancy gimcracks, even brick; beats everything else hollow, except stone. Then they've got candles. We went on last night about the luxury of oil-lamps. They don't bring 'em in here!"

"*We* do in our prairie and Southern country churches."

"I know. But look at those altar lights." The Boy was too busy looking at Sister Winifred. "I tell you, sir, a man never made a finer thing than a tall wax candle."

"Sh! Mustn't talk in church."

The Colonel stared a moment at the Boy's presumption, drew himself up a little pompously, and crossed his arms over his huge chest.

"Why, they've got an organ!" The Boy forgot his strict views on church etiquette as the sudden sweetness swelled in the air. Brother Paul, with head thrown back and white face lifted, was playing, slowly, absently, like one who listens to some great choir invisible, and keeps their time with a few obedient but unnecessary chords. And yet——

"The fella can play," the Colonel admitted.

The native choir, composed entirely of little dark-faced boys, sang their way truly through the service, Father Brachet celebrating Mass.

"Brother Paul's ill, isn't he? Look!" The lay-brother had swayed, and drooped forward over the keyboard, but his choir sang steadily on. He recovered himself, and beckoned one of the boys to his side. When he rose, the child nodded and took the organist's place, playing quite creditably to the end. Brother Paul sat in the corner with bowed head.

Coming out, they were in time to confront Sister Winifred, holding back the youngest children, eager to anticipate their proper places in the procession.

The Boy looked fixedly at her, wondering. Suddenly meeting the clear eyes, he smiled, and then shrank inwardly at his forwardness. He could not tell if she remembered him.

The Colonel, finding himself next her at the door, bowed, and stood back for her to pass.

"No," she said gently; "my little children must wait for the older ones."

"You have them under good discipline, madam." He laid his hand on the furry shoulder of the smallest.

The Boy stood behind the Colonel, unaccountably shy in the presence of the only white woman he had seen in nearly seven months. She couldn't be any older than he, and yet she was a nun. What a gulf opened at the word! Sister Winifred and her charges fell into rank at the tail of the little procession, and vanished in the falling snow.

At breakfast the Colonel would not sit down till he was presented to Brother Paul.

"Sir," he said in his florid but entirely sincere fashion, "I should like to thank you for the pleasure of hearing that music to-day. We were much impressed, sir, by the singing. How old is the boy who played the organ?"

"Ten," said Brother Paul, and for the first time the Boy saw him smile. "Yes, I think he has music in him, our little Jerome."

"And how well *all* your choir has the service by heart! Their unison is perfect."

"Yes," said Father Brachet from the head of the table, "our music has never been so good as since Paul came among us." He lifted his hand, and every one bowed his head.

After grace Father Richmond took the floor, conversationally, as seemed to be his wont, and breakfast went on, as supper had the night before, to the accompaniment of his shrewd observations and lively anecdotes. In the midst of all the laughter and good cheer Brother Paul sat at the end of the board, eating absently, saying nothing, and no one speaking to him.

Father Richmond especially, but, indeed, all of them, seemed arrant worldlings beside the youngest of the lay-brethren. The Colonel could more easily imagine Father Richmond walking the streets of Paris or of Rome, than "hitting the Yukon trail." He marvelled afresh at the devotion that brought such a man to wear out his fine attainments, his scholarship, his energy, his wide and Catholic knowledge, in travelling winter after winter, hundreds of miles over the ice from one Indian village to another. You could not divorce Father Richmond in your mind from the larger world outside; he spoke with its accent, he looked with his humourous, experienced eyes. You found it natural to think of him in very human relations. You wondered about his people, and what brought him to this.

Not so with Brother Paul. He was one of those who suggest no country upon any printed map. You have to be reminded that you do not know his birthplace or his history. It was this same Brother Paul who, after breakfast and despite the Pymeut incident, offered to show the gold-seekers over the school. The big recitation-room was full of natives and decidedly stuffy. They did not stay long. Upstairs, "I sleep here in the dormitory," said the Brother, "and I live with the pupils —as much as I can. I often eat with them," he added as one who mounts a climax. "They have to be taught *everything,* and they have to be taught it over again every day."

"Except music, apparently."

"Except music—and games. Brother Vincent teaches them football and baseball, and plays with them and works with them. Part of each day is devoted to manual training and to sport."

He led the way to the workshop.

"One of our brothers is a carpenter and master mechanic."

He called to a pupil passing the door, and told him the strangers would like to inspect the school work. Very proudly the lad obeyed. He himself was a carpenter, and showed his half-finished table. The Boy's eye fell on a sled.

"Yes," said the lad, "that kind better. Your kind no good." He had evidently made intimate acquaintance with the Boy's masterpiece.

"Yours is splendid," admitted the unskilled workman.

"Will you sell it?" the Colonel asked Brother Paul.

"They make them to sell," was the answer, and the transaction was soon effected.

*   *   *   *   *   *   *

"It has stopped snowing and ze wind is fallen," said Father Brachet, going to the reception-room window an hour or so after they had come in from dinner.

The Colonel exchanged looks with the Boy, and drew out his watch.

"Later than I thought."

"Much," the Colonel agreed, and sat considering, watch in hand.

"I sink our friends must see now ze girls' school, and ze laundry, hein?"

"To be sure," agreed Father Richmond. "I will take you over and give you into the hands of our Mother Superior."

"Why, it's much warmer," said the Boy as they went by the cross; and Father Richmond greeted the half-dozen native boys, who were packing down the fresh snow under their broad shoes, laughing and shouting to one another as they made anew the familiar mission trails.

The door of the two-story house, on the opposite side of the settlement, was opened by Sister Winifred.

"Friends of ours from the White Camp below."

She acknowledged the nameless introduction, smiling; but at the request that followed, "Ah, it is too bad that just to-day—the Mother Superior—she is too faint and weak to go about. Will you see her, Father?"

"Yes, if you will show these strangers the school and laundry and——"

"Oh, yes, I will show them."

She led the way into the cheerful schoolroom, where big girls and little girls were sitting about, amusing themselves in the quiet of a long Sunday afternoon. Several of the younger children ran to her as she came in, and stood holding fast to the folds of her black habit, staring up at the strangers, while she explained the kind of instruction given, the system, and the order reigning in each department. Finally, she persuaded a little girl, only six years old, to take her dusky face out of the long flowing veil of the nun, and show how quickly she could read a sentence that Sister Winifred wrote on the black-board. Then others were called on, and gave examples of their accomplishments in easy arithmetic and spelling. The children must have been very much bored with themselves that stormy Sunday, for they entered into the examination with a quite unnatural zest.

Two of the elder girls recited, and some specimens of pen-manship and composition were shown. The delicate complex-ion of the little nun flushed to a pretty wild-rose pink as these pupils of hers won the Colonel's old fashioned compliments.

"And they are taught most particularly of all," she hastened to say, "cooking, housekeeping, and sewing."

Whereupon specimens of needlework were brought out and cast like pearls before the swine's eyes of the ignorant men. But they were impressed in their benighted way, and said so.

"And we teach them laundry-work." She led the way, with the children trooping after, to the washhouse. "No, run back. You'll take cold. Run back, and you shall sing for the stran-gers before they go."

She smiled them away—a happy-faced, clean little throng, striking contrast to the neglected, filthy children seen in the native villages. As they were going into the laundry, Father Richmond came out of the house, and stopped to point out to the Colonel a snow-covered enclosure—"the Sisters' garden"—and he told how marvellously, in the brief summer, some of the hardier vegetables flourished there.

"They spring up like magic at the edge of the snow-drifts, and they do not rest from their growing all night. If the time is short, they have twice as much sunlight as with you. They drink it in the whole summer night as well as all the day. And over here is the Fathers' garden." Talking still, he led the way towards a larger enclosure on the other side of the Cross.

Sister Winifred paused a moment, and then, as they did not turn back, and the Boy stood waiting, she took him into the drying-room and into the ironing-room, and then returned to the betubbed apartment first invaded. There was only one blot on the fairness of that model laundry—a heap of torn and dirty canvas in the middle of the floor.

The Boy vaguely thought it looked familiar, before the Sister, blushing faintly, said: "We hope you won't go before we have time to repair it."

"Why, it's our old sled-cover!"

"Yes; it is very much cut and torn. But you do not go at once?"

"Yes, to-morrow."

"Oh! Father Brachet thought you would stay for a few days, at least."

"We have no time."

"You go, like the rest, for gold?"

"Like the rest."

"But you came before to help poor Nicholas out of his trouble."

"He was quite able to help himself, as it turned out."

"Why will you go so far, and at such risk?" she said, with a suddenness that startled them both.

"I—I—well, I think I go chiefly because I want to get my home back. I lost my home when I was a little chap. Where is your home?"

"Here."

"How long have you been here?"

"Nearly two years."

"Then how can you call it home?"

"I do that only that I may—speak your language. Of course, it is not my real home."

"Where is the real home?"

"I hope it is in heaven," she said, with a simplicity that took away all taint of cant or mere phrase-making.

"But where do you come from?"

"I come from Montreal."

"Oh! and don't you ever go back to visit your people?"

"No, I never go back."

"But you will some time?"

"No; I shall never go back."

"Don't you *want* to?"

She dropped her eyes, but very steadfastly she said:

"My work is here."

"But you are young, and you may live a great, great many years."

She nodded, and looked out of the open door. The Colonel and the Travelling Priest were walking in Indian file the new-made, hard-packed path.

"Yes," she said in a level voice, "I shall grow old here, and here I shall be buried."

"I shall never understand it. I have such a longing for my home. I came here ready to bear anything that I might be able to get it back."

She looked at him steadily and gravely.

"I may be wrong, but I doubt if you would be satisfied even if you got it back—now."

"What makes you think that?" he said sharply.

"Because"—and she checked herself as if on the verge of something too personal—"you can never get back a thing you've lost. When the old thing is there again, you are not as you were when you lost it, and the change in you makes the old thing new—and strange."

"Oh, it's plain I am very different from you," but he said it with a kind of uneasy defiance. "Besides, in any case, I shall do it for my sister's sake."

"Oh, you have a sister?"

He nodded.

"How long since you left her?"

"It's a good while now."

"Perhaps your sister won't want that particular home any more than you when you two meet again." Then, seeming not to notice the shade on her companion's face: "I promised my children they should sing for you. Do you mind? Will your friend come in, too?" And, looking from the door after the Colonel and the Father as they turned to rejoin them: "He is odd, that big friend of yours," she said—quite like a human being, as the Boy thought instantly.

"He's not odd, I assure you."

"He called me 'madam.'" She spoke with a charming piqued childishness.

"You see, he didn't know your name. What is your name?"

"Sister Winifred."

"But your real name?" he said, with the American's insistence on his own point of view.

"That is my only name," she answered with dignity, and led the way back into the schoolroom. Another, older, nun was there, and when the others rejoined them they made the girls sing.

"Now we have shown you enough," said Father Richmond, rising; "boasted to you enough of the very little we are able to accomplish here. We must save something for to-morrow."

"Ah, to-morrow we take to the trail again," said the Colonel, and added his "Good-bye, madam."

Sister Winifred, seeing he expected it, gave him her hand.

"Good-bye, and thank you for coming."

"For your poor," he said shyly, as he turned away and left a gift in her palm.

"Thank you for showing us all this," the Boy said, lingering, but not daring to shake hands. "It—it seems very wonderful. I had no idea a mission meant all this."

"Oh, it means more—more than anything you can *see*."

"Good-bye."

"Good-bye."

In the early evening the reception-room was invaded by the lads' school for their usual Sunday night entertainment. Very proudly these boys and young men sang their glees and choruses, played the fiddle, recited, even danced.

"Pity Mac isn't here!"

"Awful pity. Sunday, too."

Brother Etienne sang some French military songs, and it came out that he had served in the French army. Father Roget sang, also in French, explaining himself with a humourous skill in pantomime that set the room in a roar.

"Well," said the Colonel when he stood up to say goodnight, "I haven't enjoyed an evening so much for years."

"It is very early still," said Father Brachet, wrinkling up his face in a smile.

"Ah, but we have to make such an early start."

The Colonel went up to bed, leaving the Boy to go to Father Richmond's room to look at his Grammar of the Indian language.

The instant the door was shut, the priest set down the lamp, and laid his hands on the young man's shoulders.

"My son, you must not go on this mad journey."

"I must, you know."

"You must *not*. Sit there." He pushed him into a chair. "Let me tell you. I do not speak as the ignorant. I have in my day travelled many hundreds of miles on the ice; but I've done it in the season when the trail's at its best, *with dogs,* my son, and with tried native servants."

"I know it is pleasanter that way, but——"

"Pleasanter? It is the way to keep alive."

"But the Indians travel with hand-sleds."

"For short distances, yes, and they are inured to the climate. You? You know nothing of what lies before you."

"But we'll find out as other people have." The Boy smiled confidently.

"I assure you, my son, it is madness, this thing you are trying to do. The chances of either of you coming out alive, are one in fifty. In fifty, did I say? In five hundred."

"I don't think so, Father. We don't mean to travel when——"

"But you'll have to travel. To stay in such places as you'll find yourself in will be to starve. Or if by any miracle you escape the worst effects of cold and hunger, you'll get caught in the ice in the spring break-up, and go down to destruction on a floe. You've no conception what it's like. If you were six weeks earlier, or six weeks later, I would hold my peace."

The Boy looked at the priest and then away. *Was* it going to be so bad? Would they leave their bones on the ice? Would they go washing by the mission in the great spring flood, that all men spoke of with the same grave look? He had a sudden vision of the torrent as it would be in June. Among the whirling ice-masses that swept by—two bodies, swollen, unrecognisable. One gigantic, one dressed gaily in chaparejos. And neither would lift his head, but, like men bent grimly upon some great errand, they would hurry on, past the tall white cross with never a sign—on, on to the sea.

"Be persuaded, my son."

Dimly the Boy knew he was even now borne along upon a current equally irresistible, this one setting northward, as that other back to the south. He found himself shaking his head under the Jesuit's remonstrant eyes.

"We've lost so much time already. We couldn't possibly turn back—now."

"Then here's my Grammar." With an almost comic change of tone and manner the priest turned to the table where the lamp stood, among piles of neatly tied-up and docketed papers.

He undid one of the packets, with an ear on the sudden sounds outside in the passage.

"Brother Paul's got it in the schoolhouse."

Brother Paul! He hadn't been at the entertainment, and no one seemed to have missed him.

"How did Sister Winifred know?" asked another voice.

"Old Maria told her."

Father Richmond got up and opened the door.

"What is it?"

"It's a new-born Indian baby." The Father looked down as if it might be on the threshold. "Brother Paul found it below at the village all done up ready to be abandoned."

"Tell Sister Winifred I'll see about it in the morning."

"She says—pardon me, Father—she says that is like a man. If I do not bring the little Indian in twenty minutes she will come herself and get it."

Father Richmond laughed.

"Good-night, my son;" and he went downstairs with the others.

*　　　*　　　*　　　*　　　*　　　*　　　*

"Colonel, you asleep?" the Boy asked softly.

"No."

He struggled in silence with his mucklucks. Presently, "Isn't it frightfully strange," he mused aloud. "Doesn't it pull a fella up by the roots, somehow, to see Americans on this old track?"

The Colonel had the bedclothes drawn up to his eyes. Under the white quilt he made some undistinguishable sound, but he kept his eyes fastened on his pardner.

"Everything that we Americans have done, everything that we are, is achieved by the grace of goin' bang the other way." The Boy pulled off a muckluck and threw it half across the room. "And yet, and yet——"

He sat with one stocking-foot in his hand and stared at the candle.

"I wonder, Colonel, if it *satisfies* anybody to be a hustler and a millionaire."

"Satisfies?" echoed the Colonel, pushing his chin over the bed-clothes. "Who expects to be satisfied?"

"Why, every man, woman and child on the top o' the earth; and it just strikes me I've never, personally, known anybody get there but these fellas at Holy Cross."

The Colonel pushed back the bedclothes a little farther with his chin.

"Haven't you got the gumption to see why it is this place and these men take such a hold on you? It's because you've eaten, slept, and lived for half a year in a space the size of this bedroom. We've got so used to narrowing life down, that the first result of a little larger outlook is to make us dizzy. Now, you hurry up and get to bed. You'll sleep it off."

* * * * * * *

The Boy woke at four o'clock, and after the match-light, by which he consulted his watch, had flickered out, he lay a long time staring at the dark.

Silence still reigned supreme, when at last he got up, washed and dressed, and went downstairs. An irresistible restlessness had seized hold of him.

He pulled on his furs, cautiously opened the door, and went out—down, over the crisp new crust, to the river and back in the dimness, past the Fathers' House to the settlement behind, then to the right towards the hillside. As he stumbled up the slope he came to a little burial-ground. Half hidden in the snow, white wooden crosses marked the graves. "And here I shall be buried," she had said—"here." He came down the hill and round by the Sisters' House.

That window! That was where a light had shone the evening they arrived, and a nun—Sister Winifred—had stood drawing the thick curtains, shutting out the world.

He thought, in the intense stillness, that he heard sounds from that upper room. Yes, surely an infant's cry.

A curious, heavy-hearted feeling came upon him, as he turned away, and went slowly back towards the other house.

He halted a moment under the Cross, and stared up at it. The door of the Fathers' House opened, and the Travelling Priest stood on the threshold. The Boy went over to him, nodding good-morning.

"So you are all ready—eager to go from us?"

"No; but, you see——"

"I see."

He held the door open, and the Boy went in.

"I don't believe the Colonel's awake yet," he said, as he took off his furs. "I'll just run up and rouse him."

"It is very early"—the priest laid his hand on the young man's arm—"and he will not sleep so well for many a night to come. It is an hour till breakfast."

Henry had lit the fire, and now left it roaring. The priest took a chair, and pushed one forward for his guest.

The Boy sat down, stretched his legs out straight towards the fire, and lifting his hands, clasped them behind his head. The priest read the homesick face like a book.

"Why are you up here?" Before there was time for reply he added: "Surely a young man like you could find, nearer home, many a gate ajar. And you must have had glimpses through of—things many and fair."

"Oh, yes, I've had glimpses of those things."

"Well——"

"What I wanted most I never saw."

"You wanted——"

"To be—*sure*."

"Ah! it is one of the results of agnosticism."

The Boy never saw the smile.

"I've said—and I was not lying—that I came away to shorten the business of fortune-making—to buy back an old place we love, my sister and I; but——"

"Which does she love best, the old place or the young brother?"

"Oh, she cares about me—no doubt o' that." He smiled the smile of faith.

"Has she . . . an understanding heart?"

"The most I know."

"Then she would be glad to know you had found a home for the spirit. A home for the body, what does it matter?"

In the pause, Father Brachet opened the door, but seemed suddenly to remember some imperative call elsewhere. The Boy jumped up, but the Superior had vanished without even "Good-morning." The Boy sat down again.

"Of course," he went on, with that touch of pedantry so common in American youth, "the difficulty in my case is an intellectual one. I think I appreciate the splendid work you do, and I see as I never saw before——" He stopped.

"You strike your foot against the same stone of stumbling over which the Pharisees fell, when the man whom Jesus healed by the way replied to their questioning: 'Whether He be a sinner or no, I know not. One thing I know, that whereas I was blind, now I see.'"

"I don't deny that the life here has been a revelation to me. I'm not talkin' about creeds (for I don't know much about them, and I don't think it's in me to care much); but so far as the work here is concerned——" He paused.

"We can take little credit for that; it is the outcome of our Order."

The Boy failed to catch the effect of the capital letter.

"Yes, it's just that—the order, the good government! A fella would be a bigot if he couldn't see that the system is as nearly perfect as a human institution can be."

"That has been said before of the Society of Jesus." But he spoke with the wise man's tolerance for the discoveries of the young. Still, it was not to discuss the merits of his Order that he had got up an hour before his time. "I understand, maybe better than yourself, something of the restlessness that drove you here."

"You understand?"

The priest nodded.

"You had the excuse of the old plantation and the sister——"

The Boy sat up suddenly, a little annoyed.

The priest kept on: "But you felt a great longing to make a breach in the high walls that shut you in. You wanted to fare away on some voyage of discovery. Wasn't that it?" He paused now in his turn, but the Boy looked straight before him, saying nothing. The priest leaned forward with a deeper gravity.

"It will be a fortunate expedition, this, my son, *if thou discover thyself*—and in time!" Still the Boy said nothing. The other resumed more lightly: "In America we combine our travels with business. But it is no new idea in the world that a young man should have his Wanderjahr before he finds what he wants, or even finds acquiescence. It did not need Wilhelm Meister to set the feet of youth on that trail; it did not need the Crusades. It's as old as the idea of a Golden Fleece or a Promised Land. It was the first man's first inkling of heaven."

The Boy pricked his ears. Wasn't this heresy?

"The old idea of the strenuous, to leave home and comfort and security, and go out to search for wisdom, or holiness, or happiness—whether it is gold or the San Grael, the instinct of Search is deep planted in the race. It is this that the handful of men who live in what they call 'the world'—it is this they forget. Every hour in the greater world outside, someone, somewhere, is starting out upon this journey. He may go only as far as Germany to study philosophy, or to the nearest mountain-top, and find there the thing he seeks; or he may go to the ends of the earth, and still not find it. He may travel in a Hindu gown or a Mongolian tunic, or he comes, like Father Brachet, out of his vineyards in 'the pleasant land of France,' or, like you, out of a country where all problems are to be solved by machinery. But my point is, *they come!* When all the other armies of the world are disbanded, that army, my son, will be still upon the march."

They were silent awhile, and still the young face gave no sign.

"To many," the Travelling Priest went on, "the impulse is a blind one or a shy one, shrinking from calling itself by the old names. But none the less this instinct for the Quest is still the gallant way of youth, confronted by a sense of the homelessness they cannot think will last."

"That's it, Father! That's it!" the Boy burst out. "Homelessness! To feel that is to feel something urging you——" He stopped, frowning.

"——urging you to take up your staff," said the priest.

They were silent a moment, and then the same musical voice tolled out the words like a low bell: "But with all your journeying, my son, you will come to no Continuing City."

"It's no use to say this to me. You see, I am——"

"I'll tell you why I say it." The priest laid a hand on his arm. "I see men going up and down all their lives upon this Quest. Once in a great while I see one for whom I think the journey may be shortened."

"How shortened?"

A heavy step on the stair, and the Boy seemed to wake from a dream.

"Good-morning," said the Colonel, coming in cheerily, rubbing his hands.

"I am very jealous!" He glanced at the Boy's furs on the floor. "You have been out, seeing the rest of the mission without me."

"No—no, we will show you the rest—as much as you care for, after breakfast."

"I'm afraid we oughtn't to delay——"

But they did—"for a few minutes while zey are putting a little fresh meat on your sled," as Father Brachet said. They went first to see the dogs fed. For they got breakfast when they were at home, those pampered mission dogs.

"And now we will show you our store-house, our caches——"

While Father Brachet looked in the bunch for the key he wanted, a native came by with a pail. He entered the low building on the left, leaving wide the door.

"What? No! Is it really? No, not *really!*" The Colonel was more excited than the Boy had ever seen him. Without the smallest ceremony he left the side of his obliging host, strode to the open door, and disappeared inside.

"What on earth's the matter?"

"I cannot tell. It is but our cow-house."

They followed, and, looking in at the door, the Boy saw a picture that for many a day painted itself on his memory. For inside the dim, straw-strewn place stood the big Kentuckian, with one arm round the cow, talking to her and rubbing her nose, while down his own a tear trickled.

"Hey? Well, yes! Just my view, Sukey. Yes, old girl, Alaska's a funny kind o' place for you and me to be in, isn't it? Hey? Ye-e-yes." And he stroked the cow and sniffed back the salt water, and called out, seeing the Boy, "Look! They've got a thoroughbred bull, too, an' a heifer. Lord, I haven't been in any place so like home for a coon's age! You go and look at the caches. I'll stay here while Sambo milks her."

"My name is Sebastian."

"Oh, all right; reckon you can milk her under that name, too."

When they came back, the Colonel was still there exchanging views about Alaska with Sukey, and with Sebastian about the bull. Sister Winifred came hurrying over the snow to the cow-house with a little tin pail in her hand.

"Ah, but you are slow, Sebastian!" she called out almost petulantly. "Good-morning," she said to the others, and with a quick clutch at a respectful and submissive demeanour, she added, half aside: "What do you think, Father Brachet? They forgot that baby because he is good and sleeps late. They drink up all the milk."

"Ah, there is very little now."

"Very little, Father," said Sebastian, returning to the task from which the Colonel's conversation had diverted him.

"I put aside some last night, and they used it. I send you to bring me only a little drop"—she was by Sebastian now, holding out the small pail, unmindful of the others, who were talking stock—"and you stay, and stay——"

"Give me your can." The Boy took it from her, and held it inside the big milk-pail, so that the thin stream struck it sharply.

"There; it is enough."

Her shawl had fallen. The Colonel gathered it up.

"I will carry the milk back for you," said the Boy, noticing how red and cold the slim hands were. "Your fingers will be frostbitten if you don't wrap them up." She pulled the old shawl closely round her, and set a brisk pace back to the Sisters' House.

"I must go carefully or I might slip, and if I spilt the milk——"

"Oh, you mustn't do that!"

She paused suddenly, and then went on, but more slowly than before. A glaze had formed on the hard-trodden path, and one must needs walk warily. Once she looked back with anxiety, and, seeing that the precious milk was being carried with due caution, her glance went gratefully to the Boy's face. He felt her eyes.

"I'm being careful," he laughed, a little embarrassed and not at first lifting his bent head. When, after an instant, he did so, he found the beautiful calm eyes full upon him. But no self-consciousness there. She turned away, gentle and reflective, and was walking on when some quick summons seemed to reach her. She stopped quite still again, as if seized suddenly by a detaining hand. Her own hands dropped straight at her sides, and the rusty shawl hung free. A second time she turned, the Boy thought to him again; but as he glanced up, wondering, he saw that the fixed yet serene look went past him like a homing-dove. A neglected, slighted feeling came over him. She wasn't thinking of him the least in the world, nor even of the milk he was at such pains to carry for her. What was she staring at? He turned his head over his right shoulder. Nothing. No one. As he came slowly on, he kept glancing at her. She, still with upturned face, stood there in the attitude of an obedient child receiving admonition. One cold little hand fluttered up to her silver cross. Ah! He turned again, under-

233

standing now the drift, if not the inner meaning, of that summons that had come.

"Your friend said something——" She nodded faintly, riverwards, towards the mission sign. "Did you feel like that about it—when you saw it first?"

"Oh—a—I'm not religious like the Colonel."

She smiled, and walked on.

At the door, as she took the milk, instead of "Thank you," "Wait a moment."

She was back again directly.

"You are going far beyond the mission . . . so carry this with you. I hope it will guide you as it guides us."

On his way back to the Fathers' House, he kept looking at what Sister Winifred had given him—a Latin cross of silver scarce three inches long. At the intersection of the arms it bore a chased lozenge on which was a mitre; above it, the word "Alaska," and beneath, the crossed keys of St. Peter and the letters, "P. T. R."

As he came near to where the Colonel and his hosts were, he slipped the cross into his pocket. His fingers encountered Muckluck's medal. Upon some wholly involuntary impulse, he withdrew Sister Winifred's gift, and transferred it to another pocket. But he laughed to himself. "Both sort o' charms, after all." And again he looked at the big cross and the heaven above it, and down at the domain of the Inua, the jealous god of the Yukon.

Twenty minutes later the two travellers were saying goodbye to the men of Holy Cross, and making their surprised and delighted acknowledgments for the brand-new canvas cover they found upon the Colonel's new sled.

"Oh, it is not we," said Father Brachet; "it is made by ze Sisters. Zey shall know zat you were pleased."

Father Richmond held the Boy's hand a moment.

"I see you go, my son, but I shall see you return."

"No, Father, I shall hardly come this way again."

Father Brachet, smiling, watched them start up the long trail.

"I sink we shall meet again," were his last words.

"What does he mean?" asked the Colonel, a little high and mightily. "What plan has he got for a meeting?"

"Same plan as you've got, I s'pose. I believe you both call it 'Heaven.'"

The Holy Cross thermometer had registered twenty degrees

below zero, but the keen wind blowing down the river made it seem more like forty below. When they stopped to lunch, they had to crouch down behind the sled to stand the cold, and the Boy found that his face and ears were badly frost-bitten. The Colonel discovered that the same thing had befallen the toes of his left foot. They rubbed the afflicted members, and tried not to let their thoughts stray backwards. The Jesuits had told them of an inhabited cabin twenty-three miles up the river, and they tried to fix their minds on that. In a desultory way, when the wind allowed it, they spoke of Minóok, and of odds and ends they'd heard about the trail. They spoke of the Big Chimney Cabin, and of how at Anvik they would have their last shave. The one subject neither seemed anxious to mention was Holy Cross. It was a little "marked," the Colonel felt; but he wasn't going to say the first word, since he meant to say the last.

About five o'clock the gale went down, but it came on to snow. At seven the Colonel said decidedly: "We can't make that cabin to-night."

"Why not?"

"Because I'm not going any further, with this foot——" He threw down the sled-rope, and limped after wood for the fire.

The Boy tilted the sled up by an ice-hummock, and spread the new canvas so that it gave some scant shelter from the snow. Luckily, for once, the wind how grown quite lamb-like—for the Yukon. It would be thought a good stiff breeze almost anywhere else.

Directly they had swallowed supper the Colonel remarked: "I feel as ready for my bed as I did Saturday night."

Ah! Saturday night—that was different. They looked at each other with the same thought.

"Well, that bed at Holy Cross isn't any whiter than this," laughed the Boy.

But the Colonel was not to be deceived by this light and airy reference. His own unwilling sentiments were a guide to the Boy's, and he felt it incumbent upon him to restore the Holy Cross incident to its proper proportions. Those last words of Father Brachet's bothered him. Had they been "gettin' at" the Boy?

"You think all that mission business mighty wonderful—just because you run across it in Alaska."

"And isn't it wonderful at all?"

The Boy spoke dreamily, and, from force of old habit, held out his mittened hands to the unavailing fire.

The Colonel gave a prefatory grunt of depreciation, but he was pulling his blankets out from under the stuff on the sled.

The Boy turned his head, and watched him with a little smile. "I'll admit that I always *used* to think the Jesuits were a shady lot——"

"So they are—most of 'em."

"Well, I don't know about 'most of 'em.' You and Mac used to talk a lot about the 'motives' of the few I do know. But as far as I can see, every creature who comes up to this country comes to take something out of it—except those Holy Cross fellas. They came to bring something."

The Colonel had got the blankets out now, but where was the rubber sheet? He wouldn't sleep on it in this weather, again, for a kingdom, but when the thaws came, if those explorer fellas were right——

In his sense of irritation at a conscientious duty to perform and no clear notion of how to discharge it, he made believe it was the difficulty in finding the rubber sheet he didn't want that made him out of sorts.

"It's bitter work, anyhow, this making beds with your fingers stiff and raw," he said.

"Is it?"

Dignity looked at Impudence sitting in the shelter, smiling.

"Humph! Just try it," growled the Colonel.

"I s'pose the man over the fire cookin' supper does *look* better off than the 'pore pardner' cuttin' down trees and makin' beds in the snow. But he isn't."

"Oh, isn't he?" It was all right, but the Big Chimney boss felt he had chosen the lion's share of the work in electing to be woodman; still, it wasn't *that* that troubled him. Now, what was it he had been going to say about the Jesuits? Something very telling.

"If you mean that you'd rather go back to the cookin'," the Boy was saying, "*I'm* agreeable."

"Well, you start in to-morrow, and see if you're so agreeable."

"All right. I think I dote on one job just about as much as I do on t'other."

But still the Colonel frowned. He couldn't remember that

excellent thing he had been going to say about Romanists. But he sniffed derisively, and flung over his shoulder:

"To hear you goin' on, anybody'd think the Jesuits were the only Christians. As if there weren't others, who——"

"Oh, yes, Christians with gold shovels and Winchester rifles. I know 'em. But if gold hadn't been found, how many of the army that's invaded the North—how many would be here, if it hadn't been for the gold? But all this Holy Cross business would be goin' on just the same, as it has done for years and years."

With a mighty tug the Colonel dragged out the rubber blanket, flung it down on the snow, and squared himself, back to the fire, to make short work of such views.

"I'd no notion you were such a sucker. You can bet," he said darkly, "those fellas aren't making a bad thing out of that 'Holy Cross business,' as you call it."

"I didn't mean business in that sense."

"What else could they do if they didn't do this?"

"Ask the same of any parson."

But the Colonel didn't care to.

"I suppose," he said severely, "you could even make a hero out of that hang-dog Brother Etienne."

"No, but he *could* do something else, for he's served in the French army."

"Then there's that mad Brother Paul. What good would he be at anything else?"

"Well, I don't know."

"Brachet and Wills are decent enough men, but where else would they have the power and the freedom they have at Holy Cross? Why, they live there like feudal barons."

"Father Richmond could have done anything he chose."

"Ah, Father Richmond——" The Colonel shut his mouth suddenly, turned about, and proceeded to crawl under his blankets, feet to the fire.

"Well?"

No answer.

"Well?" insisted the Boy.

"Oh, Father Richmond must have seen a ghost."

"*What!*"

"Take my word for it. *He* got frightened somehow. A man like Father Richmond has to be scared into a cassock."

The Boy's sudden laughter deepened the Colonel's own impression that the instance chosen had not been fortunate. One man of courage knows another man of courage when he sees him, and the Colonel knew he had damned his own argument.

"Wouldn't care for the job myself," the Boy was saying.

"What job?"

"Scarin' Father Richmond."

The Boy sat watching the slow wet snow-flakes fall and die in the fire. His clothes were pretty damp, but he was warm after a chilly fashion, as warmth goes on the trail.

The Colonel suddenly put his head out from under the marmot-skin to say discontentedly, "What you sittin' up for?"

"Oh . . . for instance!" But aside from the pertness of the answer, already it was dimly recognised as an offence for one to stay up longer than the other.

"Can't think how it is," the Colonel growled, "that you don't see that their principle is wrong. Through and through mediæval, through and through despotic. They make a virtue of weakness, a fetich of vested authority. And it isn't American authority, either."

The Boy waited for him to quiet down. "What's the first rule," demanded the Colonel, half sitting up, "of the most powerful Catholic Order? Blind obedience to an old gentleman over in Italy."

"I said last night, you know," the Boy put in quite meekly, "that it all seemed very un-American."

"Huh! Glad you can see that much." The Colonel drove his huge fist at the provision-bag, as though to beat the stiff-necked beans into a feathery yielding. "Blind submission don't come easy to most Americans. The Great Republic was built upon revolt;" and he pulled the covers over his head.

"I know, I know. We jaw an awful lot about freedom and about what's American. There's plenty o' free speech in America and plenty o' machinery, but there's a great deal o' human nature, too, I guess." The Boy looked out of the corner of his eye at the blanketed back of his big friend. "And maybe there'll always be some people who—who think there's something in the New Testament notion o' sacrifice and service."

The Colonel rolled like an angry leviathan, and came to the surface to blow. But the Boy dashed on, with a fearful joy in his own temerity. "The difference between us, Colonel, is that I'm an unbeliever, and I know it, and you're a cantankerous old heathen, and you *don't* know it." The Colonel sat suddenly bolt upright. "Needn't look at me like that. You're as bad as anybody—rather worse. Why are you *here?* Dazzled and lured by the great gold craze. An' you're not even poor. You want *more* gold. You've got a home to stay in; but you weren't satisfied, not even in the fat lands down below."

"Well," said the Colonel solemnly, blinking at the fire, "I hope I'm a Christian, but as to bein' satisfied——"

"Church of England can't manage it, hey?"

"Church of England's got nothing to do with it. It's a question o' character. Satisfied! We're little enough, God knows, but we're too big for that."

The Boy stood up, back to the fire, eyes on the hilltops whitening in the starlight.

"Perhaps—not—all of us."

"Yes, sah, all of us." The Colonel lifted his head with a fierce look of most un-Christian pride. Behind him the hills, leaving the struggling little wood far down the slope, went up and up into dimness, reaching to the near-by stars, and looking down to the far-off camp fire by the great ice-river's edge.

"Yes, sah," the Colonel thundered again, "all that have got good fightin' blood in 'em, like you and me. 'Tisn't as if we came of any worn-out, frightened, servile old stock. You and I belong to the free-livin', hard-ridin', straight-shootin' Southerners. The people before us fought bears, and fought Indians, and beat the British, and when there wasn't anything else left to beat, turned round and began to beat one another. It was the one battle we found didn't pay. We finished that job up in '65, and since then we've been lookin' round for something else to beat. We've got down now to beatin' records, and foreign markets, and breedin' prize bulls; but we don't breed cowards—yet; and we ain't lookin' round for any asylums. The Catholic Church is an asylum. It's for people who never had any nerve, or who have lost it."

The Colonel turned about, wagged his head defiantly at the icy hills and the night, and in the after-stillness fell sound asleep in the snow.

CHAPTER XII

THE GREAT WHITE SILENCE

"——paa dit Firmament
Den klare Nordlyslampe tændt. . . ."

INNOCENTLY thinking that they had seen Arctic travelling at its worst, and secretly looking upon themselves as highly accomplished trailmen, they had covered the forty-one miles from Holy Cross to Anvik in less than three days.

The Colonel made much of the pleasant and excellent man at the head of the Episcopal mission there, and the Boy haunted Benham's store, picking up a little Ingalik and the A. C. method of trading with the Indians, who, day and night, with a number of stranded Klondykers, congregated about the grateful warmth of the big iron stove.

The travellers themselves did some business with the A. C. agent, laying in supplies of fresh meat, and even augmenting their hitherto carefully restricted outfit, for they were going far beyond the reach of stores, or even of missions. Anvik was the last white settlement below Nulato; Nulato was said to be over two hundred miles to the northward.

And yet after all their further preparation and expense, each man kept saying in his heart, during those first days out from Anvik, that the journey would be easy enough but for their "comforts"—the burden on the sled. By all the rules of arithmetic, the daily subtraction of three meals from the store should have lightened the load. It seemed to have the opposite effect. By some process of evil enchantment every ounce grew to weigh a pound, every pound a hundredweight. The sled itself was bewitched. Recall how lightsomely it ran down the snowy slope, from the Big Chimney Cabin to the river trail, that morning they set forth. The Boy took its pretty impetuosity for a happy augury—the very sled was eager for the mighty undertaking.

But never in all that weary march did it manifest again any

such modest alacrity. If, thereafter, in the long going "up river" there came an interval of downhill, the sled turned summersaults in the air, wound its forward or backward rope round willow scrub or alder, or else advanced precipitately with an evil, low-comedy air, bottom side up, to attack its master in the shins. It either held back with a power superhuman, or it lunged forward with a momentum that capsized its weary conductor. Its manners grew steadily worse as the travellers pushed farther and farther into the wilderness, beyond the exorcising power of Holy Cross, beyond the softening influences of Christian hospitality at Episcopal Anvik, even beyond Tischsocket, the last of the Indian villages for a hundred miles.

The two who had been scornful of the frailty of temper they had seen common in men's dealings up here in the North, began to realize that all other trials of brotherhood pale before the strain of life on the Arctic trail. Beyond any question, after a while something goes wrong with the nerves. The huge drafts on muscular endurance have, no doubt, something to do with it. They worked hard for fourteen, sometimes seventeen, hours at a stretch; they were ill-fed, suffering from exposure, intense cold, and a haunting uncertainty of the end of the undertaking. They were reasonable fellows as men go, with a respect for each other, but when hardship has got on the nerves, when you are suffering the agonies of snow-blindness, sore feet, and the pangs of hunger, you are not, to put it mildly, at your best as a member of the social order. They sometimes said things they were ashamed to remember, but both men grew carefuller at crucial moments, and the talkative one more silent as time went on.

By the rule of the day the hard shift before dinner usually fell to the Boy. It was the worst time in the twenty-four hours, and equally dreaded by both men. It was only the first night out from Anvik, after an unusually trying day, the Boy was tramping heavily ahead, bent like an old man before the cutting sleet, fettered like a criminal, hands behind back, rope-wound, stiff, straining at the burden of the slow and sullen sled. On a sudden he stopped, straightened his back, and remonstrated with the Colonel in unprintable terms, for putting off the halt later than ever they had yet, "after such a day."

"Can't make fire with green cotton-wood," was the Colonel's rejoiner.

"Then let's stop and rest, anyhow."

"Nuh! We know where that would land us. Men who stop to rest, go to sleep in the snow, and men who go to sleep in the snow on empty stomachs don't wake up."

They pushed on another mile. When the Colonel at last called the halt, the Boy sank down on the sled too exhausted to speak. But it had grown to be a practice with them not to trust themselves to talk at this hour. The Colonel would give the signal to stop, simply by ceasing to push the sled that the boy was wearily dragging. The Boy had invariably been feeling (just as the Colonel had before, during his shift in front) that the man behind wasn't helping all he might, whereupon followed a vague, consciously unreasonable, but wholly irresistible rage against the partner of his toil. But however much the man at the back was supposed to spare himself, the man in front had never yet failed to know when the impetus from behind was really removed.

The Boy sat now on the sled, silent, motionless, while the Colonel felled and chopped and brought the wood. Then the Boy dragged himself up, made the fire and the beef-tea. But still no word even after that reviving cup—the usual signal for a few remarks and more social relations to be established. To-night no sound out of either. The Colonel changed his foot-gear and the melted snow in the pot began to boil noisily. But the Boy, who had again betaken himself to the sled, didn't budge. No man who really knows the trail would have dared, under the circumstances, to remind his pardner that it was now his business to get up and fry the bacon. But presently, without looking up, the hungry Colonel ventured:

"Get your dry things!"

"Feet aren't wet."

"Don't talk foolishness; here are your things." The Colonel flung in the Boy's direction the usual change, two pairs of heavy socks, the "German knitted" and "the felt."

"Not wet," repeated the Boy.

"You know you are."

"Could go through water in these mucklucks."

"I'm not saying the wet has come in from outside; but you know as well as I do a man sweats like a horse on the trail."

Still the Boy sat there, with his head sunk between his shoulders.

"First rule o' this country is to keep your feet dry, or else pneumonia, rheumatism—God knows what!"

"First rule o' this country is mind your own business, or else —God knows what!"

The Colonel looked at the Boy a moment, and then turned his back. The Boy glanced up conscience-stricken, but still only half alive, dulled by the weight of a crushing weariness. The Colonel presently bent over the fire and was about to lift off the turbulently boiling pot. The Boy sprang to his feet, ready to shout, "You do your work, and keep your hands off mine," but the Colonel turned just in time to say with unusual gentleness:

"If you *like*, I'll make supper to-night;" and the Boy, catching his breath, ran forward, swaying a little, half blind, but with a different look in his tired eyes.

"No, no, old man. It isn't as bad as that."

And again it was two friends who slept side by side in the snow.

The next morning the Colonel, who had been kept awake half the night by what he had been thinking was neuralgia in his eyes, woke late, hearing the Boy calling:

"I say, Kentucky, aren't you *ever* goin' to get up?"

"Get up?" said the Colonel. "Why should I, when it's pitch-dark?"

"*What?*"

"Fire clean out, eh?" But he smelt the tea and bacon, and sat up bewildered, with a hand over his smarting eyes. The Boy went over and knelt down by him, looking at him curiously.

"Guess you're a little snow-blind, Colonel; but it won't last, you know."

"Blind!"

"No, no, only *snow*-blind. Big difference;" and he took out his rag of a handkerchief, got some water in a tin cup, and the eyes were bathed and bandaged.

"It won't last, you know. You'll just have to take it easy for a few days."

The Colonel groaned.

For the first time he seemed to lose heart. He sat during breakfast with bandaged eyes, and a droop of the shoulders, that seemed to say old age had come upon him in a single night. The day that followed was pretty dark to both men. The Boy had to do all the work, except the monotonous, blind, pushing from behind, in whatever direction the Boy dragged the sled.

Now, snow-blindness is not usually dangerous, but it is horribly painful while it lasts. Your eyes swell up and are stabbed continually by cutting pains; your head seems full of acute neuralgia, and often there is fever and other complications. The Colonel's was a bad case. But he was a giant for strength and "sound as a dollar," as the Boy reminded him, "except for this little bother with your eyes, and you're a whole heap better already."

At a very slow rate they plodded along.

They had got into a region where there was no timber; but, as they couldn't camp without a fire, they took an extra rest that day at four o'clock, and regaled themselves on some cold grub. Then they took up the line of march again. But they had been going only about half an hour when the Colonel suddenly, without warning, stopped pushing the sled, and stood stock-still on the trail. The Boy, feeling the removal of the pressure, looked round, went back to him, and found nothing in particular was the matter, but he just thought he wouldn't go any further.

"We can camp here."

"No, we can't," says the Boy; "there isn't a tree in sight."

But the Colonel seemed dazed. He thought he'd stop anyhow—"right where he was."

"Oh, no," says the Boy, a little frightened; "we'll camp the minute we come to wood." But the Colonel stood as if rooted. The Boy took his arm and led him on a few paces to the sled. "You needn't push hard, you know. Just keep your hand there so, without looking, you'll know where I'm going." This was very subtle of the Boy. For he knew the Colonel was blind as a bat and as sensitive as a woman. "We'll get through all right yet," he called back, as he stooped to take up the sled-rope. "I bet on Kentucky."

Like a man walking in his sleep, the Colonel followed, now holding on to the sled and unconsciously pulling a little, and when the Boy, very nearly on his last legs, remonstrated, leaning against it, and so urging it a little forward.

Oh, but the wood was far to seek that night!

Concentrated on the two main things—to carry forward his almost intolerable load, and to go the shortest way to the nearest wood—the Boy, by-and-by, forgot to tell his tired nerves to take account of the unequal pressure from behind. If he felt it—well, the Colonel was a corker; if he didn't feel it—well, the Colonel was just about tuckered out. It was very late when at last the Boy raised a shout. Behind the cliff overhanging the river-bed that they were just rounding, there, spread out in the sparkling starlight, as far as he could see, a vast primeval forest. The Boy bettered his lagging pace.

"Ha! you haven't seen a wood like this since we left 'Frisco. It's all right now, Kentucky;" and he bent to his work with a will.

When he got to the edge of the wood, he flung down the rope and turned—to find himself alone.

"Colonel! Colonel! Where are you? *Colonel!*"

He stood in the silence, shivering with a sudden sense of desolation. He took his bearings, propped a fallen fir sapling aslant by the sled, and, forgetting he was ready to drop, he ran swiftly back along the way he came. They had travelled all that afternoon and evening on the river ice, hard as iron, retaining no trace of footprint or of runner possible to verify even in daylight. The Yukon here was fully three miles wide. They had meant to hug the right bank, but snow and ice refashion the world and laugh at the trustful geography of men. A traveller on this trail is not always sure whether he is following the mighty Yukon or some slough equally mighty for a few miles, or whether, in the protracted twilight, he has not wandered off upon some frozen swamp.

On the Boy went in the ghostly starlight, running, stumbling, calling at regular intervals, his voice falling into a melancholy monotony that sounded foreign to himself. It occurred to him that were he the Colonel he wouldn't recognise it, and he began instead to call "Kentucky! Ken-tuck-kee!" sounding those fine barbaric syllables for the first time, most like, in that world of ice and silence.

He stood an instant after his voice died, and listened to the quiet. Yes, the people were right who said nothing was so hard to bear in this country of hardship—nothing ends by being so ghastly—as the silence. No bird stirs. The swift-flashing fish are sealed under ice, the wood creatures gone to their underground sleep. No whispering of the pointed firs, stiff, snow-clotted; no swaying of the scant herbage sheathed in ice or muffled under winter's wide white blanket. No greater hush can reign in the interstellar spaces than in winter on the Yukon.

"Colonel!"

Silence—like a negation of all puny things, friendship, human life——

"Colonel!"

Silence. No wonder men went mad up here, when they didn't drown this silence in strong drink.

On and on he ran, till he felt sure he must have passed the Colonel, unless—yes, there were those air-holes in the river ice . . . He felt choked and stopped to breathe. Should he go back? It was horrible to turn. It was like admitting that the man was not to be found—that this was the end.

"Colonel!"

He said to himself that he would go back, and build a fire for a signal, and return; but he ran on farther and farther away from the sled and from the forest. Was it growing faintly light? He looked up. Oh, yes; presently it would be brighter still. Those streamers of pale light dancing in the North; they would be green and scarlet and orange and purple, and the terrible white world would be illuminated as by conflagration. He stopped again. That the Colonel should have dropped so far back as this, and the man in front not know—it was incredible. What was that? A shadow on the ice. A frozen hummock? No, a man. Was it really . . . ? Glory hallelujah —it *was!* But the shadow lay there ghastly still and the Boy's greeting died in his throat. He had found the Colonel, but he had found him delivered over to that treacherous sleep that seldom knows a waking. The Boy dropped down beside his friend, and wasn't far off crying. But it was a tonic to young nerves to see how, like one dead, the man lay there, for all the calling and tugging by the arm. The Boy rolled the body over, pulled open the things at the neck, and thrust his hand down, till he could feel the heart beating. He jumped up, got a handful of snow, and rubbed the man's face with it. At last a feeble protest—an effort to get away from the Boy's rude succour.

"Thank God! Colonel! Colonel! wake up!"

He shook him hard. But the big man only growled sullenly, and let his leaden weight drop back heavily on the ice. The Boy got hold of the neck of the Colonel's parki and pulled him frantically along the ice a few yards, and then realised that only the terror of the moment gave him the strength to do that much. To drag a man of the Colonel's weight all the way to the wood was stark impossibility. He couldn't get him eighty yards. If he left him and went for the sled and fuel, the man would be dead by the time he got back. If he stayed, they would both be frozen in a few hours. It was pretty horrible.

He felt faint and dizzy. It occurred to him that he would pray. He was an agnostic all right, but the Colonel was past praying for himself; and here was his friend—an agnostic—here he was on his knees. He hadn't prayed since he was a little chap down in the South. How did the prayers go? "Our Father"—he looked up at the reddening aurora—"Our Father, who art in heaven——" His eyes fell again on his friend. He leapt to his feet like a wild animal, and began to go at the Colonel with his fists. The blows rained thick on the chest of the prostrate man, but he was too well protected to feel more than the shock. But now they came battering down, under the ear—right, left, as the man turned blindly to avoid them—on the jaw, even on the suffering eyes, and that at last stung the sleeper into something like consciousness.

He struggled to his feet with a roar like a wounded bull, lunging heavily forward as the Boy eluded him, and he would have pounded the young fellow out of existence in no time had he stood his ground. That was exactly what the Boy didn't mean to do—he was always just a little way on in front; but as the Colonel's half-insane rage cooled, and he slowed down a bit, the Boy was at him again like some imp of Satan. Sound and lithe and quick-handed as he was, he was no match for the Colonel at his best. But the Colonel couldn't see well, and his brain was on fire. He'd kill that young devil, and then he'd lie down and sleep again.

Meanwhile Aurora mounted the high heavens; from a great corona in the zenith all the sky was hung with banners, and the snow was stained as if with blood. The Boy looked over his shoulder, and saw the huge figure of his friend, bearing down upon him, with his discoloured face rage-distorted, and murder in his tortured eyes. A moment's sense of the monstrous spectacle fell so poignant upon the Boy, that he felt dimly he must have been full half his life running this race with death, followed by a maniac bent on murder, in a world whose winter was strangely lit with the leaping fires of hell.

At last, on there in front, the cliff! Below it, the sharp bend in the river, and although he couldn't see it yet, behind the cliff the forest, and a little hand-sled bearing the means of life.

The Colonel was down again, but it wasn't safe to go near him just yet. The Boy ran on, unpacked the sled, and went, axe in hand, along the margin of the wood. Never before was a fire made so quickly. Then, with the flask, back to the Colonel, almost as sound asleep as before.

The Boy never could recall much about the hours that followed. There was nobody to help, so it must have been he who somehow got the Colonel to the fire, got him to swallow some food, plastered his wounded face over with the carbolic ointment, and got him into bed, for in the morning all this was seen to have been done.

They stayed in camp that day to "rest up," and the Boy shot a rabbit. The Colonel was coming round; the rest, or the ointment, or the tea-leaf poultice, had been good for snow-blindness. The generous reserve of strength in his magnificent physique was quick to announce itself. He was still "frightfully bunged up," but "I think we'll push on to-morrow," he said that night, as he sat by the fire smoking before turning in.

"Right you are!" said the Boy, who was mending the sled-runner. Neither had referred to that encounter on the river-ice, that had ended in bringing the Colonel where there was succour. Nothing was said, then or for long after, in the way of deliberate recognition that the Boy had saved his life. It wasn't necessary; they understood each other.

But in the evening, after the Boy had finished mending the sled, it occurred to him he must also mend the Colonel before they went to bed. He got out the box of ointment and bespread the strips of torn handkerchief.

"Don't know as I need that to-night," says the Colonel. "Musn't waste ointment."

But the Boy brought the bandages round to the Colonel's side of the fire. For an instant they looked at each other by the flickering light, and the Colonel laid his hand on the Boy's arm. His eyes looked worse for the moment, and began to water. He turned away brusquely, and knocked the ashes out of his pipe on a log.

"What in hell made you think of it?"

"Ask me an easy one," says the Boy. "But I know what the Jesuit Fathers would say."

"Jesuits and George Warren! Humph! precious little we'd agree about."

"You would about this. It flashed over me when I looked back and saw you peltin' after me."

"Small wonder I made for you! I'm not findin' fault, but

248

what on earth put it into your head to go at me with your fists like that?"

"You'll never prove it by me. But when I saw you comin' at me like a mad bull, I thought to myself, thinks I, the Colonel and the Jesuits, they'd both of 'em say this was a direct answer to prayer."

CHAPTER XIII

THE PIT

"L'humanité a commencé tout entière par le crime. . . . C'était le vieux nourricier des hommes des cavernes."—ANATOLE FRANCE.

AN old story now, these days of silent plodding through the driving snow.

But if outward conditions lacked variety, not so their cumulative effect upon poor human nature. A change was going on in the travellers that will little commend them to the sentimentalist.

"I've come to think a snow-storm's all right to travel in, all right to sleep in," said the Colonel one morning; "but to cook in, eat in, make or break camp in—it's the devil's champion invention." For three days they had worked like galley-slaves, and yet covered less than ten miles a day. "And you never get rested," the Colonel went on; "I get up as tired as I go to bed."

Again the Boy only nodded. His body, if not his temper, had got broken into the trail, but for a talkative person he had in these days strangely little to say. It became manifest that, in the long run, the Colonel would suffer the most physically; but his young companion, having less patience and more ambition, more sheer untamed vitality in him, would suffer the most in spirit. Every sense in him was becoming numbed, save the gnawing in his stomach, and that other, even more acute ache, queer compound of fatigue and anger. These two sensations swallowed up all else, and seemed to grow by what they fed on.

The loaded sled was a nightmare. It weighed a thousand tons. The very first afternoon out from Anvik, when in the desperate hauling and tugging that rescued it from a bottomless snow-drift, the lashing slipped, the load loosened, tumbled off, and rolled open, the Colonel stood quite still and swore till his half-frozen blood circulated freely again. When it came to repacking, he considered in detail the items that made up the intolerable weight, and fell to wondering which of them they could do without.

250

The second day out from Anvik they had decided that it was absurd, after all, to lug about so much tinware. They left a little saucepan and the extra kettle at that camp. The idea, so potent at Anvik, of having a tea-kettle in reserve— well, the notion lost weight, and the kettle seemed to gain.

Two pairs of boots and some flannels marked the next stopping-place.

On the following day, when the Boy's rifle kept slipping and making a brake to hold back the sled, "I reckon you'll have to plant that rifle o' yours in the next big drift," said the Colonel; "one's all we need, anyway."

"One's all you need, and one's all I need," answered the Boy stiffly.

But it wasn't easy to see immediate need for either. Never was country so bare of game, they thought, not considering how little they hunted, and how more and more every faculty, every sense, was absorbed in the bare going forward.

The next time the Colonel said something about the uselessness of carrying two guns, the Boy flared up: "If you object to guns, leave yours."

This was a new tone for the Boy to use to the Colonel.

"Don't you think we'd better hold on to the best one?"

Now the Boy couldn't deny that the Colonel's was the better, but none the less he had a great affection for his own old 44 Marlin, and the Colonel shouldn't assume that he had the right to dictate. This attitude of the "wise elder" seemed out of place on the trail.

"A gun's a necessity. I haven't brought along any whim-whams."

"Who has?"

"Well, it wasn't me that went loadin' up at Anvik with fool thermometers and things."

"Thermometer! Why, it doesn't weigh——"

"Weighs something, and it's something to pack; frozen half the time, too. And when it isn't, what's the good of havin' it hammered into us how near we are to freezin' to death." But it annoyed him to think how very little in argument a thermometer weighed against a rifle.

They said no more that day about lightening the load, but with a double motive they made enormous inroads upon their provisions.

A morning came when the Colonel, packing hurriedly in the

biting cold, forgot to shove his pardner's gun into its accustomed place.

The Boy, returning from trail-breaking to the river, kicked at the butt to draw attention to the omission. The Colonel flung down the end of the ice-coated rope he had lashed the load with, and, "Pack it yourself," says he.

The Boy let the rifle lie. But all day long he felt the loss of it heavy on his heart, and no reconciling lightness in the sled.

The Colonel began to have qualms about the double rations they were using. It was only the seventeenth night after turning their backs on the Big Chimney, as the Colonel tipped the pan, pouring out half the boiled beans into his pardner's plate, "That's the last o' the strawberries! Don't go expectin' any more," says he.

"What!" ejaculated the Boy, aghast; then quickly, to keep a good face: "You take my life when you do take the beans, whereby I live."

When the Colonel had disposed of his strawberries, "Lord!" he sighed, trying to rub the stiffness out of his hands over the smoke, "the appetite a fella can raise up here is something terrible. You eat and eat, and it doesn't seem to make any impression. You're just as hungry as ever."

"And the stuff a fella can eat!"

The Colonel recalled that speech of the Boy's the very next night, when, after "a hell of a time" getting the fire alight, he was bending forward in that attitude most trying to maintain, holding the frying-pan at long range over the feebly-smoking sticks. He had to cook, to live on snow-shoes nowadays, for the heavy Colonel had illustrated oftener than the Boy, that going without meant breaking in, floundering, and, finally, having to call for your pardner to haul you out. This was one of the many uses of a pardner on the trail. The last time the Colonel had trusted to the treacherous crust he had gone in head foremost, and the Boy, happening to look round, saw only two snow-shoes, bottom side up, moving spasmodically on the surface of the drift. The Colonel was nearly suffocated by the time he was pulled out, and after that object-lesson he stuck to snow-shoes every hour of the twenty-four, except those spent in the sleeping-bag.

But few things on earth are more exasperating than trying to work mounted on clumsy, long web-feet that keep jarring against, yet holding you off from, the tree you are felling, or the fire you are cooking over. You are constrained to stand wholly out of natural relation to the thing you are trying to do—the thing you've got to do, if you mean to come out alive.

The Colonel had been through all this time and time again, But as he squatted on his heels to-night, cursing the foot and a half of snow-shoe that held him away from the sullen fire, straining every muscle to keep the outstretched frying-pan over the best of the blaze, he said to himself that what had got him on the raw was that speech of the Boy's yesterday about the stuff he had to eat. If the Boy objected to having his rice par-boiled in smoked water he was damned unreasonable, that was all.

The culprit reappeared at the edge of the darkening wood. He came up eagerly, and flung down an armful of fuel for the morning, hoping to find supper ready. Since it wasn't, he knew that he mustn't stand about and watch the preparations. By this time he had learned a good deal of the trail-man's unwritten law. On no account must you hint that the cook is incompetent, or even slow, any more than he may find fault with your moment for calling halt, or with your choice of timber. So the woodman turned wearily away from the sole spot of brightness in the waste, and went back up the hill in the dark and the cold, to busy himself about his own work, even to spin it out, if necessary, till he should hear the gruff "Grub's ready!" And when that dinner-gong sounds, don't you dally! Don't you wait a second. You may feel uncomfortable if you find yourself twenty minutes late for a dinner in London or New York, but to be five minutes late for dinner on the Winter Trail is to lay up lasting trouble.

By the time the rice and bacon were done, and the flap-jack, still raw in the middle, was burnt to charcoal on both sides, the Colonel's eyes were smarting, in the acrid smoke, and the tears were running down his cheeks.

"Grub's ready!"

The Boy came up and dropped on his heels in the usual attitude. The Colonel tore a piece off the half-charred, half-raw pancake.

"Maybe you'll think the fire isn't thoroughly distributed, but *that's* got to do for bread," he remarked severely, as if in reply to some objection.

The Boy saw that something he had said or looked had been misinterpreted.

"Hey? Too much fire outside, and not enough in? Well, sir, I'll trust *my* stomach to strike a balance. Guess the heat'll get distributed all right once I've swallowed it."

When the Colonel, mollified, said something about cinders in the rice, the Boy, with his mouth full of grit, answered: "I'm pretendin' it's sugar."

Not since the episode of the abandoned rifle had he shown himself so genial.

"Never in all my bohn life," says the Colonel after eating steadily for some time—"never in a year, sah, have I thought as much about food as I do in a day on this —— trail."

"Same here."

"And it's quantity, not quality."

"Ditto."

The Boy turned his head sharply away from the fire. "Hear that?"

No need to ask. The Colonel had risen upright on his cramped legs, red eyes starting out of his head. The Boy got up, turned about in the direction of the hollow sound, and made one step away from the fire.

"You stay right where you are!" ordered the Colonel, quite in the old way.

"Hey?"

"That's a bird-song."

"Thought so."

"Mr. Wolf smelt the cookin'; want's the rest of the pack to know there's something queer up here on the hill." Then, as the Boy moved to one side in the dark: "What you lookin' for?"

"My gun."

"Mine's here."

Oh yes! His own old 44 Marlin was lying far down the river under eight-and-fifty hours of snow. It angered him newly and more than ever to remember that if he had a shot at anything now it must needs be by favour of the Colonel.

They listened for that sound again, the first since leaving Anvik not made by themselves.

"Seems a lot quieter than it did," observed the Colonel by-and-bye.

The Boy nodded.

Without preface the Colonel observed:

"It's five days since I washed my face and hands."

"What's the good o' rememberin'?" returned the Boy sharply. Then more mildly: "People talk about the bare necessaries o' life. Well, sir, when they're really bare you find there ain't but three—food, warmth, sleep."

Again in the distance that hollow baying.

"Food, warmth, sleep," repeated the Colonel. "We've about got down to the wolf basis.

He said it half in defiance of the trail's fierce lessoning; but it was truer than he knew.

They built up the fire to frighten off the wolves, but the Colonel had his rifle along when they went over and crawled into their sleeping-bag. Half in, half out, he laid the gun carefully along the right on his snow-shoes. As the Boy buttoned the fur-lined flap down over their heads he felt angrier with the Colonel than he had ever been before.

"Took good care to hang on to his own shootin'-iron. Suppose anything should happen"; and he said it over and over.

Exactly what could happen he did not make clear; the real danger was not from wolves, but it was *something*. And he would need a rifle. . . . And he wouldn't have one. . . . And it was the Colonel's fault.

*   *   *   *   *   *   *

Now, it had long been understood that the woodman is lord of the wood. When it came to the Colonel's giving unasked advice about the lumber business, the Boy turned a deaf ear, and thought well of himself for not openly resenting the interference.

"The Colonel talks an awful lot, anyway. He has more hot air to offer than muscle."

When they sighted timber that commended itself to the woodman, if *he* thought well of it, why, he just dropped the sled-rope without a word, pulled the axe out of the lashing, trudged up the hillside, holding the axe against his shirt underneath his parki, till he reached whatever tree his eye had marked for his own. Off with the fur mitt, and bare hand protected by the inner mitt of wool, he would feel the axe-head, for there was always the danger of using it so cold that the steel would chip and fly. As soon as he could be sure the proper molecular change had been effected, he would take up his awkward attitude before the selected spruce, leaning far forward on his snow-shoes, and seeming to deliver the blows on tip-toe.

But the real trouble came when, after felling the dead tree, splitting an armful of fuel and carrying it to the Colonel, he returned to the task of cutting down the tough green spruce for their bedding. Many strained blows must be delivered before he could effect the chopping of even a little notch. Then he would shift his position and cut a corresponding notch further round, so making painful circuit of the bole. To-night, what with being held off by his snow-shoes, what with utter weariness and a dulled axe, he growled to himself that he was "only gnawin' a ring round the tree like a beaver!"

"Damn the whole—— Wait!" Perhaps the cursed snow was packed enough now to bear. He slipped off the web-feet, and standing gingerly, but blessedly near, made effectual attack. Hooray! One more good 'un and the thing was down. Hah! ugh! Woof-ff! The tree was down, but so was he, floundering breast high, and at every effort to get out only breaking down more of the crust and sinking deeper.

This was not the first time such a thing had happened. Why did he feel as if it was for him the end of the world? He lay still an instant. It would be happiness just to rest here and go to sleep. The Colonel! Oh, well, the Colonel had taken his rifle. Funny there should be orange-trees up here. He could smell them. He shut his eyes. Something shone red and glowing. Why, that was the sun making an effect of stained glass as it shone through the fat pine weather-boarding of his little bedroom on the old place down in Florida. Suddenly a face. *Ah, that face!* He must be up and doing. He knew perfectly well how to get out of this damn hole. You lie on your side and roll. Gradually you pack the softness tight till it bears—not if you stand up on your feet, but bears the length of your body, while you worm your way obliquely to the top, and feel gingerly in the dimness after your snow-shoes.

But if it happens on a pitch-dark night, and your pardner has chosen camp out of earshot, you feel that you have looked close at the end of the Long Trail.

On getting back to the fire, he found the Colonel annoyed at having called "Grub!" three times—"yes, sah! three times, sah!"

And they ate in silence.

"Now I'm going to bed," said the Boy, rising stiffly.

"You just wait a minute."

"No."

Now, the Colonel himself had enunciated the law that whenever one of them was ready to sleep the other must come too. He didn't know it, but it is one of the iron rules of the Winter Trail. In absence of its enforcement, the later comer brings into the warmed up sleeping-bag not only the chill of his own body, he lets in the bitter wind, and brings along whatever snow and ice is clinging to his boots and clothes. The melting and warming-up is all to be done again.

But the Colonel was angry.

"Most unreasonable," he muttered—"damned unreasonable!"

Worse than the ice and the wet in the sleeping-bag, was this lying in such close proximity to a young jackanapes who wouldn't come when you called "Grub!" and wouldn't wait a second till you'd felt about in the dimness for your gun. Hideous to lie so close to a man who snored, and who'd deprived you of your 44 Marlin. Although it meant life, the Boy grudged the mere animal heat that he gave and that he took. Full of grudging, he dropped asleep. But the waking spirit followed him into his dreams. An ugly picture painted itself upon the dark, and struggling against the vision, he half awoke. With the first returning consciousness came the oppression of the yoke, the impulse to match the mental alienation with that of the body—strong need to move away.

You can't move away in a sleeping-bag.

In a city you may be alone, free.

On the trail, you walk in bonds with your yoke-fellow, make your bed with him, with him rise up, and with him face the lash the livelong day.

* * * * * * *

"Well," sighed the Colonel, after toiling onward for a couple of hours the next morning, "this is the worst yet."

But by the middle of the afternoon, "What did I say? Why, this morning—*everything* up till now has been child's play." He kept looking at the Boy to see if he could read any sign of halt in the tense, scarred face.

Certainly the wind was worse, the going was worse. The sled kept breaking through and sinking to the level of the load. There it went! in again. They tugged and hauled, and only dragged the lashing loose, while the sled seemed soldered to the hard-packed middle of the drift. As they reloaded, the thermometer came to light. The Colonel threw it out, with never a word. They had no clothes now but what they stood in, and only one thing on the sled they could have lived without —their money, a packet of trading stores. But they had thrown away more than they knew. Day by day, not flannels and boots alone, not merely extra kettle, thermometer and gun went overboard, but some grace of courtesy, some decency of life had been left behind.

About three o'clock of this same day, dim with snow, and dizzy in a hurricane of wind, "We can't go on like this," said the Boy suddenly.

"Wish I knew the way we *could* go on," returned the Colonel, stopping with an air of utter helplessness, and forcing his rigid hands into his pockets. The Boy looked at him. The man of dignity and resource, who had been the boss of the Big Chimney Camp—what had become of him? Here was only a big, slouching creature, with ragged beard, smoke-blackened countenance, and eyes that wept continually.

"Come on," said his equally ruffianly-looking pardner, "we'll both go ahead."

So they abandoned their sled for awhile, and when they had forged a way, came back, and one pulling, the other pushing, lifting, guiding, between them, with infinite pains they got their burden to the end of the beaten track, left it, and went ahead again—travelling three miles to make one.

"What's the matter now?"

The Boy was too tired to turn his head round and look back, but he knew that the other man wasn't doing his share. He remembered that other time when the Colonel had fallen behind. It seemed years ago, and even further away was the vague recollection of how he'd cared. How horribly frightened he'd been! Wasn't he frightened now? No. It was only a dull curiosity that turned him round at last to see what it was that made the Colonel peg out this time. He was always peggin' out. Yes, there he was, stoppin' to stroke himself. Trailman? An old woman! Fit only for the chimney-corner. And even when they went on again he kept saying to himself as he bent to the galling strain, "An old woman—just an old woman!" till he made a refrain of the words, and in the level places marched to the tune. After that, whatever else his vague thought went off upon, it came back to "An old woman—just an old woman!"

It was at a bad place towards the end of that forced march that the Colonel, instead of lifting the back of the sled, bore hard on the handle-bar. With a vicious sound it snapped. The Boy turned heavily at the noise. When he saw the Colonel standing, dazed, with the splintered bar in his hand, his dull eyes flashed. With sudden vigour he ran back to see the extent of the damage.

"Well, it's pretty discouragin'," says the Colonel very low.

The Boy gritted his teeth with suppressed rage. It was only a chance that it hadn't happened when he himself was behind, but he couldn't see that. No; it was the Colonel's bungling—tryin' to spare himself; leanin' on the bar instead o' liftin' the sled, as he, the Boy, would have done.

With stiff hands they tried to improvise a makeshift with a stick of birch and some string.

"Don't know what you think," says the Colonel presently, "but I call this a desperate business we've undertaken."

The Boy didn't trust himself to call it anything. With a bungled job they went lamely on. The loose snow was whirling about so, it was impossible to say whether it was still falling, or only hurricane-driven.

To the Colonel's great indignation it was later than usual before they camped.

Not a word was spoken by either till they had finished their first meal, and the Colonel had melted a frying-pan full of snow preparatory to the second. He took up the rice-bag, held it by the top, and ran his mittened hand down the gathered sack till he had outlined the contents at the bottom.

"Lord! That's all there is."

The boy only blinked his half-shut eyes. The change in him, from talkativeness to utter silence, had grown horribly oppressive to the Colonel. He often felt he'd like to shake him till he shook some words out. "I told you days ago," he went on, "that we ought to go on rations."

Silence.

"But no! you knew so much better."

The Boy shut his eyes, and suddenly, like one struggling against sleep or swooning, he roused himself.

"I thought I knew the more we took off the damn sled the lighter it'd be. 'Tisn't so."

"And we didn't either of us think we'd come down from eighteen miles a day to six," returned the Colonel, a little mollified by any sort of answer. "I don't believe we're going to put this job through."

Now this was treason.

Any trail-man may think that twenty times a day, but no one ought to say it. The Boy set his teeth, and his eyes closed. The whole thing was suddenly harder—doubt of the issue had been born into the world. But he opened his eyes again. The Colonel had carefully poured some of the rice into the smoky water of the pan. What was the fool doing? Such a little left, and making a second supper?

Only that morning the Boy had gone a long way when mentally he called the boss of the Big Chimney Camp "an old woman." By night he was saying in his heart, "The Colonel's a fool." His pardner caught the look that matched the thought.

"No more second helpin's," he said in self-defence; "this'll freeze into cakes for luncheon."

No answer. No implied apology for that look. In the tone his pardner had come to dread the Colonel began: "If we don't strike a settlement to-morrow——"

"Don't *talk!*"

The Boy's tired arm fell on the handle of the frying-pan. Over it went—rice, water, and all in the fire. The culprit sprang up speechless with dismay, enraged at the loss of the food he was hungry for—enraged at "the fool fry-pan"—enraged at the fool Colonel for balancing it so badly.

A column of steam and smoke rose into the frosty air between the two men. As it cleared away a little the Boy could see the Colonel's bloodshot eyes. The expression was ill to meet.

When they crouched down again, with the damped-out fire between them, a sense of utter loneliness fell upon each man's heart.

*   *   *   *   *   *   *

The next morning, when they came to digging the sled out of the last night's snow-drift, the Boy found to his horror that he was weaker—yes, a good deal. As they went on he kept stumbling. The Colonel fell every now and then. Sometimes he would lie still before he could pull himself on his legs again.

In these hours they saw nothing of the grim and splendid waste; nothing of the ranks of snow-laden trees; nothing of sun course or of stars, only the half-yard of dazzling trail in front of them, and—clairvoyant—the little store of flour and bacon that seemed to shrink in the pack while they dragged it on.

Apart from partial snow-blindness, which fell at intervals upon the Colonel, the tiredness of the eyes was like a special sickness upon them both. For many hours together they never raised their lids, looking out through slits, cat-like, on the world.

They had not spoken to each other for many days—or was it only hours?—when the Colonel, looking at the Boy, said:

"You've got to have a face-guard. Those frostbites are eating in."

" 'Xpect so."

"You ought to stop it. Make a guard."

"Out of a snow-ball, or chunk o' ice?"

"Cut a piece out o' the canvas o' the bag." But he didn't.

The big sores seemed such small matters beside the vast overshadowing doubt, Shall we come out of this alive?—doubt never to be openly admitted by him, but always knocking, knocking——

"You can't see your own face," the Colonel persisted.

"One piece o' luck, anyhow."

The old habit of looking after the Boy died hard. The Colonel hesitated. For the last time he would remonstrate. "I used to think frost*bite* was a figure o' speech," said he, "but the teeth were set in *your* face, sonny, and they've bitten deep; they'll leave awful scars."

"Battles do, I b'lieve." And it was with an effort that he remembered there had been a time when they had been uncomfortable because they hadn't washed their faces. Now, one man was content to let the very skin go if he could keep the flesh on his face, and one was little concerned even for that. Life—life! To push on and come out alive.

The Colonel had come to that point where he resented the Boy's staying power, terrified at the indomitable young life in him. Yes, the Colonel began to feel old, and to think with vague wrath of the insolence of youth.

Each man fell to considering what he would do, how he would manage if he were alone. And there ceased to be any terror in the thought.

"If it wasn't for him"—so and so; till in the gradual deadening of judgment all the hardship was somehow your pardner's fault. Your nerves made him responsible even for the snow and the wind. By-and-by he was The Enemy. Not but what each had occasional moments of lucidity, and drew back from the pit they were bending over. But the realisation would fade. No longer did even the wiser of the two remember that this is that same abyss out of which slowly, painfully, the race has climbed. With the lessened power to keep from falling in, the terror of it lessened. Many strange things grew natural. It was no longer difficult or even shocking to conceive one's partner giving out and falling by the way. Although playing about the thought, the one thing that not even the Colonel was able actually to realise, was the imminent probability of death for himself. Imagination always pictured the other fellow down, one's self somehow forging ahead.

This obsession ended on the late afternoon when the Colonel broke silence by saying suddenly:

"We must camp; I'm done." He flung himself down under a bare birch, and hid his face.

The Boy remonstrated, grew angry; then, with a huge effort at self-control, pointed out that since it had stopped snowing this was the very moment to go on.

"Why, you can see the sun. Three of 'em! Look, Colonel!"

But Arctic meteorological phenomena had long since ceased to interest the Kentuckian. Parhelia were less to him than covered eyes, and the perilous peace of the snow. It seemed a long time before he sat up, and began to beat the stiffness out of his hands against his breast. But when he spoke, it was only to say:

"I mean to camp."

"For how long?"

"Till a team comes by—or something."

The Boy got up abruptly, slipped on his snow-shoes, and went round the shoulder of the hill, and up on to the promontory, to get out of earshot of that voice, and determine which of the two ice-roads, stretching out before them, was main channel and which was tributary.

He found on the height only a cutting wind, and little enlightenment as to the true course. North and east all nimbus still. A brace of sun-dogs following the pale God of Day across the narrow field of primrose that bordered the duncoloured west. There would be more snow to-morrow, and meanwhile the wind was rising again. Yes, sir, it was a mean outlook.

As he took Mac's aneroid barometer out of his pocket, a

sudden gust cut across his raw and bleeding cheek. He turned abruptly; the barometer slipped out of his numb fingers. He made a lunge to recover it, clutched the air, and, sliding suddenly forward, over he went, flying headlong down the steep escarpment.

He struck a jutting rock, only half snowed under, that broke the sheer face of the promontory, and he bounded once like a rubber ball, struck a second time, caught desperately at a solitary clump of ice-sheathed alders, crashed through the snow-crust just below them, and was held there like a mudlark in its cliff nest, halfway between bluff and river.

His last clear thought had been an intense anxiety about his snow-shoes as they sailed away, two liberated kites, but as he went on falling, clutching at the air—falling—and felt the alder twigs snap under his hands, he said to himself, "This is death," but calmly, as if it were a small matter compared to losing one's snow-shoes.

It was only when he landed in the snow, that he was conscious of any of the supposed natural excitement of a man meeting a violent end. It was then, before he even got his breath back, that he began to struggle frantically to get a foothold; but he only broke down more of the thin ice-wall that kept him from the sheer drop to the river, sixty or seventy feet below. He lay quite still. Would the Colonel come after him? If he did come, would he risk his life to—— If he did risk his life, was it any use to try to—— He craned his neck and looked up, blinked, shut his eyes, and lay back in the snow with a sound of far-off singing in his head. "Any use?" No, sir; it just about wasn't. That bluff face would be easier to climb up than to climb down, and either was impossible.

Then it was, that a great tide of longing swept over him—a flood of passionate desire for more of this doubtful blessing, life. All the bitter hardship—why, how sweet it was, after all, to battle and to overcome! It was only this lying helpless, trapped, that was evil. The endless Trail? Why, it was only the coming to the end that a man minded.

Suddenly the beauty that for days had been veiled shone out. Nothing in all the earth was glorious with the glory of the terrible white North. And he had only just been wakened to it. Here, now, lying in his grave, had come this special revelation of the rapture of living, and the splendour of the visible universe.

The sky over his head—he had called it "a mean outlook," and turned away. It was the same sky that bent over him now with a tenderness that made him lift his cramped arms with tears, as a sick child might to its mother. The haloed sun with his attendant dogs—how little the wonder had touched him! Never had he seen them so dim and sad as to-night . . . saying good-bye to one who loved the sun.

The great frozen road out of sight below, road that came winding, winding down out of the Arctic Circle—what other highway so majestic, mysterious?—shining and beckoning on. An earthly Milky Way, leading to the golden paradise he had been travelling towards since summer.

And he was to go no further?——not till the June rains and thaws and winds and floods should carry him back, as he had foreseen, far below there at Holy Cross.

With a sharp contraction of the heart he shut his eyes again. When he opened them they rested on the alder-twig, a couple of yards above, holding out mocking finger-tips, and he turned his head in the snow till again he could see the mock-suns looking down.

"As well try to reach the sky as reach the alder-bush. What did that mean? That he was really going to lie there till he died? *He* die, and the Colonel and everybody else go on living?

He half rose on his elbow at the monstrous absurdity of the idea. "I won't die!" he said out loud.

Crack, crack! warned the ice-crust between him and that long fall to the river. With horror at his heart he shrank away and hugged the face of the precipice. Presently he put out his hand and broke the ice-crust above. With mittened fists and palms he pounded firm a little ledge of snow. Reaching out further, he broke the crust obliquely just above, and having packed the snow as well as he could immediately about, and moving lengthwise with an infinite caution, he crawled up the few inches to the narrow ledge, balancing his stiff body with a nicety possible only to acrobat or sleep-walker.

It was in no normal state of ordinary waking senses that the work went on—with never a downward look, nor even up, eyes riveted to the patch of snow on which the mittened hands fell as steady and untrembling as steel hammers. In the seconds of actual consciousness of his situation that twice visited him, he crouched on the ledge with closed eyes, in the clutch of an overmastering horror, absolutely still, like a bird in the talons of a hawk. Each time when he opened his eyes he would stare at the snow-ledge till hypnotised into disregard of danger, balance his slight body, lift one hand, and go on pounding firm another shallow step. When he reached the alder-bush his heart gave a great leap of triumph. Then, for the first time since starting, he looked up. His heart fell down. It seemed farther than ever, and the light waning.

But the twilight would be long, he told himself, and in that other, beneficent inner twilight he worked on, packing the snow, and crawling gingerly up the perilous stair a half-inch at a time.

At last he was on the jutting rock, and could stand secure. But here he could see that the top of the bluff really did shelve over. To think so is so common an illusion to the climber that the Boy had heartened himself by saying, when he got there he would find it like the rest, horribly steep, but not impossible. Well, it *was* impossible. After all his labour, he was no better off on the rock than in the snow-hole below the alder, down there where he dared not look. The sun and his dogs had travelled down, down. They touched the horizon while he sat there; they slipped below the world's wide rim. He said in his heart, "I'm freezing to death." Unexpectedly to himself his despair found voice:

"Colonel!"

"Hello!"

He started violently.

Had he really heard that, or was imagination playing tricks with echo?

"Colonel!"

"Where the devil——"

A man's head appeared out of the sky.

"Got the rope?"

Words indistinguishable floated down—the head withdrawn —silence. The Boy waited a very long time, but he stamped his feet, and kept his blood in motion. The light was very grey when the head showed again at the sky-line. He couldn't hear what was shouted down, and it occurred to him, even in his huge predicament, that the Colonel was "giving him hot air" as usual, instead of a life-line. Down the rope came, nearer, and stopped about fifteen feet over his head.

"Got the axe? Let her down."

* * * * * * *

The night was bright with moonlight when the Boy stood again on the top of the bluff.

"Humph!" says the Colonel, with agreeable anticipation; "you'll be glad to camp for a few days after this, I reckon."

"Reckon I won't."

* * * * * * *

In their colossal fatigue they slept the clock round; their watches run down, their sense of the very date blurred. Since the Colonel had made the last laconic entry in the journal— was it three days or two—or twenty?

In spite of a sensation as of many broken bones, the Boy put on the Colonel's snow-shoes, and went off looking along the foot of the cliff for his own. No luck, but he brought back some birch-bark and a handful of willow-withes, and set about making a rude substitute.

Before they had despatched breakfast the great red moon arose, so it was not morning, but evening. So much the better. The crust would be firmer. The moon was full; it was bright enough to travel, and travel they must.

"No!" said the Colonel, with a touch of his old pompous authority, "we'll wait awhile."

The Boy simply pointed to the flour-bag. There wasn't a good handful left.

They ate supper, studiously avoiding each other's eyes. In the background of the Boy's mind: "He saved my life, but he ran no risk. . . . And I saved his. We're quits." In the Colonel's, vague, insistent, stirred the thought, "I might have left him there to rot, half-way up the precipice. Oh, he'd go! *And he'd take the sled!* No!" His vanished strength flowed back upon a tide of rage. Only one sleeping-bag, one kettle, one axe, one pair of snow-shoes . . . *one gun!* No, by the living Lord! not while I have a gun. *Where's* my gun?" He looked about guiltily, under his lowered lids. What? No! Yes! It was gone! Who packed at the last camp? Why, he —himself, and he'd left it behind. "Then it was because I didn't see it; the Boy took care I shouldn't see it! Very likely he buried it so that I shouldn't see it! He—yes—if I refuse to go on, he——"

And the Boy, seeing without looking, taking in every move, every shade in the mood of the broken-spirited man, ready to die here, like a dog, in the snow, instead of pressing on as long as he could crawl—the Boy, in a fever of silent rage, called him that "meanest word in the language—a quitter." And as, surreptitiously, he took in the vast discouragement of the older man, there was nothing in the Boy's changed heart to say, "Poor fellow! if he can't go on, I'll stay and die with him"; but only, "He's *got* to go on! . . . and if he refuses . . . well——" He felt about in his deadened brain, and the best he could bring forth was: "I won't leave him—*yet*."

* * * * * * *

A mighty river-jam had forced them up on the low range of hills. It was about midnight to judge by the moon—clear of snow and the wind down. The Boy straightened up at a curious sight just below them. Something black in the moonlight. The Colonel paused, looked down, and passed his hand over his eyes.

The Boy had seen the thing first, and had said to himself, "Looks like a sled, but it's a vision. It's come to seeing things now."

When he saw the Colonel stop and stare, he threw down his rope and began to laugh, for there below were the blackened remains of a big fire, silhouetted sharply on the snow.

"Looks like we've come to a camp, Boss!"

He hadn't called the Colonel by the old nickname for many a day. He stood there laughing in an idiotic kind of way, wrapping his stiff hands in his parki, Indian fashion, and looking down to the level of the ancient river terrace, where the weather-stained old Indian sled was sharply etched on the moonlit whiteness.

Just a sled lying in the moonlight. But the change that can be wrought in a man's heart upon sight of a human sign! it may be idle to speak of that to any but those who have travelled the desolate ways of the North.

Side by side the two went down the slope, slid and slipped and couldn't stop themselves, till they were below the landmark. Looking up, they saw that a piece of soiled canvas or a skin, held down with a drift-log, fell from under the sled, portière-wise from the top of the terrace, straight down to the sheltered level, where the camp fire had been. Coming closer, they saw the curtain was not canvas, but dressed deerskin.

"Indians!" said the Colonel.

But with the rubbing out of other distinctions this, too, was curiously faint. Just so there were human beings it seemed enough. Within four feet of the deerskin door the Colonel stopped, shot through by a sharp misgiving. What was behind? A living man's camp, or a dead man's tomb? Succour, or some stark picture of defeat, and of their own oncoming doom?

The Colonel stood stock-still waiting for the Boy. For the first time in many days even he hung back. He seemed to lack the courage to be the one to extinguish hope by the mere drawing of a curtain from a snow-drift's face. The Kentuckian pulled himself together and went forward. He lifted his hand to the deerskin, but his fingers shook so he couldn't take hold: "Hello!" he called. No sound. Again: "Hello!"

"Who's there?"

The two outside turned and looked into each other's faces— but if you want to know all the moment meant, you must travel the Winter Trail.

CHAPTER · XIV

KURILLA

" And I swear to you Athenians—by the dog I swear !—for I must tell you the truth——."—SOCRATES.

THE voice that had asked the question belonged to one of two stranded Klondykers, as it turned out, who had burrowed a hole in the snow and faced it with drift-wood. They had plenty of provisions, enough to spare, and meant to stay here till the steamers ran, for the younger of the pair had frosted his feet and was crippled.

The last of their dogs had been frozen to death a few miles back on the trail, and they had no idea, apparently, how near they were to that "first Indian settlement this side of Kaltag" reached by the Colonel and the Boy after two days of rest and one day of travel.

No one ever sailed more joyfully into the Bay of Naples, or saw with keener rapture Constantinople's mosques and minarets arise, than did these ice-armoured travellers, rounding the sharp bend in the river, sight the huts and hear the dogs howl on the farther shore.

"First thing I do, sah, is to speculate in a dog-team," said the Colonel.

Most of the bucks were gone off hunting, and most of the dogs were with them. Only three left in the village—but they were wonderful fellows those three! Where were they? Well, the old man you see before you, "*me*—got two."

He led the way behind a little shack, a troop of children following, and there were two wolf-dogs, not in the best condition, one reddish, with a white face and white forelegs, the other grey with a black splotch on his chest and a white one on his back.

"How much?"

"Fiftee dolla."

"And this one?"

"Fiftee dolla." As the Colonel hesitated, the old fellow added: "Bohf eightee dolla."

"Oh, eightee for the two?"

He nodded.

"Well, where's the other?"

"Hein?"

"The other—the third dog. Two are no good."

"Yes. Yes," he said angrily, "heap good dog."

"Well, I'll give you eighty dollars for these" (the Ingalik, taking a pipe out of his parki, held out one empty hand); "but who's got the other?"

For answer, a head-shake, the outstretched hand, and the words, "Eightee dolla—tabak—tea."

"Wait," interrupted the Boy, turning to the group of children; "where's the other dog?"

Nobody answered. The Boy pantomimed. "We want *three* dogs." He held up as many fingers. "We got two—see?— must have one more." A lad of about thirteen turned and began pointing with animation towards a slowly approaching figure.

"Peetka—him got."

The old man began to chatter angrily, and abuse the lad for introducing a rival on the scene. The strangers hailed the new-comer.

"How much is your dog?"

Peetka stopped, considered, studied the scene immediately before him, and then the distant prospect.

"You got dog?"

He nodded.

"Well, how much?"

"Sixty dolla."

"*One* dog, sixty?"

He nodded.

"But this man says the price is eighty for two."

"My dog—him Leader."

After some further conversation, "Where is your dog?" demanded the Colonel.

The new-comer whistled and called. After some waiting, and well-simulated anger on the part of the owner, along comes a dusky Siwash, thin, but keen-looking, and none too mild-tempered.

KURILLA

The children all brightened and craned, as if a friend, or at least a highly interesting member of the community, had appeared on the scene.

"The Nigger's the best!" whispered the Boy.

"Him bully," said the lad, and seemed about to pat him, but the Siwash snarled softly, raising his lip and showing his gleaming fangs. The lad stepped back respectfully, but grinned, reiterating, "Bully dog."

"Well, I'll give you fifty for him," said the Colonel.

"Sixty."

"Well, all right, since he's a leader. Sixty."

The owner watched the dog as it walked round its master smelling the snow, then turning up its pointed nose interrogatively and waving its magnificent feathery tail. The oblique eyes, acute angle of his short ears, the thick neck, broad chest, and heavy forelegs, gave an impression of mingled alertness and strength you will not see surpassed in any animal that walks the world. Jet-black, except for his grey muzzle and broad chest, he looks at you with the face of his near ancestor, the grizzled wolf. If on short acquaintance you offer any familiarity, as the Colonel ventured to do, and he shows his double row of murderous-looking fangs, the reminder of his fierce forefathers is even more insistent. Indeed, to this day your Siwash of this sort will have his moments of nostalgia, in which he turns back to his wild kinsfolk, and mates again with the wolf.

When the Leader looked at the Colonel with that indescribably horrid smile, the owner's approval of the proud beast seemed to overcome his avarice.

"Me no sell," he decided abruptly, and walked off in lordly fashion with his dusky companion at his side, the Leader curling his feathery tail arc-like over his back, and walking with an air princes might envy.

The Colonel stood staring. Vainly the Boy called, "Come back. Look here! Hi!" Neither Siwash nor Ingalik took the smallest notice. The Boy went after them, eliciting only airs of surly indifference and repeated "Me no sell." It was a bitter disappointment, especially to the Boy. He liked the looks of that Nigger dog. When, plunged in gloom, he returned to the group about the Colonel, he found his pardner asking about "feed." No, the old man hadn't enough fish to spare even a few days' supply. Would anybody here sell fish?

No, he didn't think so. All the men who had teams were gone to the hills for caribou; there was nobody to send to the Summer Caches. He held out his hand again for the first instalment of the "eightee dolla," in kind, that he might put it in his pipe.

"But dogs are no good to us without something to feed 'em."

The Ingalik looked round as one seeking counsel.

"Get fish tomalla."

"No, sir. To-day's the only day in my calendar. No buy dogs till we get fish."

When the negotiations fell through the Indian took the failure far more philosophically than the white men, as was natural. The old fellow could quite well get on without "eightee dolla"—could even get on without the tobacco, tea, sugar, and matches represented by that sum, but the travellers could not without dogs get to Minóok. It had been very well to feel set up because they had done the thing that everybody said was impossible. It had been a costly victory. Yes, it had come high. "And, after all, if we don't get dogs we're beaten."

"Oh, beaten be blowed! We'll toddle along somehow."

"Yes, we'll toddle along *if* we get dogs."

And the Boy knew the Colonel was right.

They inquired about Kaltag.

"I reckon we'd better push ahead while we can," said the Colonel. So they left the camp that same evening intending to "travel with the moon." The settlement was barely out of sight when they met a squaw dragging a sled-load of salmon. Here was luck! "And now we'll go back and get those two dogs."

As it was late, and trading with the natives, even for a fish, was a matter of much time and patience, they decided not to hurry the dog deal. It was bound to take a good part of the evening, at any rate. Well, another night's resting up was welcome enough.

While the Colonel was re-establishing himself in the best cabin, the Boy cached the sled and then went prowling about. As he fully intended, he fell in with the Leader—that "bully Nigger dog." His master not in sight—nobody but some dirty children and the stranger there to see how the Red Dog, in a moment of aberration, dared offer insolence to the Leader. It all happened through the Boy's producing a fish, and presenting it on bended knee at a respectful distance. The Leader bestowed a contemptuous stare upon the stranger and pointedly turned his back. The Red Dog came "loping" across the snow. As he made for the fish the Leader quietly headed him off, pointed his sharp ears, and just looked the other fellow out of countenance. Red said things under his breath as he turned away. The more he thought the situation over the more he felt himself outraged. He looked round over his shoulder. There they still were, the stranger holding out the fish, the Leader turning his back on it, but telegraphing Red at the same time *not to dare!* It was more than dog-flesh could bear; Red bounded back, exploding in snarls. No sound out of the Leader. Whether this unnatural calm misled Red, he came up closer, braced his forelegs, and thrust his tawny muzzle almost into the other dog's face, drew back his lips from all those shining wicked teeth, and uttered a muffled hiss.

Well, it was magnificently done, and it certainly looked as if the Leader was going to have a troubled evening. But he didn't seem to think so. He "fixed" the Red Dog as one knowing the power of the master's eye to quell. Red's reply, unimaginably bold, was, as the Boy described it to the Colonel, "to give the other fella the curse." The Boy was proud of Red's pluck—already looking upon him as his own—but he jumped up from his ingratiating attitude, still grasping the dried fish. It would be a shame if that Leader got chewed up! And there was Red, every tooth bared, gasping for gore, and with each passing second seeming to throw a deeper damnation into his threat, and to brace himself more firmly for the hurling of the final doom.

At that instant, the stranger breathing quick and hard, the elder children leaning forward, some of the younger drawing back in terror—if you'll believe it, the Leader blinked in a bored way, and sat down on the snow. A question only of last moments now, poor brute! and the bystanders held their breath. But no! Red, to be sure, broke into the most awful demonstrations, and nearly burst himself with fury; but he backed away, as though the spectacle offered by the Leader were too disgusting for a decent dog to look at. He went behind the shack and told the Spotty One. In no time they were back, approaching the Boy and the fish discreetly from behind. Such mean tactics roused the Leader's ire. He got up and flew at them. They made it hot for him, but still the Leader seemed to be doing pretty well for himself, when the old Ingalik (whom the Boy had sent a child to summon) hobbled up with a raw-hide whip, and laid it on with a practised hand, separating the combatants, kicking them impartially all round, and speaking injurious words.

"Are your two hurt?" inquired the future owner anxiously. The old fellow shook his head.

"Fur thick," was the reassuring answer; and once more the Boy realised that these canine encounters, though frequently ending in death, often look and sound much more awful than they are.

As the Leader feigned to be going home, he made a dash in passing at the stranger's fish. It was held tight, and the pirate got off with only a fragment. Leader gave one swallow and looked back to see how the theft was being taken. That surprising stranger simply stood there laughing, and holding out the rest of a fine fat fish! Leader considered a moment, looked the alien up and down, came back, all on guard for sudden rushes, sly kicks, and thwackings, to pay him out. But nothing of the kind. The Nigger dog said as plain as speech could make it:

"You cheechalko person, you look as if you're actually offering me that fish in good faith. But I'd be a fool to think so."

The stranger spoke low and quietly.

They talked for some time.

The owner of the two had shuffled off home again, with Spotty and Red at his heels.

The Leader came quite near, looking almost docile; but he snapped suddenly at the fish with an ugly gleam of eye and fang. The Boy nearly made the fatal mistake of jumping, but he controlled the impulse, and merely held tight to what was left of the salmon. He stood quite still, offering it with fair words. The Leader walked all round him, and seemed with difficulty to recover from his surprise. The Boy felt that they were just coming to an understanding, when up hurries Peetka, suspicious and out of sorts.

"*My dog!*" he shouted. "No sell white man my dog. Huh! ho—*oh* no!" He kicked the Leader viciously, and drove him home, abusing him all the way. The wonder was that the wolfish creature didn't fly at his master's throat and finish him.

Certainly the stranger's sympathies were all with the four-legged one of the two brutes.

"—— something about the Leader——" the Boy said sadly,

telling the Colonel what had happened. "Well, sir, I'd give a hundred dollars to own that dog."

"So would I," was the dry rejoinder, "if I were a millionaire like you."

* * * * * * *

After supper, their host, who had been sent out to bring in the owner of Red and Spotty, came back saying, "He come. All come. Me tell—you from below Holy Cross!" He laughed and shook his head in a well-pantomimed incredulity, representing popular opinion outside. Some of the bucks, he added, who had not gone far, had got back with small game.

"And dogs?"

"No. Dogs in the mountains. Hunt moose—caribou."

The old Ingalik came in, followed by others. "Some" of the bucks? There seemed no end to the throng.

Opposite the white men the Indians sat in a semicircle, with the sole intent, you might think, of staring all night at the strangers. Yet they had brought in Arctic hares and grouse, and even a haunch of venison. But they laid these things on the floor beside them, and sat with grave unbroken silence till the strangers should declare themselves. They had also brought, or permitted to follow, not only their wives and daughters, but their children, big and little.

Behind the semicircle of men, three or four deep, were ranged the ranks of youth—boys and girls from six to fourteen —standing as silent as their elders, but eager, watchful, carrying king salmon, dried deer-meat, boot-soles, thongs for snow-shoes, rabbits, grouse. A little fellow of ten or eleven had brought in the Red Dog, and was trying to reconcile him to his close quarters. The owner of Red and Spotty sat with empty hands at the semicircle's farthest end. But he was the capitalist of the village, and held himself worthily, yet not quite with the high and mighty unconcern of the owner of the Leader.

Peetka came in late, bringing in the Nigger dog against the Nigger dog's will, just to tantalise the white men with the sight of something they couldn't buy from the poor Indian. Everybody made way for Peetka and his dog, except the other dog. Several people had to go to the assistance of the little boy to help him to hold Red.

"Just as well, perhaps," said the Colonel, "that we aren't likely to get all three."

"Oh, if they worked together they'd be all right," answered the Boy. "I've noticed that before." But the Leader, meanwhile, was flatly refusing to stay in the same room with Red. He howled and snapped and raged. So poor Red was turned out, and the little boy mourned loudly.

Behind the children, a row of squaws against the wall, with and without babies strapped at their backs. Occasionally a young girl would push aside those in front of her, craning and staring to take in the astonishing spectacle of the two white men who had come so far without dogs—pulling a hand-sled a greater distance than any Indian had ever done—if they could be believed!

Anyhow, these men with their sack of tea and magnificent bundle of matches, above all with their tobacco—they could buy out the town—everything except Peetka's dog.

The Colonel and the Boy opened the ball by renewing their joint offer of eighty dollars for Red and Spotty. Although this had been the old Ingalik's own price, it was discussed fully an hour by all present before the matter could be considered finally settled, even then the Colonel knew it was safest not to pay till just upon leaving. But he made a little present of tobacco in token of satisfactory arrangement. The old man's hands trembled excitedly as he pulled out his pipe and filled it. The bucks round him, and even a couple of the women at the back, begged him for some. He seemed to say, "Do your own deal; the strangers have plenty more."

By-and-by, in spite of the limited English of the community, certain facts stood out: that Peetka held the white man in avowed detestation, that he was the leading spirit of the place, that they had all been suffering from a tobacco famine, and that much might be done by a judicious use of Black Jack and Long Green. The Colonel set forth the magnificent generosity of which he would be capable, could he secure a good Leader. But Peetka, although he looked at his empty pipe with bitterness, shook his head.

Everybody in the village would profit, the Colonel went on; everybody should have a present if——

Peetka interrupted with a snarl, and flung out low words of contemptuous refusal.

The Leader waked from a brief nap cramped and uneasy, and began to howl in sympathy. His master stood up, the better to deliver a brutal kick. This seemed to help the Leader to put up with cramp and confinement, just as one great discomfort will help his betters to forget several little ones. But the Boy had risen with angry eyes. Very well, he said impulsively; if he and his pardner couldn't get a third dog (two were very little good) they would not stock fresh meat here. In vain the Colonel whispered admonition. No, sir, they would wait till they got to the next village.

"Belly far," said a young hunter, placing ostentatiously in front his brace of grouse.

"We're used to going belly far. Take all your game away, and go home."

A sorrowful silence fell upon the room. They sat for some time like that, no one so much as moving, till a voice said, "We want tobacco," and a general murmur of assent arose. Peetka roused himself, pulled out of his shirt a concave stone and a little woody-looking knot. The Boy leaned forward to see what it was. A piece of dried fungus—the kind you sometimes see on the birches up here. Peetka was hammering a fragment of it into powder, with his heavy clasp-knife, on the concave stone. He swept the particles into his pipe and applied to one of the fish-selling women for a match, lit up, and lounged back against the Leader, smiling disagreeably at the strangers. A little laugh at their expense went round the room. Oh, it wasn't easy to get ahead of Peetka! But even if he chose to pretend that he didn't want cheechalko tobacco, it was very serious—it was desperate—to see all that Black Jack going on to the next village. Several of the hitherto silent bucks remonstrated with Peetka—even one of the women dared raise her voice. She had not been able to go for fish: where was *her* tobacco and tea?

Peetka burst into voluble defence of his position. Casting occasional looks of disdain upon the strangers, he addressed most of his remarks to the owner of Red and Spotty. Although the Colonel could not understand a word, he saw the moment approaching when that person would go back on his bargain. With uncommon pleasure he could have throttled Peetka.

The Boy, to create a diversion, had begun talking to a young hunter in the front row about "the Long Trail," and, seeing that several others craned and listened, he spoke louder, more slowly, dropping out all unnecessary or unusual words. Very soon he had gained an audience and Peetka had lost one. As the stranger went on describing their experiences the whole room listened with an attentiveness that would have been flattering had it been less strongly dashed with unbelief. From beyond Anvik they had come? Like that—with no dogs? What! From below Koserefsky? Not really? Peetka grunted and shook his head. Did they think the Ingaliks were children? Without dogs that journey was impossible. Low whispers and gruff exclamations filled the room. White men were great liars. They pretended that in their country the bacon had legs, and could run about, and one had been heard to say he had travelled in a thing like a steamboat, only it could go without water under it—ran over the dry land on strips of iron—ran quicker than any steamer! Oh, they were awful liars. But these two, who pretended they'd dragged a sled all the way from Holy Cross, they were the biggest liars of all. Just let them tell that yarn to Unookuk. They all laughed at this, and the name ran round the room.

"Who is Unookuk?"

"Him guide."

"*Him* know."

"Where is him?" asked the Boy.

"Him sick."

But there was whispering and consultation. This was evidently a case for the expert. Two boys ran out, and the native talk went on, unintelligible save for the fact that it centred round Unookuk. In a few minutes the boys came back with a tall, fine-looking native, about sixty years old, walking lame, and leaning on a stick. The semicircle opened to admit him. He limped over to the strangers, and stood looking at them gravely, modestly, but with careful scrutiny.

The Boy held out his hand.

"How do you do?"

"How do you do?" echoed the new-comer, and he also shook hands with the Colonel before he sat down.

"Are you Unookuk?"

"Yes. How far you come?"

Peetka said something rude, before the strangers had time to answer, and all the room went into titters. But Unookuk listened with dignity while the Colonel repeated briefly the story already told. Plainly it stumped Unookuk.

"Come from Anvik?" he repeated.

"Yes; stayed with Mr. Benham."

"Oh, Benham!" The trader's familiar name ran round the

room with obvious effect. "It is good to have A. C. Agent for friend," said Unookuk guardedly. "Everybody know Benham."

"He is not A. C. Agent much longer," volunteered the Boy. "That so?"

"No; he will go 'on his own' after the new agent gets in this spring."

"It is true," answered Unookuk gravely, for the first time a little impressed, for this news was not yet common property. Still, they could have heard it from some passer with a dogteam. The Boy spoke of Holy Cross, and Unookuk's grave unbelief was painted on every feature.

"It was good you get to Holy Cross before the big storm," he said, with a faint smile of tolerance for the white man's tall story. But Peetka laughed aloud.

"What good English you speak!" said the Boy, determined to make friends with the most intelligent-appearing native he had seen.

"Me; I am Kurilla!" said Unookuk, with a quiet magnificence. Then, seeing no electric recognition of the name, he added: "You savvy Kurilla!"

The Colonel with much regret admitted that he did not.

"But I am Dall's guide—*Kurilla*."

"Oh, Dall's guide, are you," said the Boy, without a glimmer of who Dall was, or for what, or to what, he was "guided." "Well, Kurilla, we're pleased and proud to meet you," adding with some presence of mind, "And how's Dall?"

"It is long I have not hear. We both old now. I hurt my knee on the ice when I come down from Nulato for caribou."

"Why do you have two names?"

"Unookuk, Nulato name. My father big Nulato Shamán. Him killed, mother killed, everybody killed in Koyukuk massacre. They forget kill me. Me kid. Russians find Unookuk in big wood. Russians give food. I stay with Russians—them call Unookuk 'Kurilla.' Dall call Unookuk 'Kurilla.'"

"Dall—Dall," said the Colonel to the Boy; "was that the name of the explorer fella——"

Fortunately the Boy was saved from need to answer.

"First white man go down Yukon to the sea," said Kurilla with pride. "Me Dall's guide."

"Oh, wrote a book, didn't he? Name's familiar somehow," said the Colonel.

Kurilla bore him out.

"Mr. Dall great man. Thirty year he first come up here with Survey people. Make big overland tel-ee-grab."

"Of course. I've heard about that." The Colonel turned to the Boy. "It was just before the Russians sold out. And when a lot of exploring and surveying and pole-planting was done here and in Siberia, the Atlantic cable was laid and knocked the overland scheme sky-high."

Kurilla gravely verified these facts.

"And me, Dall's chief guide. Me with Dall when he make portage from Unalaklik to Kaltag. He see the Yukon first time. He run down to be first on the ice. Dall and the coast natives stare, like so'—Kurilla made a wild-eyed, ludicrous face—"and they say: 'It is not a river—it is another sea!'"

"No wonder. I hear it's ten miles wide up by the flats, and even a little below where we wintered, at Ikogimeut, it's four miles across from bank to bank."

Kurilla looked at the Colonel with dignified reproach. Why did he go on lying about his journey like that to an expert?

"Even at Holy Cross——" the Boy began, but Kurilla struck in:

"When you there?"

"Oh, about three weeks ago."

Peetka made remarks in Ingalik.

"Father MacManus, him all right?" asked Kurilla, politely cloaking his cross-examination.

"MacManus? Do you mean Wills, or the Superior, Father Brachet?"

"Oh yes! MacManus at Tanana." He spoke as though inadvertently he had confused the names. As the strangers gave him the winter's news from Holy Cross, his wonder and astonishment grew.

Presently, "Do you know my friend Nicholas of Pymeut?" asked the Boy.

Kurilla took his empty pipe out of his mouth and smiled in broad surprise. "Nicholas!" repeated several others. It was plain the Pymeut pilot enjoyed a wide repute.

The Boy spoke of the famine and Ol' Chief's illness.

"It is true," said Unookuk gravely, and turning, he added something in Ingalik to the company. Peetka answered back as surly as ever. But the Boy went on, telling how the Shamán had cured Ol' Chief, and that turned out to be a surprisingly popular story. Peetka wouldn't interrupt it, even to curse the Leader for getting up and stretching himself. When the dog—feeling that for some reason discipline was relaxed—dared to leave his cramped quarters, and come out into the little open space between the white men and the close-packed assembly, the Boy forced himself to go straight on with his story as if he had not observed the liberty the Leader was taking. When, after standing there an instant, the dog came over and threw himself down at the stranger's feet as if publicly adopting him, the white story-teller dared not meet Peetka's eye. He was privately most uneasy at the Nigger dog's tactless move, and he hurried on about how Brother Paul caught the Shamán, and about the Penitential Journey—told how, long before that, early in the Fall, Nicholas had got lost, making the portage from St. Michael's, and how the white camp had saved him from starvation; how in turn the Pymeuts had pulled the speaker out of a blow-hole; what *tremendous* friends the Pymeuts were with these particular, very good sort of white men. Here he seemed to allow by implication for Peetka's prejudice—there were two kinds of pale-face strangers—and on an impulse he drew out Muckluck's medal. He would have them to know, so highly were these present specimens of the doubtful race regarded by the Pymeuts—such friends were they, that Nicholas' sister had given him this for an offering to Yukon Inua, that the Great Spirit might help them on their way. He owned himself wrong to have delayed this sacrifice. He must to-morrow throw it into the first blow-hole he came to—unless indeed . . . his eye caught Kurilla's. With the help of his stick the old Guide pulled his big body up on his one stout leg, hobbled nearer and gravely eyed Muckluck's offering as it swung to and fro on its walrus-string over the Leader's head. The Boy, quite conscious of some subtle change in the hitherto immobile face of the Indian, laid the token in his hand. Standing there in the centre of the semicircle between the assembly and the dog, Kurilla turned the Great Katharine's medal over, examining it closely, every eye in the room upon him.

When he lifted his head there was a rustle of expectation and a craning forward.

"It is the same." Kurilla spoke slowly like one half in a dream. "When I go down river, thirty winter back, with the Great Dall, he try buy this off Nicholas's mother. She wear it on string red Russian beads. Oh, it is a thing to remember!" He nodded his grey head significantly, but he went on with the bare evidence: "When *John J. Healy* make last trip down this fall—Nicholas pilot you savvy—they let him take his sister, Holy Cross to Pymeut. I see she wear this round neck."

The weight of the medal carried the raw-hide necklace slipping through his fingers. Slowly now, with even impulse, the silver disc swung right, swung left, like the pendulum of a clock. Even the Nigger dog seemed hypnotised, following the dim shine of the tarnished token.

"I say Nicholas's sister: 'It is thirty winters I see that silver picture first; I give you two dolla for him.' She say 'No.' I say, 'Gi' fi' dolla.' 'No.' I sit and think far back—thirty winters back. 'I gi' ten dolla,' I say. She say, 'I no sell; no —not for a hunner'—but she *give* it him! for to make Yukon Inua to let him go safe. Hein? Savvy?" And lapsing into Ingalik, he endorsed this credential not to be denied.

"It is true," he wound up in English. The "Autocratrix Russorum" was solemnly handed back. "You have make a brave journey. It is I who unnerstan'—I, too, when I am young, I go with Dall on the Long Trail. *We had dogs.*" All the while, from all about the Leader's owner, and out of every corner of the crowded room, had come a spirited punctuation of Kurilla's speech—nods and grunts. "Yes, perhaps *these* white men deserved dogs—even Peetka's!"

Kurilla limped back to his place, but turned to the Ingaliks before he sat down, and bending painfully over his stick, "Not Kurilla," he said, as though speaking of one absent—"not *Dall* make so great journey, no dogs. Kurilla? Best guide in Yukon forty year. Kurilla say: 'Must have dogs—men like that!'" He limped back again and solemnly offered his hand to each of the travellers in turn. "Shake!" says he. Then, as though fascinated by the silver picture, he dropped down by the Boy, staring absently at the Great Katharine's effigy. The general murmur was arrested by a movement from Peetka— he took his pipe out of his mouth and says he, handsomely:

"No liars. Sell dog," adding, with regretful eye on the apostate Leader, "Him bully dog!"

And that was how the tobacco famine ended, and how the white men got their team.

CHAPTER XV

THE ESQUIMAUX HORSE

" Plus je connais les hommes, plus j'aime les chiens."

IT doesn't look hard to drive a dog-team, but just you try it. In moments of passion, the first few days after their acquisition, the Colonel and the Boy wondered why they had complicated a sufficiently difficult journey by adding to other cares a load of fish and three fiends.

"Think how well they went for Peetka."

"Oh yes; part o' their cussedness. They know we're green hands, and they mean to make it lively."

Well, they did. They sat on their haunches in the snow, and grinned at the whip-crackings and futile "Mush, mush!" of the Colonel. They snapped at the Boy and made sharp turns, tying him up in the traces and tumbling him into the snow. They howled all night long, except during a blessed interval of quiet while they ate their seal-skin harness. But man is the wiliest of the animals, and the one who profits by experience. In the end, the Boy became a capital driver; the dogs came to know he "meant business," and settled into submission. "Nig," as he called the bully dog for short, turned out "the best leader in the Yukon."

They were much nearer Kaltag than they had realised, arriving after only two hours' struggle with the dogs at the big Indian village on the left bank of the river. But their first appearance here was clouded by Nig's proposal to slay all the dogs in sight. He was no sooner unharnessed than he undertook the congenial job. It looked for a few minutes as if Peetka's bully dog would chew up the entire canine population, and then lie down and die of his own wounds. But the Kaltags understood the genus Siwash better than the white man, and took the tumult calmly.

It turned out that Nig was not so much bloodthirsty as "bloody-proud"—one of those high souls for ever concerned about supremacy. His first social act, on catching sight of his

283

fellow, was to howl defiance at him. And even after they have fought it out and come to some sort of understanding, the first happy thought of your born Leader on awakening is to proclaim himself boss of the camp.

No sooner has he published this conviction of high calling than he is set upon by the others, punishes them soundly, or is himself vanquished and driven off. Whereupon he sits on his haunches in the snow, and, with his pointed nose turned sky-ward, howls uninterruptedly for an hour or two, when all is forgiven and forgotten—till the next time.

Order being restored, the travellers got new harness for the dogs, new boots for themselves, and set out for the white trad-ing post, thirty miles above.

Here, having at last come into the region of settlements, they agreed never again to overtax the dogs. They "travelled light" out of Nulato towards the Koyukuk.

The dogs simply flew over those last miles. It was glorious going on a trail like glass.

They had broken the back of the journey now, and could well afford, they thought, to halt an hour or two on the island at the junction of the two great rivers, stake out a trading post, and treat themselves to town lots. Why town lots, in Heav-en's name! when they were bound for Minóok, and after that the Klondyke, hundreds of miles away? Well, partly out of mere gaiety of heart, and partly, the Colonel would have told you gravely, that in this country you never know when you have a good thing. They had left the one white layman at Nulato seething with excitement over an Indian's report of still another rich strike up yonder on the Koyukuk, and this point, where they were solemnly staking out a new post, the Nulato Agent had said, was "dead sure to be a great centre." That almost unknown region bordering the great tributary of the Yukon, haunt of the fiercest of all the Indians of the North, was to be finally conquered by the white man. It had been left practically unexplored ever since the days when the bloodthirsty Koyukons came down out of their fastnesses and perpetrated the great Nulato massacre, doing to death with ghastly bar-barity every man, woman, and child at the post, Russian or Indian, except Kurilla, not sparing the unlucky Captain Bar-nard or his English escort, newly arrived here in their search for the lost Sir John Franklin. But the tables were turned now, and the white man was on the trail of the Indian.

While the Colonel and the Boy were staking out this future stronghold of trade and civilisation it came on to snow; but "Can't last this time o' year," the Colonel consoled himself, and thanked God "the big, unending snows are over for this season."

So they pushed on. But the Colonel seemed to have thanked God prematurely. Down the snow drifted, soft, sticky, unending. The evening was cloudy, and the snow increased the dimness overhead as well as the heaviness under foot. They never knew just where it was in the hours between dusk and dark that they lost the trail. The Boy believed it was at a certain steep incline that Nig did his best to rush down.

"I thought he was at his tricks," said the Boy ruefully some hours after. "I believe I'm an ass, and Nig is a gentleman and a scholar. He knew perfectly what he was about."

"Reckon we'll camp, pardner."

"Reckon we might as well."

After unharnessing the dogs, the Boy stood an instant looking enviously at them as he thawed out his stiff hands under his parki. Exhausted and smoking hot, the dogs had curled down in the snow as contented-looking as though on a hearthrug before a fire, sheltering their sharp noses with their tails.

"Wish I had a tail to shelter my face," said the Boy, as if a tail were the one thing lacking to complete his bliss.

"You don't need any shelter *now*," answered the Colonel. "Your face is gettin' well——" And he stopped suddenly, carried back to those black days when he had vainly urged a face-guard. He unpacked their few possessions, and watched the Boy take the axe and go off for wood, stopping on his way, tired as he was, to pull Nig's pointed ears. The odd thing about the Boy was that it was only with these Indian curs— Nig in particular, who wasn't the Boy's dog at all—only with these brute-beasts had he seemed to recover something of that buoyancy and ridiculous youngness that had first drawn the Colonel to him on the voyage up from 'Frisco. It was also clear that if the Boy now drew away from his pardner ever so little, by so much did he draw nearer to the dogs.

He might be too tired to answer the Colonel; he was seldom too tired to talk nonsense to Nig, never too tired to say, "Well, old boy," or even "Well, *pardner*," to the dumb brute. It was, perhaps, this that the Colonel disliked most of all.

Whether the U. S. Agent at Nulato was justified or not in

saying all the region hereabouts was populous in the summer
with Indian camps, the native winter settlements, the half-
buried ighloo, or the rude log-hut, where, for a little tea, tobacco, or sugar, you could get as much fish as you could carry,
these welcome, if malodorous, places seemed, since they lost
the trail, to have vanished off the face of the earth. No question of the men sharing the dogs' fish, but of the dogs sharing
the men's bacon and meal. That night the meagre supper was
more meagre still that the "horses" might have something, too.
The next afternoon it stopped snowing and cleared, intensely
cold, and that was the evening the Boy nearly cried for joy
when, lifting up his eyes, he saw, a good way off, perched on
the river bank, the huts and high caches of an Indian village
etched black against a wintry sunset—a fine picture in any eye,
but meaning more than beauty to the driver of hungry dogs.

"Fish, Nig!" called out the Boy to his Leader. "You hear
me, you Nig? *Fish*, old fellow! Now, look at that, Colonel!
you tell me that Indian dog doesn't understand English. I
tell you what: we had a mean time with these dogs just at first,
but that was only because we didn't understand one another."

The Colonel preserved a reticent air.

"You'll come to my way of thinking yet. The Indian dog—
he's a daisy."

"Glad you think so." The Colonel, with some display of
temper, had given up trying to drive the team only half an hour
before, and was still rather sore about it.

"When you get to *understand* him," persisted the Boy, "he's
the most marvellous little horse ever hitched in harness. He
pulls, pulls, pulls all day long in any kind o' weather——"

"Yes, pulls you off your legs or pulls you the way you don't
want to go."

"Oh, that's when you rile him! He's just like any other
American gentleman: he's got his feelin's. Ain't you got feelin's, Nig? Huh! rather. I tell you what, Colonel, many a
time when I'm pretty well beat and ready to snap at anybody, I've looked at Nig peggin' away like a little man, on a
rotten trail, with a blizzard in his eyes, and it's just made me
sick after that to hear myself grumblin'. Yes, sir, the Indian
dog is an example to any white man on the trail." The Boy
seemed not to relinquish the hope of stirring the tired Colonel to
enthusiasm. "Don't you like the way, after the worst sort of
day, when you stop, he just drops down in the snow and rolls

about a little to rest his muscles, and then lies there as patient as anything till you are ready to unharness him and feed him?"

"—— and if you don't hurry up, he saves you the trouble of unharnessing by eating the traces and things."

"Humph! So would you if that village weren't in sight, if you were sure the harness wouldn't stick in your gizzard. And think of what a dog gets to reward him for his plucky day: one dried salmon or a little meal-soup when he's off on a holiday like this. Works without a let-up, and keeps in good flesh on one fish a day. Doesn't even get anything to drink; eats a little snow after dinner, digs his bed, and sleeps in a drift till morning."

"When he doesn't howl all night."

"Oh, that's when he meets his friends, and they talk about old times before they came down in the world."

"Hey?"

"Yes; when they were wolves and made us run instead of our making them. Make any fellow howl. Instead of carrying our food about we used to carry theirs, and run hard to keep from giving it up, too."

"Nig's at it again," said the Colonel. "Give us your whip."

"No," said the Boy; "I begin to see now why he stops and goes for Red like that. Hah! Spot's gettin it, too, this time. They haven't been pullin' properly. You just notice: if they aren't doin' their share Nig 'll turn to every time and give 'em 'Hail, Columbia!' You'll see, when he's freshened 'em up a bit we'll have 'em on a dead run." The Boy laughed and cracked his whip.

"They've got keen noses. *I* don't smell the village this time. Come on, Nig, Spot's had enough; he's sorry, good and plenty. Cheer up, Spot! Fish, old man! You hear me talkin' to you, Red? *Fish!* Caches full of it. Whoop!" and down they rushed, pell-mell, men and dogs tearing along like mad across the frozen river, and never slowing till it came to the stiff pull up the opposite bank.

"Funny I don't hear any dogs," panted the Boy.

They came out upon a place silent as the dead—a big deserted village, emptied by the plague, or, maybe, only by the winter; caches emptied, too; not a salmon, not a pike, not a lusk, not even a whitefish left behind.

It was a bitter blow. They didn't say anything; it was too bad to talk about. The Colonel made the fire, and fried a little bacon and made some mush: that was their dinner. The bacon-rinds were boiled in the mush-pot with a great deal of snow and a little meal, and the "soup" so concocted was set out to cool for the dogs. They were afraid to sleep in one of the cabins; it might be plague-infected. The Indians had cut all the spruce for a wide radius round about—no boughs to make a bed. They hoisted some tent-poles up into one of the empty caches, laid them side by side, and on this bed, dry, if hard, they found oblivion.

The next morning a thin, powdery snow was driving about. Had they lost their way in the calendar as well as on the trail, and was it December instead of the 29th of March? The Colonel sat on the packed sled, undoing with stiff fingers the twisted, frozen rope. He knew the axe that he used the night before on the little end of bacon was lying, pressed into the snow, under one runner. But that was the last thing to go on the pack before the lashing, and it wouldn't get lost pinned down under the sled. Nig caught sight of it, and came over with a cheerful air of interest, sniffed bacon on the steel, and it occurred to him it would be a good plan to lick it.

A bitter howling broke the stillness. The Boy came tearing up with a look that lifted the Colonel off the sled, and there was Nig trying to get away from the axe-head, his tongue frozen fast to the steel, and pulled horribly long out of his mouth like a little pink rope. The Boy had fallen upon the agonized beast, and forced him down close to the steel. Holding him there between his knees, he pulled off his outer mits and with hands and breath warmed the surface of the axe, speaking now and then to the dog, who howled wretchedly, but seemed to understand something was being done for him, since he gave up struggling. When at last the Boy got him free, the little horse pressed against his friend's legs with a strange new shuddering noise very pitiful to hear.

The Boy, blinking hard, said: "Yes, old man, I know, that was a mean breakfast; and he patted the shaggy chest. Nig bent his proud head and licked the rescuing hand with his bleeding tongue.

"An' you say that dog hasn't got feelin's!"

They hitched the team and pushed on. In the absence of a trail, the best they could do was to keep to the river ice. By-and-bye:

"Can you see the river bank?"

"I'm not sure," said the Boy.

"I thought you were going it blind."

"I believe I'd better let Nig have his head," said the Boy, stopping; "he's the dandy trail-finder. Nig, old man, I takes off my hat to you!"

They pushed ahead till the half-famished dogs gave out. They camped under the lee of the propped sled, and slept the sleep of exhaustion.

The next morning dawned clear and warm. The Colonel managed to get a little wood and started a fire. There were a few spoonfuls of meal in the bottom of the bag and a little end of bacon, mostly rind. The sort of soup the dogs had had yesterday was good enough for men to-day. The hot and watery brew gave them strength enough to strike camp and move on. The elder man began to say to himself that he would sell his life dearly. He looked at the dogs a good deal, and then would look at the Boy, but he could never catch his eye. At last: "They say, you know, that men in our fix have sometimes had to sacrifice a dog."

"Ugh!" The Boy's face expressed nausea at the thought.

"Yes, it is pretty revolting."

"We could never do it."

"N-no," said the Colonel.

The three little Esquimaux horses were not only very hungry, their feet were in a bad condition, and were bleeding. The Boy had shut his eyes at first at the sight of their red tracks in the snow. He hardly noticed them now.

An hour or so later: "Better men than we," says the Colonel significantly, "have had to put their feelings in their pockets." As if he found the observation distinctly discouraging, Nig at this moment sat down in the melting snow, and no amount of "mushing" moved him.

"Let's give him half an hour's rest, Colonel. Valuable beast, you know—altogether best team on the river," said the Boy, as if to show that his suggestion was not inspired by mere pity for the bleeding dogs. "And you look rather faded yourself, Colonel. Sit down and rest."

Nothing more was said for a full half-hour, till the Colonel, taking off his fur hat, and wiping his beaded forehead on the back of his hand, remarked: "Think of the Siege of Paris."

"Eh? What?" The Boy stared as if afraid his partner's brain had given way.

"When the horses gave out they had to eat dogs, cats, *rats* even. Think of it—rats!"

"The French are a dirty lot. Let's mush, Colonel. I'm as fit as a fiddle." The Boy got up and called the dogs. In ten minutes they were following the blind trail again. But the sled kept clogging, sticking fast and breaking down. After a desperate bout of ineffectual pulling, the dogs with one mind stopped again, and lay down in their bloody tracks.

The men stood silent for a moment; then the Colonel remarked:

"Red is the least valuable"—a long pause—"but Nig's feet are in the worst condition. That dog won't travel a mile further. Well," added the Colonel after a bit, as the Boy stood speechless studying the team, "what do you say?"

"Me?" He looked up like a man who has been dreaming and is just awake. "Oh, I should say our friend Nig here has had to stand more than his share of the racket."

"Poor old Nig!" said the Colonel, with a somewhat guilty air. "Look here: what do you say to seeing whether they can go if we help 'em with that load?"

"Good for you, Colonel!" said the Boy, with confidence wonderfully restored. "I was just thinking the same."

They unlashed the pack, and the Colonel wanted to make two bundles of the bedding and things; but whether the Boy really thought the Colonel was giving out, or whether down in some corner of his mind he recognised the fact that if the Colonel were not galled by this extra burden he might feel his hunger less, and so be less prone to thoughts of poor Nig in the pot—however it was, he said the bundle was his business for the first hour. So the Colonel did the driving, and the Boy tramped on ahead, breaking trail with thirty-five pounds on his back. And he didn't give it up, either, though he admitted long after it was the toughest time he had ever put in in all his life.

"Haven't you had about enough of this?" the Colonel sang out at dusk.

"Pretty nearly," said the Boy in a rather weak voice. He flung off the pack, and sat on it.

"Get up," says the Colonel; "give us the sleepin'-bag." When it was undone, the Norfolk jacket dropped out. He rolled it up against the sled, flung himself down, and heavily dropped his head on the rough pillow. But he sprang up.

"What? Yes. By the Lord!" He thrust his hand into the

capacious pocket of the jacket, and pulled out some broken ship's biscuit. "Hard tack, by the living Jingo!" He was up, had a few sticks alight, and the kettle on, and was melting snow to pour on the broken biscuit. "It swells, you know, like thunder!"

The Boy was still sitting on the bundle of "trade" tea and tobacco. He seemed not to hear; he seemed not to see the Colonel, shakily hovering about the fire, pushing aside the green wood and adding a few sticks of dry.

There was a mist before the Colonel's eyes. Reaching after a bit of seasoned spruce, he stumbled, and unconsciously set his foot on Nig's bleeding paw. The dog let out a yell and flew at him. The Colonel fell back with an oath, picked up a stick, and laid it on. The Boy was on his feet in a flash.

"Here! stop that!" He jumped in between the infuriated man and the infuriated dog.

"Stand back!" roared the Colonel.

"It was your fault; you trod——"

"Stand back, damn you! or you'll get hurt."

The stick would have fallen on the Boy; he dodged it, calling excitedly, "Come here, Nig! Here!"

"He's my dog, and I'll lamm him if I like. You——" The Colonel couldn't see just where the Boy and the culprit were. Stumbling a few paces away from the glare of the fire, he called out, "I'll kill that brute if he snaps at me again!"

"Oh yes," the Boy's voice rang passionately out of the gloom, "I know you want him killed."

The Colonel sat down heavily on the rolled-up bag. Presently the bubbling of boiling snow-water roused him. He got up, divided the biscuit, and poured the hot water over the fragments. Then he sat down again, and waited for them to "swell like thunder." He couldn't see where, a little way up the hillside, the Boy sat on a fallen tree with Nig's head under his arm. The Boy felt pretty low in his mind. He sat crouched together, with his head sunk almost to his knees. It was a lonely kind of a world after all. Doing your level best didn't seem to get you any forrader. What was the use? He started. Something warm, caressing, touched his cold face just under one eye. Nig's tongue.

"Good old Nig! You feel lonesome, too?" He gathered the rough beast up closer to him.

Just then the Colonel called, "Nig!"

"Sh! sh! Lie quiet!" whispered the Boy.

"Nig! Nig!"

"Good old boy! Stay here! He doesn't mean well **by you.** *Sh!* quiet! *Quiet,* I say!"

"Nig!" and the treacherous Colonel gave the peculiar whistle both men used to call the dogs to supper. The dog struggled to get away, the Boy's stiff fingers lost their grip, and "the best leader in the Yukon" was running down the bank as hard as he could pelt, to the camp fire—to the cooking-pot.

The Boy got up and floundered away in the opposite direction. He must get out of hearing. He toiled on, listening for the expected gunshot—hearing it, too, and the yawp of a wounded dog, in spite of a mitten clapped at each ear.

"That's the kind of world it is! Do your level best, drag other fellas' packs hundreds o' miles over the ice with a hungry belly and bloody feet, and then—— Poor old Nig!—'cause you're lame—poor old Nig!" With a tightened throat and hot water in his eyes, he kept on repeating the dog's name as he stumbled forward in the snow. "Nev' mind, old boy; it's a lonely kind o' world, and the right trail's hard to find." Suddenly he stood still. His stumbling feet were on a track. He had reached the dip in the saddle-back of the hill, and—yes! this was the *right* trail; for down on the other side below him were faint lights—huts—an Indian village! with fish and food for everybody. And Nig—Nig was being——

The Boy turned as if a hurricane had struck him, and tore back down the incline—stumbling, floundering in the snow, calling hoarsely: "Colonel, Colonel! don't do it! There's a village here, Colonel! Nig! Colonel, don't do it!"

He dashed into the circle of firelight, and beheld Nig standing with a bandaged paw, placidly eating softened biscuit out of the family frying-pan.

It was short work getting down to the village. They had one king salmon and two white fish from the first Indian they saw, who wanted hootch for them, and got only tabak.

In the biggest of the huts, nearly full of men, women, and children, coughing, sickly-looking, dejected, the natives made room for the strangers. When the white men had supped they handed over the remains of their meal (as is expected) to the head of the house. This and a few matches or a little tobacco on parting, is all he looks for in return for shelter, room for beds on the floor, snow-water laboriously melted, use of the fire, and as much wood as they like to burn, even if it is a barren place, and fuel is the precious far-travelled "drift."

It is curious to see how soon travellers get past that first cheechalko feeling that it is a little "nervy," as the Boy had said, to walk into another man's house uninvited, an absolute stranger, and take possession of everything you want without so much as "by your leave." You soon learn it is the Siwash* custom.

Nothing would have seemed stranger now, or more inhuman, than the civilized point of view.

The Indians trailed out one by one, all except the old buck to whom the hut belonged. He hung about for a bit till he was satisfied the travellers had no hootch, not even a little for the head of the house, and yet they seemed to be fairly decent fellows. Then he rolls up his blankets, for there is a premium on sleeping-space, and goes out, with never a notion that he is doing more than any man would, anywhere in the world, to find a place in some neighbour's hut to pass the night.

He leaves the two strangers, as Indian hospitality ordains, to the warmest places in the best hut, with two young squaws, one old one, and five children, all sleeping together on the floor, as a matter of course.

The Colonel and the Boy had flung themselves down on top of their sleeping-bag, fed and warmed and comforted. Only the old squaw was still up. She had been looking over the travellers' boots and "mitts," and now, without a word or even a look being exchanged upon the subject, she sat there in the corner, by the dim, seal-oil light, sewing on new thongs, patching up holes, and making the strange men tidy—men she had never seen before and would never see again. And this, no tribute to the Colonel's generosity or the youth and friendly manners of the Boy. They knew the old squaw would have done just the same had the mucklucks and the mitts belonged to "the tramp of the Yukon," with nothing to barter and not a cent in his pocket. This, again, is a Siwash custom.

The old squaw coughed and wiped her eyes. The children coughed in their sleep.

The dogs outside were howling like human beings put to torture. But the sound no longer had power to freeze the blood of the trail-men.

* Siwash, corruption of French-Canadian *sauvage*, applied all over the North to the natives, their possessions and their customs.

The Colonel merely damned them. The Boy lifted his head, and listened for Nig's note. The battle raged nearer; a great scampering went by the tent.

"Nig!"

A scuffling and snuffing round the bottom of the tent. The Boy, on a sudden impulse, reached out and lifted the flap.

"Got your bandage on? Come here."

Nig brisked in with the air of one having very little time to waste.

"Lord! I should think you'd be glad to lie down. *I* am. Let's see your paw. Here, come over to the light." He stepped very carefully over the feet of the other inhabitants till he reached the old woman's corner. Nig, following calmly, walked on prostrate bodies till he reached his friend.

"Now, your paw, pardner. F-ith! Bad, ain't it?" he appealed to the toothless squaw. Her best friend could not have said her wizened regard was exactly sympathetic, but it was attentive. She seemed intelligent as well as kind.

"Look here," whispered the Boy, "let that muckluck string o' mine alone." He drew it away, and dropped it between his knees. "Haven't you got something or other to make some shoes for Nig? Hein? He pantomimed, but she only stared. "Like this." He pulled out his knife, and cut off the end of one leg of his "shaps," and gathered it gently round Nig's nearest foot. "Little dog-boots. See? Give you some bully tabak if you'll do that for Nig. Hein?"

She nodded at last, and made a queer wheezy sound, whether friendly laughing or pure scorn, the Boy wasn't sure. But she set about the task.

"Come 'long, Nig," he whispered. "You just see if I don't shoe my little horse." And he sneaked back to bed, comfortable in the assurance that the Colonel was asleep. Nig came walking after his friend straight over people's heads.

One of the children sat up and whimpered. The Colonel growled sleepily.

"You black devil!" admonished the Boy under his breath. "Look what you're about. Come here, sir." He pushed the devil down between the sleeping-bag and the nearest baby.

The Colonel gave a distinct grunt of disapproval, and then, "Keepin' that brute in here?"

"He's a lot cleaner than our two-legged friends," said the Boy sharply, as if answering an insult.

"Right," said the Colonel with conviction.

His pardner was instantly mollified. "If you wake another baby, you'll get a lickin'," he said genially to the dog; and then he stretched out his feet till they reached Nig's back, and a feeling of great comfort came over the Boy.

"Say, Colonel," he yawned luxuriously, "did you know that —a—to-night—when Nig flared up, did you know you'd trodden on his paw?"

"Didn't know it till you told me," growled the Colonel.

"I thought you didn't. Makes a difference, doesn't it?"

"You needn't think," says the Colonel a little defiantly, "that I've weakened on the main point just because I choose to give Nig a few cracker-crumbs. If it's a question between a man's life and a dog's life, only a sentimental fool would hesitate."

"I'm not talking about that; we can get fish now. What I'm pointin' out is that Nig didn't fly at you for nothin'."

"He's got a devil of a temper, that dog."

"It's just like Nicholas of Pymeut said." The Boy sat up, eager in his advocacy and earnest as a judge. "Nicholas of Pymeut said: 'You treat a Siwash like a heathen, and he'll show you what a hell of a heathen he can be.'"

"Oh, go to sleep."

"I'm goin', Colonel."

CHAPTER XVI

MINÓOK

"For whatever . . . may come to pass, it lies with me to have it serve me."—EPICTETUS.

THE Indians guided them back to the trail. The Colonel and the Boy made good speed to Novikakat, laid in supplies at Korkorines, heard the first doubtful account of Minóok at Tanana, and pushed on. Past camps Stoneman and Woodworth, where the great Klondyke Expeditions lay fast in the ice; along the white strip of the narrowing river, pent in now between mountains black with scant, subarctic timber, or gray with fantastic weather-worn rock—on and on, till they reached the bluffs of the Lower Ramparts.

Here, at last, between the ranks of the many-gabled heights, Big Minóok Creek meets Father Yukon. Just below the junction, perched jauntily on a long terrace, up above the frozen river-bed, high and dry, and out of the coming trouble when river and creek should wake—here was the long, log-built mining town, Minóok, or Rampart, for the name was still undetermined in the spring of 1898.

It was a great moment.

"Shake, pardner," said the Boy. The Colonel and he grasped hands. Only towering good spirits prevented their being haughty, for they felt like conquerors, and cared not a jot that they looked like gaol-birds.

It was two o'clock in the morning. The Gold Nugget Saloon was flaring with light, and a pianola was perforating a tune. The travellers pushed open a frosted door, and looked into a long, low, smoke-veiled room, hung with many kerosene lamps, and heated by a great red-hot iron stove.

"Hello!" said a middle-aged man in mackinaws, smoking near the door-end of the bar.

"Hello! Is Blandford Keith here? There are some letters for him."

"Say, boys!" the man in mackinaws shouted above the pia-nola, "Windy Jim's got in with the mail."

The miners lounging at the bar and sitting at the faro-tables looked up laughing, and seeing the strangers through the smoke-haze, stopped laughing to stare.

"Down from Dawson?" asked the bar-tender hurrying for-ward, a magnificent creature in a check waistcoat, shirt-sleeves, four-in-hand tie, and a diamond pin.

"No, t'other way about. Up from the Lower River."

"Oh! May West or Muckluck crew? Anyhow, I guess you got a thirst on you," said the man in the mackinaws. "Come and licker up."

The bar-tender mixed the drinks in style, shooting the liquor from a height into the small gin-sling glasses with the dexterity that had made him famous.

When their tired eyes had got accustomed to the mingled smoke and glare, the travellers could see that in the space be-yond the card-tables, in those back regions where the pianola reigned, there were several couples twirling about—the clum-sily-dressed miners pirouetting with an astonishing lightness on their moccasined feet. And women! White women!

They stopped dancing and came forward to see the new arrivals.

The mackinaw man was congratulating the Colonel on "get-tin' back to civilization."

"See that plate-glass mirror?" He pointed behind the bar, below the moose antlers. "See them ladies? You've got to a place where you can rake in the dust all day, and dance all night, and go buckin' the tiger between whiles. Great place, Minóok. Here's luck!" He took up the last of the gin slings set in a row before the party.

"Have you got some property here?" asked the Boy.

The man, without putting down his glass, simply closed one eye over the rim.

"We've heard some bad accounts of these diggin's," said the Colonel.

"I ain't sayin' there's millions for *every*body. You've got to get the inside track. See that feller talkin' to the girl? Billy Nebrasky tipped him the wink in time to git the inside track, just before the Fall Stampede up the gulch."

"Which gulch?"

He only motioned with his head. "Through havin' that tip,

he got there in time to stake number three Below Discovery. He's had to hang up drinks all winter, but he's a millionaire all right. He's got a hundred thousand dollars *in sight,* only waitin' for runnin' water to wash it out."

"Then there *is* gold about here?"

"There is gold? Say, Maudie," he remarked in a humourous half-aside to the young woman who was passing with No-thumb-Jack, "this fellow wants to know if there is gold here."

She laughed. "Guess he ain't been here long."

Now it is not to be denied that this rejoinder was susceptible of more than one interpretation, but the mackinaw man seemed satisfied, so much so that he offered Maudie the second gin-sling which the Colonel had ordered "all round." She eyed the strangers over the glass. On the hand that held it a fine diamond sparkled. You would say she was twenty-six, but you wouldn't have been sure. She had seemed at least that at a distance. Now she looked rather younger. The face wore an impudent look, yet it was delicate, too. Her skin showed very white and fine under the dabs of rouge. The blueness was not yet faded out of her restless eyes.

"Minóok's all right. No josh about that," she said, setting down her glass. Then to the Boy, "Have a dance?"

"Not much," he replied rather roughly, and turned away to talk about the diggin's to two men on the other side.

Maudie laid her hand on the Colonel's arm, and the diamond twitched the light. *"You* will," she said.

"Well, you see, ma'am"—the Colonel's smile was charming in spite of his wild beard—"we've done such a lot o' dancin' lately—done nothin' else for forty days; and after seven hundred miles of it we're just a trifle tired, ma'am."

She laughed good-naturedly.

"Pity you're tired," said the mackinaw man. "There's a pretty good thing goin' just now, but it won't be goin' long."

The Boy turned his head round again with reviving interest in his own group.

"Look here, Si," Maudie was saying: "if you want to let a lay on your new claim to *anybody,* mind it's got to be me."

But the mackinaw man was glancing speculatively over at another group. In haste to forestall desertion, the Boy inquired:

"Do you know of anything good that isn't staked yet?"

"Well, mebbe I don't—and mebbe I do." Then, as if to

prove that he wasn't overanxious to pursue the subject: "Say, Maudie, ain't that French Charlie over there?" Maudie put her small nose in the air. "Ain't you made it up with Charlie yet?"

"No, I ain't."

"Then we'll have another drink all round."

While he was untying the drawstring of his gold sack, Maudie said, half-aside, but whether to the Colonel or the Boy neither could tell: "Might do worse than keep your eye on Si McGinty." She nodded briskly at the violet checks on the mackinaw back. "Si's got a cinch up there on Glory Hallelujah, and nobody's on to it yet."

The pianola picked out a polka. The man Si McGinty had called French Charlie came up behind the girl and said something. She shook her head, turned on her heel, and began circling about in the narrow space till she found another partner, French Charlie scowling after them, as they whirled away between the faro-tables back into the smoke and music at the rear. McGinty was watching Jimmie, the man at the gold scales, pinch up some of the excess dust in the scale-pan and toss it back into the brass blower.

"Where did that gold come from?" asked the Colonel.

"Off a claim o' mine"; and he lapsed into silence.

You are always told these fellows are so anxious to rope in strangers. This man didn't seem to be. It made him very interesting. The Boy acted strictly on the woman's hint, and kept an eye on the person who had a sure thing up on Glory Hallelujah. But when the lucky man next opened his mouth it was to say:

"Why, there's Butts down from Circle City."

"Butts?" repeated the Boy, with little affectation of interest.

"Yep. Wonder what the son of a gun is after *here*." But he spoke genially, even with respect.

"Who's Butts?"

"Butts? Ah—well—a—Butts is the smartest fellow with his fingers in all 'laska"; and McGinty showed his big yellow teeth in an appreciative smile.

"Smart at washin' gold out?"

"Smarter at pickin' it out." The bartender joined in Si's laugh as that gentleman repeated, "Yes, *sir!* handiest feller with his fingers I ever seen."

"What does he do with his fingers?" asked the Boy, with impatient suspicion.

"Well, he don't dare do much with 'em up here. 'Tain't popular."

"What ain't?"

"Butts's little game. But Lord! he *is* good at it." Butts had been introduced as a stalking-horse, but there was no doubt about Si's admiration of his "handiness." "Butts is wasted up here," he sighed. "There's some chance for a murderer in Alaska, but a thief's a goner."

"Oh, well; you were sayin' that gold o' yours came from——"

"Poor old Butts! Bright feller, too.

"How far off is your——"

"I tell you, sir, Butts is brains to his boots. Course you know Jack McQuestion?"

"No, but I'd like to hear a little about your——"

"Y' don' know Jack McQuestion? Well, sir, Jack's the biggest man in the Yukon. Why, he built Fort Reliance six miles below the mouth of the Klondyke in '73; he discovered gold on the Stewart in '85, and established a post there. *Everybody* knows Jack McQuestion; an"—quickly, as he saw he was about to be interrupted—"you heard about that swell watch we all clubbed together and give him? No? Well, sir, there ain't an eleganter watch in the world. Is there?"

"Guess not," said the bartender.

"Repeater, you know. Got twenty-seven di'mon's in the case. One of 'em's this size." He presented the end of a gnarled and muscular thumb. "And inside, the case is all wrote in—a lot of soft sawder; but Jack ain't got *any*thing he cares for so much. You can see he's always tickled to death when anybody asks him the time. But do you think he ever lets that watch out'n his own hands? Not *much*. Let's anybody *look* at it, and keeps a holt o' the stem-winder. Well, sir, we was all in a saloon up at Circle, and that feller over there—Butts —he bet me fifty dollars that he'd git McQuestion's watch away from him before he left the saloon. An' it was late. McQuestion was thinkin' a'ready about goin' home to that squaw wife that keeps him so straight. Well, sir, Butts went over and began to gas about outfittin', and McQuestion answers and figures up the estimates on the counter, and, by Gawd! in less 'n quarter of an hour Butts, just standin' there

and listenin', as you'd think—he'd got that di'mon' watch off'n
the chain an' had it in his pocket. I knew he done it, though I
ain't exactly seen *how* he done it. The others who were in
the game, they swore he hadn't got it yet, but, by Gawd, Butts
says he'll think over McQuestion's terms, and wonders what
time it is. He takes that di'mon' watch out of his pocket,
glances at it, and goes off smooth as cream, sayin' 'Good-
night.' Then he come a grinnin' over to us. 'Jest you go an'
ask the Father o' the Yukon Pioneers what time it is, will yer?'
An' I done it. Well, sir, when he put his hand in his pocket,
by Gawd! I wish y' could a' saw McQuestion's face. Yes, sir,
Butts is brains to his boots."

"How far out are the diggin's?"

"What diggin's?"

"Yours."

"Oh—a—my gulch ain't fur."

There was a noise about the door. Someone bustled in with
a torrent of talk, and the pianola was drowned in a pandemonium of shouts and laughter.

"Windy Jim's reely got back!"

Everybody crowded forward. Maudie was at the Colonel's
elbow explaining that the little yellow-bearded man with the
red nose was the letter-carrier. He had made a contract early
in the winter to go to Dawson and bring down the mail for
Minóok. His agreement was to make the round trip and be
back by the middle of February. Since early March the standing gag in the camp had been: "Well, Windy Jim got in last
night."

The mild jest had grown stale, and the denizens of Minóok
had given up the hope of ever laying eyes on Windy again,
when lo! here he was with twenty-two hundred letters in his
sack. The patrons of the Gold Nugget crowded round him
like flies round a lump of sugar, glad to pay a dollar apiece
on each letter he handed out. "And you take *all* that's addressed
to yer at that price or you get none." Every letter there had
come over the terrible Pass. Every one had travelled twelve
hundred miles by dog-team, and some had been on the trail
seven months.

"Here, Maudie, me dear." The postman handed her two
letters. "See how he dotes on yer."

"Got anything fur—what's yer names?" says the mackinaw
man, who seemed to have adopted the Colonel and the Boy.

He presented them without embarrassment to "Windy Jim Wilson, of Hog'em Junction, the best trail mail-carrier in the 'nited States."

Those who had already got letters were gathered in groups under the bracket-lights reading eagerly. In the midst of the lull of satisfaction or expectancy someone cried out in disgust, and another threw down a letter with a shower of objurgation.

"Guess you got the mate to mine, Bonsor," said a bystander with a laugh, slowly tearing up the communication he had opened with fingers so eager that they shook.

"You pay a dollar apiece for letters from folks you never heard of, asking you what you think of the country, and whether you'd advise 'em to come out."

"Huh! don't I wish they would!"

"It's all right. *They will.*"

"And then trust Bonsor to git even."

Salaman, "the luckiest man in camp," who had come in from his valuable Little Minóok property for the night only, had to pay fifteen dollars for his mail. When he opened it, he found he had one home letter, written seven months before, eight notes of inquiry, and six advertisements.

Maudie had put her letters unopened in her pocket, and told the man at the scales to weigh out two dollars to Windy, and charge to her. Then she began to talk to the Colonel.

The Boy observed with scant patience that his pardner treated Maudie with a consideration he could hardly have bettered had she been the first lady in the land. "Must be because she's little and cute-lookin'. The Colonel's a sentimental ol' goslin'."

"What makes you so polite to that dance-hall girl?" muttered the Boy aside. "She's no good."

"Reckon it won't make her any better for me to be impolite to her," returned the Colonel calmly.

But finding she could not detach the Kentuckian from his pardner, Maudie bestowed her attention elsewhere. French Charlie was leaning back against the wall, his hands jammed in his pockets, and his big slouch-hat pulled over his brows. Under the shadow of the wide brim furtively he watched the girl. Another woman came up and asked him to dance. He shook his head.

"Reckon we'd better go and knock up Blandford Keith and

get a bed," suggested the Boy regretfully, looking round for the man who had a cinch up on Glory Hallelujah, and wouldn't tell you how to get there.

"Reckon we'd better," agreed the Colonel.

But they halted near Windy Jim, who was refreshing himself, and at the same time telling Dawson news, or Dawson lies, as the company evidently thought. And still the men crowded round, listening greedily, just as everybody devours certain public prints without ceasing to impeach their veracity. Lacking newspapers at which to pish! and pshaw! they listened to Windy Jim, disbelieving the only unvarnished tale that gentleman had ever told. For Windy, with the story-teller's instinct, knew marvellous enough would sound the bare recital of those awful Dawson days when the unprecedented early winter stopped the provision boats at Circle, and starvation stared the over-populated Klondyke in the face.

Having disposed of their letters, the miners crowded round the courier to hear how the black business ended—matter of special interest to Minóok, for the population here was composed chiefly of men who, by the Canadian route, had managed to get to Dawson in the autumn, in the early days of the famine scare, and who, after someone's panic-proposal to raid the great Stores, were given free passage down the river on the last two steamers to run.

When the ice stopped them (one party at Circle, the other at Fort Yukon), they had held up the supply boats and helped themselves under the noses of Captain Ray and Lieutenant Richardson, U. S. A.

"Yes, sir," McGinty had explained, "we Minóok boys was all in that picnic. But we give our bond to pay up at midsummer, and after the fun was over we dropped down here."

He pushed nearer to Windy to hear how it had fared with the men who had stayed behind in the Klondyke—how the excitement flamed and menaced; how Agent Hansen of the Alaska Commercial Company, greatest of the importers of provisions and Arctic equipment, rushed about, half crazy, making speeches all along the Dawson River front, urging the men to fly for their lives, back to the States or up to Circle, before the ice stopped moving!

But too many of these men had put everything they had on earth into getting here; too many had abandoned costly outfits on the awful Pass, or in the boiling eddies of the White Horse

Rapids, paying any price in money or in pain to get to the gold-fields before navigation closed. And now! here was Hansen, with all the authority of the A. C., shouting wildly: "Quick, quick! go up or down. It's a race for life!"

Windy went on to tell how the horror of the thing dulled the men, how they stood about the Dawson streets helpless as cattle, paralysed by the misery that had overtaken them. All very well for Hansen to try to relieve the congestion at the Klondyke—the poor devils knew that to go either way, up or down, as late as this meant death. Then it was whispered how Captain Constantine of the Mounted Police was getting ready to drive every man out of the Klondyke, at the point of the bayonet, who couldn't show a thousand pounds of provisions. Yet most of the Klondykers still stood about dazed, silent, waiting for the final stroke.

A few went up, over the way they had come, to die after all on the Pass, and some went down, their white, despairing faces disappearing round the Klondyke bend as they drifted with the grinding ice towards the Arctic Circle, where the food was caught in the floes. And how one came back, going by without ever turning his head, caring not a jot for Golden Dawson, serene as a king in his capital, solitary, stark on a little island of ice.

"Lord! it was better, after all, at the Big Chimney."

"Oh, it wasn't so bad," said Windy cheerfully. "About the time one o' the big companies announced they was sold out o' everything but sugar and axe-handles, a couple o' steamers pushed their way in through the ice. After all, just as old J. J. Healy said, it was only a question of rations and proper distribution. Why, flour's fell from one hundred and twenty dollars a sack to fifty! And there's a big new strike on the island opposite Ensley Creek. They call it Monte Cristo; pay runs eight dollars to the pan. Lord! Dawson's the greatest gold camp on the globe."

But no matter what befell at Dawson, business must be kept brisk at Minóok. The pianola started up, and Buckin' Billy, who called the dances, began to bawl invitations to the company to come and waltz.

Windy interrupted his own music for further refreshment, pausing an instant, with his mouth full of dried-apple pie to say:

"Congress has sent out a relief expedition to Dawson."

"No!"

"Fact! Reindeer."

"Ye mean peacocks."

"Mean reindeer! It's all in the last paper come over the Pass. A Reindeer Relief Expedition to save them poor starvin' Klondykers."

"Haw, haw! Good old Congress!"

"Well, did you find any o' them reindeer doin' any relievin' round Dawson?"

"Naw! What do *you* think? Takes more'n Congress to git over the Dalton Trail"; and Windy returned to his pie.

Talking earnestly with Mr. Butts, French Charlie pushed heavily past the Boy on his way to the bar. From his gait it was clear that he had made many similar visits that evening. In his thick Canadian accent Charlie was saying:

"I blowed out a lot o' dust for dat girl. She's wearin' my di'mon' now, and won't look at me. Say, Butts, I'll give you twenty dollars if you sneak dat ring."

"Done with you," says Butts, as calm as a summer's day. In two minutes Maudie was twirling about with the handy gentleman, who seemed as accomplished with his toes as he was reputed to be with his fingers.

He came up with her presently and ordered some wine.

"Wine, b-gosh!" muttered Charlie in drunken appreciation, propping himself against the wall again, and always slipping sideways. "Y' tink he's d' fines' sor' fella, don't you? Hein? Wai' 'n see!"

The wine disappears and the two go off for another dance. Inside of ten minutes up comes Butts and passes something to French Charlie. That gentleman laughs tipsily, and, leaning on Butts's arm, makes his way to the scales.

"Weigh out twen' dollars dis gen'man," he ordered.

Butts pulled up the string of his poke and slipped to one side, as noise reached the group at the bar of a commotion at the other end of the saloon.

"My ring! it's gone! My diamond ring! Now, you've got it"; and Maudie came running out from the dancers after one of the Woodworth gentlemen.

Charlie straightened up and grinned, almost sobered in excess of joy and satisfied revenge. The Woodworth gentleman is searched and presently exonerated. Everybody is told of the loss, every nook and corner investigated. Maudie goes down on hands and knees, even creeping behind the bar.

"I know'd she go on somethin' awful," said Charlie, so glee-fully that Bonsor, the proprietor of the Gold Nugget, began to look upon him with suspicion.

When Maudie reappeared, flushed, and with disordered hair, after her excursion under the counter, French Charlie confronted her.

"Looky here. You treated me blame mean, Maudie; but wha' d' you say if I's to off' a rewar' for dat ring?"

"Reward! A healthy lot o' good that would do."

"Oh, very well; 'f you don' wan' de ring back——"

"I *do,* Charlie."

He hammered on the bar.

"Ev'body gottah look fur ring. I give a hunner 'n fifty dollah rewar'."

Maudie stared at the princely offer. But instantly the commotion was greater than ever. "Ev'body" did what was expected of them, especially Mr. Butts. They flew about, looking in possible and impossible places, laughing, screaming, tumbling over one another. In the midst of the uproar French Charlie lurches up to Maudie.

"Dat look anyt'in' like it?"

"Oh, *Charlie!*"

She looked the gratitude she could not on the instant speak.

In the midst of the noise and movement the mackinaw man said to the Boy:

"Don't know as you'd care to see my new prospect hole?"

"Course I'd like to see it."

"Well, come along to-morrow afternoon. Meet me here 'bout two. Don't *say* nothin' to nobody," he added still lower. "We don't want to get overrun before we've recorded."

The Boy could have hugged that mackinaw man.

Outside it was broad day, but still the Gold Nugget lights were flaring and the pianola played.

They had learned from the bar-tender where to find Blandford Keith—"In the worst-looking shack in the camp." But "It looks good to me," said the Boy, as they went in and startled Keith out of his first sleep. The man that brings you letters before the ice goes out is your friend. Keith helped them to bring in their stuff, and was distinctly troubled because the travellers wouldn't take his bunk. They borrowed some dry blankets and went to sleep on the floor.

It was after two when they woke in a panic, lest the mackinaw man should have gone without them. While the Colonel got breakfast the Boy dashed round to the Gold Nugget, found Si McGinty playing craps, and would have brought him back in triumph to breakfast—but no, he would "wait down yonder below the Gold Nugget, and don't you say nothin' yit about where we're goin', or we'll have the hull town at our heels."

About twelve miles "back in the mountains" is a little gulch that makes into a big one at right angles.

"That's the pup where my claim is."

"The what?"

"Little creek; call 'em pups here."

Down in the desolate hollow a ragged A tent, sagged away from the prevailing wind. Inside, they found that the canvas was a mere shelter over a prospect hole. A rusty stove was almost buried by the heap of earth and gravel thrown up from a pit several feet deep.

"This is a winter diggins y' see," observed the mackinaw man with pride. "It's only while the ground is froze solid you can do *this* kind o' minin'. I've had to burn the ground clean down to bed-rock. Yes, sir, thawed my way inch by inch to the old channel."

"Well, and what have you found?"

"S'pose we pan some o' this dirt and see."

His slow caution impressed his hearers. They made up a fire, melted snow, and half filled a rusty pan with gravel and soil from the bottom of the pit.

"Know how to pan?"

The Colonel and the Boy took turns. They were much longer at it than they ever were again, but the mackinaw man seemed not in the least hurry. The impatience was all theirs. When they had got down to fine sand, "Look!" screamed the Boy.

"By the Lord!" said the Colonel softly.

"*Is* that——"

"Looks like you got some colours there. Gosh! Then I ain't been dreamin' after all."

"Hey? Dreamin'? What? Look! Look!"

"That's why I brought you gen'l'men out," says the mackinaw man. "I was afraid to trust my senses—thought I was gettin' wheels in my head."

"Lord! *look* at the gold!"

They took about a dollar and twenty cents out of that pan.

"Now see here, you gen'l'men jest lay low about this strike." His anxiety seemed intense. They reassured him.

"I don't suppose you mind our taking up a claim apiece next you," pleaded the Boy, "since the law don't allow you to stake more'n one."

"Oh, that's all right," said the mackinaw man, with an air of princely generosity. "And I don't mind if you like to let in a few of your particular pals, if you'll agree to help me organise a district. An' I'll do the recordin' fur ye."

Really, this mackinaw man was a trump. The Colonel took twenty-five dollars out of a roll of bills and handed it to him.

"What's this fur?"

"For bringing us out—for giving us the tip. I'd make it more, but till I get to Dawson——"

"Oh!" laughed the mackinaw man, "*that's* all right," and indifferently he tucked the bills into his baggy trousers.

The Colonel felt keenly the inadequacy of giving a man twenty-five dollars who had just introduced him to hundreds of thousands—and who sat on the edge of his own gold-mine— but it was only "on account."

The Colonel staked No. 1 Above the Discovery, and the Boy was in the act of staking No. 1 Below when——

"No, no," says that kind mackinaw man, "the heavier gold will be found further up the gulch—stake No. 2 Above"; and he told them natural facts about placer-mining that no after expert knowledge could ever better. But he was not as happy as a man should be who has just struck pay.

"Fact is, it's kind of upsettin' to find it so rich here."

"Give you leave to upset me that way all day."

"Y' see, I bought another claim over yonder where I done a lot o' work last summer and fall. Built a cabin and put up a sluice. I *got* to be up there soon as the ice goes out. Don't see how I *got* time to do my assessment here too. Wish I was twins."

"Why don't you sell this?"

"Guess I'll have to part with a share in it." He sighed and looked lovingly into the hole. "Minin's an awful gamble," he said, as though admonishing Si McGinty; "but we *know* there's gold just there."

The Colonel and the Boy looked at their claims and felt the pinch of uncertainty.

"What do you want for a share in your claim, Mr. Mc-Ginty?"

"Oh, well, as I say, I'll let it go reasonable to a feller who'd do the assessment, *on account* o' my having that other property. Say three thousand dollars."

The Colonel shook his head.

"Why, it's dirt-cheap! Two men can take a hundred and fifty dollars a day out of that claim without outside help. And properly worked, the summer ought to show forty thousand dollars."

On the way home McGinty found he could let the thing go for "two thousand spot cash."

"Make it quarter shares," suggested the Boy, thrilled at such a chance, "and the Colonel and I together 'll raise five hundred and do the rest of the assessment work for you."

But they were nearly back at Minóok before McGinty said, "Well, I *ain't* twins, and I can't personally work two gold-mines, so we'll call it a deal." And the money passed that night.

And the word passed, too, to an ex-Governor of a Western State and his satellites, newly arrived from Woodworth, and to a party of men just down from Circle City. McGinty seemed more inclined to share his luck with strangers than with the men he had wintered amongst. "Mean lot, these Minóok fellers." But the return of the ex-Governor and so large a party from quietly staking their claims, roused Minóok to a sense that "somethin' was goin' on."

By McGinty's advice, the strangers called a secret meeting, and elected McGinty recorder. All the claim-holders registered their properties and the dates of location. The Recorder gave everybody his receipt, and everybody felt it was cheap at five dollars. Then the meeting proceeded to frame a code of Laws for the new district, stipulating the number of feet permitted each claim (being rigidly kept by McGinty within the limits provided by the United States Laws on the subject), and decreeing the amount of work necessary to hold a claim a year, settling questions of water rights, etc., etc.

Not until Glory Hallelujah Gulch was a full-fledged mining district did Minóok in general know what was in the wind. The next day the news was all over camp.

If McGinty's name inspired suspicion, the Colonel's and the ex-Governor's reassured, the Colonel in particular (he had already established that credit that came so easy to him) being triumphantly quoted as saying, "Glory Hallelujah Gulch was the richest placer he'd ever struck." Nobody added that it was also the only one. But this matter of a stampede is not controlled by reason; it is a thing of the nerves; while you are ridiculing someone else your legs are carrying you off on the same errand.

In a mining-camp the saloon is the community's heart. However little a man cares to drink, or to dance, or to play cards, he goes to the saloon as to the one place where he may meet his fellows, do business, and hear the news. The saloon is the Market Place. It is also the Café, the Theatre, the Club, the Stock Exchange, the Barber's Shop, the Bank—in short, you might as well be dead as not be a patron of the Gold Nugget.

Yet neither the Colonel nor the Boy had been there since the night of their arrival. On returning from that first triumphant inspection of McGinty's diggings, the Colonel had been handed a sealed envelope without address.

"How do you know it's for me?"

"She said it was for the Big Chap," answered Blandford Keith.

The Colonel read:

*"Come to the Gold Nugget as soon as you get this, and hear something to your advantage.—*MAUDIE.*"*

So he had stayed away, having plenty to occupy him in helping to organise the new district. He was strolling past the saloon the morning after the Secret Meeting, when down into the street, like a kingfisher into a stream, Maudie darted, and held up the Colonel.

"Ain't you had my letter?"

"Oh—a—yes—but I've been busy."

"Guess so!" she said with undisguised scorn. "Where's Si McGinty?"

"Reckon he's out at the gulch. I've got to go down to the A. C. now and buy some grub to take out." He was moving on.

"Take where?" She followed him up.

"To McGinty's gulch."

"What for?"

"Why, to live on, while my pardner and I do the assessment work."

"Then it's true! McGinty's been fillin' you full o' guff."
The Colonel looked at her a little haughtily.

"See here: I ain't busy, as a rule, about other folks' funerals,
but——" She looked at him curiously. "It's cold here; come
in a minute." There was no hint of vulgar nonsense, but something very earnest in the pert little face that had been so pretty.
They went in. "Order drinks," she said aside, "and don't talk
before Jimmie."

She chaffed the bartender, and leaned idly against the counter. When a group of returned stampeders came in, she sat
down at a rough little faro-table, leaned her elbows on it, sipped
the rest of the stuff in her tumbler through a straw, and in the
shelter of her arms set the straw in a knot-hole near the table-
leg, and spirited the bad liquor down under the board.

"Don't give me away," she said.

The Colonel knew she got a commission on the drinks, and
was there to bring custom. He nodded.

"I hoped I'd see you in time," she went on hurriedly—"in
time to warn you that McGinty was givin' you a song and
dance."

"Hey?"

"Tellin' you a ghost story."

"You mean——"

"Can't you understand plain English?" she said, irritated at
such obtuseness. "I got worried thinkin' it over, for it was
me told that pardner o' yours——" She smiled wickedly. "I
expected McGinty'd have some fun with the young feller, but
I didn't expect *you'd* be such a Hatter." She wound up with
the popular reference to lunacy.

The Colonel pulled up his great figure with some pomposity.

"I don't understand."

"Any feller can see that. You're just the kind the McGintys
are layin' for." She looked round to see that nobody was
within earshot. "Si's been layin' round all winter waitin' for
the spring crop o' suckers."

"If you mean there isn't gold out at McGinty's gulch, you're
wrong; I've seen it."

"Course you have."

He paused. She, sweeping the Gold Nugget with vigilant
eye, went on in a voice of indulgent contempt.

"Some of 'em load up an old shot-gun with a little charge
o' powder and a quarter of an ounce of gold-dust on top, fire

the prospect hole a dozen times or so, and then take
I bet Si didn't take any
more trouble with me colours in his mouth,
to spit in the shovel or the pan, when you wasn't lookin'—just
enough to drive you crazy, and get you to boost him into a
Recordership. Why, he's cleaned up a tub o' money in fees
since you struck the town."

The Colonel moved uneasily, but faith with him died hard.
"McGinty strikes me as a very decent sort of man, with a
knowledge of practical mining and of mining law——"

Maudie made a low sound of impatience, and pushed her
empty glass aside.

"Oh, very well, go your own way! Waste the whole spring
doin' Si's assessment for him. And when the bottom drops
out o' recordin', you'll see Si gettin' some cheechalko to buy an
interest in that rottin' hole o' his——"

Her jaw fell as she saw the Colonel's expression.

"He's got you too!" she exclaimed.

"Well, didn't you say yourself that night you'd be glad if
McGinty 'd let you a lay?"

"Pshaw! I was only givin' you a song and dance. Not you
neither, but that pardner o' yours. I thought I'd learn that
young man a lesson. But I didn't know *you'd* get flim-flammed
out o' your boots. Thought you looked like you got some
sense."

Unmoved by the Colonel's aspect of offended dignity, faintly
dashed with doubt, she hurried on:

"Before you go shellin' out any more cash, or haulin' stuff
to Glory Hallelujah, just you go down that prospect hole o'
McGinty's when McGinty ain't there, and see how many
colours you can ketch."

The Colonel looked at her.

"Well, I'll do it," he said slowly, "and if you're right——"

"Oh, *I'm* all right," she laughed; "an' I know my McGinty
backwards. But"—she frowned with sudden anger—"it ain't
Maudie's pretty way to interfere with cheechalkos gettin' fooled.
I ain't proud o' the trouble I've taken, and I'll thank you not
to mention it. Not to that pardner o' yours—not to nobody."

She stuck her nose in the air, and waved her hand to French
Charlie, who had just then opened the door and put his head
in. He came straight over to her, and she made room for him
on the bench.

MINÓOK

The Colonel went out full of thought. He listened attentively when the ex-Governor, that evening at Keith's, said something about the woman up at the Gold Nugget—"Maudie —what's the rest of her name?"

"Don't believe anybody knows. Oh, yes, they must, too; it'll be on her deeds. She's got the best hundred by fifty foot lot in the place. Held it down last fall herself with a six-shooter, and she owns that cabin on the corner. Isn't a better business head in Minóok than Maudie's. She got a lay on a good property o' Salaman's last fall, and I guess she's got more ready dust even now, before the washin' begins, than anybody here except Salaman and the A. C. There ain't a man in Minóok who wouldn't listen respectfully to Maudie's views on any business proposition —once he was sure she wasn't fooling."

And Keith told a string of stories to show how the Minóok miners admired her astuteness, and helped her unblushingly to get the better of one another.

The Colonel stayed in Minóok till the recording was all done, and McGinty got tired of living on flap-jacks at the gulch.

The night McGinty arrived in town the Colonel, not even taking the Boy into his confidence, hitched up and departed for the new district.

He came back the next day a sadder and a wiser man. They had been sold.

McGinty was quick to gather that someone must have given him away. It had only been a question of time, after all. He had lined his pockets, and could take the new turn in his affairs with equanimity.

"Wait till the steamers begin to run," Maudie said; "McGinty 'll play that game with every new boat-load. Oh, McGinty 'll make another fortune. Then he'll go to Dawson and blow it in. Well, Colonel, sorry you ain't cultivatin' rheumatism in a damp hole up at Glory Hallelujah?"

"I—I am very much obliged to you for saving me from———"

She cut him short. "You see you've got time now to look about you for something really good, if there *is* anything outside of Little Minóok."

"It was very kind of you to———"

"No it wasn't," she said shortly.

The Colonel took out a roll of bank bills and selected one,

folded it small, and passed it towards her under the ledge of the table. She glanced down.

"Oh, I don't want that."

"Yes, please."

"Tell you I don't."

"You've done me a very good turn; saved me a lot of time and expense."

Slowly she took the money, as one thinking out something.

"Where do you come from?" he asked suddenly.

"'Frisco. I was in the chorus at the Alcazar."

"What made you go into the chorus?"

"Got tired o' life on a sheep-ranch. All work and no play. Never saw a soul. Seen plenty since."

"Got any people belonging to you?"

"Got a kind of a husband."

"A kind of a husband?"

"Yes—the kind you'd give away with a pound o' tea."

The little face, full of humourous contempt and shrewd scorn, sobered; she flung a black look round the saloon, and her eyes came back to the Colonel's face.

"I've got a girl," she said, and a sudden light flashed across her frowning as swiftly as a meteor cuts down along a darkened sky. "Four years old in June. *She* ain't goin' into no chorus, bet your life! *She's* going to have money, and scads o' things I ain't never had."

That night the Colonel and the Boy agreed that, although they had wasted some valuable time and five hundred and twenty-five dollars on McGinty, they still had a chance of making their fortunes before the spring rush.

The next day they went eight miles out in slush and in alternate rain and sunshine, to Little Minóok Creek, where the biggest paying claims were universally agreed to be. They found a place even more ragged and desolate than McGinty's, where smoke was rising sullenly from underground fires and the smell of burning wood filled the air, the ground turned up and dotted at intervals with piles of frozen gravel that had been hoisted from the shafts by windlass, forlorn little cabins and tents scattered indiscriminately, a vast number of empty bottles and cans sown broadcast, and, early as it was, a line of sluices upon Salaman's claim.

They had heard a great deal about the dark, keen-looking young Oregon lawyer, for Salaman was the most envied man in Minóok. "Come over to my dump and get some nuggets," says Mr. Salaman, as in other parts of the world a man will say, "Come into the smoking-room and have a cigar."

The snow was melted from the top of Salaman's dump, and his guests had no difficulty in picking several rough little bits of gold out of the thawing gravel. It was an exhilarating occupation.

"Come down my shaft and see my cross-cuts"; and they followed him.

He pointed out how the frozen gravel made solid wall, or pillar, and no curbing was necessary. With the aid of a candle and their host's urging, they picked out several dollars' worth of coarse gold from the gravel "in place" at the edge of the bed-rock. When he had got his guests thoroughly warmed up:

"Yes, I took out several thousand last fall, and I'll have twenty thousand more out of my first summer clean-up."

"And after that?"

"After that I'm going home. I wouldn't stay here and work this way and live this way another winter, not for twenty millions."

"I'm surprised to hear *you* talking like that, sah."

"Well, you won't be once you have tried it yourself. Mining up here's an awful gamble. Colours pretty well everywhere, and a few flakes of flour gold, just enough to send the average cheechalko crazy, but no real 'pay' outside of this little gulch. And even here, every inch has been scrambled for—and staked, too—and lots of it fought over. Men died here in the fall defending their ground from the jumpers—ground that hadn't a dollar in it."

"Well, your ground was worth looking after, and John Dillon's. Which is his claim?"

Salaman led the way over the heaps of gravel and round a windlass to No. 6, admitting:

"Oh, yes, Dillon and I, and a few others, have come out of it all right, but Lord! it's a gamble."

Dillon's pardner, Kennedy, did the honours, showing the Big Chimney men the very shaft out of which their Christmas heap of gold had been hoisted. It was true after all. For the faoured there *was* "plenty o' gold—plenty o' gold."

"But," said Salaman, "there are few things more mysterious than its whereabouts or why it should be where it is. Don't talk to me about mining experts—we've had 'em here. But who can explain the mystery of Minóok? There are six claims in all this country that pay to work. The pay begins in No. 5; before that, nothing. Just up yonder, above No. 10, the pay-streak pinches out. No mortal knows why. A whole winter's toiling and moiling, and thousands of dollars put into the ground, haven't produced an ounce of gold above that claim or below No. 5. I tell you it's an awful gamble. Hunter Creek, Hoosier, Bear, Big Minóok, I You, Quail, Alder, Mike Hess, Little Nell—the whole blessed country, rivers, creeks, pups, and all, staked for a radius of forty miles just because there's gold here, where we're standing."

"You don't mean there's *nothing* left!"

"Nothing within forty miles that somebody hasn't either staked or made money by abandoning."

"Made money?"

Salaman laughed.

"It's money in your pocket pretty nearly every time you don't take up a claim. Why, on Hunter alone they've spent twenty thousand dollars this winter."

"And how much have they taken out?"

With index-finger and thumb Salaman made an "O," and looked shrewdly through it.

"It's an awful gamble," he repeated solemnly.

"It doesn't seem possible there's *nothing* left," reiterated the Boy, incredulous of such evil luck.

"Oh, I'm not saying you may not make something by getting on some other fellow's property, if you've a mind to pay for it. But you'd better not take anything on trust. I wouldn't trust my own mother in Alaska. Something in the air here that breeds lies. You can't believe anybody, yourself included." He laughed, stooped, and picked a little nugget out of the dump. "You'll have the same man tell you an entirely different story about the same matter within an hour. Exaggeration is in the air. The best man becomes infected. You lie, he lies, they all lie. Lots of people go crazy in Alaska every year—various causes, but it's chiefly from believing their own lies."

They returned to Rampart.

It was decidedly inconvenient, considering the state of their finances, to have thrown away that five hundred dollars on McGinty. They messed with Keith, and paid their two-thirds of the household expenses; but Dawson prices reigned, and it was plain there were no Dawson prizes.

"Well," said the Colonel in the morning, "we've got to live somehow till the ice goes out." The Boy sat thinking. The Colonel went on: "And we can't go to Dawson cleaned out. No tellin' whether there are any proper banks there or whether my Louisville instructions got through. Of course, we've got the dogs yet."

"Don't care how soon we sell Red and Spot."

After breakfast the Boy tied Nig up securely behind Keith's shack, and followed the Colonel about with a harassed and watchful air.

"No market for dogs now," seemed to be the general opinion, and one person bore up well under the news.

But the next day a man, very splashed and muddy, and obviously just in from the gulches, stopped, in going by Keith's, and looked at Nig.

"Dog market's down," quoted the Boy internally to hearten himself.

"That mahlemeut's for sale," observed the Colonel to the stranger.

"These are." The Boy hastily dragged Red and Spot upon the scene.

"How much?"

"Seventy-five dollars apiece."

The man laughed. "Ain't you heard the dog season's over?"

"Well, don't you count on livin' to the next?"

The man pushed his slouch over his eyes and scratched the back of his head.

"Unless I can git 'em reasonable, dogs ain't worth feedin' till next winter."

"I suppose not," said the Boy sympathetically; "and you can't get fish here."

"Right. Feedin' yourn on bacon, I s'pose, at forty cents a pound?"

"Bacon and meal."

"Guess you'll get tired o' that."

"Well, we'd sell you the red dog for sixty dollars," admitted the Boy.

The man stared. "Give you thirty for that black brute over there."

"Thirty dollars for Nig!"

"And not a —— cent more. Dogs is down." He could get a dozen as good for twenty-five dollars.

"Just you try." But the Colonel, grumbling, said thirty dollars was thirty dollars, and he reckoned he'd call it a deal. The Boy stared, opened his mouth to protest, and shut it without a sound.

The Colonel had untied Nig, and the Leader, unmindful of the impending change in his fortunes, dashed past the muddy man from the gulch with such impetuosity that he knocked that gentleman off his legs. He picked himself up scowling, and was feeling for his gold sack.

"Got scales here?"

"No need of scales." The Boy whipped out a little roll of money, counted out thirty dollars, and held it towards the Colonel. "I can afford to keep Nig awhile if that's his figure."

The stranger was very angry at this new turn in the dog deal. He had seen that Siwash out at the gulch, heard he was for sale, and came in "a purpose to git him."

"The dog season's over," said the Boy, pulling Nig's ears and smiling.

"Oh, *is* it? Well, the season for eatin' meals ain't over. How 'm I to git grub out to my claim without a dog?"

"We are offerin' you a couple o' capital draught dogs."

"I bought that there Siwash, and I'd a paid fur him if he hadn't a knocked me down." He advanced threateningly. "An' if you ain't huntin' trouble——"

The big Colonel stepped in and tried to soothe the stranger, as well as to convince him that this was not the party to try bullying on.

"I'll give you forty dollars for the dog," said the muddy man sulkily to the Boy.

"No."

"Give you fifty, and that's my last word."

"I ain't sellin' dogs."

He cursed, and offered five dollars more.

"Can't you see I *mean* it? I'm goin' to keep that dog—awhile."

"S'pose you think you'll make a good thing o' hirin' him out?"

He hadn't thought of it, but he said: "Why not? Best dog in the Yukon."

"Well, how much?"

"How much 'll you give?"

"Dollar a day."

"Done."

So Nig was hired out, Spot was sold for twenty dollars, and Red later for fifteen.

"Well," said the Colonel when they went in, "I didn't know you were so smart. But you can't live *here* on Nig's seven dollars a week."

The Boy shook his head. Their miserable canned and salted fare cost about four dollars a day per man.

"I'm goin' to take Nig's tip," he said—"goin' to work."

Easier said than done. In their high rubber boots they splashed about Rampart in the mild, thawing weather, "tryin' to scare up a job," as one of them stopped to explain to every likely person: "Yes, sah, lookin' for any sort of honourable employment till the ice goes out."

"Nothin' doin'."

"Everything's at a standstill."

"Just keepin' body and soul together myself till the boats come in."

They splashed out to the gulch on the same errand.

Yes, wages were fifteen dollars a day when they were busy. Just now they were waiting for the thorough thaw.

"Should think it was pretty thorough without any waitin'."

Salaman shook his head. "Only in the town and tundra. The frost holds on to the deep gulch gravel like grim death. And the diggin's were already full of men ready to work for their keep—at least, they say so," Salaman added.

Not only in the great cities is human flesh and blood held cheaper than that of the brutes. Even in the off season, when dogs was down, Nig could get his dollar a day, but his masters couldn't get fifty cents.

CHAPTER XVII

THE GREAT STAMPEDE

"Die Menchen suchen und suchen, wollen immer was Besseres finden
. . . Gott geb' ihnen nur Geduld ! "

MEN in the Gold Nugget were talking about some claims, staked and recorded in due form, but on which the statutory work had not been done.

"What about 'em?"

"They're jumpable at midnight."

French Charlie invited the Boy to go along, but neither he nor the Colonel felt enthusiastic.

"They're no good, those claims, except to sell to some sucker, and we're not in that business *yet,* sah."

They had just done twenty miles in slush and mire, and their hearts were heavier than their heels. No, they would go to bed while the others did the jumpin', and next day they would fill Keith's wood-bin.

"So if work does turn up we won't have to worry about usin' up his firin'."

In the chill of the next evening they were cording the results of the day's chopping, when Maudie, in fur coat, skirts to the knee, and high rubber boots, appeared behind Keith's shack. Without deigning to notice the Boy, "Ain't seen you all day," says she to the Colonel.

"Busy," he replied, scarcely looking up.

"Did you do any jumpin' last night?"

"No."

"*That's* all right."

She seated herself with satisfaction on a log. She looked at the Boy impudently, as much as to say, "When that blot on the landscape is removed, I'll tell you something." The Boy had not the smallest intention of removing the blot.

Grudgingly he admitted to himself that, away from the un-savory atmosphere of the Gold Nugget, there was nothing in

Maudie positively offensive. At this moment, with her shrewd little face peering pertly out from her parki-hood, she looked more than ever like an audacious child, or like some strange, new little Arctic animal with a whimsical human air.

"Look here, Colonel," she said presently, either despairing of getting rid of the Boy or ceasing to care about it: "you got to get a wiggle on to-morrow."

"What for?"

She looked round, first over one shoulder, then over the other. "Well, it's on the quiet."

The Kentuckian nodded. But she winked her blue eyes suspiciously at the Boy.

"Oh, *he's* all right."

"Well, you been down to Little Minóok, ain't you?"

"Yes."

"And you seen how the pay pinches out above No. 10?"

"Yes."

"Well, now, if it ain't above No. 10, where is it?" No answer. "Where does it *go?*" she repeated severely, like a schoolmarm to a class of backward boys.

"That's what everybody 'd like to know."

"Then let 'em ask Pitcairn."

"What's Pitcairn say?"

She got up briskly, moved to another log almost at the Colonel's feet, and sat looking at him a moment as if making up her mind about something serious. The Colonel stood, fists at his sides, arrested by that name Pitcairn.

"You know Pitcairn's the best all-round man we got here," she asserted rather than asked.

The Colonel nodded.

"He's an *Idaho miner*, Pitcairn is!"

"I know."

"Well, he's been out lookin' at the place where the gold gives out on Little Minóok. There's a pup just there above No. 10 —remember?"

"Perfectly."

"And above the pup, on the right, there's a bed of gravel."

"Couldn't see much of that for the snow."

"Well, sir, that bed o' gravel's an *old channel*."

"No!"

She nodded. "Pitcairn's sunk a prospect, and found colours in his first pan."

"Oh, colours!"

"But the deeper he went, the *better* prospects he got." She stood up now, close to the Colonel. The Boy stopped work and leaned on the wood pile, listening. "Pitcairn told Charlie and me (on the strict q. t.) that the gold channel crossed the divide at No. 10, and the only gold on Little Minóok is just what spilt down on those six claims as the gold went crossin' the gulch. The real placer is that old channel above the pup, and boys"—in her enthusiasm she even included the Colonel's objectionable pardner—"boys, it's rich as blazes!"

"I wonder——" drawled the Colonel, recovering a little from his first thrill.

"I wouldn't advise you to waste much time wonderin'," she said with fire. "What I'm tellin' you is scientific. Pitcairn is straight as a string. You won't get any hymns out o' Pitcairn, but you'll get fair and square. His news is worth a lot. If you got any natchral gumption anywhere about you, you can have a claim worth anything from ten to fifty thousand dollars this time to-morrow."

"Well, well! Good Lord! Hey, Boy, what we goin' to do?"

"Well, you don't want to get excited," admonished the queer little Arctic animal, jumping up suddenly; "but you can bunk early and get a four a.m. wiggle on. Charlie and me 'll meet you on the Minóok Trail. Ta-ta!" and she whisked away as suddenly as a chipmunk.

They couldn't sleep. Some minutes before the time named they were quietly leaving Keith's shack. Out on the trail there were two or three men already disappearing towards Little Minóok, and here was Maudie, all by herself, sprinting along like a good fellow, on the thin surface of the last night's frost. She walked in native water-boots, but her snow-shoes stuck out above the small pack neatly lashed on her straight little shoulders. They waited for her.

She came up very brisk and businesslike. To their good-mornings she only noddde in a funny, preoccupied way, never opening her lips.

"Charlie gone on?" inquired the Colonel presently.

She shook her head. "Knocked out."

"Been fightin'?"

"No; ran a race to Hunter."

"To jump that claim?"

She nodded.

"Did he beat?"

She laughed. "Butts had the start. They got there together at nine o'clock!"

"Three hours before jumpin' time?"

Again she nodded. "And found four more waitin' on the same fool errand."

"What did they do?"

"Called a meetin'. Couldn't agree. It looked like there'd be a fight, and a fast race to the Recorder among the survivors. But before the meetin' was adjourned, those four that had got there first (they were pretty gay a'ready), they opened some hootch, so Butts and Charlie knew they'd nothing to fear except from one another."

On the top of the divide that gave them their last glimpse of Rampart she stopped an instant and looked back. The quick flash of anxiety deepening to defiance made the others turn. The bit they could see of the water-front thoroughfare was alive. The inhabitants were rushing about like a swarm of agitated ants.

"What's happening?"

"It's got out," she exploded indignantly. "They're comin', too!"

She turned, flew down the steep incline, and then settled into a steady, determined gait, that made her gain on the men who had got so long a start. Her late companions stood looking back in sheer amazement, for the town end of the trail was black with figures. The Boy began to laugh.

"Look! if there isn't old Jansen and his squaw wife."

The rheumatic cripple, huddled on a sled, was drawn by a native man and pushed by a native woman. They could hear him swearing at both impartially in broken English and Chinook.

The Colonel and the Boy hurried after Maudie. It was some minutes before they caught up. The Boy, feeling that he couldn't be stand-offish in the very act of profiting by her acquaintance, began to tell her about the crippled but undaunted Swede. She made no answer, just trotted steadily on. The Boy hazarded another remark—an opinion that she was making uncommon good time for a woman.

"You'll want all the wind you got before you get back," she said shortly, and silence fell on the stampeders.

Some of the young men behind were catching up. Maudie

set her mouth very firm and quickened her pace. This spectacle touched up those that followed; they broke into a canter, floundered in a drift, recovered, and passed on. Maudie pulled up.

"*That's* all right! Let 'em get good and tired, half-way. We got to save all the run we got in us for the last lap."

The sun was hotter, the surface less good.

She loosened her shoulder-straps, released her snow-shoes, and put them on. As she tightened her little pack the ex-Governor came puffing up with apoplectic face.

"Why, she can throw the diamond hitch!" he gasped with admiration.

"S'pose you thought the squaw hitch would be good enough for me."

"Well, it is for *me*," he laughed breathlessly.

"That's 'cause you're an ex-Governor"; and steadily she tramped along.

In twenty minutes Maudie's party came upon those same young men who had passed running. They sat in a row on a fallen spruce. One had no rubber boots, the other had come off in such a hurry he had forgotten his snow-shoes. Already they were wet to the waist.

"Step out, Maudie," said one with short-breathed hilarity; "we'll be treadin' on your heels in a minute;" but they were badly blown.

Maudie wasted not a syllable. Her mouth began to look drawn. There were violet shadows under the straight-looking eyes.

The Colonel glanced at her now and then. Is she thinking about that four-year-old? Is Maudie stampedin' through the snow so that other little woman need never dance at the Alcazar? No, the Colonel knew well enough that Maudie rather liked this stampedin' business.

She had passed one of those men who had got the long start of her. He carried a pack. Once in a while she would turn her strained-looking face over her shoulder, glancing back, with the frank eyes of an enemy, at her fellow-citizens labouring along the trail.

"Come on, Colonel!" she commanded, with a new sharpness. "Keep up your lick."

But the Colonel had had about enough of this gait. From now on he fell more and more behind. But the Boy was with her neck and neck.

"Guess you're goin' to get there."

"Guess I am."

Some men behind them began to run. They passed. They had pulled off their parkis, and left them where they fell. They threw off their caps now, and the sweat rolled down their faces. Not a countenance but wore that immobile look, the fixed, unseeing eye of the spent runner, who is overtaxing heart and lungs. Not only Maudie now, but everyone was silent. Occasionally a man would rouse himself out of a walk, as if out of sleep, and run a few yards, going the more weakly after. Several of the men who had been behind caught up.

Where was Kentucky?

If Maudie wondered, she wasted no time over the speculation. For his own good she had admonished him to keep up his lick, but of course the main thing was that Maudie should keep up hers.

"What i fthis is the great day of my life!" thought the Boy. "Shall I always look back to this? Why, it's Sunday. Wonder if Kentucky remembers?" Never pausing, the Boy glanced back, vaguely amused, and saw the Colonel plunging heavily along in front of half a dozen, who were obviously out of condition for such an expedition—eyes bloodshot, lumbering on with nervous "whisky gait," now whipped into a breathless gallop, now half falling by the way. Another of the Gold Nugget women with two groggy-looking men, and somewhere down the trail, the crippled Swede swearing at his squaw. A dreamy feeling came over the Boy. Where in the gold basins of the North was this kind of thing not happening—finished yesterday, or planned for to-morrow? Yes, it was typical. Between patches of ragged black spruce, wide stretches of snow-covered moss, under a lowering sky, and a mob of men floundering through the drifts to find a fortune. "See how they run!" —mad mice. They'd been going on stampedes all winter, and would go year in, year out, until they died. The prizes were not for such as they. As for himself—ah, it was a great day for him! He was going at last to claim that gold-mine he had come so far to find. This was the decisive moment of his life. At the thought he straightened up, and passed Maudie. She gave him a single sidelong look, unfriendly, even fierce. That was because he could run like sixty, and keep it up. "When I'm a millionaire I shall always remember that I'm rich because I won the race." A dizzy feeling came over him. He seemed to be running through some softly resisting medium like water—no, like wine jelly. His heart was pounding up in his throat. "What if something's wrong, and I drop dead on the way to my mine? Well, Kentucky 'll look after things."

Maudie had caught up again, and here was Little Minóok at last! A couple of men, who from the beginning had been well in advance of everyone else, and often out of sight, had seemed for the last five minutes to be losing ground. But now they put on steam, Maudie too. She stepped out of her snow-shoes, and flung them up on the low roof of the first cabin. Then she ducked her head, crooked her arms at the elbow, and, with fists uplifted, she broke into a run, jumping from pile to pile of frozen pay, gliding under sluice-boxes, scrambling up the bank, slipping on the rotting ice, recovering, dashing on over fallen timber and through waist-deep drifts, on beyond No. 10 up to the bench above.

When the Boy got to Pitcairn's prospect hole, there were already six claims gone. He proceeded to stake the seventh, next to Maudie's. That person, with flaming cheeks, was driving her last location-post into a snow-drift with a piece of water-worn obsidian.

The Colonel came along in time to stake No. 14 Below, under Maudie's personal supervision.

Not much use, in her opinion, "except that with gold, it's where you find it, and that's all any man can tell you."

As she was returning alone to her own claim, behold two brawny Circle City miners pulling out her stakes and putting in their own. She flew at them with remarks unprintable.

"You keep your head shut," advised one of the men, a big, evil-looking fellow. "This was our claim first. We was here with Pitcairn yesterday. Somebody's took away our location-posts."

"You take me for a cheechalko?" she screamed, and her blue eyes flashed like smitten steel. She pulled up her sweater and felt in her belt. "You —— —— take your stakes out! Put mine back, unless you want——" A murderous-looking revolver gleamed in her hand.

"Hold on!" said the spokesman hurriedly. "Can't you take a joke?"

"No; this ain't my day for jokin'. You want to put them stakes o' mine back." She stood on guard till it was done. "And now I'd advise you, like a mother, to back-track home. You'll find this climate very tryin' to your health."

They went farther up the slope and marked out a claim on the incline above the bench.

In a few hours the mountain-side was staked to the very top, and still the stream of people struggled out from Rampart to the scene of the new strike. All day long, and all the night, the trail was alive with the coming or the going of the five hundred and odd souls that made up the population. In the town itself the excitement grew rather than waned. Men talked themselves into a fever, others took fire, and the epidemic spread like some obscure nervous disease. Nobody slept, everybody drank and hurrahed, and said it was the greatest night in the history of Minóok. In the Gold Nugget saloon, crowded to suffocation, Pitcairn organized the new mining district, and named it the Idaho Bar. French Charlie and Keith had gone out late in the day. On their return, Keith sold his stake to a woman for twenty-five dollars, and Charlie advertised a half-interest in his for five thousand. Between these two extremes you could hear Idaho Bar quoted at any figure you liked.

Maudie was in towering spirits. She drank several cocktails, and in her knee-length "stampedin' skirt" and her scarlet sweater she danced the most audacious jig even Maudie had ever presented to the Gold Nugget patrons. The miners yelled with delight. One of them caught her up and put her on the counter of the bar, where, no whit at a loss, she curveted and spun among the bottles and the glasses as lightly as a dragonfly dips and whirls along a summer brook. The enthusiasm grew delirious. The men began to throw nuggets at her, and Maudie, never pausing in the dance, caught them on the fly.

Suddenly she saw the Big Chap turn away, and, with his back to her, pretend to read the notice on the wall, written in charcoal on a great sheet of brown wrapping-paper:

"Minook,
April 30.

"To who it may concern:
  "know all men by these presents that I, James McGinty,
now of Minóok (or Rampart City), Alaska, do hereby
give notice of my intention to hold and claim a lien by
virtue of the statue in such case——"

He had read so far when Maudie, having jumped down off the bar with her fists full of nuggets, and dodging her admirers, wormed her way to the Colonel. She thrust her small person in between the notice and the reader, and scrutinised the tanned face, on which the Rochester burners shed a flood of light.

"You lookin' mighty serious," she said.

"Am I?"

"M-hm! Thinkin' 'bout home sweet home?"

"N-no—not just then."

"Say, I told you 'bout—a—'bout *me*. You ain't never told me nothin'."

He seemed not to know the answer to that, and pulled at his ragged beard. She leaned back against McGinty's notice, and blurred still more the smudged intention "by virtue of the statue."

"Married, o' course," she said.

"No."

"Widder?"

"No."

"Never hitched up yet?"

He shook his head.

"Never goin' to, I s'pose."

"Oh, I don't know," he laughed, and turned his head over his shoulder to the curious scene between them and the bar. It was suddenly as if he had never seen it before; then, while Maudie waited, a little scornful, a little kind, his eyes went through the window to the pink and orange sunrise. As some change came over the Colonel's face, "She died!" said Maudie.

"No—no—she didn't *die;*" then half to himself, half to forestall Maudie's crude probing, "but I lost her," he finished.

"Oh, you lost her!"

He stood, looking past the ugliness within to the morning majesty without. But it was not either that he saw. Maudie studied him.

"Guess you ain't give up expectin' to find her some day?"

"No—no, not quite."

"Humph! Did you guess you'd find her here?"

"No," and his absent smile seemed to remove him leagues away. "No, not here."

"*I* could a' told you——" she began savagely. "I don't know for certain whether any—what you call good women come up here, but I'm dead sure none stay."

"When do you leave for home, Maudie?" he said gently.

But at the flattering implication the oddest thing happened. As she stood there, with her fists full of gold, Maudie's eyes filled. She turned abruptly and went out. The crowd began to melt away. In half an hour only those remained who had more hootch than they could carry off the premises. They made themselves comfortable on the floor, near the stove, and the greatest night Minóok had known was ended.

CHAPTER XVIII

A MINERS' MEETING

> " Leiden oder triumphiren
> Hammer oder Amboss sein."
>
> GOETHE.

IN a good-sized cabin, owned by Bonsor, down near the A. C., Judge Corey was administering Miners' Law. The chief magistrate was already a familiar figure, standing on his dump at Little Minóok, speculatively chewing and discussing "glayshal action," but most of the time at the Gold Nugget, chewing still, and discussing more guardedly the action some Minóok man was threatening to bring against another. You may treat a glacier cavalierly, but Miners' Law is a serious matter. Corey was sitting before a deal table, littered with papers strewn round a central bottle of ink, in which a steel pen stuck upright. The Judge wore his usual dilapidated business suit of brown cheviot that had once been snuff-coloured and was now a streaky drab. On his feet, stretched out under the magisterial table till they joined the jury, a pair of moccasins; on his grizzled head a cowboy hat, set well back. He could spit farther than any man in Minóok, and by the same token was a better shot. They had unanimously elected him Judge.

The first-comers had taken possession of the chairs and wooden stools round the stove. All the later arrivals, including Keith and his friends, sat on the floor.

"There's a good many here."

"They'll keep comin' as long as a lean man can scrouge in."

"Yes," said Keith, "everybody's got to come, even if it's only the usual row between pardners, who want to part and can't agree about dividing the outfit."

"*Got* to come?"

Keith laughed. "That's the way everybody feels. There'll be a debate and a chance to cast a vote. Isn't your true-born American always itching to hold a meeting about something?"

"Don't know about that," said McGinty, "but I do know there's more things happens in a minute to make a man mad in Alaska, than happens in a year anywhere else." And his sentiment was loudly applauded. The plaintiff had scored a hit.

"I don't know but two partnerships," the ex-Governor was saying, "of all those on my ship and on the *Muckluck* and the *May West*—just two, that have stood the Alaska strain. Everyone that didn't break on the boats, or in camp, went to smash on the trail."

They all admitted that the trail was the final test. While they smoked and spat intoi or at the stove, and told trail yarns, the chief magistrate arranged papers, conferred with the clerk and another man, wrinkled deeply his leathery forehead, consulted his Waterbury, and shot tobacco-juice under the table.

"Another reason everybody comes," whispered Keith, "is because the side that wins always takes the town up to the Nugget and treats to hootch. Whenever you see eighty or ninety more drunks than usual, you know there's either been a stampede or else justice has been administered."

"Ain't Bonsor late?" asked someone.

"No, it's a quarter of."

"Why do they want Bonsor?"

"His case on the docket—McGinty *v.* Burt Bonsor, proprietor of the Gold Nugget."

"If they got a row on——"

"*If* they got a row? Course they got a row. Weren't they pardners?"

"But McGinty spends all his time at the Gold Nugget."

"Well, where would he spend it?"

"A Miners' Meetin's a pretty poor machine," McGinty was saying to the ex-Governor, "but it's the best we got."

"——in a country bigger than several of the nations of Europe put together," responded that gentleman, with much public spirit.

"A *Great* Country!"

"Right!"

"You bet!"

"——a country that's paid for its purchase over and over again, even before we discovered gold here."

"Did she? Good old 'laska."

"——and the worst treated part o' the Union."

"That's so."

"After this, when I read about Russian corruption and Chinese cruelty, I'll remember the way Uncle Sam treats the natives up——"

"——and us, b'gosh! White men that are openin' up this great, rich country fur Uncle Sam——"

"——with no proper courts—no Government protection—no help—no justice—no nothin'."

"Yer forgittin' them reindeer!" And the court-room rang with derisive laughter.

"Congress *started* that there Relief Expedition all right," the josher went on, "only them blamed reindeer had got the feed habit, and when they'd et up everything in sight they set down on the Dalton Trail—and there they're settin' yit, just like *they* was Congress. But I don't like to hear no feller talkin' agin' the Gover'ment."

"Yes, it's all very funny," said McGinty gloomily, "but think o' the fix a feller's in wot's had a wrong done him in the fall, and knows justice is thousands o' miles away, and he can't even go after her for eight months; and in them eight months the feller wot robbed him has et up the money, or worked out the claim, and gone dead-broke."

"No, sir! we don't wait, and we don't go trav'lin'. We stay at home and call a meetin'."

The door opened, and Bonsor and the bar-tender, with great difficulty, forced their way in. They stood flattened against the wall. During the diversion McGinty was growling disdainfully, "Rubbidge!"

"Rubbidge? Reckon it's pretty serious rubbidge."

"Did you ever know a Miners' Meetin' to make a decision that didn't become law, with the whole community ready to enforce it if necessary? *Rubbidge!*"

"Oh, we'll hang a man if we don't like his looks," grumbled McGinty; but he was overborne. There were a dozen ready to uphold the majesty of the Miners' Meetin'.

"No, sir! No funny business about *our* law! This tribunal's final."

"I ain't disputin' that it's final. I ain't talkin' about law. I was mentionin' Justice."

"The feller that loses is always gassin' 'bout Justice. When you win you don't think there's any flies on the Justice."

"Ain't had much experience with winnin'. We all knows who wins in these yere Meetin's."

"Who?" But they turned their eyes on Mr. Bonsor, over by the door.

"Who wins?" repeated a Circle City man.

"The feller that's got the most friends."

"It's so," whispered Keith.

"——same at Circle," returned the up-river man.

McGinty looked at him. Was this a possible adherent?

"You got a Push at Circle?" he inquired, but without genuine interest in the civil administration up the river. "Why, 'fore this yere town was organised, when we hadn't got no Court of Arbitration to fix a boundary, or even to hang a thief, we had our 'main Push,' just like we was 'Frisco." He lowered his voice, and leaned towards his Circle friend. "With Bonsor's help they 'lected Corey Judge o' the P'lice Court, and Bonsor ain't never let Corey forgit it."

"What about the other?" inquired a Bonsorite, "the shifty Push that got you in for City Marshal?"

"What's the row on to-night?" inquired the Circle City man.

"Oh, Bonsor, over there, he lit out on a stampede 'bout Christmas, and while he was gone a feller by the name o' Lawrence quit the game. Fanned out one night at the Gold Nugget. I seen for days he was wantin' to be a angil, and I kep' a eye on 'im. Well, when he went to the boneyard, course it was my business, bein' City Marshal, to take possession of his property fur his heirs!"

There was unseemly laughter behind the stove-pipe.

"Among his deeds and traps," McGinty went on, unheeding, "there was fifteen hundred dollars in money. Well, sir, when Bonsor gits back he decides he'd like to be the custodian o' that cash. Mentions his idee to me. I jest natchrally tell him to go to hell. No, sir, he goes to Corey over there, and gits an order o' the Court makin' Bonsor administrator o' the estate o' James Lawrence o' Noo Orleens, lately deceased. Then Bonsor comes to me, shows me the order, and demands that fifteen hundred."

"Didn't he tell you you could keep all the rest o' Lawrence's stuff?" asked the Bonsorite.

McGinty disdained to answer this thrust.

"But I knows my dooty as City Marshal, and I says, 'No,' and Bonsor says, says he, 'If you can't git the idee o' that fifteen hundred dollars out o' your head, I'll git it out fur ye with a bullet,' an' he draws on me."

"An' McGinty weakens," laughed the mocker behind the stove-pipe.

"Bonsor jest pockets the pore dead man's cash," says Mc-Ginty, with righteous indignation, "and I've called this yer meetin' t' arbitrate the matter."

"Minóok doesn't mind arbitrating," says Keith low to the Colonel, "but there isn't a man in camp that would give five cents for the interest of the heirs of Lawrence in that fifteen hundred dollars."

A hammering on the clerk's little table announced that it was seven p.m.

The Court then called for the complaint filed by McGinty v. Bonsor, the first case on the docket. The clerk had just risen when the door was flung open, and hatless, coatless, face aflame, Maudie stood among the miners.

"Boys!" said she, on the top of a scream, "I been robbed."

"Hey?"

"Robbed?"

"Golly!"

"*Maudie robbed?*" They spoke all together. Everybody had jumped up.

"While we was on that stampede yesterday, somebody found my—all my——" She choked, and her eyes filled. "Boys! my nuggets, my dust, my dollars—they're gone!"

"Where did you have 'em?"

"In a little place under—in a hole." Her face twitched, and she put her hand up to hide it.

"Mean shame."

"Dirt mean."

"We'll find him, Maudie."

"An' when we do, we'll hang him on the cottonwood."

"Did anybody know where you kept your——"

"I didn't think so, unless it was—— No!" she screamed hysterically, and then fell into weak crying. "Can't think *who* could have been such a skunk."

"But who do you suspect?" persisted the Judge.

"How do I know?" she retorted angrily. "I suspect every-body till—*till I know*." She clenched her hands.

That a thief should be "operating" in Minóok on somebody who wasn't dead yet, was a matter that came home to the busi-ness and the bosoms of all the men in the camp. In the midst of the babel of speculation and excitement, Maudie, still crying and talking incoherently about skunks, opened the door. The men crowded after her. Nobody suggested it, but the entire Miners' Meeting with one accord adjourned to the scene of the crime. Only a portion could be accommodated under Maudie's roof, but the rest crowded in front of her door or went and examined the window. Maudie's log-cabin was a cheerful place, its one room, neatly kept, lined throughout with red and white drill, hung with marten and fox, carpeted with wolf and caribou. The single sign of disorder was that the bed was pulled out a little from its place in the angle of the wall above the patent condenser stove. Behind the oil-tank, where the patent condensation of oil into gas went on, tiers of shelves, enamelled pots and pans ranged below, dishes and glasses above. On the very top, like a frieze, gaily labelled ranks of "tinned goods." On the table under the window a pair of gold scales. A fire burned in the stove. The long-lingering sunlight poured through the "turkey-red" that she had tacked up for a half-curtain, and over this, one saw the slouch-hats and fur caps of the outside crowd.

Clutching Judge Corey by the arm, Maudie pulled him after her into the narrow space behind the head-board and the wall.

"It was here—see?" She stooped down.

Some of the men pulled the bed farther out, so that they, too, could pass round and see.

"This piece o' board goes down so slick you'd never know it lifted out." She fitted it in with shaking hands, and then with her nails and a hairpin got it out. "And way in, under-neath, I had this box. *I* always set it on a flat stone." She spoke as if this oversight were the thief's chief crime. "See? Like that."

She fitted the cigar-box into unseen depths of space and then brought it out again, wet and muddy. The ground was full of springs hereabouts, and the thaw had loosed them.

"Boys!" She stood up and held out the box. "Boys! it was *full*."

Eloquently she turned it upside down.

"How much do you reckon you had?" She handed the muddy box to the nearest sympathiser, sat down on the fur-covered bed, and wiped her eyes.

"Any idea?"

"I weighed it all over again after I got in from the Gold Nugget the night we went on the stampede."

335

As she sobbed out the list of her former possessions, Judge Corey took it down on the back of a dirty envelope. So many ounces of dust, so many in nuggets, so much in bills and coin, gold and silver. Each item was a stab.

"Yes, all that—all that!" she jumped up wildly, "and it's gone! But we got to find it. What you hangin' round here for? Why, if you boys had any natchral spunk you'd have the thief strung up by now."

"We got to find him fust."

"You won't find him standin' here."

They conferred afresh.

"It must have been somebody who knowed where you kept the stuff."

"N-no." Her red eyes wandered miserably, restlessly, to the window. Over the red half-curtain French Charlie and Butts looked in. They had not been to the meeting.

Maudie's face darkened as she caught sight of the Canadian.

"Oh, yes, you can crow over me now," she shouted shrilly above the buzz of comment and suggestion. The Canadian led the way round to the door, and the two men crowded in.

"You just get out," Maudie cried in a fury. "Didn't I turn you out o' this and tell you never——"

"Hol' on," said French Charlie in a conciliatory tone. "This true 'bout your losin'——"

"*Yes*, it's true; but I ain't askin' *your* sympathy!"

He stopped short and frowned.

"Course not, when you can get *his*." Under his slouch-hat he glowered at the Colonel.

Maudie broke into a volley of abuse. The very air smelt of brimstone. When finally, through sheer exhaustion, she dropped on the side of the bed, the devil prompted French Charlie to respond in kind. She jumped up and turned suddenly round upon Corey, speaking in a voice quite different, low and hoarse: "You asked me, Judge, if anybody knew where I kept my stuff. Charlie did."

The Canadian stopped in the middle of a lurid remark and stared stupidly. The buzz died away. The cabin was strangely still.

"Wasn't you along with the rest up to Idaho Bar?" inquired the Judge in a friendly voice.

"Y-yes."

"Not when we all were! No!" Maudie's tear-washed eyes

were regaining a dangerous brightness. "I wanted him to come with me. He wouldn't, and we quarrelled."

"We didn't."

"You *didn't* quarrel?" put in the Judge.

"We did," said Maudie, breathless.

"Not about that. It was because she wanted another feller to come, too." Again he shot an angry glance at the Kentuckian.

"And Charlie said if I gave the other feller the tip, *he* wouldn't come. And he'd get even with me, if it took a leg!"

"Well, it looks like he done it."

"Can't you prove an alibi? Thought you said you was along with the rest to Idaho Bar?" suggested Windy Jim.

"So I was."

"I didn't see you," Maudie flashed.

"When were you there?" asked the Judge.

"Last night."

"Oh, yes! When everybody else was comin' home. You all know if that's the time Charlie usually goes on a stampede!"

"You——"

If words could slay, Maudie would have dropped dead, riddled with a dozen mortal wounds. But she lived to reply in kind. Charlie's abandonment of coherent defence was against him. While he wallowed blindly in a mire of offensive epithet, his fellow-citizens came to dark conclusions. He had an old score to pay off against Maudie, they all knew that. Had he chosen this way? What other so effectual? He might even say most of that dust was his, anyway. But it was an alarming precedent.

The fire of Maudie's excitement had caught and spread. Eve the less inflammable muttered darkly that it was all up with Minóok, if a person couldn't go on a stampede without havin' his dust took out of his cabin. The crowd was pressing Charlie, and twenty cross-questions were asked him in a minute. He, beside himself with rage, or fear, or both, lost all power except to curse.

The Judge seemed to be taking down damning evidence on the dirty envelope. Some were suggesting:

"Bring him over to the court."

"Yes, try him straight away."

No-Thumb-Jack was heard above the din, saying it was all gammon wasting time over a trial, or even—in a plain case like this—for the Judge to require the usual complaint made in writing and signed by three citizens.

Two men laid hold of the Canadian, and he turned ghastly white under his tan.

"*Me?* Me *tief?* You—let me alone!" He began to struggle. His terrified eyes rolling round the little cabin, fell on Butts.

"I don' know but one tief in Minóok," he said wildly, like a man wandering in a fever, and unconscious of having spoken, till he noticed there was a diversion of some sort. People were looking at Butts. A sudden inspiration pierced the Canadian's fog of terror.

"You know what Butts done to Jack McQuestion. You ain't forgot how he sneaked Jack's watch!" The incident was historic.

Every eye on Butts. Charlie caught up breath and courage.

"An' t'odder night w'en Maudie treat me like she done"— he shot a blazing glance at the double-dyed traitor—"I fixed it up with Butts. Got him to go soft on 'er and nab 'er ring."

"You didn't!" shouted Maudie.

With a shaking finger Charlie pointed out Jimmie, the cashier.

"Didn't I tell you to weigh me out twenty dollars for Butts that night?"

"Right," says Jimmie.

"It was to square Butts fur gittin' that ring away from Maudie."

"You put up a job like that on me?" To be fooled publicly was worse than being robbed.

Charlie paid no heed to her quivering wrath. The menace of the cotton-wood gallows outrivalled even Maudie and her moods.

"Why should I pay Butts twenty dollars if I could work dat racket m'self? If I want expert work, I go to a man like Butts, who knows his business. I'm a *miner*—like the rest o' yer!"

The centre of gravity had shifted. It was very grave indeed in the neighbourhood of Mr. Butts.

"Hold on," said the Judge, forcing his way nearer to the man whose fingers had a renown so perilous. " 'Cause a man plays a trick about a girl's ring don't prove he stole her money. This thing happened while the town was emptied out on the Little Minóok trail. Didn't you go off with the rest yesterday morning?"

"No."

"Ha!" gasped Maudie, as though this were conclusive—"had business in town, did you?"

Mr. Butts declined to answer.

"You thought the gold-mine out on the gulch could wait—and the gold-mine in my cabin couldn't."

"You lie!" remarked Mr. Butts.

"What time did you get to Idaho Bar?" asked Corey.

"Didn't get there at all."

"Where were you?"

"Here in Rampart."

"What?"

"Wait! Wait!" commanded the Judge, as the crowd rocked towards Butts: "P'raps you'll tell us what kept you at home?"

Butts shut his mouth angrily, but a glance at the faces nearest him made him think an answer prudent.

"I was tired."

The men, many of them ailing, who had nearly killed themselves to get to Idaho Bar, sneered openly.

"I'd been jumpin' a claim up at Hunter."

"So had Charlie. But he joined the new stampede in the afternoon."

"Well, I didn't."

"Why, even the old cripple Jansen went on *this* stampede."

"Can't help that."

"Mr. Butts, you're the only able-bodied white man in the district that stayed at home." Corey spoke in his most judicial style.

Mr. Butts must have felt the full significance of so suspicious a fact, but all he said was:

"Y' ought to fix up a notice. Anybody that don't join a stampede will be held guilty o' grand larceny." Saying this Butts had backed a step behind the stove-pipe, and with incredible quickness had pulled out a revolver. But before he had brought it into range, No-Thumb-Jack had struck his arm down, and two or three had sprung at the weapon and wrested it away.

"Search him!"

"No tellin' what else he's got!"

"——and he's so damned handy!"

"Search him!"

Maudie pressed forward as the pinioned man's pockets were

turned out. Only tobacco, a small buckskin bag with less than four ounces of dust, a pipe, and a knife.

"Likely he'd be carrying my stuff about on him!" said she, contemptuous of her own keen interest.

"Get out a warrant to search Butts' premises," said a voice in the crowd.

"McGinty and Johnson are down there now!"

"Think he'd leave anything layin' round?"

Maudie pressed still closer to the beleaguered Butts.

"Say, if I make the boys let you go back to Circle, will you tell me where you've hid my money?"

"Ain't got your money!"

"Look at 'im," whispered Charlie, still so terrified he could hardly stand.

"Butts ain't borrowin' no trouble."

And this formulating of the general impression did Butts no good. As they had watched the calm demeanour of the man, under suspicion of what was worse, in their eyes, than murder, there had come over the bystanders a wave of that primitive cruelty that to this hour will wake in modern men and cry as loud as in Judean days, or in the Saga times of Iceland, "Retribution! Let him suffer! Let him pay in blood!" And here again, on the Yukon, that need of visible atonement to right the crazy injustice of the earth.

Even the women—the others had crowded in—were eager for Butts' instant expiation of the worst crime such a community knows. They told one another excitedly how they'd realised all along it was only a question of time before Butts would be tryin' his game up here. Nobody was safe. Luckily they were on to him. But look! *He* didn't care a curse. It would be a good night's job to make him care.

Three men had hold of him, and everybody talked at once. Minnie Bryan was sure she had seen him skulking round Maudie's after that lady had gone up the trail, but everybody had been too excited about the stampede to notice particularly.

The Judge and Bonsor were shouting and gesticulating, Butts answering bitterly but quietly still. His face was pretty grim, but it looked as if he were the one person in the place who hadn't lost his head. Maudie was still crying at intervals, and advertising to the newcomers that wealth she had hitherto kept so dark, and between whiles she stared fixedly at Butts, as conviction of his guilt deepened to a rage to see him suffer for his crime.

She would rather have her nuggets back, but, failing that— let Butts pay! He owed her six thousand dollars. Let him pay!

The miners were hustling him to the door—to the Court House or to the cotton-wood—a toss-up which.

"Look here!" cried out the Colonel; "McGinty and Johnson haven't got back!"

Nobody listened. Justice had been sufficiently served in sending them. They had forced Butts out across the threshold, the crowd packed close behind. The only men who had not pressed forward were Keith, the Colonel, and the Boy, and No-Thumb-Jack, still standing by the oil-tank.

"What are they going to do with him?" The Colonel turned to Keith with horror in his face.

Keith's eyes were on the Boy, who had stooped and picked up the block of wood that had fitted over the treasure-hole. He was staring at it with dilated eyes. Sharply he turned his head in the direction where No-Thumb-Jack had stood. Jack was just making for the door on the heels of the last of those pressing to get out.

The Boy's low cry was drowned in the din. He lunged forward, but the Colonel gripped him. Looking up, he saw that Kentucky understood, and meant somehow to manage the business quietly.

Jack was trying, now right, now left, to force his way through the congestion at the door, like a harried rabbit at a wattled fence. A touch on the shoulder simultaneously with the click of a trigger at his ear brought his face round over his shoulder. He made the instinctive pioneer motion to his hip, looked into the bore of the Colonel's pistol, and under Keith's grip dropped his "gun-hand" with a smothered oath.

Or was it that other weapon in the Colonel's left that bleached the ruddy face? Simply the block of wood. On the under side, dried in, like a faint stain, four muddy finger-prints, index joint lacking. Without a word the Colonel turned the upper side out. A smudge?—no—the grain of human skin clean printed—a distorted palm without a thumb. Only one man in Minóok could make that sign manual!

The last of the crowd were over the threshold now, and still no word was spoken by those who stayed behind, till the Colonel said to the Boy:

"Go with 'em, and look after Butts. Give us five minutes; *more if you can!*"

He laid the block on a cracker-box, and, keeping pistol and eye still on the thief, took his watch in his left hand, as the Boy shot through the door.

Butts was making a good fight for his life, but he was becoming exhausted. The leading spirits were running him down the bank to where a crooked cotton-wood leaned cautiously over the Never-Know-What, as if to spy out the river's secret.

But after arriving there, they were a little delayed for lack of what they called tackle. They sent a man off for it, and then sent another to hurry up the man. The Boy stood at the edge of the crowd, a little above them, watching Maudie's door, and with feverish anxiety turning every few seconds to see how it was with Butts.

Up in the cabin No-Thumb-Jack had pulled out of the usual capacious pockets of the miner's brown-duck—pockets that fasten with a patent snap—a tattered pocket-book, fat with bills. He plunged deeper and brought up Pacific Coast eagles and five-dollar pieces, Canadian and American gold that went rolling out of his maimed and nervous hand across the tablet to the scales and set the brass pans sawing up and down.

Keith, his revolver still at full cock, had picked up a trampled bit of paper near the stove. Corey's list. Left-handedly he piled up the money, counting, comparing.

"Quick! the dust!" ordered the Colonel. Out of a left hip-pocket a long, tight-packed buckskin bag. Another from a side-pocket, half the size and a quarter as full.

"That's mine," said Jack, and made a motion to recover.

"Let it alone. Turn out everything. Nuggets!"

A miner's chamois belt unbuckled and flung heavily down. The scales jingled and rocked; every pocket in the belt was stuffed.

"Where's the rest?"

"There ain't any rest. That's every damned pennyweight."

"Maybe we ought to weigh it, and see if he's lying?"

"'Fore God it's all! Let me go!" He had kept looking through the crack of the door.

"Reckon it's about right," said Keith.

"'Tain't right! There's more there'n I took. My stuff's there too. For Christ's sake, let me go!"

"Look here, Jack, *is* the little bag yours?"

Jack wet his dry lips and nodded "Yes."

The Colonel snatched up the smaller bag and thrust it into the man's hands. Jack made for the door. The Colonel stopped him.

"Better take to the woods," he said, with a motion backwards the window. The Colonel opened the half-closed door and looked out, as Jack pushed aside the table, tore away the red curtain, hammered at the sash, then, desperate, set his shoulder at it and forced the whole thing out. He put his maimed hand on the sill and vaulted after the shattered glass.

They could see him going like the wind up towards his own shack at the edge of the wood, looking back once or twice, doubling and tacking to keep himself screened by the haphazard, hillside cabins, out of sight of the lynchers down at the river.

"Will you stay with this?" the Colonel had asked Keith hurriedly, nodding at the treasure-covered table, and catching up the finger-marked block before Jack was a yard from the window.

"Yes," Keith had said, revolver still in hand and eyes on the man Minóok was to see no more. The Colonel met the Boy running breathless up the bank.

"Can't hold 'em any longer," he shouted; "you're takin' it pretty easy while a man's gettin' killed down here."

"Stop! Wait!" The Colonel floundered madly through the slush and mud, calling and gesticulating, "I've got the thief!"

Presto all the backs of heads became faces.

"Got the *money?*" screamed Maudie, uncovering her eyes. She had gone to the execution, but after the rope was brought, her nerve failed her, and she was sobbing hysterically into her two palms held tight over her eyes.

"Oh, *you* had it, did you?" called out McGinty with easy insolence.

"Look here!" The Colonel held up the bit of flooring with rapid explanation.

"Where is he?"

"Got him locked up?"

Everybody talked at once. The Colonel managed to keep them going for some moments before he admitted.

"Reckon he's lit out." And then the Colonel got it hot and strong for his clumsiness.

"Which way'd he go?"

The Colonel turned his back to the North Pole, and

made a fine large gesture in the general direction of the Equator.

"Where's my money?"

"Up in your cabin. Better go and count it."

A good many were willing to help since they'd been cheated out of a hanging, and even defrauded of a shot at a thief on the wing. Nobody seemed to care to remain in the neighbourhood of the crooked cotton-wood. The crowd was dispersing somewhat sheepishly.

Nobody looked at Butts, and yet he was a sight to see. His face and his clothes were badly mauled. He was covered with mud and blood. When the men were interrupted in trying to get the noose over his head, he had stood quite still in the midst of the crowd till it broke and melted away from him. He looked round, passed his hand over his eyes, threw open his torn coat, and felt in his pockets.

"Who's got my tobacco?" says he.

Several men turned back suddenly, and several pouches were held out, but nobody met Butts' eyes. He filled his pipe, nor did his hand shake any more than those that held the tobacco-bags. When he had lit up, "Who's got my Smith and Wesson?" he called out to the backs of the retiring citizens. Windy Jim stood and delivered. Butts walked away to his cabin, swaying a little, as if he'd had more hootch than he could carry.

"What would you have said," demanded the Boy, "if you'd hung the wrong man?"

"Said?" echoed McGinty. "Why, we'd 'a' said *that* time the corpse had the laugh on us."

A couple of hours later Keith put an excited face into his shack, where the Colonel and the Boy were just crawling under their blankets.

"Thought you might like to know, that Miners' Meeting that was interrupted is having an extra session."

They followed him down to the Court through a fine rain. The night was heavy and thick. As they splashed along Keith explained:

"Of course, Charlie knew there wasn't room enough in Alaska now for Butts and him; and he thought he'd better send Butts home. So he took his gun and went to call."

"Don't tell me that poor devil's killed after all."

"Not a bit. Butts is a little bunged up, but he's the handier man, even so. He drew the first bead."

"Charlie hurt?"

"No, he isn't *hurt*. He's dead. Three or four fellows had just looked in, on the quiet, to kind of apologise to Butts. They're down at Corey's now givin' evidence against him."

"So Butts 'll have to swing after all. Is he in Court?"

"Yes—been a busy day for Butts."

A confused noise came suddenly out of the big cabin they were nearing. They opened the door with difficulty, and forced their way into the reeking, crowded room for the second time that night. Everybody seemed to be talking—nobody listening. Dimly through dense clouds of tobacco-smoke "the prisoner at the Bar" was seen to be—what—no! Yes—shaking hands with the Judge.

"Verdict already?"

"Oh, that kind o' case don't take a feller like Corey long."

"What's the decision?"

"Prisoner discharged. Charlie Le Gros committed suicide."

"Suicide!"

"—— by goin' with his gun to Butts' shack lookin' f trouble."

CHAPTER XIX

THE ICE GOES OUT

" I am apart of all that I have seen."

IT had been thawing and freezing, freezing and thawing, for so long that men lost account of the advance of a summer coming, with such balked, uncertain steps. Indeed, the weather variations had for several weeks been so great that no journey, not the smallest, could be calculated with any assurance. The last men to reach Minóok were two who had made a hunting and prospecting trip to an outlying district. They had gone there in six days, and were nineteen in returning.

The slush was waist-deep in the gulches. On the benches, in the snow, holes appeared, as though red-hot stones had been thrown upon the surface. The little settlement by the mouth of the Minóok sat insecurely on the boggy hillside, and its inhabitants waded knee-deep in soaking tundra moss and mire.

And now, down on the Never-Know-What, water was beginning to run on the marginal ice. Up on the mountains the drifted snow was honey-combed. Whole fields of it gave way and sunk a foot under any adventurous shoe. But although these changes had been wrought slowly, with backsets of bitter nights, when everything was frozen hard as flint, the illusion was general that summer came in with a bound. On the 9th of May, Minóok went to bed in winter, and woke to find the snow almost gone under the last nineteen hours of hot, unwinking sunshine, and the first geese winging their way up the valley—sight to stir men's hearts. Stranger still, the eight months' Arctic silence broken suddenly by a thousand voices. Under every snow-bank a summer murmur, very faint at first, but hourly louder—the sound of falling water softly singing over all the land.

As silence had been the distinguishing feature of the winter, so was noise the sign of the spring. No ear so dull but now was full of it. All the brooks on all the hills, tinkling, tumbling, babbling of some great and universal joy, all the streams of all the gulches joining with every little rill to find the old way, or to carve a new, back to the Father of Waters.

And the strange thing had happened on the Yukon. The shore-edges of the ice seemed sunken, and the water ran yet deeper there. But of a certainty the middle part had risen! The cheechalkos thought it an optical illusion. But old Brandt from Forty-Mile had seen the ice go out for two-and-twenty years, and he said it went out always so—"humps his back, an' gits up gits, and when he's a gitten', jest look out!" Those who, in spite of warning, ventured in hip-boots down on the Never-Know-What, found that, in places, the under side of the ice was worn nearly through. If you bent your head and listened, you could plainly hear that greater music of the river running underneath, low as yet, but deep, and strangely stirring—dominating in the hearer's ears all the clear, high clamour from gulch and hill.

In some men's hearts the ice "went out" at the sound, and the melting welled up in their eyes. Summer and liberty were very near.

"Oh, hurry, Yukon Inua; let the ice go out and let the boats come in."

But the next few days hung heavily. The river-ice humped its back still higher, but showed no disposition to "git." The wonder was it did not crack under the strain; but Northern ice ahs the air of being strangely flexile. Several feet in depth, the water ran now along the margin.

More geese and ducks appeared, and flocks of little birds—Canada jays, robins, joined the swelling chorus of the waters.

Oh, hurry, hurry Inua, and open the great highway! Not at Minóok alone: at every wood camp, mining town and mission, at every white post and Indian village, all along the Yukon, groups were gathered waiting the great moment of the year.

No one had ever heard of the ice breaking up before the 11th of May or later than the 28th. And yet men had begun to keep a hopeful eye on the river from the 10th of April, when a white ptarmigan was reported wearing a collar of dark-brown feathers, and his wings tipped brown. That was a month ago, and the great moment could not possibly be far now.

The first thing everybody did on getting up, and the last

thing everybody did on going to bed, was to look at the river. It was not easy to go to bed; and even if you got so far it was not easy to sleep. The sun poured into the cabins by night as well as by day, and there was nothing to divide one part of the twenty-four hours from another. You slept when you were too tired to watch the river. You breakfasted, like as not, at six in the evening; you dined at midnight. Through all your waking hours you kept an eye on the window overlooking the river. In your bed you listened for that ancient Yukon cry, "The ice is going out!"

For ages it had meant to the timid: Beware the fury of the shattered ice-fields; beware the caprice of the flood. Watch! lest many lives go out with the ice as aforetime. And for ages to the stout-hearted it had meant: Make ready the kyaks and the birch canoes; see that tackle and traps are strong—for plenty or famine wait upon the hour. As the white men waited for boats to-day, the men of the older time had waited for the salmon—for those first impatient adventurers that would force their way under the very ice-jam, tenderest and best of the season's catch, as eager to prosecute that journey from the ocean to the Klondyke as if they had been men marching after the gold boom.

No one could settle to anything. It was by fits and starts that the steadier hands indulged even in taget practice, with a feverish subconsciousness that events were on the way that might make it inconvenient to have lost the art of sending a bullet straight. After a diminutive tin can, hung on a tree, had been made to jump at a hundred paces, the marksman would glance at the river and forget to fire. It was by fits and starts that they even drank deeper or played for higher stakes.

The Wheel of Fortune, in the Gold Nugget, was in special demand. It was a means of trying your luck with satisfactory despatch "between drinks" or between long bouts of staring at the river. Men stood in shirt-sleeves at their cabin doors in the unwinking sunshine, looking up the valley or down, betting that the "first boat in" would be one of those nearest neighbours, *May West* or *Muckluck,* coming up from Wood-worth; others as ready to back heavily their opinion that the first blast of the steam whistle would come down on the flood from Circle or from Dawson.

The Colonel had bought and donned a new suit of "store

clothes," and urged on his companion the necessity of at least a whole pair of breeches in honour of his entrance into the Klondyke. But the Boy's funds were low and his vanity chastened. Besides, he had other business on his mind.

After sending several requests for the immediate return of his dog, requests that received no attention, the Boy went out to the gulch to recover him. Nig's new master paid up all arrears of wages readily enough, but declined to surrender the dog. "Oh, no, the ice wasn't thinkin' o' goin' out yit."

"I want my dog."

"You'll git him sure."

"I'm glad you understand that much."

"I'll bring him up to Rampart in time for the first boat."

"Where's my dog?"

No answer. The Boy whistled. No Nig. Dread masked itself in choler. He jumped on the fellow, forced him down, and hammered him till he cried for mercy.

"Where's my dog, then?"

"He—he's up to Idyho Bar," whimpered the prostrate one. And there the Boy found him, staggering under a pair of saddle-bags, hired out to Mike O'Reilly for a dollar and a half a day. Together they returned to Rampart to watch for the boat.

Certainly the ice was very late breaking up this year. The men of Rampart stood about in groups in the small hours of the morning of the 16th of May; as usual, smoking, yarning, speculating, inventing elaborate joshes. Somebody remembered that certain cheechalkos had gone to bed at midnight. Now this was unprecedented, even impertinent. If the river is not open by the middle of May, your Sour-dough may go to bed—only he doesn't. Still, he may do as he lists. But your cheechalko—why, this is the hour of his initiation. It was as if a man should yawn at his marriage or refuse to sleep at his funeral. The offenders were some of those Woodworth fellows, who, with a dozen or so others, had built shacks below "the street" yet well above the river. At two in the morning Sour-dough Saunders knocked them up.

"The ice is goin' out!"

In a flash the sleepers stood at the door.

"Only a josh." One showed fight.

"Well, it's true what I'm tellin' yer," persisted Saunders seriously: "the ice *is* goin' out, and it's goin' soon, and when you're washed out o' yer bunks ye needn't blame me, fur I warned yer."

"You don't mean the flood 'll come up *here?*"

"Mebbe you've arranged so she won't *this* year."

The cheechalkos consulted. In the end, four of them occupied the next two hours (to the infinite but masked amusement of the town) in floundering about in the mud, setting up tents in the boggy wood above the settlement, and with much pains transporting thither as many of their possessions as they did not lose in the bottomless pit of the mire.

When the business was ended, Minóok self-control gave way. The cheechalkos found themselves the laughing-stock of the town. The others, who had dared to build down on the bank, but who "hadn't scared worth a cent," sauntered up to the Gold Nugget to enjoy the increased esteem of the Sour-doughs, and the humiliation of the men who had thought "the Yukon was goin' over the Ramparts this year—haw, haw!"

It surprises the average mind to discover that one of civilization's most delicate weapons is in such use and is so potently dreaded among the roughest frontier spirits. No fine gentleman in a drawing-room, no sensitive girl, shrinks more from what Meredith calls "the comic laugh," none feels irony more keenly than your ordinary American pioneer. The men who had moved up into the soaking wood saw they had run a risk as great to them as the fabled danger of the river—the risk of the josher's irony, the dire humiliation of the laugh. If a man up here does you an injury, and you kill him, you haven't after all taken the ultimate revenge. You might have "got the laugh on him," and let him live to hear it.

While all Minóok was "jollying" the Woodworth men, Maudie made one of her sudden raids out of the Gold Nugget. She stood nearly up to the knees of her high rubber boots in the bog of "Main Street," talking earnestly with the Colonel. Keith and the Boy, sitting on a store box outside of the saloon, had looked on at the fun over the timid cheechalkos, and looked on now at Maudie and the Colonel. It crossed the Boy's mind that they'd be putting up a josh on his pardner pretty soon, and at the thought he frowned.

Keith had been saying that the old miners had nearly all got "squawed." He had spoken almost superstitiously of the queer, lasting effect of the supposedly temporary arrangement. "No, they don't leave their wives as often as you'd expect,

350

but in most cases it seems to kill the pride of the man. He gives up all idea of ever going home, and even if he makes a fortune, they say, he stays on here. And year by year he sinks lower and lower, till he's farther down in the scale of things human than his savage wife."

"Yes, it's awful to think how the life up here can take the stiffening out of a fella."

He looked darkly at the two out there in the mud. Keith nodded.

"Strong men have lain down on the trail this winter and cried." But it wasn't that sort of thing the other meant.

Keith followed his new friend's glowering looks.

"Yes. That's just the kind of man that gets taken in."

"What?" said the Boy brusquely.

"Just the sort that goes and marries some flighty creature."

"Well," said his pardner haughtily, *"he* could afford to marry 'a flighty creature.' *The Colonel's got both feet on the ground."* And Keith felt properly snubbed. But what Maudie was saying to the Colonel was:

"You're goin' up in the first boat, I s'pose?"

"Yes."

"Looks like I'll be the only person left in Minóok."

"I don't imagine you'll be quite alone."

"No? Why, there's only between five and six hundred expectin' to board a boat that'll be crowded before she gets here."

"Does everybody want to go to Dawson?"

"Everybody except a few boomers who mean to stay long enough to play off their misery on someone else before they move on."

The Colonel looked a trifle anxious.

"I hadn't thought of that. I suppose there *will* be a race for the boat."

"There'll be a race all the way up the river for all the early boats. Ain't half enough to carry the people. But you look to me like you'll stand as good a chance as most, and anyhow, you're the one man I know, I'll trust my dough to."

The Colonel stared.

"You see, I want to get some money to my kiddie, an' besides, I got m'self kind o' scared about keepin' dust in my cabin. I want it in a bank, so 's if I should kick the bucket (there'll be some pretty high rollin' here when there's been a few boats in, and my life's no better than any other feller's), I'd feel a lot easier if I knew the kiddie 'd have six thousand clear, even if I *did* turn up my toes. See?"

"A—yes—I see. But——"

The door of the cabin next the saloon opened suddenly. A graybeard with a young face came out rubbing the sleep from his eyes. He stared interrogatively at the river, and then to the world in general:

"What time is it?"

"Half-past four."

"Mornin' or evenin'?" and no one thought the question strange.

Maudie lowered her voice.

"No need to mention it to pardners and people. You don't want every feller to know you're goin' about loaded; but will you take my dust up to Dawson and get it sent to 'Frisco on the first boat?"

"The ice! the ice! It's moving!"

"The ice is going out!"

"Look! the ice!"

From end to end of the settlement the cry was taken up. People darted out of cabins like beavers out of their burrows. Three little half-breed Indian boys, yelling with excitement, tore past the Gold Nugget, crying now in their mother's Minóok, now in their father's English, "The ice is going out!" From the depths of the store-box whereon his master had sat, Nig darted, howling excitedly and waving a muddy tail like a draggled banner, saying in Mahlemeut: "The ice is going out! The fish are coming in." All the other dogs waked and gave tongue, running in and out among the huddled rows of people gathered on the Ramparts.

Every ear full of the rubbing, grinding noise that came up out of the Yukon—noise not loud, but deep—an undercurrent of heavy sound. As they stood there, wide-eyed, gaping, their solid winter world began to move. A compact mass of ice, three-quarters of a mile wide and four miles long, with a great grinding and crushing went down the valley. Some distance below the town it jammed, building with incredible quickness a barrier twenty feet high.

The people waited breathless. Again the ice-mass trembled. But the watchers lifted their eyes to the heights above. Was that thunder in the hills? No, the ice again; again crushing, grinding, to the low accompaniment of thunder that seemed to come from far away.

Sections a mile long and half a mile wide were forced up, carried over the first ice-pack, and summarily stopped below the barrier. Huge pieces, broken off from the sides, came crunching their way angrily up the bank, as if acting on some independent impulse. There they sat, great fragments, glistening in the sunlight, as big as cabins. It was something to see them come walking up the shelving bank! The cheechalkos who laughed before are contented now with running, leaving their goods behind. Sour-dough Saunders himself never dreamed the ice would push its way so far.

In mid-channel a still unbroken sheet is bent yet more in the centre. Every now and then a wide crack opens near the margin, and the water rushes out with a roar. Once more the mass is nearly still, and now all's silent. Not till the water, dammed and thrown back by the ice, not until it rises many feet and comes down with a volume and momentum irresistible, will the final conflict come.

Hour after hour the people stand there on the bank, waiting to see the barrier go down. Unwillingly, as the time goes on, this one, that one, hurries away for a few minutes to prepare and devour a meal, back again, breathless, upon rumour of that preparatory trembling, that strange thrilling of the ice. The grinding and the crushing had begun again.

The long tension, the mysterious sounds, the sense of some great unbridled power at work, wrought on the steadiest nerves. People did the oddest things. Down at the lower end of the town a couple of miners, sick of the scurvy, had painfully clambered on their roof—whether to see the sights or be out of harm's way, no one knew. The stingiest man in Minóok, who had refused to help them in their cabin, carried them food on the roof. A woman made and took them the Yukon remedy for their disease. They sat in state in sight of all men, and drank spruce tea.

By one o'clock in the afternoon the river had risen eight feet, but the ice barrier still held. The people, worn out, went away to sleep. All that night the barrier held, though more ice came down and still the water rose. Twelve feet now. The ranks of shattered ice along the shore are claimed again as the flood widens and licks them in. The cheechalkos' cabins are flooded to the eaves. Stout fellows in hip-boots take a boat and rescue the scurvy-stricken from the roof. And still the barrier held.

People began to go about their usual avocations. The empty

Gold Nugget filled again. Men sat, as they had done all the winter, drinking, and reading the news of eight months before, out of soiled and tattered papers.

Late the following day everyone started up at a new sound. Again miners, Indians, and dogs lined the bank, saw the piled ice masses tremble, heard a crashing and grinding as of mountains of glass hurled together, saw the barrier give way, and the frozen wastes move down on the bosom of the flood. Higher yet the water rose—the current ran eight miles an hour. And now the ice masses were less enormous, more broken. Somewhere far below another jam. Another long bout of waiting.

Birds are singing everywhere. Between the white snow-drifts the Arctic moss shows green and yellow, white flowers star the hills.

Half the town is packed, ready to catch the boat at five minutes' notice. With door barred and red curtain down, Maudie is doing up her gold-dust for the Colonel to take to Dawson. The man who had washed it out of a Birch Creek placer, and "blowed it in fur the girl"—up on the hillside he sleeps sound.

The two who had broken the record for winter travel on the Yukon, side by side in the sunshine, on a plank laid across two mackerel firkins, sit and watch the brimming flood. They speak of the Big Chimney men, picture them, packed and waiting for the *Oklahoma*, wonder what they have done with Kaviak, and what the three months have brought them.

"When we started out that day from the Big Chimney, we thought we'd be made if only we managed to reach Minóok."

"Well, we've got what we came for—each got a claim."

"Oh, yes."

"A good claim, too."

"Guess so."

"Don't you *know* the gold's there?"

"Yes; but where are the miners? You and I don't propose to spend the next ten years in gettin' that gold out."

"No; but there are plenty who would if we gave 'em the chance. All we have to do is to give the right ones the chance."

The Colonel wore an air of reflection.

"The district will be opened up," the Boy went on cheerfully, "and we'll have people beggin' us to let 'em get out our gold, and givin' us the lion's share for the privilege."

"Do you altogether like the sound o' that?"

"I expect, like other people, I'll like the result."

"We ought to see some things clearer than other people. We had our lesson on the trail," said the Colonel quietly. "Nobody ought ever to be able to fool us about the power and the value of the individual apart from society. Seems as if association *did* make value. In the absence of men and markets a pit full of gold is worth no more than a pit full of clay."

"Oh, yes; I admit, till the boats come in, we're poor men."

"Nobody will stop here this summer—they'll all be racing on to Dawson."

"Dawson's 'It,' beyond a doubt."

The Colonel laughed a little ruefully.

"We used to say Minóok."

"I said Minóok, just to sound reasonable, but, of course, I *meant* Dawson."

And they sat there thinking, watching the ice-blocks meet, crash, go down in foam, and come up again on the lower reaches, the Boy idly swinging the great Katharine's medal to and fro. In his buckskin pocket it has worn so bright it catches at the light like a coin fresh from the mint.

No doubt Muckluck is on the river-bank at Pymeut; the one-eyed Prince, the story-teller Yagorsha, even Ol' Chief—no one will be indoors to-day.

Sitting there together, they saw the last stand made by the ice, and shared that moment when the final barrier, somewhere far below, gave way with boom and thunder. The mighty flood ran free, tearing up trees by their roots as it ran, detaching masses of rock, dissolving islands into swirling sand and drift, carving new channels, making and unmaking the land. The water began to fall. It had been a great time: it was ended.

"Pardner," says the Colonel, "we've seen the ice go out."

"No fella can call you and me cheechalkos after to-day."

"No, sah. We've travelled the Long Trail, we've seen the ice go out, and we're friends yet."

The Kentuckian took his pardner's brown hand with a gentle solemnity, seemed about to say something, but stopped, and turned his bronzed face to the flood, carried back upon some sudden tide within himself to those black days on the trail, that he wanted most in the world to forget. But in his heart he knew that all dear things, all things kind and precious—his home, a woman's face—all, all would fade before he forgot those last days on the trail. The record of that journey was burnt into the brain of the men who had made it. On that stretch of the Long Trail the elder had grown old, and the younger had forever lost his youth. Not only had the roundness gone out of his face, not only was it scarred, but such lines were graven there as commonly takes the antique pencil half a score of years to trace.

"Something has happened," the Colonel said quite low. "We aren't the same men who left the Big Chimney."

"Right!" said the Boy, with a laugh, unwilling as yet to accept his own personal revelation, preferring to put a superficial interpretation on his companion's words. He glanced at the Colonel, and his face changed a little. But still he would not understand. Looking down at the chaparejos that he had been so proud of, sadly abbreviated to make boots for Nig, jagged here and there, and with fringes now not all intentional, it suited him to pretend that the "shaps" had suffered most.

"Yes, the ice takes the kinks out."

"Whether the thing that's happened is good or evil, I don't pretend to say," the other went on gravely, staring at the river. "I only know something's happened. There were possibilities—in me, anyhow—that have been frozen to death. Yes, we're different."

The Boy roused himself, but only to persist in his misinterpretation.

"You ain't different to hurt. If I started out again to-morrow——"

"The Lord forbid!"

"Amen. But if I had to, you're the only man in Alaska—in the world—I'd want for my pardner."

"Boy——!" he wrestled with a slight bronchial huskiness, cleared his throat, tried again, and gave it up, contenting himself with, "Beg your pardon for callin' you 'Boy.' You're a seasoned old-timer, sah." And the Boy felt as if some Sovereign had dubbed him Knight.

In a day or two now, from north or south, the first boat must appear. The willows were unfolding their silver leaves. The alder-buds were bursting; geese and teal and mallard swarmed about the river margin. Especially where the equisetæ showed the tips of their feathery green tails above the mud, ducks flocked and feasted. People were too excited, "too busy," they said, looking for the boats, to do much shooting. The shy birds waxed daring. Keith, standing by his shack, knocked over a mallard within forty paces of his door.

It was eight days after that first cry, "The ice is going out!" four since the final jam gave way and let the floes run free, that at one o'clock in the afternoon the shout went up, "A boat! a boat!"

Only a lumberman's bateau, but two men were poling her down the current with a skill that matched the speed. They swung her in. A dozen hands caught at the painter and made fast. A young man stepped ashore and introduced himself as Van Alen, Benham's "Upper River pardner, on the way to Anvik."

His companion, Donovan, was from Circle City, and brought appalling news. The boats depended on for the early summer traffic, *Bella*, and three other N. A. T. and T. steamers, as well as the A. C.'s *Victoria* and the *St. Michael*, had been lifted up by the ice "like so many feathers," forced clean out of the channel, and left high and dry on a sandy ridge, with an ice wall eighty feet wide and fifteen high between them and open water.

"All the crews hard at work with jackscrews," said Donovan; "and if they can get skids under, and a channel blasted through the ice, they *may* get the boats down here in fifteen or twenty days."

A heavy blow. But instantly everyone began to talk of the *May West* and the *Muckluck* as though all along they had looked for succour to come up-stream rather than down. But as the precious hours passed, a deep dejection fastened on the camp. There had been a year when, through one disaster after another, no boats had got to the Upper River. Not even the arrival from Dawson of the Montana Kid, pugilist and gambler, could raise spirits so cast down, not even though he was said to bring strange news from outside.

There was war in the world down yonder—war had been formally declared between America and Spain.

Windy slapped his thigh in humourous despair.

"Why hadn't *he* thought o' gettin' off a josh like that?"

To those who listened to the Montana Kid, to the fretted spirits of men eight months imprisoned, the States and her foreign affairs were far away indeed, and as for the other party to the rumoured war—*Spain?* They clutched at school memories of Columbus, Americans finding through him the way to Spain, as through him Spaniards had found the way to America. So Spain was not merely a State historic! She was still in the active world. But what did these things matter? Boats mattered: the place where the Klondykers were caught, this Minóok, mattered. And so did the place they wanted to reach —Dawson mattered most of all. By the narrowed habit of long months, Dawson was the centre of the universe.

More little boats going down, and still nothing going up. Men said gloomily:

"We're done for! The fellows who go by the Canadian route will get everything. The Dawson season will be half over before we're in the field—if we *ever* are!"

The 28th of May! Still no steamer had come, but the mosquitoes had—bloodthirsty beyond any the temperate climates know. It was clear that some catastrophe had befallen the Woodworth boats. And Nig had been lured away by his quondam master! No, they had not gone back to the gulch— that was too easy. The man had a mind to keep the dog, and, since he was not allowed to buy him, he would do the other thing.

He had not been gone an hour, rumour said—had taken a scow and provisions, and dropped down the river. Utterly desperate, the Boy seized his new Nulato gun and somebody else's canoe. Without so much as inquiring whose, he shot down the swift current after the dog-thief. He roared back to the remonstrating Colonel that he didn't care if an up-river steamer *did* come while he was gone—he was goin' gunnin'.

At the same time he shared the now general opinion that a Lower River boat would reach them first, and he was only going to meet her, meting justice by the way.

He had gone safely more than ten miles down, when suddenly, as he was passing an island, he stood up in his boat, balanced himself, and cocked his gun.

Down there, on the left, a man was standing knee-deep in the water, trying to free his boat from a fallen tree; a Siwash dog watched him from the bank.

The Boy whistled. The dog threw up his nose, yapped and whined. The man had turned sharply, saw his enemy and the levelled gun. He jumped into the boat, but she was filling while he bailed; the dog ran along the island, howling fit to raise the dead. When he was a little above the Boy's boat he plunged into the river. Nig was a good swimmer, but the current here would tax the best. The Boy found himself so occupied with saving Nig from a watery grave, while he kept the canoe from capsizing, that he forgot all about the thief till a turn in the river shut him out of sight.

The canoe was moored, and while trying to restrain Nig's dripping caresses, his master looked up, and saw something queer off there, above the tops of the cottonwoods. As he looked he forgot the dog—forgot everything in earth or heaven except that narrow cloud wavering along the sky. He sat immovable in the round-shouldered attitude learned in pulling a hand-sled against a gale from the Pole. If you are moderately excited you may start, but there is an excitement that "nails you."

Nig shook his wolf's coat and sprayed the water far and wide, made little joyful noises, and licked the face that was so still. But his master, like a man of stone, stared at that long gray pennon in the sky. If it isn't a steamer, what is it? Like an echo out of some lesson he had learned and long forgot, "Up-bound boats don't run the channel: they have to hunt for easy water. " Suddenly he leaped up. The canoe tipped, and Nig went a second time into the water. Well for him that they were near the shore; he could jump in without help this time. No hand held out, no eye for him. His master had dragged the painter free, seized the oars, and, saying harshly, "Lie down, you black devil!" he pulled back against the current with every ounce he had in him. For the gray pennon was going round the other side of the island, and the Boy was losing the boat to Dawson.

Nig sat perkily in the bow, never budging till his master, running into the head of the island, caught up a handful of tough root fringes, and, holding fast by them, waved his cap, and shouted like one possessed, let go the fringes, caught up his gun, and fired. Then Nig, realising that for once in a way noise seemed to be popular, pointed his nose at the big object hugging the farther shore, and howled with a right goodwill.

"They see! They see! Hooray!"

The Boy waved his arms, embraced Nig, then snatched up the oars. The steamer's engines were reversed; now she was still. The Boy pulled lustily. A crowded ship. Crew and passengers pressed to the rails. The steamer canted, and the Captain's orders rang out clear. Several cheechalkos laid their hands on their guns as the wild fellow in the ragged buckskins shot round the motionless wheel, and brought his canoe 'long-side, while his savage-looking dog still kept the echoes of the Lower Ramparts calling.

"Three cheers for the *Oklahoma!*"

At the sound of the Boy's voice a red face hanging over the stern broke into a broad grin.

"Be the Siven! Air ye the little divvle himself, or air ye the divvle's gran'fatherr?"

The apparition in the canoe was making fast and preparing to board the ship.

"Can't take another passenger. Full up!" said the Captain. He couldn't hear what was said in reply, but he shook his head. "Been refusin' 'em right along." Then, as if reproached by the look in the wild young face, "We thought you were in trouble."

"So I am if you won't——"

"I tell you we got every ounce we can carry."

"Oh, take me back to Minóok, anyway!"

He said a few words about fare to the Captain's back. As that magnate did not distinctly say "No"—indeed, walked off making conversation with the engineer—twenty hands helped the new passenger to get Nig and the canoe on board.

"Well, got a gold-mine?" asked Potts.

"Yes, *sir*."

"Where's the Colonel?" Mac rasped out, with his square jaw set for judgment.

"Colonel's all right—at Minóok. We've got a gold-mine apiece."

"Anny gowld in 'em?"

"Yes, sir, and no salt, neither."

"Sorry to see success has gone to your head," drawled Potts, eyeing the Boy's long hair. "I don't see any undue signs of it elsewhere."

"Faith! I do, thin. He's turned wan o' thim hungry, grabbin' millionaires."

"What makes you think that?" laughed the Boy, poking his brown fingers through the knee-hole of his breeches.

"Arre ye contint wid that gowld-mine at Minóok? No, be the Siven! What's wan gowld-mine to a millionaire? What forr wud ye be prospectin that desert oiland, you and yer faithful man Froyday, if ye wasn't rooned intoirely be riches?"

The Boy tore himself away from his old friends, and followed the arbiter of his fate. The engines had started up again, and they were going on.

"I'm told," said the Captain rather severely, "that Minóok's a busted camp."

"Oh, *is* it?" returned the ragged one cheerfully. Then he remembered that this Captain Rainey had grub-staked a man in the autumn—a man who was reported to know where to look for the Mother Lode, the mighty parent of the Yukon placers. "I can tell you the *facts* about Minóok." He followed the Captain up on the hurricane-deck, giving him details about the new strike, and the wonderful richness of Idaho Bar. "Nobody would know about it to-day, but that the *right* man went prospecting there." (One in the eye for whoever said Minóok was "busted," and another for the prospector Rainey had sent to look for——) "You see, men like Pitcairn have given up lookin' for the Mother Lode. They say you might as well look for Mother Eve; you got to make out with her descendants. Yukon gold, Pitcairn says, comes from an older rock series than this" —he stood in the shower of sparks constantly spraying from the smoke-stack to the fireproof deck, and he waved his hand airily at the red rock of the Ramparts—"far older than any of these. The gold up here has all come out o'rock that went out o' the rock business millions o' years ago. Most o' that Mother Lode the miners are lookin' for is sand now, thirteen hundred miles away in Norton Sound."

"Just my luck," said the Captain gloomily, going a little for'ard, as though definitely giving up mining and returning to his own proper business.

"But the rest o' the Mother Lode, the gold and magnetic iron, was too heavy to travel. That's what's linin' the gold basins o' the North—linin' Idaho Bar *thick*."

The Captain sighed.

"Twelve," a voice sang out on the lower deck.

"Twelve," repeated the Captain.

"Twelve," echoed the pilot at the wheel.

"Twelve and a half," from the man below, a tall, lean fellow, casting the sounding-pole. With a rhythmic nonchalance he plants the long black and white staff at the ship's side, draws it up dripping, plunges it down again, draws it up, and sends it down hour after hour. He never seems to tire; he never seems to see anything but the water-mark, never to say anything but what he is chanting now, "Twelve and a half," or some variation merely numerical. You come to think him as little human as the calendar, only that his numbers are told off with the significance of sound, the suggested menace of a cry. If the "sounding" comes too near the steamer's draught, or the pilot fails to hear the reading, the Captain repeats it. He often does so when there is no need; it is a form of conversation, non-committal, yet smacking of authority.

"Ten."

"Ten," echoed the pilot, while the Captain was admitting that he had been mining vicariously "for twenty years, and never made a cent. Always keep thinkin' I'll soon be able to give up steamboatin' and buy a farm."

He shook his head as one who sees his last hope fade.

But his ragged companion turned suddenly, and while the sparks fell in a fresh shower, "Well, Captain," says he, "you've got the chance of your life right now."

"Ten and a half."

"Just what they've all said. Wish I had the money I've wasted on grub-stakin'."

The ragged one thrust his hands in the pockets of his chaparejos.

"*I* grub-staked myself, and I'm very glad I did."

"Nobody in with you?"

"No."

"Nine."

Echo, "Nine."

"Ten."

"Pitcairn says, somehow or other, there's been gold-washin' goin' on up here pretty well ever since the world began."

"Indians?"

"No; seems to have been a bigger job than even white men could manage. Instead o' stamp-mills, glaciers grindin' up the Mother Lode; instead o' little sluice-boxes, rivers; instead o' riffles, gravel bottoms. Work, work, wash, wash, day and night, every summer for a million years. Never a clean-up since the foundation of the world. No, sir, waitin' for us to do that— waitin' now up on Idaho Bar."

The Captain looked at him, trying to conceal the envy in his soul. They were sounding low water, but he never heard. He looked round sharply as the course changed.

"I've done my assessment," the ragged man went on joyously, "and I'm going to Dawson."

This was bad navigation. He felt instantly he had struck a snag. The Captain smiled, and passed on sounding: "Nine and a half."

"But I've got a fortune on the Bar. I'm not a boomer, but I believe in the Bar."

"Six."

"Six. Gettin' into low water."

Again the steamer swung out, hunting a new channel.

"Pitcairn's opinion is thought a lot of. The Geologic Survey men listen to Pitcairn. He helped them one year. He's one of those extraordinary old miners who can tell from the look of things, without even panning. When he saw that pyrites on Idaho Bar he stopped dead. 'This looks good to me!' he said, and, Jee-rusalem! it *was* good!"

They stared at the Ramparts growing bolder, the river hurrying like a mill-race, the steamer feeling its way slow and cautiously like a blind man with a stick.

"Seven."

"Seven."

"Seven."

"Six and a half."

"Pitcairn says gold is always thickest on the inside of an elbow or turn in the stream. It's in a place like that my claim is."

The steamer swerved still further out from the course indicated on the chart. The pilot was still hunting a new channel, but still the Captain stood and listened, and it was not to the sounding of the Yukon Bar.

"They say there's no doubt about the whole country being glaciated."

"Hey?"

"Signs of glacial erosion everywhere."

The Captain looked sharply about as if his ship might be in some new danger.

"No doubt the gold is all concentrates."

"Oh, is that so?" He seemed relieved on the whole.

"Eight and a half," from below.

"Eight and a half," from the Captain.

"Eight and a half," from the pilot-house.

"Concentrates, eh?"

Something arresting, rich-sounding, in the news—a triple essence of the perfume of riches.

With the incantation of technical phrase over the witch-brew of adventure, gambling, and romance, that simmers in the mind when men tell of finding gold in the ground, with the addition of this salt of science comes a savour of homely virtue, an aroma promising sustenance and strength. It confounds suspicion and sees unbelief, first weaken, and at last do reverence. There is something hypnotic in the terminology. Enthusiasm, even backed by fact, will scare off your practical man, who yet will turn to listen to the theory of "the mechanics of erosion" and one of its proofs—"up there before our eyes, the striation of the Ramparts."

But Rainey was what he called "an old bird." His squinted pilot-eye came back from the glacier track and fell on the outlandish figure of his passenger. And with an inward admiration of his quality of extreme old-birdness, the Captain struggled against the trance.

"Didn't I hear you say something about going to Dawson?"

"Y-yes. I think Dawson 'll be worth seeing."

"Holy Moses, yes! There's never been anything like Dawson before."

"And I want to talk to the big business men there. I'm not a miner myself. I mean to put my property on the market." As he said the words it occurred to him unpleasantly how very like McGinty they sounded. But he went on: "I didn't dream of spending so much time up here as I've put in already. I've got to get back to the States."

"You had any proposition yet?" The Captain led the way to his private room.

"About my claim? Not yet; but once I get it on the market——"

So full was he of a scheme of his own he failed to see that he had no need to go to Dawson for a buyer.

The Captain set out drinks, and still the talk was of the Bar. It had come now to seem impossible, even to an old bird, that, given those exact conditions, gold should not be gathered thick along that Bar.

"I regard it as a sure thing. Anyhow, it's recorded, and the assessment's done. All the district wants now is capital to develop it."

"Districts like that all over the map," said the old bird, with a final flutter of caution. "Even if the capital's found—if everything's ready for work, the summer's damn short. But if it's a question of goin' huntin' for the means of workin'——"

"There's time," returned the other quietly, "but there's none to waste. You take me and my pardner——"

"Thought you didn't have a pardner," snapped the other, hot over such duplicity.

"Not in ownership; he's got another claim. But you take my pardner and me to Dawson——"

The Captain stood on his legs and roared:

"I *can't*, I tell you!"

"You can if you will—you will if you want that farm!"

Rainey gaped.

"Take us to Dawson, and I'll get a deed drawn up in Minóok turning over one-third of my Idaho Bar property to John R. Rainey."

John R. Rainey gaped the more, and then finding his tongue:

"No, no. I'd just as soon come in on the Bar, but it's true what I'm tellin' you. There simply ain't an unoccupied inch on the *Oklahoma* this trip. It's been somethin' awful, the way I've been waylaid and prayed at for a passage. People starvin' with bags o' money waitin' for 'em at the Dawson Bank! Settlements under water—men up in trees callin' to us to stop for the love of God—men in boats crossin' our channel, headin' us off, thinkin' nothin' o' the risk o' bein' run down. 'Take us to Dawson!' it's the cry for fifteen hundred miles."

"Oh, come! you stopped for me."

The Captain smiled shrewdly.

"I didn't think it necessary at the time to explain. We'd struck bottom just then—new channel, you know; it changes a lot every time the ice goes out and the floods come down. I reversed our engines and went up to talk to the pilot. We backed off just after you boarded us. I must have been rattled to take you even to Minóok."

"No. It was the best turn you've done yourself in a long while."

The Captain shook his head. It was true: the passengers of the *Oklahoma* were crowded like cattle on a Kansas stock-car. He knew he ought to unload and let a good portion wait at Minóok for that unknown quantity the next boat. He would issue the order, but that he knew it would mean a mutiny.

"I'll get into trouble for overloading as it is."

"You probably won't; people are too busy up here. If you do, I'm offerin' you a good many thousand dollars for the risk."

"God bless my soul! where'd I put you? There ain't a bunk."

"I've slept by the week on the ice."

"There ain't room to lie down."

"Then we'll stand up."

Lord, Lord! what could you do with such a man? Owner of Idaho Bar, too. "Mechanics of erosion," "Concentrates," "a third interest"—it all rang in his head. "I've got nine fellers sleepin' in here," he said helplessly, "in *my* room."

"Can we come if we find our own place, and don't trouble you?"

"Well, I won't have any pardner—but perhaps you——"

"Oh, pardner's got to come too."

Whatever the Captain said the nerve-tearing shriek of the whistle drowned. It was promptly replied to by the most horrible howls.

"Reckon that's Nig! He's got to come too," said this dreadful ragged man.

"God bless me, this must be Minóok!"

The harassed Captain hustled out.

"You must wait long enough here to get that deed drawn, Captain!" called out the other, as he flew down the companionway.

Nearly six hundred people on the bank. Suddenly controlling his eagerness, the Boy contented himself with standing back and staring across strange shoulders at the place he knew so well. There was "the worst-lookin' shack in the town," that had been his home, the A. C. store looming importantly, the Gold Nugget, and hardly a face to which he could not give a name and a history: Windy Jim and the crippled Swede; Bonsor, cheek by jowl with his enemy, McGinty; Judge Corey spitting straight and far; the gorgeous bartender, all checks and diamonds, in front of a pitiful group of the scurvy-stricken (thirty of them in the town waiting for rescue by the steamer); Butts, quite bland, under the crooked cottonwood, with never a thought of how near he had come, on that very spot, to missing the first boat of the year, and all the boats of all the years to follow.

Maudie, Keith and the Colonel stood with the A. C. agent at the end of the baggage-bordered plank-walk that led to the landing. Behind them, at least four hundred people packed and waiting with their possessions at their feet, ready to be put aboard the instant the *Oklahoma* made fast. The Captain had called out "Howdy" to the A. C. Agent, and several greetings were shouted back and forth. Maudie mounted a huge pile of baggage and sat there as on a throne, the Colonel and Keith

366

perching on a heap of gunny-sacks at her feet. That woman almost the only person in sight who did not expect, by means of the *Oklahoma*, to leave misery behind! The Boy stood thinking "How will they bear it when they know?"

The *Oklahoma* was late, but she was not only the first boat—she might conceivably be the last.

Potts and O'Flynn had spotted the man they were looking for, and called out "Hello! Hello!" as the big fellow on the pile of gunnies got up and waved his hat.

Mac leaned over the rail, saying gruffly, "That you, Colonel?" trying, as the Boss of the Big Chimney saw—"tryin' his darndest not to look pleased," and all the while O'Flynn was waving his hat and howling with excitement:

"How's the gowld? How's yersilf?"

The gangway began its slow swing round preparatory to lowering into place. The mob on shore caught up boxes, bundles, bags, and pressed forward.

"No, no! Stand back!" ordered the Captain.

"*Take* your time!" said people trembling with excitement. "There's no rush."

"There's no room!" called out the purser to a friend.

"*No room?*" went from mouth to mouth, incredulous that the information could concern the speaker. He was only one. There was certainly room for him; and every man pushed the harder to be the sole exception to the dreadful verdict.

"Stand back there! Can't take even a pound of freight. Loaded to the guards!"

A whirlwind of protest and appeal died away in curses. Women wept, and sick men turned away their faces. The dogs still howled, for nothing is so lacerating to the feelings of your Siwash as a steam-whistle blast. The memory of it troubles him long after the echo of it dies. Suddenly above the din Maudie's shrill voice:

"I *thought* that was Nig!"

Before the gangway had dropped with a bang her sharp eyes had picked out the Boy.

"Well I'll be—— See who that is behind Nig? Trust *him* to get in on the ground-floor. *He* ain't worryin' for fear his pardner 'll lose the boat," she called to the Colonel, who was pressing forward as Rainey came down the gangway.

"How do you do, Captain?"

The man addressed never turned his head. He was forcing his way through the jam up to the A. C. Store.

"You may recall me, sah; I am——"

"If you are a man wantin' to go to Dawson, it doesn't matter who you are. I can't take you."

"But, sah——" It was no use.

A dozen more were pushing their claims, every one in vain. The *Oklahoma* passengers, bent on having a look at Minóok, crowded after the Captain. Among those who first left the ship, the Boy, talking to the purser, hard upon Rainey's heels. The Colonel stood there as they passed, the Captain turning back to say something to the Boy, and then they disappeared together through the door of the A. C.

Never a word for his pardner, not so much as a look. Bitterness fell upon the Colonel's heart. Maudie called to him, and he went back to his seat on the gunny-sacks.

"He's in with the Captain now," she said; "he's got no more use for us."

But there was less disgust than triumph in her face.

O'Flynn was walking over people in his frantic haste to reach the Colonel. Before he could accomplish his design he had three separate quarrels on his hands, and was threatening with fury to "settle the hash" of several of his dearest new friends.

Potts meanwhile was shaking the Big Chimney boss by the hand and saying, "Awfully sorry we can't take you on with us;" adding lower: "We had a mighty mean time after you lit out."

Then Mac thrust his hand in between the two, and gave the Colonel a monkey-wrench grip that made the Kentuckian's eyes water.

"Kaviak? Well, I'll tell you."

He shouldered Potts out of his way, and while the talk and movement went on all round Maudie's throne, Mac, ignoring her, set forth grimly how, after an awful row with Potts, he had adventured with Kaviak to Holy Cross. "An awful row, indeed," thought the Colonel, "to bring Mac to that;" but the circumstances had little interest for him, beside the fact that his pardner would be off to Dawson in a few minutes, leaving him behind and caring "not a sou markee."

Mac was still at Holy Cross. He had seen a woman there— "calls herself a nun—evidently swallows those priests whole. Kind of mad, believes it all. Except for that, good sort of girl. The kind to keep her word"—and she had promised to look after Kaviak, and never let him away from her till Mac came back to fetch him.

"Fetch him?"

"Fetch him!"

"Fetch him where?"

"Home!"

"When will that be?"

"Just as soon as I've put through the job up yonder." He jerked his head up the river, indicating the common goal.

And now O'Flynn, roaring as usual, had broken away from those who had obstructed his progress, and had flung himself upon the Colonel. When the excitement had calmed down a little, "Well," said the Colonel to the three ranged in front of him, Maudie looking on from above, "what you been doin' all these three months?"

"Doin'?"

"Well—a——"

"Oh, we done a lot."

They looked at one another out of the corners of their eyes and then they looked away.

"Since the birds came," began Mac in the tone of one who wishes to let bygones be bygones.

"Och, yes; them burruds was foine!"

Potts pulled something out of his trousers pocket—a strange collapsed object. He took another of the same description out of another pocket. Mac's hands and O'Flynn's performed the same action. Each man seemed to have his pockets full of these——

"What are they?"

"Money-bags, me bhoy! Made out o' the fut o' the 'Lasky swan, God bless 'em! Mac cahls 'em some haythen name, but everybuddy else cahls 'em illegant money-bags!"

*   *   *   *   *   *   *

In less than twenty minutes the steamer whistle shrieked. Nig bounded out of the A. C., frantic at the repetition of the insult; other dogs took the quarrel up, and the Ramparts rang.

The Boy followed the Captain out of the A. C. store. All the motley crew that had swarmed off to inspect Minóok, swarmed back upon the *Oklahoma*. The Boy left the Captain this time, and came briskly over to his friends, who were taking leave of the Colonel.

"So you're all goin' on but me!" said the Colonel very sadly.

The Colonel's pardner stopped short, and looked at the pile of baggage.

"Got your stuff all ready!" he said.

"Yes." The answer was not free from bitterness. "I'll have the pleasure of packin' it back to the shack after you're gone."

"So you were all ready to go off and leave me," said the Boy.

The Colonel could not stoop to the obvious retort. His pardner came round the pile and his eyes fell on their common sleeping-bag, the two Nulato rifles, and other "traps," that meant more to him than any objects inanimate in all the world.

"What? you were goin' to carry off my things too?" exclaimed the Boy.

"That's all you get," Maudie burst out indignantly—"all you get for packin' his stuff down to the landin', to have it all ready for him, and worryin' yourself into shoe-strings for fear he'd miss the boat."

Mac, O'Flynn, and Potts condoled with the Colonel, while the fire of the old feud flamed and died.

"Yes," the Colonel admitted, "I'd give five hundred dollars for a ticket on that steamer."

He looked in each of the three faces, and knew the vague hope behind his words was vain. But the Boy had only laughed, and caught up the baggage as the last whistle set the Rampart echoes flying, piping, like a lot of frightened birds.

"Come along, then."

"Look here!" the Colonel burst out. "That's my stuff."

"It's all the same. You bring mine. I've got the tickets. You and me and Nig's goin' to the Klondyke."

CHAPTER XX

THE KLONDYKE

" Poverty is an odious calling."
BURTON'S *Anatomy of Melancholy.*

ON Monday morning, the 6th of June, they crossed the British line; but it was not till Wednesday, the 8th, at four in the afternoon, just ten months after leaving San Francisco, that the *Oklahoma's* passengers saw between the volcanic hills on the right bank of the Yukon a stretch of boggy tundra, whereon hundreds of tents gleamed, pink and saffron. Just beyond the bold wooded height, wearing the deep scar of a landslide on its breast, just round that bend, the Klondyke river joins the Yukon—for this is Dawson, headquarters of the richest Placer Diggings the world has seen, yet wearing more the air of a great army encampment.

For two miles the river-bank shines with sunlit canvas—tents, tents everywhere, as far as eye can see, a mushroom growth masking the older cabins. The water-front swarms with craft, scows and canoes, birch, canvas, peterboro; the great bateaux of the northern lumberman, neat little skiffs, clumsy rafts; heavy "double-enders," whip-sawed from green timber, with capacity of two to five tons; lighters and barges carrying as much as forty tons—all having come through the perils of the upper lakes and shot the cañon rapids.

As the *Oklahoma* steams nearer, the town blossoms into flags; a great murmur increases to a clamour; people come swarming down to the water-front, waving Union Jacks and Stars and Stripes as well—— What does it all mean? A cannon booms, guns are fired, and as the *Oklahoma* swings into the bank a band begins to play; a cheer goes up from fifteen thousand throats: "Hurrah for the first steamer!"

The *Oklahoma* has opened the Klondyke season of 1898!

They got their effects off the boat, and pitched the old tent up on the Moosehide; then followed days full to overflowing, breathless, fevered, yet without result beyond a general stringing up of nerves. The special spell of Dawson was upon them all—the surface aliveness, the inner deadness, the sense of being cut off from all the rest of the world, as isolated as a man is in a dream, with no past, no future, only a fantastic, intensely vivid Now. This was the summer climate of the Klondyke.

The Colonel, the Boy, and Captain Rainey maintained the illusion of prosecuting their affairs by frequenting the offices, stores, and particularly saloons, where buyers and sellers most did congregate. Frequent mention was made of a certain valuable piece of property.

Where was it?

"Down yonder at Minóok;" and then nobody cared a straw.

It was true there was widespread dissatisfaction with the Klondyke. Everyone agreed it had been overdone. It would support one-quarter of the people already here, and tens of thousands on their way! "Say Klondyke, and instantly your soberest man goes mad; say anything else, and he goes deaf."

Minóok was a good camp, but it had the disadvantage of lying outside the magic district. The madness would, of course, not last, but meanwhile the time went by, and the people poured in day and night. Six great steamers full came up from the Lower River, and still the small craft kept on flocking like coveys of sea-fowl through the Upper Lakes, each party saying, "The crowd is behind."

On the 14th of June a toy whistle sounded shrill above the town, and in puffed a Liliputian "steel-hull" steamer that had actually come "on her own" through the cañon and shot the White Horse Rapids. A steamer from the Upper River! after that, others. Two were wrecked, but who minded? And still the people pouring in, and still that cry, "The crowd's behind!" and still the clamour for quicker, ampler means of transport to the North, no matter what it cost. The one consideration "to get there," and to get there "quickly," brought most of the horde by the Canadian route; yet, as against the two ocean steamers—all-sufficient the year before to meet the five river boats at St. Michael's—now, by the All-American route alone, twenty ocean steamers and forty-seven river boats, double-deckers, some two hundred and twenty-five feet long, and every one crowded to the guards with people coming to the Klondyke.

Meanwhile, many of those already there were wondering why they came and how they could get home. In the tons of " mail matter" for Dawson, stranded at Skaguay, must be those "instructions" from the Colonel's bank, at home, to the Canadian Bank of Commerce, Dawson City. He agreed with the Boy that if—very soon now—they had not disposed of the Minóok property, they would go to the mines.

"What's the good?" rasped Mac. "Every foot staked for seventy miles."

"For my part," admitted the Boy, "I'm less grand than I was. I meant to make some poor devil dig out my Minóok gold for me. It'll be the other way about: I'll dig gold for any man on Bonanza that'll pay me wages."

They sat slapping at the mosquitoes till a whistle screamed on the Lower River. The Boy called to Nig, and went down to the town to hear the news. By-and-by Mac came out with a pack, and said he'd be back in a day or two. After he had disappeared among the tents—a conquering army that had forced its way far up the hill by now—the Colonel got up and went to the spring for a drink. He stood there a long time looking out wistfully, not towards the common magnet across the Klondyke, but quite in the other direction towards the nearer gate of exit—towards home.

"What special brand of fool am I to be here?"

Down below, Nig, with hot tongue hanging out of the side of his mouth, now followed, now led, his master, coming briskly up the slope.

"That was the *Weare* we heard whistlin'," said the Boy, breathless. "And who d'you think's aboard?"

"Who?"

"Nicholas o' Pymeut, pilot. An' he's got Princess Muckluck along."

"No," laughed the Colonel, following the Boy to the tent. "What's the Princess come for?"

"How should I know?"

"Didn't she say?"

"Didn't stop to hear."

"Reckon she was right glad to see you," chaffed the Colonel. "Hey? Wasn't she?"

"I—don't think she noticed I was there."

"What! you bolted?" No reply. "See here, what you doin'?"

"Packin' up."

"Where you goin'?"

"Been thinkin' for some time I ain't wealthy enough to live

in this metropolis. There may be a place for a poor man, but Dawson isn't It."

"Well, I didn't think you were that much of a coward— turnin' tail like this just because a poor little Esquimaux—— Besides, she *may* have got over it. Even the higher races do." And he went on poking his fun till suddenly the Boy said:

"You're in such high spirits, I suppose you must have heard Maudie's up from Minóok."

"You're jokin'!"

"It ain't my idea of a joke. She's comin' up here soon 's she's landed her stuff."

"She's not comin' up here!"

"Why not? Anybody can come up on the Moosehide, and everybody's doin' it. I'm goin' to make way for some of 'em."

"Did she see you?"

"Well, she's seen Potts, anyhow."

"You're right about Dawson," said the Colonel suddenly; "it's too rich for my blood."

They pinned a piece of paper on the tent-flap to say they were "Gone prospecting: future movements uncertain."

Each with a small pack, and sticking out above it the Klondyke shovel that had come all the way from San Francisco, Nig behind with provisions in his little saddle-bags, and tongue farther out than ever, they turned their backs on Dawson, crossed the lower corner of Lot 6, behind the Government Reserve, stared with fresh surprise at the young market-garden flourishing there, down to the many-islanded Klondyke, across in the scow-ferry, over the Corduroy, that cheers and deceives the new-comer for that first mile of the Bonanza Trail, on through pool and morass to the thicket of white birches, where the Colonel thought it well to rest awhile.

"Yes, he felt the heat," he said, as he passed the time of day with other men going by with packs, pack-horses, or draught-dogs, cursing at the trail and at the Government that taxed the miners so cruelly and then did nothing for them, not even making a decent highway to the Dominion's source of revenue. But out of the direct rays of the sun the traveller found refreshment, and the mosquitoes were blown away by the keen breeze that seemed to come from off some glacier. And the birds sang loud, and the wild-flowers starred the birch-grove, and the briar-roses wove a tangle on either side the swampy trail.

On again, dipping to a little valley—Bonanza Creek! They stood and looked.

"Well, here we are."

"Yes, this is what we came for."

And it was because of "this" that so vast a machinery of ships, engines, and complicated human lives had been set in motion. What was it? A dip in the hills where a little stream was caught up into sluices. On either side of every line of boxes, heaps and windrows of gravel. Above, high on log-cabin staging, windlasses. Stretching away on either side, gentle slopes, mossed and flower starred. Here and there upon this ancient moose pasture, tents and cabins set at random. In the bed of the creek, up and down in every direction, squads of men sweating in the sun—here, where for untold centuries herds of leisurely and majestic moose had come to quench their thirst. In the older cabins their horns still lorded it. Their bones were bleaching in the fire-weed.

On from claim to claim the new-comers to these rich pastures went, till they came to the junction of the El Dorado, where huddles the haphazard settlement of the Grand Forks, only twelve miles from Dawson. And now they were at the heart of "the richest Placer Mining District the world has seen." But they knew well enough that every inch was owned, and that the best they could look for was work as unskilled labourers, day shift or night, on the claims of luckier men.

They had brought a letter from Ryan, of the North-West Mounted Police, to the Superintendent of No. 0, Above Discovery, a claim a little this side of the Forks. Ryan had warned them to keep out of the way of the part-owner, Scoville Austin, a surly person naturally, so exasperated at the tax, and so enraged at the rumour of Government spies masquerading as workmen, checking his reports, that he was "a first-rate man to avoid." But Seymour, the Superintendent, was, in the words of the soothing motto of the whole American people, "All right."

They left their packs just inside the door of the log-cabin, indicated as "Bunk House for the men on No. 0, Above"—a fearsome place, where, on shelf above shelf, among long unwashed bedclothes, the unwashed workmen of a prosperous company lay in the stupor of sore fatigue and semi-asphyxiation. Someone stirred as the door opened, and out of the foetid dusk of the unventilated, closely-shuttered cabin came a voice:

"Night shift on?"

"No."

"Then, damn you! shut the door."

As the never-resting sun "forced" the Dawson market-garden and the wild-roses of the trail, so here on the creek men must follow the strenuous example. No pause in the growing or the toiling of this Northern world. The day-gang on No. o was hard at it down there where lengthwise in the channel was propped a line of sluice-boxes, steadied by regularly spaced poles laid from box to bank on gravel ridge. Looking down from above, the whole was like a huge fish-bone lying along the bed of the creek. A little group of men with picks, shovels, and wheelbarrows were reducing the "dump" of winter pay, piled beside a windlass, conveying it to the sluices. Other men in line, four or five feet below the level of the boxes, were "stripping," picking, and shovelling the gravel off the bed-rock—no easy business, for even this summer temperature thawed but a few inches a day, and below, the frost of ten thousand years cemented the rubble into iron.

"Where is the Superintendent?"

"That's Seymour in the straw hat."

It was felt that even the broken and dilapidated article mentioned was a distinction and a luxury.

Yes, it was too hot up here in the Klondyke.

They made their way to the man in authority, a dark, quiet-mannered person, with big, gentle eyes, not the sort of Super-intendent they had expected to find representing such a man as the owner of No. o.

Having read Ryan's letter and slowly scanned the appli-cants: "What do you know about it?" He nodded at the sluice.

"All of nothing," said the Boy.

"Does it call for any particular knowing?" asked the Colonel.

"Calls for muscle and plenty of keep-at-it." His voice was soft, but as the Colonel looked at him he realized why a hard fellow like Scoville Austin had made this Southerner Superin-tendent.

"Better just try us."

"I can use one more man on the night shift, a dollar and a half an hour."

"All right," said the Boy.

The Colonel looked at him. "Is this job yours or mine?"
The Superintendent had gone up towards the dam.
"Whichever you say."

The Boy did not like to suggest that the Colonel seemed little fit for this kind of exercise. They had been in the Klondyke long enough to know that to be in work was to be in luck.

"I'll tell you," the younger man said quickly, answering something unspoken, but plain in the Colonel's face; "I'll go up the gulch and see what else there is."

It crossed his mind that there might be something less arduous than this shovelling in the wet thaw or picking at frozen gravel in the hot sun. If so, the Colonel might be induced to exchange. It was obvious that, like so many Southerners, he stood the sun very ill. While they were agreeing upon a rendezvous the Superintendent came back.

"Our bunk-house is yonder," he said, pointing. A kind of sickness came over the Kentuckian as he recalled the place. He turned to his pardner.

"Wish we'd got a pack-mule and brought our tent out from Dawson." Then, apologetically, to the Superintendent: "You see, sah, there are men who take to bunk-houses just as there are women who want to live in hotels; and there are others who want a place to call home, even if it's a tent."

The Superintendent smiled. "That's the way we feel about it in Alabama." He reflected an instant. "There's that big new tent up there on the hill, next to the Buckeyes' cabin. Good tent; belongs to a couple o' rich Englishmen, third owners in No. o. Gone to Atlin. Told me to do what I liked with that tent. You might bunk there while they're away."

"Now, that's mighty good of you, sah. Next whose cabin did you say?"

"Oh, I don't know their names. They have a lay on seventeen. Ohio men. They're called Buck One and Buck Two. Anybody 'll show you to the Buckeyes';" and he turned away to shout "Gate!" for the head of water was too strong, and he strode off towards the lock.

As the Boy tramped about looking for work he met a great many on the same quest. It seemed as if the Colonel had secured the sole job on the creek. Still, vacancies might occur any hour.

In the big new tent the Colonel lay asleep on a little camp-bed, (mercifully left there by the rich Englishmen), "gettin' ready for the night-shift." As he stood looking down upon him, a sudden wave of pity came over the Boy. He knew the Colonel didn't "really and truly *have* to do this kind of thing; he just didn't like givin' in." But behind all that there was a sense in the younger mind that here was a life unlike his own, which dimly he foresaw was to find its legitimate expression in battle and in striving. Here, in the person of the Colonel, no soldier fore-ordained, but a serene and equable soul wrenched out of its proper sphere by a chance hurt to a woman, forsooth! an imagination so stirred that, if it slept at all, it dreamed and moaned in its sleep, as now; a conscience wounded and refusing to heal. Had he not said himself that he had come up here to forget? It was best to let him have the job that was too heavy for him—yes, it was best, after all.

And so they lived for a few days, the Boy chafing and wanting to move on, the Colonel very earnest to have him stay.

"Something sure to turn up, and, anyhow, letters—my instruction——" And he encouraged the acquaintance the Boy had struck up with the Buckeyes, hoping against hope that to go over and smoke a pipe, and exchange experiences with such mighty good fellows would lighten the tedium of the long day spent looking for a job.

"I call it a very pleasant cabin," the Colonel would say as he lit up and looked about.

Anything dismaller it would be hard to find. Not clean and shipshape as the Boy kept the tent. But with double army blankets nailed over the single window it was blessedly dark, if stuffy, and in crying need of cleaning. Still, they were mighty good fellows, and they had a right to be cheerful. Up there, on the rude shelf above the stove, was a row of old tomato-cans brimful of Bonanza gold. There they stood, not even covered. Dim as the light was, you could see the little top nuggets peering out at you over the ragged tin-rims, in a never locked shanty, never molested, never bothered about. Nearly every cabin on the creek had similar chimney ornaments, but not everyone boasted an old coat, kept under the bunk, full of the bigger sort of nuggets.

The Colonel was always ready with pretended admiration of such bric-à-brac, but the truth was he cared very little about this gold he had come so far to find. His own wages, paid in dust, were kept in a jam-pot the Boy had found "lyin' round."

The growing store shone cheerfully through the glass, but its value in the Colonel's eyes seemed to be simply as an argument to prove that they had enough, and "needn't worry." When the Boy said there was no doubt this was the district in all the world the most overdone, the Colonel looked at him with sun-tired, reproachful eyes.

"You want to dissolve the pardnership—I see."

"I don't."

But the Colonel, after any such interchange, would go off and smoke by himself, not even caring for Buckeyes'. The work was plainly overtaxing him. He slept badly, was growing moody and quick to take offence. One day when he had been distinctly uncivil he apologized for himself by saying that, standing with feet always in the wet, head always in the scorching sun, he had taken a hell of a cold. Certain it was that, without sullenness, he would give in to long fits of silence; and his wide, honest eyes were heavy again, as if the snow-blindness of the winter had its analogue in a summer torment from the sun. And his sometimes unusual gentleness to his companion was sharply alternated with unusual choler, excited by a mere nothing. Enough if the Boy were not in the tent when the Colonel came and went. Of course, the Boy did the cooking. The Colonel ate almost nothing, but he made a great point of his pardner's service in doing the cooking. He would starve, he said, if he had to cook for himself as well as swing a shovel; and the Boy, acting on pure instinct, pretended that he believed this was so.

Then came the evening when the Boy was so late the Colonel got his own breakfast; and when the recreant did get home, it was to announce that a man over at the Buckeyes' had just offered him a job out on Indian River.

The Colonel set down his tea-cup and stared. His face took on an odd, rigid look. But almost indifferently he said:

"So you're goin'?"

"Of course, you know I must. I started with an outfit and fifteen hundred dollars, now I haven't a cent."

The Kentuckian raised his heavy eyes to the jam-jar. "Oh, help yourself."

The Boy laughed, and shook his head.

"I wish you wouldn't go," the other said very low.

"You see, I've got to. Why, Nig and I owe you for a week's grub already."

Then the Colonel stood up and swore—swore till he was scarlet and shaking with excitement.

"If the life up here has brought us to 'Scowl' Austin's point of view, we *are* poorly off." And he spoke of the way men lived in his part of Kentucky, where the old fashion of keeping open house survived. And didn't he know it was the same thing in Florida? "Wouldn't you do as much for me?"

"Yes, only I can't—and—I'm restless. The summer's half gone. Up here that means the whole year's half gone."

The Colonel had stumbled back into his seat, and now across the deal table he put out his hand.

"Don't go, Boy. I don't know how I'd get on without——" He stopped, and his big hand was raised as if to brush away some cloud between him and his pardner. "If you go, you won't come back."

"Oh, yes, I will. You'll see."

"I know the kind," the other went on, as if there had been no interruption. "They never come back. I don't know as I ever cared *quite* as much for my brother—little fella that died, you know." Then, seeing that his companion did not instantly iterate his determination to go, *"That's* right," he said, getting up suddenly, and leaving his breakfast barely touched. "We've been through such a lot together, let's see it out."

Without waiting for an answer, he went off to his favourite seat under the little birch-tree. But the incident had left him nervous. He would come up from his work almost on the run, and if he failed to find his pardner in the tent there was the devil to pay. The Boy would laugh to himself to think what a lot he seemed able to stand from the Colonel; and then he would grow grave, remembering what he had to make up for. Still, his sense of obligation did not extend to giving up this splendid chance down on Indian River. On Wednesday, when the fellow over at the Buckeyes' was for going back, the Boy would go along.

On Sunday morning he ran a crooked, rusty nail into his foot. Clumsily extracted, it left an ugly wound. Walking became a torture, and the pain a banisher of sleep. It was during the next few days that he found out how much the Colonel lay awake. Who could sleep in this blazing sun? Black tents were not invented then, so they lay awake and talked of many things.

The man from Indian River went back alone. The Boy

would limp after the Colonel down to the sluice, and sit on a dump-heap with Nig. Few people not there strictly on business were tolerated on No. 0, but Nig and his master had been on good terms with Seymour from the first. Now they struck up acquaintance with several of the night-gang, especially with the men who worked on either side of the Colonel. An Irish gentleman, who did the shovelling just below, said he had graduated from Dublin University. He certainly had been educated somewhere, and if the discussion were theologic, would take out of his linen-coat pocket a little testament in the Vulgate to verify a bit of Gospel. He could even pelt the man next but one in his native tongue, calling the Silesian "Uebermensch." There existed some doubt whether this were the gentleman's real name, but none at all as to his talking philosophy with greater fervour than he bestowed on the puddling-box.

The others were men more accustomed to work with their hands, but, in spite of the conscious superiority of your experienced miner, a very good feeling prevailed in the gang—a general friendliness that presently centred about the Colonel, for even in his present mood he was far from disagreeable, except now and then, to the man he cared the most for.

Seymour admitted that he had placed the Southerner where he thought he'd feel most at home. "Anyhow, the company is less mixed," he said, "than it was all winter up at twenty-three, where they had a Presbyterian missionary down the shaft, a Salvation Army captain turnin' the windlass, a nigger thief dumpin' the becket, and a dignitary of the Church of England doin' the cookin', with the help of a Chinese chore-boy. They're all there now (except one) washin' out gold for the couple of San Francisco card-sharpers that own the claim."

"Vich von is gone?" asked the Silesian, who heard the end of the conversation.

"Oh, the Chinese chore-boy is the one who's bettered himself," said the Superintendent—"makin' more than all the others put together ever made in their lives; runnin' a laundry up at Dawson."

The Boy, since this trouble with his foot, had fallen into the way of turning night into day. The Colonel liked to have him down there at the sluice, and when he thought about it, the Boy marvelled at the hours he spent looking on while others worked.

At first he said he came down only to make Scowl Austin mad. And it did make him mad at first, but the odd thing was he got over it, and used to stop and say something now and then. This attention on the part of the owner was distinctly perilous to the Boy's good standing with the gang. Not because Austin was the owner; there was the millionaire Swede, Ole Olsen—any man might talk to him. He was on the square, treated his workmen mighty fair, and when the other owners tried to reduce wages, and *did,* Ole wouldn't join them —went right along paying the highest rate on the creek.

Various stories were afloat about Austin. Oh, yes, Scowl Austin was a hard man—the only owner on the creek who wouldn't even pay the little subscription every poor miner contributed to keep the Dawson Catholic Hospital going.

The women, too, had grievances against Austin, not only "the usual lot" up at the Gold Belt, who sneered at his close fist, but some of the other sort—those few hard-working wives or "women on their own," or those who washed and cooked for this claim or that. They had stories about Austin that shed a lurid light. And so by degrees the gathered experience, good and ill, of "the greatest of all placer diggin's" flowed by the idler on the bank.

"You seem to have a lot to do," Seymour would now and then say with a laugh.

"So I have."

"What do you call it?"

"Takin' stock."

"Of us?"

"Of things in general."

"What did you mean by that?" demanded the Colonel suspiciously when the Superintendent had passed up the line.

The shovelling in was done for the time being. The water was to be regulated, and then the clean-up as soon as the owner came down.

"Better not let Austin hear you say you're takin' stock. He'll run you out o' the creek."

The Boy only smiled, and went on fillipping little stones at Nig.

"What did you mean?" the Colonel persisted, with a look as suspicious as Scowl Austin's own.

"Oh, nothin'. I'm only thinkin' out things."

"Your future, I suppose?" he said testily.

"Mine and other men's. The Klondyke's a great place to get things clear in your head."

"Don't find it so." The Colonel put up his hand with that now familiar action as if to clear away a cloud. "It's days since I had anything clear in my head, except the lesson we learned on the trail."

The Boy stopped throwing stones, and fixed his eyes on his friend, as the Colonel went on:

"We had that hammered into us, didn't we?"

"What?"

"Oh, that—you know—that—— I don't know quite how to put it so it'll sound as orthodox as it might be, bein' true; but it looks pretty clear even to me"—again the big hand brushing at the unmoted sunshine—"that the only reason men got over bein' beasts was because they began to be brothers."

"Don't," said the Boy.

"Don't what?"

"I've always known I should have to tell you some time. I won't be able to put it off if I stay . . . and I hate tellin' you now. See here: I b'lieve I'll get a pack-mule and go over to Indian River."

The Colonel looked round angrily. Standing high against the sky, Seymour, with the gateman up at the lock, was moderating the strong head of water. It began to flow sluggishly over the gravel-clogged riffles, and Scowl Austin was coming down the hill.

"I don't know what you're drivin' at, about somethin' to tell. I know one thing, though, and I learned it up here in the North: men were meant to stick to one another."

"*Don't*, I say."

"Here's Austin," whispered the Colonel.

The Silesian philosopher stood in his "gum-boots" in the puddling-box as on a rostrum; but silent now, as ever, when Scowl Austin was in sight. With the great sluice-fork, the philosopher took up, washed, and threw out the few remaining big stones that they might not clog the narrow boxes below.

Seymour had so regulated the stream that, in place of the gush and foam of a few minutes before, there was now only a scant and gently falling veil of water playing over the bright gravel caught in the riffle-lined bottoms of the boxes.

As the Boy got up and reached for his stick, Austin stood there saying, to nobody in particular, that he'd just been over to No. 29, where they were trying a new-fangled riffle.

"Don't your riffles do the trick all right?" asked the Boy.

"If you're in any doubt, come and see," he said.

They stood together, leaning over the sluice, looking in at one of the things human industry has failed to disfigure, nearly as beautiful to-day as long ago on Pactolus' banks when Lydian shepherds, with great stones, fastened fleeces in the river that they might catch and gather for King Crœsus the golden sands of Tmolus. Improving, not in beauty, but economy, quite in the modern spirit, the Greeks themselves discovered that they lost less gold if they led the stream through fleece-lined water-troughs—and beyond this device of those early placer-miners we have not progressed so far but that, in every long, narrow sluice-box in the world to-day, you may see a Lydian water-trough with a riffle in the bottom for a golden fleece.

The rich Klondyker and the poor one stood together looking in at the water, still low, still slipping softly over polished pebbles, catching at the sunlight, winking, dimpling, glorifying flint and jasper, agate and obsidian, dazzling the uncommercial eye to blind forgetfulness of the magic substance underneath.

Austin gathered up, one by one, a handful of the shining stones, and tossed them out. Then, bending down, "See?"

There, under where the stones had been, neatly caught in the lattice of the riffle, lying thick and packed by the water action, a heavy ridge of black and yellow—magnetic sand and gold.

"Riffles out!" called Seymour, and the men, who had been extracting the rusty nails that held them firm, lifted out from the bottom of each box a wooden lattice, soused it gently in the water, and laid it on the bank.

The Boy had turned away again, but stood an instant noticing how the sun caught at the countless particles of gold still clinging to the wood; for this was one of the old riffles, frayed by the action of much water and the fret of many stones. Soon it would have to be burned, and out of its ashes the careful Austin would gather up with mercury all those million points of light.

Meanwhile, Seymour had called to the gateman for more water, and himself joining the gang, armed now with flat metal scoops, they all began to turn over and throw back against the stream the débris in the bottom of the boxes, giving the water another chance to wash out the lighter stuff and clean the gold from all impurity. Away went the last of the sand, and away went the pebbles, dark or bright, away went much of the heavy magnetic iron. Scowl Austin, at the end of the line, had a corn-whisk with which he swept the floor of the box, always up-stream, gathering the contents in a heap, now on this side, now on that, letting the water play and sort and carry away, condensing, hastening the process that for ages had been concentrating gold in the Arctic placers.

"Say, look here!" shouted Austin to the Boy, already limping up the hill.

When he had reached the sluice again he found that all Scowl Austin wanted, apparently, was to show him how, when he held the water back with the whisk, it eddied softly at each side of the broad little broom, leaving exposed the swept-up pile.

"See?"

"What's all that?"

"What do you think?"

"Looks like a heap o' sawdust."

Austin actually laughed.

"See if it feels like sawdust. Take it up like this," he ordered.

His visitor obeyed, lifting a double handful out of the water and holding it over the box, dripping, gleaming, the most beautiful thing that comes out of the earth, save only life, and the assertion may stand, even if the distinction is without difference, if the crystal is born, grows old, and dies as undeniably as the rose.

The Boy held the double handful of well-washed gold up to the sunshine, feeling to the full the immemorial spell cast by the King of Metals. Nothing that men had ever made out of gold was so entirely beautiful as this.

Scowl Austin's grim gratification was openly heightened with the rich man's sense of superiority, but his visitor seemed to have forgotten him.

"Colonel! here a minute. We thought it looked wonderful enough on the Big Chimney table—but Lord! to see it like this, out o' doors, mixed with sunshine and water!"

Still he stood there fascinated, leaning heavily against the sluice-box, still with his dripping hands full, when, after a hurried glance, the Colonel returned to his own box. None of the gang ever talked in the presence of the owner.

"Guess that looks good to you." Austin slightly stressed the pronoun. He had taken a reasonless liking for the young man, who from the first had smiled into his frowning face, and treated him as he treated others. Or perhaps Austin liked him because, although the Boy did a good deal of "gassin' with the gang," he had never hung about at clean-ups. At all events, he should stay to-night, partly because when the blue devils were down on Scowl Austin nothing cheered him like showing his "luck" off to someone. And it was so seldom safe in these days. People talked. The authorities conceived unjust suspicions of a man's returns. And then, far back in his head, that vague need men feel, when a good thing has lost its early zest, to see its dimmed value shine again in an envious eye. Here was a young fellow, who, before he went lame, had been all up and down the creek for days looking for a job—probably hadn't a penny—livin' off his friend, who himself would starve but for the privilege Austin gave him of washing out Austin's gold. Let the young man stop and see the richest clean-up at the Forks.

And so it was with the acrid pleasure he had promised himself that he said to the visitor, bending over the double handful of gold, "Guess it looks good to you."

"Yes, it looks good!" But he had lifted his eyes, and seemed to be studying the man more than the metal.

A couple of newcomers, going by, halted.

"Christ!" said the younger, "look at that!"

The Boy remembered them; they had been to Seymour only a couple of hours before asking for work. One was old for that country—nearly sixty—and looked, as one of the gang had said, "as if, instid o' findin' the pot o' gold, he had got the end of the rainbow slam in his face—kind o' blinded."

At sound of the strange voice Austin had wheeled about with a fierce look, and heavily the strangers plodded by. The owner turned again to the gold. "Yes," he said curtly, "there's something about that that looks good to most men."

"What I was thinkin'," replied the Boy slowly, "was that it was the only clean gold I'd ever seen—but it isn't so clean as it was."

"What do you mean?" Austin bent and looked sharply into the full hands.

"I was thinkin' it was good to look at because it hadn't got into dirty pockets yet." Austin stared at him an instant. "Never been passed round—never bought anybody. No one had ever envied it, or refused it to help someone out of a hole. That was why I thought it looked good—because it was clean gold . . . a little while ago." And he plunged his hands in the water and washed the clinging particles off his fingers.

Austin had stared, and then turned his back with a blacker look than even "Scowl" had ever worn before.

"Gosh! guess there's goin' to be trouble," said one of the gang.

CHAPTER XXI

"He saw, and first of brotherhood had sight . . ."

IT was morning, and the night-shift might go to bed; but in the absent Englishmen's tent there was little sleep and less talk that day. The Boy, in an agony, with a foot on fire, heard the Colonel turning, tossing, growling incoherently about "the light."

It seemed unreasonable, for a frame had been built round his bed, and on it thick gray army blankets were nailed—a rectangular tent. Had he cursed the *heat* now? But no: "light," "God! the light, the light!" just as if he were lying as the Boy was, in the strong white glare of the tent. But hour after hour within the stifling fortress the giant tossed and muttered at the swords of sunshine that pierced his semi-dusk through little spark-burnt hole or nail-tear, torturing sensitive eyes.

Near three hours before he needed, the Colonel got up and splashed his way through a toilet at the tin basin. The Boy made breakfast without waiting for the usual hour. They had nearly finished when it occurred to the Colonel that neither had spoken since they went to bed. He glanced across at the absorbed face of his friend.

"You'll come down to the sluice to-night, won't you?"

"Why shouldn't I?"

"No reason on earth, only I was afraid you were broodin' over what you said to Austin."

"Austin? Oh, I'm not thinkin' about *Austin*."

"What, then? What makes you so quiet?"

"Well, I'm thinkin' I'd be better satisfied to stay here a little longer if——"

"If what?"

"If there was truth between us two."

"I thought there was."

"No. What's the reason you want me to stay here?"

388

"Reason? Why"—he laughed in his old way—"I don't defend my taste, but I kind o' like to have you round."

His companion's grave face showed no lightening. "Why do you want me round more than someone else?"

"Haven't got anyone else."

"Oh, yes, you have! Every man on Bonanza's a friend o' yours, or would be."

"It isn't just that; we understand each other."

"No, we don't."

"What's wrong?"

No answer. The Boy looked through the door across Bonanza to the hills.

"I thought we understood each other if two men ever did. Haven't we travelled the Long Trail together and seen the ice go out?"

"That's just it, Colonel. We know such a lot more than men do who haven't travelled the Trail, and some of the knowledge isn't oversweet."

A shadow crossed the kind face opposite.

"You're thinkin' about the times I pegged out—didn't do my share."

"Lord, no!" The tears sprang up in the young eyes. "I'm thinkin' o' the times—I——" He laid his head down on the rude table, and sat so for an instant with hidden face; then he straightened up. "Seems as if it's only lately there's been time to think it out. And before, as long as I could work I could get on with myself. . . . Seemed as if I stood a chance to . . . a little to make up."

"Make up?"

"But it's always just as it was that day on the *Oklahoma,* when the captain swore he wouldn't take on another pound. I was awfully happy thinkin' if I made him bring you it might kind o' make up, but it didn't."

"Made a big difference to me," the Colonel said, still not able to see the drift, but patiently brushing now and then at the dazzling mist and waiting for enlightenment.

"It's always the same," the other went on. "Whenever I've come up against something I'd hoped was goin' to make up, it's turned out to be a thing I'd have to do anyway, and there was no make up about it. For all that, I shouldn't mind stayin' on awhile since you want me to——"

The Colonel interrupted him, "*That's* right!"

"Only if I do, you've got to know—what I'd never have guessed myself, but for the Trail. After I've told you, if you can bear to see me round——" He hesitated and suddenly stood up, his eyes still wet, but his head so high an onlooker who did not understand English would have called the governing impulse pride, defiance even. "It seems I'm the kind of man, Colonel—the kind of man who could leave his pardner to die like a dog in the snow."

"If any other fella said so, I'd knock him down."

"That night before we got to Snow Camp, when you wouldn't—*couldn't* go any farther, I meant to go and leave you—take the sled, and take—I guess I meant to take everything and leave you to starve."

They looked into each other's faces, and years seemed to go by. The Colonel was the first to drop his eyes; but the other, pitilessly, like a judge arraigning a felon, his steady scrutiny never flinching: "Do you want that kind of a man round, Colonel?"

The Kentuckian turned quickly as if to avoid the stab of the other's eye, and sat hunched together, elbows on knees, head in hands.

"I knew you didn't." The Boy answered his own question. He limped over to his side of the tent, picked up some clothes, his blanket and few belongings, and made a pack. Not a word, not a sound, but some birds twittering outside in the sun and a locust making that frying sound in the fire-weed. The pack was slung on the Boy's back, and he was throwing the diamond hitch to fasten it when the Colonel at last looked round.

"Lord, what you doin'?"

"Guess I'm goin' on."

"Where?"

"I'll write you when I know; maybe I'll even send you what I owe you, but I don't feel like boastin' at the moment. Nig!"

"You can't walk."

"Did you never happen to notice that one-legged fella pluggin' about Dawson?"

He had gone down on his hands and knees to see if Nig was asleep under the camp-bed. The Colonel got up, went to the door, and let down the flap. When he turned, the traveller and the dog were at his elbow. He squared his big frame at the entrance, looking down at the two, tried to speak, but the Boy broke in: "Don't let's get sentimental, Colonel; just stand aside."

Never stirring, he found a voice to say, "I'm not askin' you to stay"—the other turned and whistled, for Nig had retired again to the seclusion of the gray blanket screen—"I only want to tell you something before you go."

The Boy frowned a little, but rested his pack against the table in that way in which the Klondyker learns to make a chair-back of his burden.

"You seem to think you've been tellin' me news," said the Colonel. "When you said that about goin' on, the night before we got to Snow Camp, I knew you simply meant you still intended to come out alive. I had thrown up my hands—at least, I thought I had. The only difference between us—I had given in and you hadn't."

The other shook his head. "There was a lot more in it than that."

"You meant to take the only means there were—to carry off the sled that I couldn't pull any farther——" The Boy looked up quickly. Something stern and truth-compelling in the dark face forced the Colonel to add: "And along with the sled you meant to carry off—the—the things that meant life to us."

"Just that——" The Boy knotted his brown fingers in Nig's hair as if to keep tight hold of one friend in the wreck.

"We *couldn't* divide," the Colonel hurried on. "It was a case of crawlin' on together, and, maybe, come out alive, or part and one die sure."

The Boy nodded, tightening his lips.

"I knew well enough you'd fight for the off-chance. But"—the Colonel came away from the door and stood in front of his companion—"*so would I*. I hadn't really given up the struggle."

"You were past strugglin', and I would have left you sick——"

"You wouldn't have left me—if I'd had my gun."

The Boy remembered that he had more than suspected that at the time, but the impression had by-and-by waxed dim. It was too utterly unlike the Colonel—a thing dreamed. He had grown as ashamed of the dream as of the thing he knew was true. The egotism of memory absorbed itself in the part he himself had played—that other, an evil fancy born of an evil time. And here was the Colonel saying it was true. The Boy dropped his eyes. It had all happened in the night. There was something in the naked truth too ghastly for the day. But the Colonel went on in a harsh whisper:

"I looked round for my gun; if I'd found it *I'd have left you behind.*"

And the Boy kept looking down at Nig, and the birds sang, and the locust whirred, and the hot sun filled the tent as hightide flushes a sea-cave.

"You've been a little hard on me, Boy, bringin' it up like this—remindin' me—— I wouldn't have gone on myself, and makin' me admit——"

"No, no, Colonel."

"Makin' me admit that before I would have let you go on I'd have shot you!"

"Colonel!" He loosed his hold of Nig.

"I rather reckon I owe you my life—and something else besides"—the Colonel laid one hand on the thin shoulder where the pack-strap pressed, and closed the other hand tight over his pardner's right—"and I hadn't *meant* even to thank you neither."

"Don't, for the Lord's sake, don't!" said the younger, and neither dared look at the other.

A scratching on the canvas, the Northern knock at the door.

"You fellers sound awake?"

A woman's voice. Under his breath, "Who the devil's that?" inquired the Colonel, brushing his hand over his eyes. Before he got across the tent Maudie had pushed the flap aside and put in her head.

"Hello!"

"*Hell*-o! How d'e do?"

He shook hands, and the younger man nodded, "Hello."

"When did you come to town?" asked the Colonel mendaciously.

"Why, nearly three weeks ago, on the *Weare.* Heard you had skipped out to Sulphur with MacCann. I had some business out that way, so that's where I been."

"Have some breakfast, won't you—dinner, I mean?"

"I put that job through at the Road House. Got to rustle around now and get my tent up. Where's a good place?"

"Well, I—I hardly know. Goin' to stay some time?"

"Depends."

The Boy slipped off his pack.

"They've got rooms at the Gold Belt," he said.

"You mean that Dance Hall up at the Forks?"

"Oh, it ain't so far. I remember you can walk."

"I can do one or two other things. Take care you don't hurt yourself worryin' about *me*."

"Hurt myself?"

"Yes. Bein' so hos*pitt*able. The way you're pressin' me to settle right down here, near's possible—why, it's real touchin'."

He laughed, and went to the entrance to tie back the door-flap, which was whipping and snapping in the breeze. Heaven be praised! the night was cooler. Nig had been perplexed when he saw the pack pushed under the table. He followed his master to the door, and stood looking at the flap-tying, ears very pointed, critical eye cocked, asking as plain as could be, "You wake me up and drag me out here into the heat and mosquitoes just to watch you doin' that? Well, I've my opinion of you."

"Colonel gone down?" inquired the Silesian, passing by.

"Not yet."

"Anything I can do?" the gentleman inside was saying with a sound of effort in his voice. The lady was not even at the pains to notice the perfunctory civility.

"Well, Colonel, now you're here, what do you think o' the Klondyke?"

"Think? Well, there's no doubt they've taken a lot o' gold out o' here."

"Reg'lar old Has Been, hey?"

"Oh, I don't say it hasn't got a future."

"What! Don't you know the boom's busted?"

"Well, no."

"Has. Tax begun it. Too many cheechalkos are finishing it. Klondyke?" She laughed. "The Klondyke's goin' to hell down-grade in a hand-car."

Scowl Austin was up, ready, as usual, to relieve Seymour of half the superintending, but never letting him off duty till he had seen the new shift at work. As the Boy limped by with the German, Austin turned his scowl significantly towards the Colonel's tent.

"Good-mornin'—good-night, I mean," laughed the lame man, just as if his tongue had not run away with him the last time the two had met. It was not often that anyone spoke so pleasantly to the owner of No. 0. Perhaps the circumstance weighed with him; at all events, he stopped short. When the German had gone on, "Foot's better," Austin asserted.

"Perhaps it is a little," though the lame man had no reason to think so.

"Lucky you heal quick. Most people don't up here—livin' on the stale stuff we get in this —— country. Seymour said anything to you about a job?"

"No."

"Well, since *you're* on time, you better come on the night shift, instead o' that lazy friend o' yours."

"Oh, *he* ain't lazy—been up hours. An old acquaintance dropped in; he'll be down in a minute."

"'Tisn't only his bein' late. You better come on the shift."

"Don't think I could do that. What's the matter?"

"Don't say there's anything very much the matter *yet*. But he's sick, ain't he?"

"Sick? No, except as we all are—sick o' the eternal glare."

The Colonel was coming slowly down the hill. Of course, a man doesn't look his best if he hasn't slept. The Boy limped a little way back to meet him.

"Anything the matter with you, Colonel?"

"Well, my Bonanza headache ain't improved."

"I suppose you wouldn' *like* me to take over the job for two or three days?"

"You? Crippled! Look here—" The Colonel flushed suddenly. "Austin been sayin' anything?"

"Oh, I was just thinkin' about the sun."

"Well, when I want to go in out of the sun, I'll say so." And, walking more quickly than he had done for long, he left his companion, marched down to the creek, and took his place near the puddling-box.

By the time the Boy got to the little patch of shade, offered by the staging, Austin had turned his back on the gang, and was going to speak to the gateman at the locks. He had evidently left the Colonel very much enraged at some curt comment.

"He meant it for us all," the Dublin gentleman was saying soothingly. By-and-by, as they worked undisturbed, serenity returned. Oh, the Colonel was all right—even more chipper than usual. What a good-looking fella he was, with that clear skin and splendid colour!

A couple of hours later the Colonel set his long shovel against the nearest of the poles steadying the sluice, and went over to the staging for a drink. He lifted the can of weak tea to his lips and took a long draught, handed the can back to the Boy, and leant against the staging. They talked a minute or two in undertones.

A curt voice behind said: "Looks like you've got a deal to attend to to-day, beside your work."

They looked round, and there was Austin. As the Colonel saw who it was had spoken, the clear colour in the tan deepened; he threw back his shoulders, hesitated, and then, without a word, went and took up his shovel.

Austin walked on. The Boy kept looking at his friend. What was the matter with the Colonel? It was not only that his eyes were queer—most of the men complained of their eyes, unless they slept in cabins. But whether through sun-blindness or shaken by anger, the Colonel was handling his shovel uncertainly, fumbling at the gravel, content with half a shovelful, and sometimes gauging the distance to the box so badly that some of the pay fell down again in the creek. As Austin came back on the other side of the line, he stopped opposite to where the Colonel worked, and suddenly called: "Seymour!"

Like so many on Bonanza, the Superintendent could not always sleep when the time came. He was walking about "showing things" to a stranger, "a newspaper woman," it was whispered—at all events, a lady who, armed with letters from the highest British officials, had come to "write up the Klondyke."

Seymour had left her at his employer's call. The lady, thin, neat, alert, with crisply curling iron-gray hair, and pleasant but unmistakably dignified expression, stood waiting for him a moment on the heap of tailings, then innocently followed her guide.

Although Austin lowered his voice, she drew nearer, prepared to take an intelligent interest in the "new riffles up on Skookum."

When Austin had first called Seymour, the Colonel started, looked up, and watched the little scene with suspicion and growing anger. Seeing Seymour's eyes turn his way, the Kentuckian stopped shovelling, and, on a sudden impulse, called out:

"See here, Austin: if you've any complaints to make, sah, you'd better make them to my face, sah."

The conversation about riffles thus further interrupted, a little silence fell. The Superintendent stood in evident fear of his employer, but he hastened to speak conciliatory words.

"No complaint at all—one of the best hands."

"May be so when he ain't sick," said Austin contemptuously.

"Sick!" the Boy called out. "Why, you're dreamin'. He's our strong man—able to knock spots out of anyone on the creek, ain't he?" appealing to the gang.

"I shall be able to spare him from my part of the creek after to-night."

"Do I understand you are dismissing me?"

"Oh, go to hell!"

The Colonel dropped his shovel and clenched his hands.

"Get the woman out o' the way," said the owner; "there's goin' to be trouble with this fire-eating Southerner."

The woman turned quickly. The Colonel, diving under the sluice-box for a plunge at Austin, came up face to face with her.

"The *lady*," said the Colonel, catching his breath, shaking with rage, but pulling off his hat—"the *lady* is quite safe, but I'm not so sure about you." He swerved as if to get by.

"Safe? I should think so!" she said steadily, comprehending all at once, and not unwilling to create a diversion.

"This is no place for a woman, not if she's got twenty letters from the Gold Commissioner."

Misunderstanding Austin's jibe at the official, the lady stood her ground, smiling into the face of the excited Kentuckian.

"Several people have asked me if I was not afraid to be alone here, and I've said no. It's quite true. I've travelled so much that I came to know years ago, it's not among men like you a woman has anything to fear."

It was funny and pathetic to see the infuriate Colonel clutching at his grand manner, bowing one instant to the lady, shooting death and damnation the next out of heavy eyes at Austin. But the wiry little woman had the floor, and meant, for peace sake, to keep it a few moments.

"At home, in the streets of London, I *have* been rudely spoken to; I have been greatly annoyed in Paris; in New York I have been subject to humorous impertinence; but in the great North-West every man has seemed to be my friend. In fact, wherever our English tongue is spoken," she wound up calmly, putting the great Austin in his place, "a woman may go alone."

Austin seemed absorbed in filling his pipe. The lady tripped on to the next claim with a sedate "Good-night" to the men on No. 0. She thought the momentary trouble past, and never turned to see how the Kentuckian, waiting till she should be out of earshot, came round in front of Austin with a low question.

The gang watched the Boy dodge under the sluice and hobble hurriedly over the chaos of stones towards the owner. Before he reached him he called breathless, but trying to laugh:

"You think the Colonel's played out, but, take my word for it, he ain't a man to fool with."

The gang knew from Austin's sneering look as he turned to strike a match on a boulder—they knew as well as if they'd been within a yard of him that Scowl had said something "pretty mean." They saw the Colonel make a plunge, and they saw him reel and fall among the stones.

The owner stood there smoking while the night gang knocked off work under his nose and helped the Boy to get the Colonel on his feet. It was no use. Either he had struck his head or he was dazed—unable, at all events, to stand. They lifted him up and started for the big tent.

Three Indians accosted the cripple leading the procession. He started, and raised his eyes. "Nicholas! Muckluck!" They shook hands, and all went on together, the Boy saying the Colonel had a little sunstroke.

* * * * * * *

The next day Scowl Austin was found lying face down among the cotton-woods above the benches on Skookum, a bullet-wound in his back. He had fainted from loss of blood, when he was picked up by the two Vermonters, the men who had twice gone by No. o the night before the quarrel, and who had enraged Austin by stopping an instant during the clean-up to look at his gold. They carried him back to Bonanza.

The Superintendent and several of the day gang got the wounded man into bed. He revived sufficiently to say he had not seen the man that shot him, but he guessed he knew him all the same. Then he turned on his side, swore feebly at the lawlessness of the South, and gave up the ghost.

Not a man on the creek but understood who Scowl Austin meant.

"Them hot-headed Kentuckians, y' know, they'd dowse a feller's glim for less 'n that."

"Little doubt the Colonel done it all right. Why, his own pardner says to Austin's face, says he, 'The Colonel's a bad man to fool with,' and just then the big chap plunged at Austin like a mad bull."

But they were sorry to a man, and said among themselves

that they'd see he was defended proper even if he hadn't nothin' but a little dust in a jam-pot.

The Grand Forks constable had put a watch on the big tent, despatched a man to inform the Dawson Chief of Police, and set himself to learn the details of the quarrel. Meanwhile the utter absence of life in the guarded tent roused suspicion. It was recalled now that since the Indians had left a little while after the Colonel was carried home, sixteen hours ago, no one had seen either of the Southerners. The constable, taking alarm at this, left the crowd at Scowl Austin's, and went hurriedly across the meadow to the new centre of interest. Just as he reached the tent the flap was turned back, and Maudie put her head out.

"Hah!" said the constable, with some relief, "they both in there?"

"The Colonel is."

Now, it was the Colonel he had wanted till he heard he was there. As the woman came out he looked in to make certain. Yes, there he was, calmly sleeping, with the gray blanket of the screen thrown up for air. It didn't look much like——

"Where's the other feller?"

"Gone to Dawson."

"With that lame leg?"

"Went on horseback."

It had as grand a sound as it would have in the States to say a man had departed in a glass coach drawn by six cream-coloured horses. But he had been "in a hell of a hurry," evidently. Men were exchanging glances.

"Funny nobody saw him."

"When'd he light out?"

"About five this morning."

Oh, that explained it. The people who were up at five were abed now. And the group round the tent whispered that Austin had done the unheard of—had gone off and left the night gang at three o'clock in the morning. They had said so as the day shift turned out.

"But how'd the young feller get such a thing as a horse?"

"Hired it off a stranger out from Dawson yesterday," Maudie answered shortly.

"Oh, that Frenchman—Count—a—Whirligig?"

But Maudie was tired of giving information and getting none. The answer came from one in the group.

"Yes, that French feller came in with a couple o' fusst-class horses. He's camped away over there beyond Muskeeter." He pointed down Bonanza.

"P'raps you won't mind just mentionin'," said Maudie with growing irritation, "*why* you're makin' yourself so busy about my friends?" (Only strong resentment could have induced the plural.)

When she heard what had happened and what was suspected she uttered a contemptuous "Tschah!" and made for the tent. The constable followed. She wheeled fiercely round.

"The man in there hasn't been out o' this tent since he was carried up from the creek last night. I can swear to it."

"Can you swear the other was here all the time?"

No answer.

"Did he say what he went to Dawson for?"

"The doctor."

One or two laughed. "Who's sick enough to send for a Dawson doctor?"

"So *you* think he's gone for a——"

"I know he is."

"And do you know what it costs to have a doctor come all the way out here?"

"Yes, beasts! won't budge till you've handed over five hundred dollars. Skunks!"

"Did your friend mention how he meant to raise the dust?"

"He's got it," she said curtly.

"Why, he was livin' off his pardner. Hadn't a red cent."

"She's shieldin' him," the men about the door agreed.

"Lord! he done it well—got away with five hundred and a horse!"

"*He* had words with Austin, himself, the night o' the clean-up. Sassed Scowl Austin! Right quiet, but, oh my! Told him to his face his gold was dirty, and washed it off his hands with a look—— Gawd! you could see Austin was mad clear through, from his shirt-buttons to his spine. You bet Scowl said something back that got the young feller's monkey up."

They all agreed that the only wonder was that Austin had lived as long—"On the other side o' the line—Gee!"

* * * * * * *

That evening the Boy, riding hard, came into camp with a doctor, followed discreetly in the rear by an N. W. M. P., really mounted this time. It had occurred to the Boy that people looked at him hard, and when he saw the groups gathered about the tent his heart contracted sharply. Had the Colonel died? He flung himself off the horse, winced as his foot cried out, told Joey Bludsoe to look after both beasts a minute, and led the Dawson doctor towards the tent.

The constable followed.

Maudie, at the door, looked at her old enemy queerly, and just as, without greeting, he pushed by, "S'pose you've heard Scowl Austin's dead?" she said in a low voice.

"No! Dead, eh? Well, there's one rattlesnake less in the woods."

The constable stopped him with a touch on the shoulder: "We have a warrant for you."

The Colonel lifted his head and stared about, in a dazed way, as the Boy stopped short and stammered, "Warr—what for?"

"For the murder of Scoville——"

"Look here," he whispered: "I—I don't know what you mean, but I'll go along with you, of course, only don't talk before this man. He's sick——" He beckoned the doctor. "This is the man I brought you to see." Then he turned his back on the wide, horrified eyes of his friend, saying, "Back in a minute, Kentucky." Outside: "Give me a second, boys, will you?" he said to the N. W. M. P.'s, "just till I hear what that doctor fella says about my pardner."

He stood there with the Buckeyes, the police, and the various day gangs that were too excited to go to bed. And he asked them where Austin was found, and other details of the murder, wearily conscious that the friendliest there felt sure that the man who questioned could best fill in the gaps in the story. When the doctor came out, Maudie at his heels firing off quick questions, the Boy hobbled forward.

"Well?"

"Temperature a hundred and four," said the Dawson doctor.

"Oh, is—is that much or little?"

"Well, it's more than most of us go in for."

"Can you tell what's the matter with him?"

"Oh, typhoid, of course."

The Boy pulled his hat over his eyes.

"Guess you won't mind my stayin' *now?*" said Maudie at his elbow, speaking low.

He looked up. "You goin' to take care of him? *Good* care?" he asked harshly.

But Maudie seemed not to mind. The tears went down her cheeks, as, with never a word, she nodded, and turned towards the tent.

"Say," he hobbled after her, "that doctor's all right—only wanted fifty." He laid four hundred-dollar bills in her hand. She seemed about to speak, when he interrupted hoarsely, "And look here: pull the Colonel through, Maudie—*pull him through!*"

"I'll do my darnedest."

He held out his hand. He had never given it to her before, and he forgot that few people would care now to take it. But she gave him hers with no grudging. Then, on a sudden impulse, "You ain't takin' him to Dawson to-night?" she said to the constable.

He nodded.

"Why, he's done the trip twice already."

"I can do it again well enough."

"Then you got to wait a minute." She spoke to the constable as if she had been Captain Constantine himself. "Better just go in and see the Colonel," she said to the Boy. "He's been askin' for you."

"N-no, Maudie; I can go to Dawson all right, but I don't feel up to goin' in there again."

"You'll be sorry if you don't. And then he knew what a temperature at a hundred and four foreboded.

He went back into the tent, dreading to face the Colonel more than he had ever dreaded anything in his life.

But the sick man lay, looking out drowsily, peacefully, through half-shut eyes, not greatly concerned, one would say, about anything. The Boy went over and stood under the gray blanket canopy, looking down with a choking sensation that delayed his question: "How you feelin' now, Kentucky?"

"All right."

"Why, that's good news. Then you—you won't mind my goin' off to—to—do a little prospectin'?"

The sick man frowned: "You stay right where you are. There's *plenty* in that jampot."

"Yes, yes! jampot's fillin' up fine."

"Besides," the low voice wavered on, "didn't we agree we'd learned the lesson o' the North?"

"The lesson o' the North?" repeated the other with filling eyes.

"Yes, sah. A man alone's a man lost. We got to stick together, Boy." The eyelids fell heavily.

"Yes, yes, Colonel." He pressed the big hand. His mouth made the motion, not the sound, "Good-bye, pardner."

CHAPTER XXII

THE GOING HOME

" Despair lies down and grovels, grapples not
With evil, casts the burden of its lot.
This Age climbs earth.
————To challenge heaven.
————Not less
The lower deeps. It laughs at Happiness."
GEORGE MEREDITH.

EVERYBODY on Bonanza knew that the Colonel had left off struggling to get out of his bed to go to work, had left off calling for his pardner. Quite in his right senses again, he could take in Maudie's explanation that the Boy was gone to Dawson, probably to get something for the Colonel to eat. For the Doctor was a crank and wouldn't let the sick man have his beans and bacon, forbade him even such a delicacy as fresh pork, though the Buckeyes nobly offered to slaughter one of their newly-acquired pigs, the first that ever rooted in Bonanza refuse, and more a terror to the passing Indian than any bear or wolf.

"But the Boy's a long time," the Colonel would say wistfully.

Before this quieter phase set in, Maudie had sent into Dawson for Potts, O'Flynn and Mac, that they might distract the Colonel's mind from the pardner she knew could not return. But O'Flynn, having married the girl at the Moosehorn Café, had excuse of ancient validity for not coming; Potts was busy breaking the faro bank, and Mac was waiting till an overdue Lower River steamer should arrive.

Nicholas of Pymeut had gone back as pilot of the *Weare,* but Princess Muckluck was still about, now with Skookum Bill, son of the local chief, now alone, trudging up and down Bonanza like one looking for something lost. The Colonel heard her voice outside the tent and had her in.

"You goin' to marry Skookum Bill, as they say?"

Muckluck only laughed, but the Indian hung about waiting the Princess's pleasure.

"When your pardner come back?" she would indiscreetly ask the Colonel. "Why he goes to Dawson?" And every few hours she would return: "Why he stay so long?"

At last Maudie took her outside and told her.

Muckluck gaped, sat down a minute, and rocked her body back and forth with hidden face, got up and called sharply: "Skookum!"

They took the trail for town. Potts said, when he passed them, they were going as if the devil were at their heels— wouldn't even stop to say how the Colonel was. So Potts had come to see for himself—and to bring the Colonel some letters just arrived.

Mac was close behind . . . but the Boy? No—no. They wouldn't let anybody see him; and Potts shook his head.

"Well, you can come in," said Maudie, "if you keep your head shut about the Boy."

The Colonel was lying flat, with that unfaltering ceiling-gaze of the sick. Now his vision dropped to the level of faces at the door. "Hello!" But as they advanced he looked behind them anxiously. Only Mac—no, Kaviak at his heels! and the sick man's disappointment lightened to a smile. He would have held out a hand, but Maudie stopped him. She took the little fellow's fingers and laid them on the Colonel's.

"Now sit down and be quiet," she said nervously.

Potts and Mac obeyed, but Kaviak had fastened his fine little hand on the weak one, and anchored so, stared about taking his bearings.

"How did *you* get to the Klondyke, Kaviak?" said the Colonel in a thin, breathy voice.

"Came up with Sister Winifred," Farva answered for him. "She was sent for to help with the epidemic. Dyin' like flies in Dawson—h'm—ahem!" (Apologetic glance at Maudie.) "Sister Winifred promised to keep Kaviak with her. Woman of her word."

"Well, what you think o' Dawson?" the low voice asked.

Kaviak understood the look at least, and smiled back, grew suddenly grave, intent, looked sharply round, loosed his hold of the Colonel, bent down, and retired behind the bed. That was where Nig was. Their foregathering added nothing to the tranquility of the occasion, and both were driven forth by Maudie.

Potts read the Colonel his letters, and helped him to sign a couple of cheques. The "Louisville instructions" had come through at last.

After that the Colonel slept, and when he woke it was only to wander away into that world where Maudie was lost utterly, and where the Colonel was at home. There was chastening in such hours for Maudie of Minóok. "Now he's found the Other One," she would say to herself—"the One he was looking for."

That same evening, as they sat in the tent in an interval of relief from the Colonel's muttering monotone, they heard Nig making some sort of unusual manifestation outside; heard the grunting of those pioneer pigs; heard sounds of a whispered "Sh! Kaviak. Shut up, Nig!" Then a low, tuneless crooning:

> " W'en yo' see a pig a-goin' along
>   Widder straw in de sider 'is mouf,
> It'll be er tuhble wintuh,
>   En yo' bettah move down Souf."

"Why, the Boy's back!" said the Colonel suddenly in a clear, collected voice.

Maudie had jumped up, but the Boy put his head in the tent, smiling, and calling out:

"They told me he was getting on all right, but I just thought maybe he was asleep." He came in and bent over his pardner. "Hello, everybody! Why, you got it so fine and dark in here, I can hardly see how well you're lookin', Colonel!" And he dropped into the nurse's place by the bedside.

"Maudie's lined the tent with black drill," said the Colonel. "You brought home anything to eat?"

"Well, no——" (Maudie telegraphed); "found it all I could do to bring myself back."

"Oh, well, *that's* the main thing," said the Colonel, battling with disappointment. Pricked by some quickened memory of the Boy's last home-coming: "I've had pretty queer dreams about you: been givin' Maudie the meanest kind of a time."

"Don't go gassin', Colonel," admonished the nurse.

"It's pretty tough, *I* can tell you," he said irritably, "to be as weak as a day-old baby, and to have to let other people——"

"Mustn't talk!" ordered Mac.

The Colonel raised his head with sudden anger. It did not mend matters that Maudie was there to hold him down before a lot of men.

"You go to Halifax," said the Boy to Mac, blustering a trifle. "The Colonel may stand a little orderin' about from Maudie—don't blame him m'self. But Kentucky ain't going to be bossed by any of us."

The Colonel lay quite still again, and when he spoke it was quietly enough.

"Reckon I'm in the kind of a fix when a man's got to take orders."

"Foolishness! Don't let him jolly you, boys. The Colonel's always sayin' he ain't a soldier, but I reckon you better look out how you rile Kentucky!"

The sick man ignored the trifling. "The worst of it is bein' so useless."

"Useless! You just wait till you see what a lot o' use we mean to make of you. No crawlin' out of it like that."

"It's quite true," said Mac harshly; "we all kind of look to you still."

"Course we do!" The Boy turned to the others. "The O'Flynns comin' all the way out from Dawson to-morrow to get Kentucky's opinion on a big scheme o' theirs. Did you ever hear what that long-headed Lincoln said when the Civil War broke out? 'I would like to have God on my side, but I *must* have Kentucky.'"

"I've been so out o' my head, I thought you were arrested."

"No 'out of your head' about it—*was* arrested. They thought I'd cleared Scowl Austin off the earth."

"Do they know who did?" Potts and Maudie asked in a breath.

"That Klondyke Indian that's sweet on Princess Muckluck."

"What had Austin done to him?"

"Nothin'. Reckon Skookum Bill was about the only man on Bonanza who had no objection to the owner of o. Said so in Court."

"What did he kill him for?"

"Well," said the Boy, "it's just one o' those topsy-turvy things that happen up here. You saw that Indian that came in with Nicholas? Some years ago he killed a drunken white man who was after him with a knife. There was no means of tryin' the Indian where the thing happened, so he was taken outside.

The Court found he'd done the killin' in self-defence, and sent him back. Well, sir, that native had the time of his life bein' tried for murder. He'd travelled on a railroad, seen a white man's city, lived like a lord, and came home to be the most famous man of his tribe. Got a taste for travel, too. Comes to the Klondyke, and his fame fires Skookum Bill. All you got to do is to kill one o' these white men, and they take you and show you all the wonders o' the earth. So he puts a bullet into Austin."

"Why didn't he own up, then, and get his reward?"

"Muckluck knew better—made him hold his tongue about it."

"And then made him own up when she saw——"

The boy nodded.

"What's goin' to happen?"

"Oh, he'll swing to-morrow instead o' me. By the way, Colonel, a fella hunted me up this mornin' who'd been to Minóok. Looked good to him. I've sold out Idaho Bar."

" 'Nough to buy back your Orange Grove?"

He shook his head. " 'Nough to pay my debts and start over again."

When the Dawson doctor left that night Maudie, as usual, followed him out. They waited a long time for her to come back.

"Perhaps she's gone to her own tent;" and the Boy went to see.

He found her where the Colonel used to go to smoke, sitting, staring out to nowhere.

As the boy looked closer he saw she had been crying, for even in the midst of honest service Maudie, like many a fine lady before her, could not forego the use of cosmetic. Her cheeks were streaked and stained.

"Five dollars a box here, too," she said mechanically, as she wiped some of the rouge off with a handkerchief. Her hand shook.

"What's the matter?"

"It's all up," she answered.

"Not with *him?*" He motioned towards the tent.

She nodded.

"Doctor says so?"

"——and I knew it before, only I wouldn't believe it."

She had spoken with little agitation, but now she flung her

arms out with a sudden anguish that oddly took the air of tossing into space Bonanza and its treasure. It was the motion of
one who renounces the thing that means the most—a final fling
in the face of the gods. The Boy stood quite still, submitting
his heart to that first quick rending and tearing asunder which
is only the initial agony of parting.

"How soon?" he said, without raising his eyes.

"Oh, he holds on—it may be a day or two."

The Boy walked slowly away towards the ridge of the low
hill. Maudie turned and watched him. On the top of the
divide he stopped, looking over. Whatever it was he saw off
there, he could not meet it yet. He flung himself down with
his face in the fire-weed, and lay there all night long.

Kaviak was sent after him in the morning, but only to say,
"Breakfast, Maudie's tent."

The Boy saw that Mac and Potts knew. For the first time
the Big Chimney men felt a barrier between them and that
one who had been the common bond, keeping the incongruous
allied and friendly. Only Nig ran in and out, unchilled by the
imminence of the Colonel's withdrawal from his kind.

Towards noon the O'Flynns came up the creek, and were
stopped near the tent by the others. They all stood talking
low till a noise of scuffling broke the silence within. They
drew nearer, and heard the Colonel telling Maudie not to turn
out Nig and Kaviak.

"I like seein' my friends. Where's the Boy?"

So they went in.

Did he know? He must know, or he would have asked
O'Flynn what the devil made him look like that! All he said
was: "Hello! How do you do, madam?" and he made a weak
motion of one hand towards Mrs. O'Flynn to do duty for that
splendid bow of his. Then, as no one spoke, "You're too late,
O'Flynn."

"Too late?"

"Had a job in your line. . . ." Then suddenly:
"Maudie's worth the whole lot of you."

They knew it was his way of saying "She's told me." They
all sat and looked at the floor. Nothing happened for a long
time. At last: "Well, you all know what my next move is;
what's yours?"

There was another silence, but not nearly so long.

"What prospects, pardners?" he repeated.

The Boy looked at Maudie. She made a little gesture of "I've done all the fightin' I'm good for." The Colonel's eyes, clear again and tranquil, travelled from face to face.

O'Flynn cleared his throat, but it was Mac who spoke.

"Yes—a—we would like to hold a last—hold a counsel o' war. We've always kind o' followed your notions—at least" —veracity pared down the compliment—"at least, you can't say but what we've always listened to you."

"Yes, you might just—a—start us as well as you can," says Potts.

The Colonel smiled a little. Each man still "starting"—forever starting for somewhere or something, until he should come to this place where the Colonel was. Even he, why, he was "starting" too. For him this was no end other than a chapter's ending. But these men he had lived and suffered with, they all wanted to talk the next move over—not his, theirs— all except the Boy, it seemed.

Mac was in the act of changing his place to be nearer the Colonel, when Potts adroitly forestalled him. The others drew off a little and made desultory talk, while Potts in an undertone told how he'd had a run of bad luck. No doubt it would turn, but if ever he got enough again to pay his passage home, he'd put it in the bank and never risk it.

"I *swear* I wouldn't! I've got to go out in the fall—goin' to get myself married Christmas; and, if she's willing, we'll come up here on the first boat in the spring—with backing this time."

He showed a picture. The Colonel studied it.

"I believe she'll come," he said.

And Potts was so far from clairvoyance that he laughed, awkwardly flattered; then anxiously: "Wish I was sure o' my passage money."

When Potts, before he meant to, had yielded place to O'Flynn, the Colonel was sworn to secrecy, and listened to excited whispers of gold in the sand off yonder on the coast of the Behring Sea. The world in general wouldn't know the authenticity of the new strike till next season. He and Mrs. O'Flynn would take the first boat sailing out of San Francisco in the spring.

"Oh, you're going outside too?"

"In the fahll—yes, yes. Ye see, I ain't like the rest. I've got Mrs. O'Flynn to consider. Dawson's great, but it ain't the place to start a famully."

"Where *you* goin', Mac?" said the Colonel to the irate one, who was making for the door. "I want a little talk with you."

Mac turned back, and consented to express his opinion of the money there was to be made out of tailings by means of a new hydraulic process. He was going to lend Kaviak to Sister Winifred again on the old terms. She'd take him along when she returned to Holy Cross, and Mac would go outside, raise a little capital, return, and make a fortune. For the moment he was broke—hadn't even passage money. Did the Colonel think he could——

The Colonel seemed absorbed in that eternal interrogation of the tent-top.

"Mine, you know"—Mac drew nearer still, and went on in the lowered voice—"mine's a special case. A man's bound to do all he can for his boys."

"I didn't know you had boys."

Mac jerked "Yes" with his square head. "Bobbie's goin' on six now."

"The others older?"

"Others?" Mac stared an instant. "Oh, there's only one more." He grinned with embarrassment, and hitched his head towards Kaviak.

"I guess you've jawed enough," said Maudie, leaving the others and coming to the foot of the bed.

"And Maudie's goin' back, too," said the sick man.

She nodded.

"And you're never goin' to leave her again?"

"No."

"Maudie's a little bit of All Right," said the patient. The Big Chimney men assented, but with sudden misgiving.

"What was that job ye said ye were wantin' me forr?"

"Oh, Maudie's got a friend of hers to fix it up."

"Fix what up?" demanded Potts.

"Little postscript to my will."

Mac jerked his head at the nurse. With that clear sight of dying eyes the Colonel understood. A meaner spirit would have been galled at the part those "Louisville Instructions" had been playing, but cheap cynicism was not in the Colonel's line. He knew the awful pinch of life up here, and he thought no less of his comrades for asking that last service of getting them home. But it was the day of the final "clean-up" for the Colonel; he must not leave misapprehension behind.

"I wanted Maudie to have my Minóok claim——"

"Got a Minóok claim o' my own."

"So I've left it to be divided——"

They all looked up.

"One-half to go to a little girl in 'Frisco, and the other half—well, I've left the other half to Kaviak. Strikes me he ought to have a little piece o' the North."

"Y-yes!"

"*Oh,* yes!"

"Good idea!"

Mac thought he'd go over to the other tent and cook some dinner. There was a general movement. As they were going out:

"Boy!"

"Yes?" He came back, Nig followed, and the two stood by the camp-bed waiting their Colonel's orders.

"Don't you go wastin' any more time huntin' gold-mines."

"I don't mean to."

"Go back to your own work; go back to your own people."

The Boy listened and looked away.

"It's good to go pioneering, but it's good to go home. Oh-h—!" the face on the pillow was convulsed for that swift passing moment—"best of all to go home. And if you leave your home too long, your home leaves you."

"Home doesn't seem so important as it did when I came up here."

The Colonel fastened one hand feverishly on his pardner's arm.

"I've been afraid of that. It's magic; break away. Promise me you'll go back and *stay.* Lord, Lord!" he laughed feebly, "to think a fella should have to be urged to leave the North alone. Wonderful place, but there's Black Magic in it. Or who'd ever come—who'd ever stay?"

He looked anxiously into the Boy's set face.

"I'm not saying the time was wasted," he went on; "I reckon it was a good thing you came."

"Yes, it was a good thing I came."

"You've learned a thing or two."

"Several."

"Specially on the Long Trail."

"Most of all on the Long Trail."

The Colonel shut his eyes. Maudie came and held a cup to his lips.

"Thank you. I begin to feel a little foggy. What was it we learned on the Trail, pardner?" But the Boy had turned away. "Wasn't it—didn't we learn how near a tolerable decent man is to bein' a villain?"

"We learned that a man can't be quite a brute as long as he sticks to another man."

"Oh, was that it?"

* * * * * * *

In the night Maudie went away to sleep. The Boy watched.

"Do you know what I'm thinking about?" the sick man said suddenly.

"About—that lady down at home?"

"Guess again."

"About—those fellas at Holy Cross?"

"No, I never was as taken up with the Jesuits as you were. No, Sah, I'm thinkin' about the Czar." (Poor old Colonel! he was wandering again.) "Did I ever tell you I saw him once?"

"No."

"Did—had a good look at him. Knew a fella in Petersburg, too, that——" He rested a moment. "That Czar's all right. Only he sends the wrong people to Siberia. Ought to go himself, and take his Ministers, for a winter on the Trail." On his face suddenly the old half-smiling, half-shrewd look. "But, Lord bless you! 'tisn't only the Czar. We all have times o' thinkin' we're some punkins. Specially Kentuckians. I reckon most men have their days when they're twelve feet high, and wouldn't stoop to say 'Thank ye' to a King. Let 'em go on the Winter Trail."

"Yes," agreed the Boy, "they'd find out—" And he stopped.

"Plenty o' use for Head Men, though." The faint voice rang with an echo of the old authority. "No foolishness, but just plain: 'I'm the one that's doin' the leadin'—like Nig here —and it's my business to lick the hind dog if he shirks.'" He held out his hand and closed it over his friend's. "I was Boss o' the Big Chimney, Boy, but you were Boss o' the Trail."

* * * * * * *

The Colonel was buried in the old moose pasture, with people standing by who knew that the world had worn a friendlier face because he had been in it. That much was clear, even before it was found that he had left to each of the Big Chimney men five hundred dollars, not to be drawn except for the purpose of going home.

They thought it was the sense of that security that made them put off the day. They would "play the game up to the last moment, and *see*——"

September's end brought no great change in fortune, but a change withal of deep significance. The ice had begun to run in the Yukon. No man needed telling it would "be a tuhble wintah, and dey'd better move down Souf." All the late boats by both routes had been packed. Those men who had failed, and yet, most tenacious, were hanging on for some last lucky turn of the wheel, knew the risk they ran. And now to-day the final boat of the year was going down the long way to the Behring Sea, and by the Canadian route, open a little longer, the Big Chimney men, by grace of that one left behind, would be on the last ship to shoot the rapids in '98.

Not only to the thousands who were going, to those who stayed behind there was something in the leaving of the last boat—something that knocked upon the heart. They, too, could still go home. They gathered at the docks and told one another they wouldn't leave Dawson for fifty thousand dollars, then looked at the "failures" with home-sick eyes, remembering those months before the luckiest Klondyker could hear from the world outside. Between now and then, what would have come to pass up here, and what down there below!

The Boy had got a place for Muckluck in the A. C. Store. She was handy at repairing and working in fur, and said she was "all right" on this bright autumn morning when the Boy went in to say good-bye. With a white woman and an Indian boy, in a little room overlooking the water-front, Muckluck was working in the intervals of watching the crowds on the wharf. Eyes more experienced than hers might well stare. Probably in no other place upon the globe was gathered as motley a crew: English, Indian, Scandinavian, French, German, Negroes, Chinese, Poles, Japs, Finns. All the fine gentlemen had escaped by earlier boats. All the smart young women with their gold-nugget buttons as big as your thumb, lucky miners from the creeks with heavy consignments of dust to take home, had been too wary to run any risk of the Never-Know-What closing inopportunely. The great majority here, on the wharf, dazed or excited, lugging miscellaneous possessions—things they had clung to in straits so desperate they knew no more how to relax their hold than dead fingers do—these were men whose last chance had been the Klondyke, and who here, as elsewhere, had failed. Many who came in young were going out old; but the odd thing was that those worst off went out game—no whining, none of the ostentatious pathos of those broken on the wheel of a great city.

A man under Muckluck's window, dressed in a moose-skin shirt, straw hat, broadcloth trousers, and carpet slippers, in one hand a tin pail, in the other something tied in a handkerchief, called out lustily to a ragged individual, cleaving a way through the throng, "Got your stuff aboard?"

"Yes, goin' to get it off. I ain't goin' home till next year."

And the face above the moose-skin shirt was stricken with a sudden envy. Without any telling, he knew just how his pardner's heart had failed him, when it came to turning his tattered back on the possibilities of the Klondyke.

"Oh, *I'm* comin' back soon 's I get a grub-stake."

"I ain't," said another with a dazed expression—a Klondyker carrying home his frying-pan, the one thing, apparently, saved out of the wreck.

"You think you ain't comin' back? Just wait! Once you've lived up here, the Outside ain't good enough fur yer."

"Right!" said an old Forty-miler, "you can try it; but Lord! how you'll miss this goll-darn Yukon."

Among the hundreds running about, talking, bustling, hauling heterogeneous luggage, sending last letters, doing last deals, a score of women either going by this boat or saying good-bye to those who were; and Potts, the O'Flynns, and Mac waiting to hand over Kaviak to Sister Winifred.

The Boy at the open window above, staring down on the tatterdemalion throng, remembered his first meeting with the Big Chimney men as the *Washington City* steamed out of San Francisco's Golden Gate a year and a month before.

Of course, even in default of finding millions, something stirring might have happened, something heroic, rewarding to the spirit, if no other how; but (his own special revelation blurred, swamped for the moment in the common wreck) he said to himself that nothing of the sort had befallen the Big Chimney men any more than to the whipped and bankrupt crew struggling down there on the wharf. They simply had failed—all alike. And yet there was between them and the common failures of the world one abiding difference: these had greatly dared. As long as the meanest in that crowd drew breath and held to memory, so long might he remember the brave and terrible days of the Klondyke Rush, and that he had borne in it his heavy share. No share in any mine save that—the knowledge that he was not among the vast majority who sit dully to the end beside what things they were born to—the earnings of other men, the savings of other women, afraid to go seeking after better lest they lose the good they have. They had failed, but it could never be said of a Klondyker that he had not tried. He might, in truth, look down upon the smug majority that smiles at unusual endeavour, unless success excuses, crowns it. No one there, after all, so poor but he had one possession treasured among kings. And he had risked it. What could a man do more?

"Good-bye, Muckluck."

"Goo'-bye? Boat Canada way no go till Thursday."

"Thursday, yes," he said absently, eyes still on the American ship.

"Then why you say goo'-bye to-day?"

"Lot to do. I just wanted to make sure you were all right."

Her creamy face was suddenly alight, but not with gratitude.

"Oh, yes, all right here," she said haughtily. "I not like much the Boston men—King George men best." It was so her sore heart abjured her country. For among the natives of the Klondyke white history stops where it began when George the Third was King. "I think"—she shot sideways a shrewd look —"I think I marry a King George man."

And at the prospect her head drooped heavily.

"Then you'll want to wear this at your wedding."

The Boy drew his hand out of his pocket, threw a walrus-string over her bent head, and when she could see clear again, her Katharine medal was swinging below her waist, and "the Boston man" was gone.

She stared with blinded eyes out of the window, till suddenly in the mist one face was clear. The Boy! Standing still down there in the hurly-burly, hands in pockets, staring at the ship.

Suddenly Sister Winifred, her black veil swirling in the wind. An orderly from St. Mary's Hospital following with a little trunk. At the gangway she is stopped by the purser, asked some questions, smiles at first and shakes her head, and then in dismay clasps her hands, seeming to plead, while the whistle shrieks.

Muckluck turned and flew down the dark little stair, threaded her way in and out among the bystanders on the wharf till she reached the Sister's side. The nun was saying that she not only had no money, but that a Yukon purser must surely know the Sisters were forbidden to carry it. He could not doubt but the passage money would be made good when they got to Holy Cross. But the purser was a new man, and when Mac and others who knew the Yukon custom expostulated, he hustled them aside and told Sister Winifred to stand back, the gangway was going up. It was then the Boy came and spoke to the man, finally drew out some money and paid the fare. The nun, not recognising him, too bewildered by this rough passage with the world even to thank the stranger, stood motionless, grasping Kaviak's hand—two children, you would say —her long veil blowing, hurrying on before her to that haven in the waste, the mission at Holy Cross.

Again the Boy was delaying the upward swing of the gangway: the nun's trunk must come on board. Two men rushed for it while he held down the gang.

"Mustn't cry," he said to Muckluck. "You'll see Sister Winifred again."

"Not for that I cry. Ah, I never shall have happiness!"

"Yes, *that* trunk!" he called.

In the babel of voices shouting from ship and shore, the Boy heard Princess Muckluck saying, with catches in her breath:

"I always knew I would get no luck!"

"Why?"

"Ah! I was a bad child. The baddest of all the Pymeut children."

"Yes, yes, they've got it now!" the Boy shouted up to the Captain. Then low, and smiling absently: "What did you do that was so bad, Princess?"

"Me? I—I mocked at the geese. It was the summer they were so late; and as they flew past Pymeut I—yes, *I mocked at them.*"

A swaying and breaking of the crowd, the little trunk flung on board, the men rushing back to the wharf, the gang lifted, and the last Lower River boat swung out into the ice-flecked stream.

Keen to piercing a cry rang out—Muckluck's:

"*Stop!* They carry him off! It is meestake! Oh! *Oh!*"

The Boy was standing for'ard, Nig beside him.

THE GOING HOME

O'Flynn rushed to the wharf's edge and screamed at the Captain to "Stop, be the Siven!" Mac issued orders most peremptory. Muckluck wept as excitedly as though there had never been question of the Boy's going away. But while the noise rose and fell, Potts drawled a "Guess he means to go that way!"

"No, he don't!"

"Stop, you —— ——, Captain!"

"Stop your —— boat!"

"Well," said a bystander, "I never seen any feller as calm as that who was bein' took the way he didn't want to go."

"D'ye mean there's a new strike?"

The suggestion flashed electric through the crowd. It was the only possible explanation.

"*He* knows what he's about."

"Lord! I wish I'd 'a' froze to him!"

"Yep," said Buck One, "never seen that young feller when he looked more like he wouldn't give a whoop in hell to change places with anybody."

As O'Flynn, back from his chase, hoarse and puffing, stopped suddenly:

"Be the Siven! Father Brachet *said* the little divil 'd be coming back to Howly Cross!"

"Where's that?"

"Lower River camp."

"Gold there?"

"No."

"Then you're talking through your hat!"

"Say, Potts, where in hell *is* he goin'?"

"Damfino!"

THE END